SIXTY

DAYS

AND

COUNTING

SIXTY

DAYS

AND

COUNTING

Kim Stanley Robinson

BANTAM BOOKS

SIXTY DAYS AND COUNTING
A Bantam Spectra Book / March 2007

Published by Bantam Dell
A Division of Random House, Inc.
New York, New York

Bantam Books, the rooster colophon, Spectra, and the portrayal of a boxed "s" are trademarks of Random House, Inc.

Library of Congress Cataloging-in-Publication Data
Robinson, Kim Stanley.
Sixty days and counting / Kim Stanley Robinson.
p.   cm.
ISBN-13: 978-0-553-80313-6
1. Global warming—Fiction.   2. Climatic changes—Fiction.   3. Scientists—Fiction.
4. Presidents—Fiction.   5. Legislators—Fiction.   6. Washington (D.C.)—Fiction.   I. Title.
PS3568.O2893S59 2007
813'.54—dc22
2006029903

Printed in the United States of America
Published simultaneously in Canada

www.bantamdell.com

BVG   10 9 8 7 6 5 4 3 2 1

CONTENTS

SIXTY

DAYS

AND

COUNTING

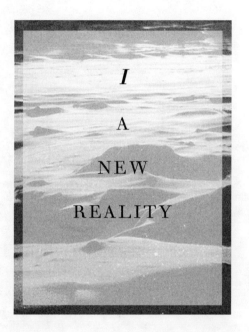

I

A

NEW

REALITY

"I believe the twenty-first century can become the
most important century of human history. I think a
new reality is emerging. Whether this view is realistic
or not, there is no harm in making an effort."

—*The Dalai Lama,*
November 15, 2005, Washington, D.C.

W hy do you do what you do?
I guess because we still kind of believe that the world can be saved.
We? The people where you work?
Yes. Not all of them. But most. Scientists are like that. I mean, we're seeing evidence that we seem to be starting a mass extinction event.
What's that?
A time when lots of species are killed off by some change in the environment. Like when that meteor struck and killed off the dinosaurs.
So people hit Earth like meteor.
Yes. It's getting to be that way for a lot of the big mammals especially. We're in the last moments already for a lot of them.
No more tigers.
That's right. No more lots of things. So . . . most of the scientists I know seem to think we ought to limit the extinctions to a minimum. Just to keep the lab working, so to speak.
The Frank Principle.
(Laughs.) I guess. Some people at work call it that. Who told you that?
Drepung tell me. Saving world so science can proceed. The Frank Principle.
Right. Well—it's like Buddhism, right? You might as well try to make a better world.
Yes. So, your National Science Foundation—very Buddhist!
Ha ha. I don't know if I'd go that far. NSF is mostly pragmatic. They have a job to do and a budget to do it with. A rather small budget.
But a big name! National—Science—Foundation. Foundation means base, right? Base of house?
Yes. It is a big name. But I don't think they regard themselves as

particularly big. Nor particularly Buddhist. Compassion and right action are not their prime motivation.

Compassion! So what? Does it matter why, if we do good things?

I don't know. Does it?

Maybe not!

Maybe not.

B Y THE TIME PHIL CHASE WAS ELECTED president, the world's climate was already far along the way to irrevocable change. There were already four hundred parts per million of carbon dioxide in the atmosphere, and another hundred parts would be there soon if civilization continued to burn its fossil carbon—and at this point there was no other option. Just as Franklin Delano Roosevelt was elected in the midst of a crisis that in some ways worsened before it got better, they were entangled in a moment of history when climate change, the destruction of the natural world, and widespread human misery were combining in a toxic and combustible mix. The new president had to contemplate drastic action while at the same time being constrained by any number of economic and political factors, not least the huge public debt left deliberately by the administrations preceding him.

It did not help that the weather that winter careened wildly from one extreme to another, but was in the main almost as cold as the previous recordbreaking year. Chase joked about it everywhere he went: "It's ten below zero, aren't you glad you elected me? Just think what it would have been like if you hadn't!" He would end speeches with a line from the poet Percy Bysshe Shelley:

"O, Wind, if Winter comes, can Spring be far behind?"

"Maybe it can," Kenzo pointed out with a grin. "We're in the Youngest Dryas, after all."

In any case, it was a fluky winter—above all windy—and the American people were in an uncertain state of mind. Chase addressed this: "The only thing we have to *fear*," he would intone, "is abrupt climate change!"

He would laugh, and people would laugh with him, understanding him to be saying that there was indeed something real to fear, but that they could do something about it.

His transition team worked with an urgency that resembled desperation.

Sea level was rising; temperatures were rising; there was no time to lose. Chase's good humor and casual style were therefore welcomed, when they were not reviled—much as it had been with FDR in the previous century. He would say, "We got ourselves into this mess and we can get out of it. The problems create an opportunity to remake our relationship to nature, and create a new dispensation. So—happy days are here again! Because we're making history, we are *seizing* the planet's history, I say, and turning it to the good."

Some scoffed; some listened and took heart; some waited to see what would happen.

As far as Frank Vanderwal's personal feelings were concerned, there was something reassuring about the world being so messed up. It tended to make his own life look like part of a trend, and a small part at that. A hill of beans in this world. Perhaps even so small as to be manageable.

Although, to tell the truth, it didn't feel that way. There were reasons to be very concerned, almost to the edge of fear. Frank's friend Caroline had disappeared on election night, chased by armed agents of some superblack intelligence agency. She had stolen her husband's plan to steal the election, and Frank had passed this plan to a friend at NSF with intelligence contacts, to what effect he could not be sure. He had helped her to escape her pursuers. To do that he had had to break a date with another friend, his boss and a woman he loved—although what that meant, given the passionate affair he was carrying on with Caroline, he did not know. There was a lot he didn't know; and he could still taste blood at the back of his throat, months after his nose had been broken. He could not think for long about the same thing. He was living a life that he called parcellated, but others might call dysfunctional: i.e., semi-homeless in Washington, D.C. He could have been back home in San Diego by now, where his teaching position was waiting for him. Instead he was a temporary guest of the embassy of the drowned nation of Khembalung. But hey, everyone had problems! Why should he be any different?

Although brain damage would be a little more than different. Brain damage meant something like—mental illness. It was a hard phrase to articulate when thinking about oneself. But it was possible his injury had exacerbated a lifelong tendency to make poor decisions. It was hard to tell. He had thought all his recent decisions had been correct, after all, in the moment he had made them. Should he not have faith that he was following a valid line of thought? He wasn't sure.

Thus it was a relief to think that all these personal problems were as nothing compared to the trouble all life on Earth now faced as a functioning biosphere. There were days in which he welcomed the bad news, and he saw that other people were doing the same. As this unpredictable winter blasted them with cold or bathed them in Caribbean balm, there grew in the city a shared interest and good cheer, a kind of solidarity.

Frank felt this solidarity also on the premises of the National Science Foundation, where he and many of his colleagues were trying to deal with the climate
problem. To do so, they had to keep trying to understand the environmental
effects of:

1) the so-far encouraging but still ambiguous results of their
   North Atlantic salting operation;
2) the equally ambiguous proliferation of a genetically modified
   "fast tree lichen" that had been released by the Russians in the
   Siberian forest;
3) the ongoing rapid detachment and flotation of the coastal
   verge of the Western Antarctic Ice Sheet;
4) the ongoing introduction of about nine billion tons of carbon
   dioxide into the atmosphere every year, ultimate source of
   many other problems;
5) the ensuing uptake of some three billion tons of carbon into the
   oceans;
6) the continuing rise of the human population by some hundred
   million people a year; and, last,
7) the cumulative impacts of all these events, gnarled together in
   feedback loops of all kinds.

It was a formidable list, and Frank worked hard on keeping his focus
on it.

But he was beginning to see that his personal problems—especially Caroline's disappearance, and the election-tampering scheme she had been tangled
in—were not going to be things he could ignore. They pressed on his mind.

She had called the Khembali embassy that night, and left a message saying
that she was okay. Earlier, in Rock Creek Park, she had told him she would be
in touch as soon as she could.

He had therefore been waiting for that contact, he told himself. But it had
not come. And Caroline's ex, who had also been her boss, had been following
her that night. Her ex had seen that Caroline knew he was following her, and
had seen also that Caroline had received help in escaping from him. He also
knew that Caroline's help had thrown a big rock right at his head.

So now this man might very well still be looking for her, and might also be
looking for that help she had gotten, as another way of hunting for her.

Or so it seemed. Frank couldn't be sure. He sat at his desk at NSF, staring
at his computer screen, trying to think it through. He could not seem to do it.
Whether it was the difficulty of the problem, or the inadequacy of his mentation, he could not be sure; but he could not do it.

So he went to see Edgardo. He entered his colleague's office and said, "Can we talk about the election result? What happened that night, and what might follow?"

"Ah! Well, that will take some time to discuss. And we were going to run today anyway. Let's talk about it while en route."

Frank took the point: no sensitive discussions to take place in their offices. Surveillance an all-too-real possibility. Frank had been on Caroline's list of surveilled subjects, and so had Edgardo.

In the locker room on the third floor they changed into running clothes. At the end of that process Edgardo took from his locker a security wand that resembled those used in airports; Caroline had used one like it. Frank was startled to see it there inside NSF, but nodded silently and allowed Edgardo to run it over him. Then he did the same for Edgardo.

They appeared to be clean of devices.

Then out on the streets.

As they ran, Frank said, "Have you had that thing for long?"

"Too long, my friend." Edgardo veered side to side as he ran, warming up his ankles in his usual extravagant manner. "But I haven't had to get it out for a while."

"Don't you worry that having it there looks odd?"

"No one notices things in the locker room."

"Are our offices bugged?"

"Yes. Yours, anyway. The thing you need to learn is that coverage is very spotty, just by the nature of the activity. The various agencies that do this have different interests and abilities, and very few even attempt total surveillance. And then only for crucial cases. Most of the rest is what you might call statistical in nature, and covers different parts of the datasphere. You can slip in and out of such surveillance."

"But—these so-called total information awareness systems, what about them?"

"It depends. Mostly by total information they mean electronic data. And then also you might be chipped in various ways, which would give your GPS location, and perhaps record what you say. Followed, filmed—sure, all that's possible, but it's expensive. But now we're clear. So tell me what's up?"

"Well—like I said. About the election results, and that program I gave you. From my friend. What happened?"

Edgardo grinned under his mustache. "We foxed that program. We forestalled it. You could say that we un-stole the vote in Oregon, right in the middle of the theft."

"We did?"

"Apparently so. The program was a stochastic tilt engine that had been installed in some of Oregon and Washington's voting machines. My friends figured that out and managed to write a disabler, and to get it introduced at the very last minute, so there wasn't any time for the people who had installed the tilter to react to the change. From the sound of it, a very neat operation."

Frank ran along feeling a glow spread through him as he tried to comprehend it. Not only the election, de-rigged and made honest—not only Phil Chase elected by a cleaned-up popular and electoral vote—but his Caroline had proved true. She had risked herself and come through for the country; for the world, really. And so—

Maybe she would come through for him too.

This train of thought led him through the glow to a new little flood of fear for her.

Edgardo saw at least some of this on his face, apparently, for he said, "So your friend is the real thing, eh?"

"Yes."

"It could get tricky for her now," Edgardo suggested. "If the tweakers try to find the leakers. As we used to say at DARPA."

"Yeah," Frank said, his pulse rate rising at the thought.

"You've sent a warning?"

"I would if I could."

"Ah!" Edgardo was nodding. "Gone away, has she?"

"Yes," Frank said; and then it was all pouring out of him, the whole story of how they had met and what had followed. This was something he had never managed to do with anyone, not even Rudra or Anna, and now it felt as if some kind of hydrostatic pressure had built up inside him, his silence like a dam that had now failed and let forth a flood.

It took a few miles to tell. The meeting in the stuck elevator, the unsuccessful hunt for her, the sighting of her on the Potomac during the flood, the brief phone call with her—her subsequent call—their meetings, their—affair.

And then, her revealing the surveillance program she was part of, in which Frank and so many others, including Edgardo, were being tracked and evaluated in some kind of virtual futures market, wherein investors, some of them computer programs, were making speculative investments, as in any other futures markets, but this time dealing in scientists doing certain kinds of biotech research.

And then how she had had to run away on election night, and how on that night he had helped her to evade her husband and his companions, who were now clearly correlated with the attempted election theft.

Edgardo bobbed along next to him as he told the tale, nodding at each new bit of information, lips pursed tightly, head tilted to the side. It was like confessing to a giant praying mantis.

"So," he said at last. "Now you're out of touch with her?"

"That's right. She said she'd call me, but she hasn't."

"But she will have to be very careful, now that her husband knows that you exist."

"Yes. But—will he be able to identify who I am, do you think?"

"I think that's very possible, if he has access to her work files. Do you know if he does?"

"She worked for him."

"So. And he knows that someone was helping her that night."

"More than one person, actually, because of the guys in the park."

"Yes. That might help you, by muddying the waters. But still, say he goes through her records to find out who she has been in contact with—will he find you?"

"I was one of the people she had under surveillance."

"But there will be a lot of those. Anything more?"

Frank tried to remember. "I don't know," he confessed. "I thought we were being careful, but..."

"Did she call you on your phone?"

"Yes, a few times. But only from pay phones."

"But she might have been chipped at the time."

"She tried to be careful about that."

"Yes, but it didn't always work, isn't that what you said?"

"Right. But"—remembering back—"I don't think she ever said my name."

"Well—if you were ever both chipped at the same time, maybe he would be able to see when you got together. And if he sourced all your cell-phone calls, some would come from pay phones, and he might be able to cross-GPS those with her."

"Are pay phones GPSed?"

Edgardo glanced at him. "They stay in one spot, which you can then GPS."

"Oh. Yeah."

Edgardo cackled and waved an elbow at Frank as they ran. "There's lots of ways to find people! There's your acquaintances in the park, for instance. If he went out there and asked around, with a photo of you, he might be able to confirm."

"I'm just Professor Nosebleed to them."

"Yes, but the correlations... So," Edgardo said after a silence had stretched out a quarter mile or more. "It seems like you probably ought to take some kind of preemptive action."

"What do you mean?"

"Well. You followed him to their apartment, right?"

"Yes."

"Not your wisest move of that night, by the way."

Frank didn't want to explain that his capacity for decision making had been possibly injured, and perhaps not good to begin with.

"—but now we can probably use that information to find out his cover identity, for a start."

"I don't know the address."

"Well, you need to get it. Also the names on the doorbell plate, if there are any. But the apartment number for sure."

"Okay, I'll go back."

"Good. Be discreet. With that information, my friends could help you take it further. Given what's happened, they might give it a pretty high priority, to find out who he really works for."

"And who do your friends work for?"

"Well. They're scattered around. It's a kind of internal check group."

"And you trust them on this kind of stuff?"

"Oh yes." There was a reptilian look in Edgardo's eye that gave Frank a shiver.

I N THE DAYS THAT FOLLOWED, Frank passed his hours feeling baffled, and, under everything else, afraid. Or maybe, he thought, the feeling would be better characterized as extreme anxiety. He would wake in the mornings, take stock, remember where he was: in the Khembali embassy house's garden shed, with Rudra snoring up on the bed and Frank on his foam mattress on the floor.

The daylight slanting through their one window would usually have roused him. He would listen to Rudra's distressed breathing, sit up and tap on his laptop, look at the headlines and the weather forecast, and Emersonforthe day.com:

> We cannot trifle with this reality, this cropping-out in our planted gardens of the core of the world. No picture of life can have any veracity that does not admit the odious facts. A man's power is hooped in by a necessity which, by many experiments, he touches on every side until he learns its arc.

Maybe Emerson too had been hit on the head. Frank wanted to look into that. And he needed to look into Thoreau, too. Recently the keepers of the site had been posting lots of Henry David Thoreau, Emerson's young friend and occasional handyman. Amazing that two such minds had lived at the same time, in the same town—even for a while the same house. Thoreau, Frank was finding in these morning reads, was the great philosopher of the forest at the edge of town, and as such extremely useful to Frank—often more so, dare he say it, than the old man himself.

Today's Thoreau was from his journal:

I never feel that I am inspired unless my body is also. It too spurns a tame and commonplace life. They are fatally mistaken who think, while they strive with their minds, that they may suffer their bodies to stagnate in luxury or sloth. A man thinks as well through his legs and arms as his brain. We exaggerate the importance and exclusiveness of the headquarters. Do you suppose they were a race of consumptives and dyspeptics who invented Grecian mythology and poetry? The poet's words are, "You would almost say the body thought!" I quite say it. I trust we have a good body then.

Except Thoreau *had* been a consumptive, active though he was in his daily life as a surveyor and wandering botanist. This passage had been written only two years before he died of tuberculosis, so he must have known by then that his lungs were compromised, and his trust in having a good body misplaced. For lack of a simple antibiotic, Thoreau had lost thirty years. Still he had lived the day, and paid ferocious attention to it, as a very respectable early scientist.

And so up and off! And up Frank would leap, thinking about what the New England pair had said, and would dress and slip out the door in a frame of mind to see the world and act in it. No matter how early he went out, he always found some of the old Khembalis already out in the vegetable garden they had planted in the backyard, mumbling to themselves as they weeded. Frank might stop to say hi to Qang if she were out there, or dip his head in the door to tell her whether he thought he would be home for dinner that night; that was hardly ever, but she liked it when he let her know.

Then off to Optimodal on foot, blinking dreamily in the morning light, Wilson Avenue all rumbly and stinky with cars on the way to work. The walk was a little long, as all walks in D.C. tended to be; it was a city built for cars, like every other city. But the walk forced him to wake up, and to look closely at the great number of trees he passed. Even here on Wilson, it was impossible to forget they lived in a forest.

Then into the gym for a quick workout to get his brain fully awake—or as fully awake as it got these days. There was something wrong there. A fog in certain areas. He found it was easiest to do the same thing every day, reducing the number of decisions he had to make. Habitual action was a ritual that could be regarded as a kind of worship of the day. And it was so much easier.

Sometimes Diane was there, a creature of habit also, and uneasily he would say hi, and uneasily she would say hi back. They were still supposed to be rescheduling a dinner to celebrate the salting of the North Atlantic, but she had said she would get back to him about a good time for it, and he was therefore waiting for her to bring it up, and she wasn't. This was adding daily to his anxiety. Who knew what anything meant, really.

———

Then at work, Diane ran them through their paces as they produced the action plan that she thought was their responsibility to the new president. They were to lay out the current moment of the abrupt climate change they were experiencing, and discuss in full whether there was any way back out of it—and if there was, what kind of policies and activities might achieve it.

One thing that she had no patience for was the idea that having restarted the Gulf Stream, they were now out of the woods. She shook her head darkly when she saw this implied in communications from other agencies, or in the media. It did not help that they were suddenly experiencing a warm spell unlike anything that had happened the previous year, when the long winter had clamped down in October and never let up until May. This year, after several hard freezes, they were experiencing a balmy and almost rain-free Indian summer. Everyone wanted to explain it by the restoration of the Gulf Stream, and there may even have been some truth to that, but there was no way to be sure. Natural variation had too great an amplitude to allow for any such one-to-one correspondence of climatic cause and effect, although unfortunately this was something the climate skeptics and carbon supporters were also always saying, so that it was tricky for Diane to try to make the distinction.

But she was persistent, even adamant. "We have to put the Gulf Stream action to one side, and take a look at all the rest of it," she commanded. "Chase is going to need that from us to go forward."

Back in his office, therefore, Frank would sit at his desk, staring at his list of Things To Do. But all in a vain attempt to take his mind off Caroline.

Ordinarily the list would be enough to distract anyone. Its length and difficulty made it all by itself a kind of blow to the head. It induced an awe so great that it resembled apathy. They had done so much and yet there was so much left to do. And as more disasters blasted into the world, their Things To Do list would lengthen. It would never shorten. They were like the Dutch boy sticking his finger into the failing dike. What had happened to Khembalung was going to happen everywhere.

But there would still be land above water. There would still be things to be done. One had to try.

Caroline had spoken of her Plan B as if she had confidence in it. She must have had a place to go, a bank account, that sort of thing.

Frank checked out the figures from the oceanography group. The oceans covered about seventy percent of the globe. About two hundred million square kilometers, therefore, and in the wake of the first really big chunks of the West Antarctic Ice Sheet floating away, sea level was reported to have risen about twenty centimeters. The oceanographers had been measuring sea level rise a millimeter at a time, mostly from water warming up and expanding, so they were blown away and spoke of this twenty centimeters' rise as of a Noah's flood. Kenzo was simply bursting with amazement and pride.

Back-of-the-envelope calculation: .2 meters times the two hundred million square kilometers, was that forty thousand cubic kilometers? A lot of water. Measurements from the last few years had Antarctica losing a hundred and fifty cubic kilometers a year, with thirty to fifty more coming off Greenland. So, now about two hundred years' worth had come off in one year. No wonder they were freaking out. The difference no doubt lay in the fact that the melt before had been actual melting, whereas now what was happening was a matter of icebergs breaking off their perch and sliding down into the ocean. Obviously it made a big difference in how fast it could happen.

Frank brought the figures in with him to the meeting of Diane's strategic group scheduled for that afternoon, and listened to the others make their presentations. They were interesting talks, if daunting. They took his mind off Caroline, one had to say that. At least most of the time.

At the end of the talks, Diane described her sense of the situation. For her, there was a lot that was good news. First, Phil Chase was certain to be more supportive of NSF, and of science in general, than his predecessor had been. Second, the salting of the North Atlantic appeared to be having the effect they had hoped for: the Gulf Stream was now running at nearly its previous strength up into the Norwegian and Greenland Seas, following its earlier path in a manner that seemed to indicate the renewed pattern was, for now, fairly robust. They were still collecting data on the deeper part of the thermohaline circulation, which ran southward underneath the northerly flow of the Gulf Stream. If the southward undercurrent was running strong, they might be okay there.

"There's so much surface pressure northward," Kenzo said. "Maybe all we'll have to do from now on is to monitor the salinity and the currents. We might be able to intervene early enough in any stall process that we wouldn't need as much salt as we applied last fall. Maybe a certain percentage of the retiring oil fleet could be mothballed, in case we needed a salt fleet to go up there again and make another application."

"It would take a change in thinking," Diane said. "Up until now, people have only wanted to pay for disasters after they've happened, to make sure the pay-out was really necessary."

Kenzo said, "But now the true costs of that strategy are becoming clear."

"When it's too late," Edgardo added, his usual refrain.

Diane wrinkled her nose at Edgardo, as she often did, and made her usual rejoinder; they had no choice but to proceed from where they were now. "So, let's follow up on that one. It would have to be a kind of insurance model, or a hedge fund. Maybe the reinsurance industry will be trying to impose something like that on the rest of the economy anyway. We'll talk to them."

She moved on to the West Antarctic Ice Sheet situation. One of Kenzo's oceanographer colleagues gave them a presentation on the latest, showing with maps and satellite photos the tabular superbergs that had detached and slipped off their underwater perch and floated away.

Diane said, "I'd like some really good 3-D graphics on this, to show the new president and Congress, and the public too."

"All very well," Edgardo said, "but what can we do about it, aside from telling people it's coming?"

Not much; or nothing. Even if they somehow managed to lower the level of atmospheric carbon dioxide, and therefore the air temperatures, the already-rising ocean temperatures would be slow to follow. There was a continuity effect.

So they couldn't stop the WAIS from detaching.

They couldn't lower the rising sea level that resulted.

And they couldn't de-acidify the ocean.

This last was a particularly troubling problem. The CO_2 they had introduced into the atmosphere had been partially taken up by the ocean; the absorption rate now was about three billion tons of carbon a year into the ocean, and one estimate of the total uptake since the industrial revolution was four hundred billion tons. As a result, the ocean had become measurably more acidic, going from 8.2 to 8.1 on the pH scale, which was a logarithmic scale, so that the 0.1 shift meant thirty percent more hydrogen ions in the water. It was felt that certain species of phytoplankton would have their very thin calcium shells in effect eaten away. They would die, a number of species would go extinct, and these very species constituted a big fraction of the bottom of the ocean's food chain.

But de-acidifying the ocean was not an option. There were fairly arcane chemistry reasons why it was easier for sea water to become more acidic than to become more basic. A Royal Society paper had calculated, for the sake of estimating the scale of the problem, that if they mined and crushed exposed limestone and marble in the British Isles, "features such as the White Cliffs of Dover would be rapidly consumed," because it would take sixty square kilometers of limestone mined a hundred meters deep, every year, just to hold the status quo. All at a huge carbon cost for the excavations, of course, exacerbating the very problem they were trying to solve. But this was just a thought experiment anyway. It wouldn't work; it was an unmitigatable problem.

And that afternoon, as they went down Diane's list together, they saw that almost all of the climate and environmental changes they were seeing, or could see coming, were not susceptible to mitigation. Their big success of the fall, the restarting of the thermohaline cycle, had been an anomaly in that sense. The Gulf Stream had rested so closely to a tipping point in its action that humans had, by an application at the largest industrial scale they commanded, managed to tip that balance—at least temporarily. And as a result (maybe) the last month on the East Coast had been markedly warmer than the previous December had been. Perhaps they had even escaped the Youngest Dryas. So now, in one of those quick leaps that humans were prone to make (although science was not), people were talking about the climate problem as if it were something that they could terraform their way out of, or even had solved already!

It wasn't true. Most of their remaining problems were so big that they had too much heft and momentum for people to find any way to slow them, much less reverse them.

So, at the end of this meeting, Edgardo shook his head. "Well, this is grim! There is not much we can do! We would need much more energy than we command right now. And it would have to be clean energy at that."

Diane agreed. "Clean power is our only way out. That means solar power, I'd say. Maybe wind, although it would take an awful lot of pylons. Maybe nuclear, just one last generation to tide us over. Maybe ocean power too, if we could properly tap into currents or tides or waves. To me—when I look at factors like technical developmental readiness, and manufacturing capability, and current costs, and dangers and damage—I'd say our best chance lies in a really hard push on solar. A kind of Manhattan Project devoted to solar power."

She raised a finger: "And when I say Manhattan Project, I don't mean the kind of silver bullet that people seem to mean when they say Manhattan Project. I mean the part of the Manhattan Project that not only designed the bomb but also entrained something like twenty percent of America's industrial capacity to make the fissionable material. About the same percent of capacity as the auto industry, and right when they needed every bit of capacity for the other parts of the war. That's the kind of commitment we need now. Because if we had good solar power—"

She made one of her characteristic gestures, one that Frank had become very fond of: an opening of the palm, turned up and held out to the world. "We might be able to stabilize the climate. Let's push all the aspects of this. Let's organize the case, and take it to Phil Chase, and get him prepped for when he takes office."

After the meeting, Frank couldn't focus. He checked his e-mail, his cell phone, his FOG phone, his office phone: no messages. Caroline had not called for yet another day. No telling where she was or what was happening.

That night he wandered north up Connecticut Avenue, past the hotel where Reagan had been shot, past the Chinese embassy with its Tibetan and Falun Gong protesters in front singing, until he crossed the big bridge over Rock Creek, guarded by its four Disneyesque lion statues. Out on the middle of the bridge there was a tiny relief from the claustrophobia of the city and forest. It was one of the only places where Rock Creek seemed like a big gorge.

He continued to the clutch of little restaurants on the far side of the bridge and chose one of the Indian ones. Ate a meal thinking about the names on the wine list. Vineyards in Bangalore, why was this surprising? He read his laptop over milk tea.

When it was late enough, he struck off to the northwest, toward Bethesda. Back streets, residential, the forest taking over. Night in the city, sound of distant sirens. For the first time in the day he felt awake. It was a long hike.

Up on Wisconsin he came into the realm of the Persian rug shops, and slowed down. It was still too early. Into a bar, afraid to drink, afraid to think. A whiskey for courage. Out again into the bright night of Wisconsin, then west into the strange tangle of streets backing it. The Metro stop had been like a fountain of money and people and buildings pouring up out of the earth, overwhelming what had been here before. Some of the old houses that still remained undemolished suggested a little urban space of the 1930s, almost like the back streets of Georgetown.

This was the Quiblers' neighborhood, but he didn't want to intrude, nor was he in the mood to be sociable. Too late for that, but not early enough for his task. Pass by and on up Woodson, off to the left, now he was in the well-remembered neighborhood of Caroline and her ex-husband. Finally it was late enough, and yet not too late: midnight. His pulse was beginning to pound a little in his neck, and he wished he hadn't had that whiskey. The streets were not entirely empty; in this city that wouldn't happen until more like two. But that was okay. Up the steps of the apartment building that Caroline's ex had gone into. The drape had been pulled back at the top window of the building. He shone his penlight on the address list under its glass, took a photo of it with his cell phone. Quite a few of the little slots had been left blank. He photoed the street address above the door as well, then turned and walked down the street, away from the streetlight he had stood under on that most fateful election night. His own fate, Caroline's, the nation's, the world's—but who knew? Probably it only felt that way. His heart was beating so hard. Fight or flight, sure; but what happened if one could neither fight nor flee?

He turned a corner and ran.

Back in his office. Late in the day. He had given Edgardo his information from Bethesda a few days before. Soon he would have to decide again what to do after work.

Unable to face that, he continued to work. If only he could work all the time he would never have to decide anything.

He typed up his notes from Diane's last two meetings. So, he thought as he looked them over, it had come to this: they had fucked up the world so badly that only the rapid invention and deployment of some kind of clean power generation much more powerful than what they had now would be enough to extricate them from the mess. If it could be done at all.

That meant solar, as Diane had concluded. Wind was too diffuse, waves and currents too hard to extract energy from. Fusion was like a mirage on a desert road, always the same distance away. Ordinary nuclear—well, that was a possibility, as Diane had pointed out. A very real possibility. It was dangerous and created waste for the ages, but it might be done. Some kinds of cost-benefit analysis might favor it.

But it was hard to imagine making it really safe. To do so they would have to become like the French (gasp!), who got ninety percent of their power from nuclear plants, all built to the same stringent standards. Not the likeliest scenario for the rest of the world, but not physically impossible. The U.S. Navy had run a safe nuclear program ever since the 1950s. Frank wrote on his notepad: *Is French nuclear power safe? Is US Navy nuclear safe? What does safe mean? Can you recycle spent fuel and guard the bomb-level plutonium that would finally reduce out of it?* All that would have to be investigated and discussed. Nothing could be taken off the table just because it might create poisons that would last fifty thousand years.

On the other hand, solar was coming along fast enough to encourage Frank to hope for even more acceleration. There were problems, but ultimately the fundamental point remained: in every moment an incredible amount of energy rained down from the sun onto the Earth. That was what oil was, after all: a small portion of the sun's energy, captured by photosynthesis over millions of years—all those plants, fixing carbon and then dying, then getting condensed into a sludge and buried rather than returning to the air. Millions of years of sunlight caught that way. Every tank of gas burned about a hundred acres of what had been a forest's carbon. Or say a hundred years of a single acre's production of forest carbon. This was a very impressive condensate! It made sense that matching it with the real-time energy input from any other system would be difficult.

But sunlight itself rained down perpetually. About seventy percent of the photosynthesis that took place on Earth was already entrained to human uses, but photosysnthesis only caught a small fraction of the total amount of solar energy striking the planet each day. Those totals, day after day, soon dwarfed even what had been caught in the Triassic fossil carbon. Every couple of months, the whole Triassic's capture was surpassed. So the potential was there.

This was true in so many areas. The potential was there, but time was required to realize the potential, and now it was beginning to seem like they did not have much time. Speed was crucial. This was the reason Diane and others were still contemplating nuclear.

It would be good if they needed less energy. Well, but this was an entirely different problem, dragging in many other issues—technology, consumption, lifestyles, values, habits—also the sheer number of humans on the planet. Perhaps seven billion was too many, perhaps six billion was too many. It was possible that three billion was too many. Their six billion could be a kind of oil bubble.

Edgardo was not calling, neither was Caroline calling.

Desperate for ways to occupy his mind—though of course he did not think of it that way, in order not to break the spell—Frank began to look into estimates of the Earth's maximum human carrying capacity. This turned out (usefully enough for his real purpose) to be an incredibly vexed topic, argued over for centuries already, with no clear answers yet found. The literature contained estimates for the Earth's human carrying capacity ranging from one hundred million to twelve trillion. Quite a spread! Although here the outliers were clearly the result of some heavily ideological analyses; the high estimate appeared to be translating the sunlight hitting the Earth directly into human calories, with no other factors included; the low estimate appeared not to like human beings, even to regard them as some kind of parasite.

The majority of serious opinion came in between two billion and thirty billion; this was satisfyingly tighter than the seven magnitudes separating the outlier estimates, but for practical purposes still a big variance, especially considering how important the real number was. If the carrying capacity of the planet was two billion, they had badly overshot and were in serious trouble, looking at a major dieback that might spiral to near extinction. If on the other hand the thirty billion figure was correct, they had some wiggle-room to maneuver.

But there were hardly any scientific or governmental organizations even looking at this issue. Zero Population Growth was one of the smallest advocacy groups in Washington, which was saying a lot; and Negative Population Growth (a bad name, it seemed to Frank) turned out to be a mom-and-pop operation run out of a garage. It was bizarre.

He read one paper, written as if by a Martian, that suggested if humanity cared to share the planet with the other species, especially the mammals—and could they really survive without them?—then they should restrict their population to something like two billion, occupying only a networked fraction of the landscape. Leaving the rest of the animals in possession of a larger networked fraction. It was a pretty persuasive paper.

As another occupier of his thoughts (though now hunger was going to drive him out into the world), he looked into theories of long-term strategic policy, thinking this might give him some tools for thinking through these things. It was another area that seemed on the face of it to be important, yet was understudied as far as Frank could tell. Most theorists in the field, he found, had agreed that the goal or method of long-term strategic thinking ought to be "robustness," which meant that you had to find things to do that would almost certainly do some good, no matter which particular future came to pass. Nice work if you could get it! Although some of the theorists actually had developed rubrics to evaluate the robustness of proposed policies. That could be useful. But when it came to generating the policies, things got more vague.

Just do the obvious things, Vanderwal. Do the necessary.

Diane was already acting in the manner suggested by most long-term strategy theory, because in any scenario conceivable, copious amounts of clean solar energy would almost certainly be a good thing. It was, therefore, a *robust plan*.

So, solar power:

1) there were the photovoltaics, in which sunlight was transformed into alternating current by way of photons stimulating piezoelectricity in silicon.
2) there were the Stirling engines, external heat engines that used mirror dishes controlled by computers to reflect sunlight onto a hydrogen-filled closed element that heated to 1,300 degrees Fahrenheit, driving pistons which generated the electricity. The engine had been designed by a Scot named Stirling in 1816.

All solar technologies had efficiency rates measured as a percentage of the sunlight's photonic energy transferred successfully to alternating current electricity. They had been getting some really good numbers from solar panels, up to twenty percent, but this Stirling engine got thirty. Given the amount of photons raining down, that was really good. That would add up fast.

Then he found a link to a site that explained that Southern California Edison had built a Stirling system to power a five-hundred-megawatt plant; most traditionally-powered plants were five hundred or a thousand megawatts, so this was full size. That meant there was some practical experience with real-world, commercial versions of this technology. Also some manufacturing ability, ready to be deployed. All good news when contemplating the need for speed.

Banishing the thought (recurrent about every hour) that they should have been doing this a long time ago, Frank called SCE and asked a long string of questions of the CPM (the Cognizant Program Manager, a useful acronym that only NSF appeared to use). This turned out to be a man who was more than happy to talk—who would have talked all day, maybe all night. With difficulty Frank got him to stop. Lots of enthusiasm for the Stirling system there.

Well, more grist for the mill. Over the past year Frank had been giving alternative energy about a quarter of his working time, and now he saw he was going to have to bump that up. Everything from now on would be jacked to emergency levels. Not a comfortable feeling, but there was no avoiding it. It was like an existential condition, as if he had become Alice's White Rabbit: I'm late! I'm late! I'm late! And most of the time he managed to obscure from his conscious train of thought the true source of his anxiety.

One day, later that week, when he was deep in work's oblivion, Diane appeared in his doorway, startling him. He was pleased, then nervous; they had not yet found a new balance. After Caroline had called Frank with her emergency situation, Frank had hastily called Diane to cancel before thinking of any plausible non-other-woman-related reason for doing so, and so had given no explanation at all—which opacity was suspicious, and probably more impolite than the cancellation per se. Opacity was seldom conducive to rapport.

"Hi, Diane," he said now, aping normality. "What's happening?"

She looked at him with a curious expression. "I just got a call from Phil Chase."

"Wow, what did he want?"

"He asked me if I would be his science advisor."

Frank found he was standing. He reached out and shook Diane's hand, then hugged her. "Now that is news we *have* to celebrate," he declared, seizing the bull by the horns. "I'm sorry about that the other night, I still owe you dinner! Can I take you out tonight?"

"Sure," she said easily, as if there had been no problem. She was so cool; maybe there never had been a problem. Frank couldn't be sure. "Meet you at," she checked her watch, "at six, okay? Now I'm going to go call my kids."

But then she stopped on her way out, and again looked at him oddly. "You must have had something to do with this," she said suddenly.

"Me? I don't think so. What do you mean?"

"Talking to Charlie Quibler, maybe?"

"Oh, no. I mean, of course I've talked to Charlie about some of our stuff, generally—"

"And he's been Chase's environment guy."

"Well yes, but you know, Charlie's just part of a large staff, and he's been staying at home with Joe, so he hasn't been a major factor with Chase for some time, as I understand it. Mostly just a voice on the phone. He says he doesn't get listened to. He says he's kind of like Jiminy Cricket was to Pinocchio, when Pinocchio's nose was at its longest."

Diane laughed. "Yeah sure. Let's meet over at Optimodal, shall we? Let's say seven instead of six. I want to run some of this off."

Now that was something he could understand. "Sure. See you there."

Frank sat in his chair feeling his chest puffed out: another cliché revealed to be an accurate account of emotion's effects on the body. Everyone was the same. It occurred to him that maybe Charlie *had* had something to do with it, after all. Someone had to have advised Chase whom to choose for this post, and as far as Frank knew, Chase and Diane had never met. So—that was interesting.

Frank went over to the Optimodal Health Club just after six, waved to Diane on the elliptical in the next room, and stomped up the Stairmaster for the equivalent of about a thousand vertical feet. After that he showered and dressed, getting into one of his "nicer" shirts for the occasion, and met Diane out in the lobby at the appointed time. She too had changed into something nice, and for a second Frank considered the possibility that she lived out of her office and Optimodal, just as he had contemplated doing before building his treehouse. What evidence did he or anyone else have to disprove it? When they arrived in the morning she was there, when they left at night she was there. There were couches in her big office, and she went to Optimodal every morning of the week, as far as he knew. . . .

But then again, she certainly had a home somewhere. Everyone did, except for him. And the bros in the park. And the fregans and ferals proliferating in the metropolis. Indeed some twenty or thirty million people in America, he had read. But one thought of everyone as having a home.

Enough—it was time to refocus on the moment and their date. It had to be called that. Their second date, in fact—the first one having occurred by accident in New York, after discussing the North Atlantic project at the UN. And now they were in a Lebanese restaurant in Georgetown that Diane had recently discovered.

And it was very nice. Now they could celebrate not only the actual salting itself, but its subsequent success in restarting the thermohaline circulation; and now, also, Diane's invitation to become the new Presidential Science Advisor.

She was pleased with this last, Frank could see. "Tell me about it," he said to her when they were settled into the main course. "Is it a good position? I mean, what does the science advisor do?" Did it have any power, in other words?

"It all depends on the president," Diane said. "I've been looking into it, and it appears the position began as Nixon's way of spanking the science community for publicly backing Johnson over Goldwater. He sent NSF packing out here to Arlington, and abolished his science advisory committee, and established this position. So it became a single advisor he could appoint without any consultation or approval mechanism, and then he could stick them on the shelf somewhere. Which is where these people have usually stayed, except in a few instances."

That didn't sound good. "But?"

"Well, in theory, if a president were listening, it could get pretty interesting. I mean, clearly there's a need for more coordination of the sciences in the federal government. We've seen that at NSF. Ideally there would be a cabinet post, you know, some kind of Department of Science, with a Secretary of Science."

"The science czar."

"Yes." She was wrinkling her nose. "Except that would create huge amounts of trouble, because really, most of the federal agencies are already supposed to be run scientifically, or have science as part of their subject, or in their operation. So if someone tried to start a Department of Science, it would poach on any number of other agencies, and none of them would stand for it. They would gang up on such an advisor and kill him, like they did to the so-called intelligence czar when they tried to coordinate the intelligence agencies."

This gave Frank a chill. "Yeah, I guess that's right."

"So, now, maybe the science advisor could act like a kind of personal advisor. You know. If we presented a menu of really robust options, and Chase chose some of them to enact, then . . . well. It would be the president himself advocating for science."

"And he might want to do that, given the situation."

"Yes, it seems that way, doesn't it? Although Washington has a way of bogging people down."

"The swamp."

"Yes, the swamp. But if the swamp freezes over"—they laughed—"then maybe we can ice-skate over the obstacles!"

Frank nodded. "Speaking of which, we were supposed to be going to try ice-skating down here, when the river froze over."

"That's right, we were. But now we've got this so-called heat spell."

"True. Return of the Gulf Stream."

"That is so crazy. I bet we will get freezing spells just like before."

"Yes. Well, until that happens maybe we can just walk the shore then, and see where you could rent ice skates when the time comes."

"Sure. I think the Georgetown Rowing Club is going to do it, we can go check it out. I read they're going to convert when the river freezes over. They're going to put out floodlights and boundary lines and everything."

"Good for them! Let's go take a look after dinner."

And so they finished the meal cheerfully, moving from one great Levantine dish to the next. Even the basics were exquisite: olives, hummus, dill—everything. And by the time they were done they had split a bottle of a dry white wine. They walked down to the Potomac arm in arm, as they had in Manhattan so very briefly; they walked the Georgetown waterfront, where the potted shrubs lining the river wall were lit by little white Christmas tree lights. All this had been overwhelmed in the great flood, and they could still see the high-water mark on the buildings behind the walk, but other than that, things were much as they had been before, the river as calm as a sheet of black silk as it poured under the Key Bridge.

Then they came to the mouth of Rock Creek, a tiny little thing. Following it upstream in his mind, Frank came to the park and his treehouse, standing right over a bend in this same creek—and thus it occurred to him to think, Here you are fooling around with another woman while your Caroline is in trouble God knows where. What would she think if she saw you?

Which was a hard thought to recover from; and Diane saw that his mood had changed. Quickly he suggested they warm up over drinks.

They retired to a bar overlooking the confluence of the creek and the river, on the Georgetown side. They ordered Irish coffees. Frank warmed up again, his sudden stab of dread dispelled by Diane's immense calmness, by the aura of reality that emanated from her. It was reassuring to be around her; precisely the opposite of the feeling he had when—

But he stayed in the moment. He agreed with Diane's comment that Irish coffee provided the perfect compound of stimulant and relaxant, sugar and fat, hydration and warmth. "It must have been invented by scientists," she said. "It's like it's made to a formula to hit all the receptors at once."

Frank said, "I remember it's what they always used to serve at the Salk Institute after their seminars. They've got a patio deck overlooking the Pacific, and everyone would go out with Irish coffees and watch the sunset."

"Nice."

Later, as Frank walked her back up through Georgetown to her car, she said, "I was wondering if you'd be interested in joining my advisory staff. It would be an extension of the work you've been doing at NSF. I mean, I know you're planning to go back to San Diego, but until then, you know . . . I could use your help."

Frank had stopped walking. Diane turned and glanced up at him, shyly it seemed, and then looked away, down M Street. The stretch they could see looked to Frank like the Platonic form of a Midwestern main street, totally unlike the rest of D.C.

"Sure," Frank heard himself say. He realized that in some sense he *had* to accept her offer. He had no choice; he was only in D.C. now because of her previous invitation to work on the climate problem, and he had been doing that for a year now. And they were friends, they were colleagues; they were . . . "I mean, I'll have to check with my department and all first, to make sure it will all be okay at UCSD. But I think it could be really interesting."

"Oh good. Good. I was hoping you'd say yes."

The next morning, at work his doorway darkened, and he swung his chair around, expecting to see Diane, there to discuss their move to the Presidential Science Advisor's offices—

"Oh! Edgardo!"

"Hi, Frank. Hey, are you up for getting a bite at the Food Factory?" Waggling his eyebrows Groucho-istically.

"Sure," Frank said, trying to sound natural. It was hard not to look around his office as he saved and shut the file he was working on.

On the way to the Food Factory, Edgardo surreptitiously ran a wand over Frank, and gave it to Frank, who did the same for him. Then they went in and stood at a bar, noisily eating chips and salsa.

"What is it?"

"A friend of mine has tracked down your friend and her husband."

"Ah ha! And?"

"They work for a unit of a black agency called Advanced Research and Development Agency Prime. The man's name is Edward Cooper, and hers is Caroline Churchland. They ran a big data-mining effort, which was a combination of the Total Information Awareness project and some other black programs in Homeland Security."

"Wait—she didn't work *for* him?"

"No. My friend says it was more like the other way around. She headed the program, but he was brought in to help when some surveillance issues cropped up. He came from Homeland Security, and before that CIA, where he was on the Afghanistan detail. My friend says the program got a lot more serious when he arrived."

"Serious?"

"Some surveillance issues. My friend didn't know what that meant. And then this attempt on the election that she tipped us to."

"But *he* worked for *her*?"

"Yes."

"And when did they get married?"

"About two years before he joined her project."

"And he worked for her."

"That's what I was told. Also, my friend thinks he probably knows where she's gone."

"What!"

"That's what he told me. On the night she disappeared, you see, there was a call from a pay phone she had used before, a call to the Khembali embassy. I take it that was to you?"

"She left a message," Frank muttered, more and more worried. "But so?"

"Well, there was another call from that pay phone, to a number in Maine. My friend found the address for that number, and it's the number of your friend's college roommate. And that roommate has a vacation home on an island up there. And the power has just been turned on for that vacation home. So he thinks that's where she may have gone, and, as I'm sure you can see, he furthermore thinks that if he can track her that well, at his remove, then her husband is likely to be even faster at it."

"Shit." Frank's feet were cold.

"Shit indeed. Possibly you should warn her. I mean, if she thinks she's hidden herself—"

"Yeah, sure," Frank said, thinking furiously. "But another thing—if her ex could find her, couldn't he find me too?"

"Maybe so."

They regarded each other.

"We have to neutralize this guy somehow," Frank said.

Edgardo shook his head. "Do not say that, my friend."

"Why not?"

"Neutralize?" He dragged out the word, his expression suddenly black. "Eliminate? Remove? Equalize? Disable? DX? Disappear? Liquidate?"

"I don't mean any of those," Frank explained. "I just meant neutralize. As in, unable to affect us. Made neutral to us."

"Hard to do," Edgardo said. "I mean, get a restraining order? You don't want to go there. It doesn't work even if you can get them."

"Well?"

"You may just have to live with it."

"*Live* with it? With *what*?"

Edgardo shrugged. "Hard to say right now."

"I can't *live with it* if he's trying to harm her, and there's a good chance of him finding her."

"I know."

"I'll have to go find her first."

Edgardo nodded, looking at him with an evaluative expression. "Maybe so."

A T THE QUIBLERS' HOUSE IN BETHESDA this unsettled winter, things were busier than ever. This was mainly because of Phil Chase's election, which of course had galvanized his Senatorial office, turning his staff into one part of a much larger transition team.

A presidential transition was a major thing, and there were famous cases of failed transitions by earlier administrations that were enough to put a spur to their rears, reminding them of the dire consequences that ineptitude in this area could have on the subsequent fates of the presidents involved. It was important to make a good running start, to craft the kind of "first hundred days" that had energized the incoming administration of Franklin Delano Roosevelt in 1933, setting the model for most presidents since to try to emulate. Critical appointments had to be made, bold new programs turned into law.

Phil was well aware of this challenge and its history, and was determined to meet it successfully. "We'll call it the First Sixty Days," he said to his staff. "Because there's no time to lose!" He had not slowed down after the election; indeed it seemed to Charlie Quibler that he had even stepped up the pace, if that was possible. Ignoring the claim of irregularities in the Oregon vote—claims which had become standard in any case ever since the tainted elections at the beginning of the century—and secure in the knowledge that the American public did not like to think about troubling news of this sort no matter who won, Phil was free to forge ahead with a nonstop schedule of meetings, meetings from dawn till midnight, and often long past it. He was lucky he was one of those people who only needed a few hours of sleep a day to get by.

Not so Charlie, who was jolted out of sleep far too often by calls from his colleague Roy Anastophoulus, Phil's new chief of staff, asking him to come down to the office and pitch in.

"Roy, I can't," Charlie would say. "I've got Joe here, Anna's off to work already, and we've got Gymboree."

"Gymboree? Am I hearing this? Charlie which is more important to the fate of the Republic, advising the president or going to Gymboree?"

"False choice," Charlie would snap. "Although Gymboree is far more important if we want Joe to sleep well at night, which we do. You're talking to me now, right? That's what telephones are for. How would this change in any way if I were down there?"

"Yeah yeah yeah yeah, hey Chucker I gotta go now, but listen you *have* to come in from the cold, this is no time to be baby-sitting, we've got the fate of the world in the balance and we need you in the office and taking one of these *crucial* jobs that no one else can fill as well as you can. Joe is around two right? So you can put him in the daycare down here at the White House, or anywhere else in the greater metropolitan region for that matter, but you have to *be here* or else you will have *missed the train,* Phil isn't going to stand for someone phoning home like E.T., lost somewhere in Bethesda when the world is sinking and freezing and drowning and burning up and everything else all at once."

"Roy. Stop. I am talking to you like once an hour, maybe more. I couldn't talk to you more if we were handcuffed together."

"Yeah it's nice it's sweet it's one of the treasured parts of my day, but *it's a face business,* you know that, and I haven't *seen* you in months, and Phil hasn't either, and I'm afraid it's getting to be a case of *not seen not heard.*"

"Are you establishing a climate-change task force?"

"Yes."

"Are you going to ask Diane Chang to be the science advisor?"

"Yes. He already did."

"And are you going to convene a meeting with all the reinsurance companies?"

"Yes."

"And you're proposing the legislative package to the Congress?"

This was Charlie's big omnibus environmental bill, brought back—in theory—from death by dismemberment.

"Of course we are."

"So how exactly am I being cut out? That's every single thing I've ever suggested to you."

"But Charlie, I'm looking *forward,* to how you *will be* cut out. You've gotta put Joe in daycare and come in out of the cold."

"But I don't want to."

"I gotta go you get a grip and get down here bye."

He sounded truly annoyed. But Charlie could speak his mind with Roy, and he wasn't going to let the election change that. And when he woke up in the morning, and considered that he could either go down to the Mall and talk policy with policy wonks all day, and get home late every night—or he could spend that day with Joe wandering the parks and bookstores of Bethesda, calling in to Phil's office from time to time to have those same policy talks in mercifully truncated form, he knew very well which day he preferred. It was an easy call, a no-brainer. He liked spending time with Joe. With all its problems and crises, he enjoyed it more than almost anything he had ever done. And Joe was growing up fast, and Charlie could see that what he enjoyed most in their life together was only going to last until preschool, if then. It went by fast!

Indeed, in the last week or so it seemed that Joe was changing so fast that Charlie's desire to spend time with him was becoming as much a result of worry as of desire for pleasure. It seemed he was dealing with a different kid. But Charlie suppressed this feeling, and tried to pretend to himself that it was only for positive reasons that he wanted to stay home.

Only occasionally, and for short periods, could he think honestly about this to himself. Nothing about the matter was obvious, even when he did try to think about it. Because ever since their trip to Khembalung, Joe had been a little different—feverish, Anna claimed, although only her closest ovulation-monitoring thermometer could find this fever—but in any case hectic, and irritable in a way that was unlike his earlier irritability, which had seemed to Charlie a kind of cosmic energy, a force chafing at its restraints. After Khembalung it had turned peevish, even pained.

All this had coincided with what Charlie regarded as undue interest in Joe on the part of the Khembalis, and Charlie had gotten Drepung to admit that the Khembalis thought that Joe was one of their great lamas, reincarnated in Joe's body. That's how it happened, to their way of thinking.

After that news, and also at Charlie's insistence, they had performed a kind of exorcism ritual (they had not put it like that) designed to drive any reincarnated soul out of Joe, leaving the original inhabitant, which was the only one Charlie wanted in there. But now he was beginning to wonder if all that had been a good idea. Maybe, he was beginning to think, his original Joe had in fact been the very personality that the Khembalis had driven out.

Not that Joe was all that different. Anna declared his fever was gone, and he was therefore more relaxed, and that his moodiness was much as before.

Only to Charlie he was clearly different, in ways he found hard to characterize to himself—but chiefly, the boy was now too content with things as they were. His Joe had never been like that, not since the very moment of his birth, which from all appearances had angered him greatly. Charlie could still remember seeing his little red face just out of Anna, royally pissed off and yelling.

But none of that now. No tantrums, no imperious commands. He was calm, he was biddable; he was even inclined to *take naps*. It just wasn't his Joe.

Given these new impressions, Charlie was not in the slightest inclined to want to put Joe in a new situation, thus confusing the issue even further. He wanted to hang out with him, see what he was doing and feeling; he wanted to *study* him. This was what parental love came down to, apparently, sometimes, especially with a toddler, a human being in one of the most transient and astonishing of all the life stages. Someone coming to consciousness!

But the world was no respecter of Charlie's feelings. Later that morning his cell phone rang again, and this time it was Phil Chase himself.

"Charlie, how are you?"

"I'm fine, Phil, how are you? Are you getting any rest?"

"Oh yeah sure. I'm still on my postcampaign vacation, so things are very relaxed."

"Uh huh, sure. That's not what Roy tells me. How's the transition coming?"

"It's coming fine, as I understand it. I thought that was your bailiwick."

Charlie laughed with a sinking feeling. Already he felt the change in Phil's status begin to weigh on him, making the conversation seem more and more surreal. He had worked for Phil for a long time, but always while Phil had been a senator; Charlie had long since gotten used to the considerable and yet highly circumscribed power that Phil as senator had wielded. It had become normalized, indeed had become kind of a running joke between them, in that Charlie often had reminded Phil just how completely circumscribed his power was.

Now that just wasn't going to work. The president of the United States might be many things, but unpowerful was not among them. Many of the administrations preceding Phil's had worked very hard to expand the powers of the executive branch beyond what the constitutional framers had intended— which campaigns made a mockery of the "strict constitutionalist" talk put out by these same people when discussing what principles the Supreme Court's justices should hold, and showed they preferred a secretive executive dictatorship to democracy, especially if the president were a puppet installed by the interested parties. But never mind; the result of their labors was an apparatus of power that if properly understood and used could in many ways rule the world. Bizarre but true: the president of the United States could rule the world, both by direct fiat and by setting the agenda that everyone else had to follow or be damned. World ruler. Not really, of course, but it was about as close as anyone could get. And how exactly did you joke about that?

"Your clothes are still visible?" Charlie inquired.

"To me they are. But look," passing on a full riposte, as being understood in advance—although Phil could no doubt see the comedy of omnipotence as well as the comedy of constraint—"I wanted to talk to you about your position in the administration. Roy says you're being a little balky, but obviously we need you."

"I'm here already. I can talk twelve hours a day, if you like."

"Well, but a lot of these jobs require more than that. They're in-person jobs, as you know."

"What do you mean, like which ones?"

"Well, like for instance head of the EPA."

"WHAT?" Charlie shouted. He reeled, literally, in that he staggered slightly to the side, then listed back to catch himself. "Don't you be scaring me, Phil! I hope you're not thinking of making appointments as stupid as that! Jesus, you know perfectly well I'm not qualified for that job! You need a first-rate scientist for that one, a major researcher with some policy and administrative experience, we've talked about this already! Every agency needs to feel appreciated and supported to keep esprit de corps and function at the highest levels, you know that! Isn't Roy reminding you? You aren't making a bunch of stupid political appointments, are you?"

Phil was cracking up. "See? That's why we need you down here!"

Charlie sucked down some air. "Oh. Ha ha. Very funny. Don't be scaring me like that, Phil."

"I was serious, Charlie. You'd be fine heading the EPA. We need someone there with a global vision of the world's environmental problems. And we'll find someone like that. But that wouldn't be the best use for you, I agree."

"Good." Charlie felt as if a bullet had just whizzed by his head. He was quivering as he said, very firmly, "Let's just keep things like they are with me."

"No, that's not what I mean, either. Listen, can you come down here and at least talk it over with me? Fit that into your schedule?"

Well, shit. How could he say no? This was his boss, also the president of the United States, speaking. But if he had to talk to him in person about it. . . . He sighed. "Yeah, yeah, of course. Your wish is my demand."

"Bring Joe, if you can, I'd enjoy seeing him. We can take him out for a spin on the Tidal Basin."

"Yeah yeah."

What else could he say?

The problem was that *yeah yeah* was pretty much the only thing you could say, when replying to the president of the United States making a polite request of you. Perhaps there had been some presidents who had established a limit there, by asking for impossible things and then seeing what happened; power could quickly bring out the latent sadism in the powerful; but if a sane and clever president wanted only ever to get yeses in response to his questions, he could certainly frame them to make it that way. That was just the way it was.

Certainly it was hard to say no to a president-elect inviting you and your toddler to paddle around the Tidal Basin in one of the shiny blue pedal boats docked on the east side of the pond.

And once on the water, it indeed proved very hard to say no to Phil. Joe was wedged between them, life-jacketed and strapped down by Secret Service agents in ways that even Anna would have accepted as safe. He was looking about blissfully; he had even been fully compliant and agreeable about getting into the life jacket and being tied down by the seat belting. It had made

Charlie a bit seasick to watch. Now it felt like Phil was doing most of the pumping on the boat's foot pedals. He was also steering.

Phil was always in a good mood on the water, rapping away about nothing, looking down at Joe, then over the water at the Jefferson Memorial, the most graceful but least emotional of the city's memorials; beaming at the day, sublimely unaware of the people on the shore path who had noticed him and were exclaiming into their cell phones or taking pictures with them. The Secret Service people had taken roost on the paddleboat dock, and there were an unusual number of men in suits walking the shore among the tourists and joggers.

"Where I need you in the room," Phil said out of the blue, "is when we gather a global-warming task force. I'll be out of my depth in that crowd, and there'll be all kinds of information and plans put forth. That's where I'll want your impressions, both real-time and afterward, to help me cross-check what I think. It won't do to have me describe these things to you after the fact. There isn't time for that, and besides I might miss the most important thing."

"Yeah, well—"

"None of that! This task force will be as close to a Department of Science or a Department for the Environment as I can make. It's going to set the agenda for a lot of what we do. It'll be my strategy group, Charlie, and I'm saying I need you in it. Now, I've looked into the daycare facilities for children at the White House. They're adequate, and we can get to work making them even better. Joe will be my target audience. You'd like to play all day with a bunch of kids, wouldn't you Joe?"

"Yeah Phil," Joe said, happy to be included in the conversation.

"We'll set up whatever system works best for you, what do you think of that?"

"I like that," Joe said.

Charlie started to mutter something about the Chinese women who buried their infants up to the neck in riverbank mud every day to leave them to go to work in the rice paddies, but Phil overrode him.

"Gymboree in the basement, if that's what it takes! Laser tag, paintball wars—you name it! You'd like paintball wars, wouldn't you Joe?"

"Big truck," Joe observed, pointing at the traffic on Independence Avenue.

"Sure, we could have big trucks too. We could have a monster truck pull right on the White House lawn."

"Monster *truck*." Joe smiled at the phrase.

Charlie sighed. It really seemed to him that Joe should be shouting *big trucks right now,* or trying to escape and crawling around among the turning pedals underfoot, or leaping overboard to go for a swim. Instead he was listening peacefully to Phil's banter, with an expression that said he understood just as much as he wanted to, and approved of it in full.

Ah well. Everyone changed. And in fact, that had been the whole point of the ceremony Charlie had asked the Khembalis to conduct! Charlie had requested it—had insisted on it, in fact! But without, he now realized, fully imagining the consequences.

Phil said, "So you'll do it?"

"I don't know."

"You more or less have to, right? I mean, you're the one who first suggested that I run, when we were over at Lincoln."

"Everyone was telling you that."

"No they weren't. Besides, you were first."

"No, you were. I just thought it would work."

"And you were right, right?"

"Apparently so."

"So you owe me. You got me into this mess."

Phil smiled, waved at some tourists as he made a broad champing turn back toward the other side of the Basin. Charlie sighed. If he agreed, he would not see Joe anywhere near as much as he was used to—an idea he hated. On the other hand, if he didn't see him as much, he wouldn't notice so often how much Joe had changed. And he hated that change.

So much to dislike! Unhappily he said, "I'll have to talk to Anna about it first. But I think she'll go for it. She's pretty pro-work. So. Shit. I'll give it a try. I'll give it a few months, and see how it goes. By that time your task force should be on their way, and I can see where things stand and go emeritus if I need to."

"Good." And Phil pedaled furiously, almost throwing Charlie's knees up into his chin with the force of his enthusiasm. He said, "Look, Joe, all the people are waving at you!"

Joe waved back. "Hi people!" he shouted. "Big truck, right there! Look! I like that big truck. That's a good truck."

And so: change. The inexorable emergence of difference in time. Becoming. One of the fundamental mysteries.

Charlie hated it. He liked being; he hated becoming. This was, he thought, an indicator of how happy he had been with the way things were, the situation as he had had it. Mister Mom—he had loved it. Just this last May he had been walking down Leland Street and had passed Djina, one of the Gymboree moms he knew, biking the other way, and he had called out to her "Happy Mother's Day!" and she had called back, "Same to you!" and he had felt a glow in him that had lasted an hour. Someone had understood.

Of course the pure-mom routine of the 1950s was an Ozzie and Harriet nightmare, a crazy-making program so effective that the surprise was there were any moms at all in that generation who had stayed sane. Most of them had gone nuts in one way or another, because in its purest form that life was too constrained to the crucial but mindless daily chores of child-rearing and house maintenance—"uncompensated labor," as the economists put it, but in a larger sense than what they meant with their idiot bean-counting. Coming in the fifties, hard on the heels of World War II's shattering of all norms, its huge chaotic space of dislocation and freedom for young women, it must have felt like a return to prison after a big long breakout.

But that wasn't the life Charlie had been leading. Along with the child care and the shopping and the housework had been his "real" work as a senatorial aide, which, even though it had been no more than a few phone conversations a day, had bolstered the "unreal" work of Mr. Momhood in a curious dual action. Eventually which work was "real" had become a moot point; the upshot was that he felt fulfilled, and the lucky and accidental recipient of a full life. Maybe even overfull! But that was what happened when Freud's short list of the important things in life—work and love—were all in play.

He had had it all. And so change be damned! Charlie wanted to live on in this life forever. Or if not forever, then as long as the stars. And he feared change, as being the probable degradation of a situation that couldn't be bettered.

But here it was anyway, and there was no avoiding it. All the repetitions in the pattern were superficial; the moment was always new. It had to be lived, and then the next moment embraced as it arrived. This was what the Khembalis were always saying; it was one of the Buddhist basics. And now Charlie had to try to believe it.

So, the day came when he got up, and Anna left for work, then Nick for school; then it was Joe and Da's time, the whole day spread before them like a big green park. But on this day, Charlie prepped them both to leave, while talking up the change in the routine. "Big day, Joe! We're off to school and work, to the White House! They have a great daycare center there, it'll be like Gymboree!"

Joe looked up. "Gymboree?"

"Yes, *like* Gymboree, but not it exactly." Charlie's mood plummeted as he considered the differences—not one hour but five, or six, or eight, or twelve—and not parents and children together, but the child alone in a crowd of strangers. And he had never even liked Gymboree!

More and more depressed, he strapped Joe into his stroller and pushed him down to the Metro. The tunnel walls were still discolored or even wet in places, and Joe checked everything out as on any other trip. This was one of their routines.

Phil himself was not installed in the White House yet, but the arrangements had been made for Joe to join the daycare there, after which Charlie would leave and walk over to the senate offices in the old Joiner's Union building. Up and out of the Metro, into warm air, under low windy clouds. People scudded underneath them, hurrying from one shelter to the next before rain hit.

Charlie had gotten out at Smithsonian, and the Mall was almost empty, only a few runners in sight. He pushed Joe along faster and faster, feeling more and more desolate—unreasonably so, almost to the point of despair—especially as Joe continued to babble on happily, energized by the Mall and the brewing storm, no doubt expecting something like their usual picnic and play session. Hours that no matter how tedious they had seemed at the time were now revealed as precious islands in eternity, as paradises lost. And it was impossible to convey to Joe that today was going to be different. "Joe, I'm going to *drop you off* at the daycare center here at the White House. You're going to get to play with the other kids and the teachers and you have to do what the teachers say for a *long time*."

"Cool Dad. Play!"

"Yeah that's right. Maybe you'll love it."

It was at least possible. Vivid in Charlie's mind was Anna's story about taking Nick to daycare for the first time, and seeing Nick's expression of stoic resignation, which had pierced her so; Charlie had seen the look himself, taking Nick in those first few times. But Joe was no stoic, and would never resign himself to anything. Charlie was anticipating something more like chaos and disorder, perhaps even mayhem, Joe moving from protest to tirade to rampage. But who knew? The way Joe was acting these days, anything was possible. He might love it. He could be gregarious, and he liked crowds and parties. It was really more a matter of liking them too much, taking them too far.

In any case, in they went. Security check, and then inside and down the hall to the daycare center, a well-appointed and very clean place. Lots of little kids running around among toys and play structures, train sets and bookshelves and Legos and all. Joe's eyes grew round. "Hey Dad! Big Gymboree!"

"That's right, like Gymboree. Except I'm going to go, Joe. I'm going to go and leave you here."

"Bye Dad!" And off he ran without a backward glance.

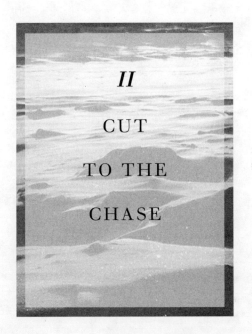

II

CUT

TO THE

CHASE

"And if you think this is utopian,
please think also why it is such."

—*Brecht*

P hil Chase was a man with a past. He was one of Congress's Vietnam vets, and that was by and large a pretty rambunctious crowd. They had license to be a little crazy, and not all of them took it, but it was there if they wanted it.

Phil had wanted it. He had always played that card to the hilt. Unconventional, unpredictable, devil-may-care, friend of McCain. And for well over a decade, his particular shtick had been to be the World's Senator, phoning in his work or jetting into D.C. at the last hour to make votes he had to make in person. All this had been laid before the people of California as an explicit policy, with the invitation to vote him out of office if they did not like it. But they did. Like a lot of California politicians who had jumped onto the national stage, his support at home was strong. High negatives, sure, but high positives, with the positives outrunning the negatives by about two to one. Now that he was president, the numbers had only polarized more, in the usual way of American politics, everyone hooked on the soap opera of cheering for or against personalities.

So a checkered past was a huge advantage in creating the spectacle. In his particular version of the clichéd list, Phil had been a reporter for the L.A. Times, a surfboard wax manufacturer (which business had bankrolled the start of his political career), a VA social worker, a college lecturer in history, a sandal maker, and an apprentice to a stonemason. From that job he had run for Congress from Marin County, and won the seat as an outsider Democrat. This was a difficult thing to do. The Democratic Party hated outsiders to join the party and win high office at the first try; they wanted everyone to start at the bottom of the ladder and work their way up until thoroughly brainwashed and obliged.

Worse yet, Phil had then jumped into a weak Senatorial race, and ridden the state's solid Democratic majority into the Senate, even though the party was still offended and not behind him.

Soon after that, his wife of twenty-three years, his high-school sweetheart, who had served in Vietnam as a nurse to be closer to him after *he was drafted, died in a car crash. It was after that that Phil had started his globe-trotting, turning into the World's Senator. Because he kept his distance from D.C. through all those years, no one in the capital knew much about his personal life. What they knew was what he gave them. From his account it was all travel, golf, and meetings with foreign politicians, often the environmental ministers, often in central Asia. "I like the Stans," he would say.*

In his frequent returns to California, he was much the same. For a while he pursued his "Ongoing Work Education program," Project OWE, because he owed it to his constituents to learn what their lives were like. Pronounced ow, however, by his staff, because of the injuries he incurred while taking on various jobs around the state for a month or three, working at them while continuing to function as senator in D.C., which irritated his colleagues no end. In that phase, he had worked as a grocery store bagger and checkout clerk, construction worker, real estate agent, plumber (or plumber's helper as he joked), barrio textile seamstress, sewage maintenance worker, trash collector, stockbroker, and a celebrated stint as a panhandler in San Francisco, during which time he had slept at undisclosed locations in Golden Gate Park and elsewhere around the city, and asked for spare change for his political fund—part of his "spare change" effort in which he had also asked California citizens to send in all the coins accumulating on their dressers, a startlingly successful plan that had weighed tons and netted him close to a million dollars, entirely funding his second run for senator, which he did on the cheap and mostly over the internet.

He had also walked from San Francisco to Los Angeles, climbed the Seven Summits (voting on the clean air bill from the top of Mt. Everest), swum from Catalina to the southern California mainland, and across Chesapeake Bay, and hiked the Appalachian trail from end to end. ("Very boring," was his judgment. "Next time the PCT.")

All these activities were extraneous to his work in the Senate, and time-consuming, and for his first two terms he was considered within the Beltway to be a celebrity freak, a party trick of a politician and a lightweight in the real world of power (i.e. money) no matter how far he could walk or swim. But even in that period his legislation had been interesting in concept (his contribution) and solidly written (his staff's contribution), and cleverly pursued and promoted by all, with much more of it being enacted into law than was usual in the Senate. This was not noted by the press, always on the lookout for bad news and ephemera, but by his third term it began to become evident to insiders that he had been playing the insider game all along, and only pretending to be an outsider, so that his committee appointments were strong, and his alliances within the Democratic Party apparatus finally strong, and across the aisle with moderate Republicans and McCain and other Vietnam vets, even stronger. He also had done a good job making his enemies, taking on flamboyantly bad senators like Winston and Reynolds and Hoof-in-mouth, whose subsequent falls from grace on corruption charges or simply failed policies had then retroactively confirmed his early judgments that these people were not just political dunderheads but also dangerous to the republic.

So ultimately, when the time came, everything he had done for twenty years and more turned out to have been as it were designed to prepare him not only for his successful run for the presidency, but for his subsequent occupancy as well, a crucial point and something that many previous candidates obviously forgot. The world travel, the global network of allies and friends, the OWE program, the legislation he had introduced and gotten passed, his committee work—it all fit a pattern, as if he had had the plan from the start.

Which he totally denied, and his staff believed him. They thought in their gossip among themselves that they had seen him come to his decision to run just a year before the campaign (at about the same time, Charlie thought but never said aloud, that he had met for twenty minutes with the Khembali leaders). Whether he had harbored thoughts all along, no one really knew. No one could read his mind, and he had no close associates. Widowed; kids grown; friends kept private and out of town: to Washington he seemed as lonely and impenetrable as Reagan, or FDR, or Lincoln—all friendly and charming people, but distant in some basic way.

In any case he was in, and ready and willing to use the office as strong presidents do—not only as the executive branch of government, whipping on the other two to get things done, but also as a bully pulpit from which to address the citizens of the country and the rest of the world. His high positive/high negative pattern continued and intensified, with the debate over him in the States more polarized than ever, at least in the media. But in the world at large, his positives were higher than any American president's since Kennedy. And interest was very high. All waited and watched through the few weeks left until his inauguration; there was a sudden feeling of stillness in the world, as if the pendulum swinging them all together helplessly this way and that had reached a height, and paused in space, just before falling the other way. People began to think that something might really happen.

IT SEEMED TO FRANK that with such a president as Phil Chase coming into office, in theory it ought to be very interesting to be the Presidential Science Advisor, or an advisor to the advisor. But there were aspects of the new job that were disturbing as well. It was going to mean increasing the distance between himself and the doing of science proper, and was therefore going to move him away from what he was good at. But that was what it meant to be moving into administration. Was there anyone who did policy well?

His intrusion on the Khembalis was another problem. Rudra's failing health was a problem. His own injury, and the uncertain mentation that had resulted (if it had), was a very central problem—perhaps *the* problem. Leaving NSF, meaning Anna and the rest of his acquaintances and routines there (except for Edgardo and Kenzo, who were also joining Diane's team), was a problem.

Problems required solutions, and solutions required decisions. And he couldn't decide. So the days were proving difficult.

Because above and beyond all the rest of his problems, there was the absolutely immediate one: he had to—*had to*—warn Caroline that her cover was insufficient to keep even a newcomer on the scene like Edgardo's friend from locating her. He had to warn her of this! But he did not know where she was. She might be on that island in Maine, but unless he went and looked he couldn't know. But if he went, he could not do anything that might expose her (and him too) to her husband. His van was chipped with a GPS transponder— Caroline was the one who had told him about it—so its identity and location could be under surveillance, and tracked wherever it went. He could easily imagine a program that would flag any time his van left the metropolitan area. This was a serious disadvantage, because his van was his shelter of last resort,

his only mobile bedroom, and all in all, the most versatile room in the disas-
sembled and modular home that he had cast through the fabric of the city.

"Can I dechip my van?" he asked Edgardo next day on their run, after
wanding them both again. "For certain? And, you know, as if by accident or
malfunction?"

"I should think so," Edgardo replied. "It might be something you would
need some help with. Let me look into it."

"Okay, but I want to go soon."

"Up to Maine?"

"Yes."

"Okay, I'll do my best. The person I want to talk to is not exactly on call. I
have to meet them in a context like this one."

But that night, as Frank was settling down in the garden shed with Rudra,
who was already asleep, Qang came out to tell him there was a man there to
see him. This caused Frank's pulse to elevate to a disturbing degree—

But it was Edgardo, and a short man, who said "hello" and after that spoke
only to Edgardo, in Spanish. "Umberto here is another porteño," Edgardo
said. "He helps me with matters such as this."

Umberto rolled his eyes dramatically. He took Frank's keys and went at the
van as if he owned it, banging around, pulling up carpet from the floor, running various diagnostics through a laptop, complaining to Edgardo all the
while. Eventually he opened the hood and after rooting around for a while,
unbolted a small box from the crowded left engine wall. When he was done he
gave the box to Frank and walked off into the dark, still berating Edgardo over
his shoulder.

"Thanks!" Frank called after him. Then to Edgardo: "Did I see how he did
that, so I can put it back in?" He peered at the engine wall, then the bolts in his
hand there with the box, then the holes the bolts had come out of. It looked
like a wrench kit would do it. "Okay, but where do I put it now?"

"You must leave it right here where it would be, so that it seems your van
is parked here. Then replace it when you return."

"Out here on the street?"

"Isn't there a driveway to this house?"

"Yeah, I can leave it there I guess. Buried in this gravel here."

"There you go."

"And other than that, I'm clean?"

"That's what Umberto said. Speaking only of the van, of course."

"Yeah. I've got the wand for my stuff. But is that enough? The van won't
look weird to toll gates for not having the box, or anything like that?"

"No. Not every vehicle has these things yet. So far, the total information
society is not yet fully online. When it is, you won't be able to do stuff like this.
You'll never be able to get off the grid, and if you did it would look so strange
it would be worse than being on the grid. Everything will have to be re-
thought."

Frank grimaced. "Well, by then I won't be involved in this kind of stuff. Listen, I think I'm going to take off now and get a few hours of driving in. It'll take me all of tomorrow to get there as it is."

"That's true. Good luck my friend. Remember—no cell-phone calls, no ATMs, no credit cards. Do you have enough cash with you?"

"I hope so," feeling the thickness of his wallet.

"You shouldn't stay away too long anyway."

"No. I guess I'm okay, then. Thanks for the help."

"Good luck. Don't call."

Grumpily Frank got in his van and drove north on 95. Transponders embedded in every vehicle's windshields... except would that really happen? Was this total information project not perhaps crazy enough to fail, ultimately? Or—could it be stopped? Could they go to Phil Chase and lay out the whole story, and get him to root out Caroline's ex and his whole operation, whatever it was? Root it out from the top down? Were the spy agencies so imbricated into the fabric of the government (and the military) that they were beyond presidential control, or even presidential knowledge? Or inquiry?

If it weren't for his going-off-grid status, he would have called up Edgardo to ask his opinion on this. As it was he could only continue to think, and worry, and drive.

Somewhere in New Jersey it occurred to him that as he was on the road north, he must therefore have decided to go. He had decided something! And without even trying. Maybe decisions now had to occur without one really noticing them happening, or wondering how. It was so hard to say. In this particular case, he really had had no choice; he *had* to warn her. So it had been more of a life override than a decision. Maybe one went through life doing the things one had to do, hooped by necessity, with decisions reserved for options and therefore not really a major factor in one's life. A bad thought or a good one? He couldn't tell.

A bad thought, he decided in the end. A bad thought in a long night of bad thoughts, as it turned out. Long past midnight he kept following the taillights ahead of him, and the traffic slowly thinned and became mostly trucks of various kinds. Over the Susquehanna, over the Hudson, otherwise tunneling on endlessly through the forest.

Finally he felt in danger of falling asleep at the wheel, got off and found a side road and a little parking lot, empty and dark and anonymous, where he felt comfortable parking under a tree and locking the doors and crawling into the back of the van to catch a few hours' sleep.

Dawn's light woke him and he drove on, north through New England, fueled by the worst 7-Eleven coffee he had ever tasted—coffee so bad it was good, in terms of waking him up. The idea that it might be poisoned gave him an extra jolt. Surely someone had poured in their battery acid as a prank.

There was too much time to think. If Caroline was the boss, and her ex worked for her, then. . . .

95 kept on coming, an endless slot through endless forest, a grass sward and two concrete strips rolling on for mile after mile. Finally he came to Bangor, Maine, and turned right, driving over hills and across small rivers, then through the standard array of franchises in Ellsworth, including an immense Wal-Mart. During the night he had driven north into full winter; a thin blanket of dirty snow covered everything. He passed a completely shut-down tourist zone, the motels, lobster shacks, antique stores, and miniature golf courses all looking miserable under their load of ice and snow, all except the Christmas knickknack barn, which had a full parking lot and was bustling with festive shoppers.

Soon after that he crossed the bridge that spanned the tidal race to Mount Desert Island. By then the round gray tops of the island's little range of peaks had appeared several times over the water of Frenchman's Bay. They were lower than Frank had expected them to be, but still, they were bare rock mountain tops, shaved into graceful curves by the immense force of the Ice Age's ice cap. Frank had googled the island on a cybercafe's rented computer, and had read quite a bit; and the information had surprised him in more ways than one. It turned out that this little island was in many ways the place where the American wilderness movement had begun, in the form of the landscape painter Frederick Church, who had come here in the 1840s to paint. In getting around the island, Church had invented what he called "rusticating," by which he meant wandering on mountainsides just for the fun of it. He also took offense at the clear-cut logging on the island, and worked to get the legislature of Maine to forbid it, in some of the nation's first environmental legislation. All this was happening at the same time Emerson and Thoreau were writing. Something had been in the air.

Eventually all that led to the national park system, and Mount Desert Island had been the third one, the first east of the Mississippi, and the only one anywhere created by citizens donating their own land. Acadia National Park now took up about two-thirds of the island, in a patchwork pattern; when Frank drove over the bridge he was on private land, but most of the seaward part of the island belonged to the park.

He slowed down, deep in forest still, following instructions printed out from a map website. The Maine coast here faced almost south. The island was roughly square, and split nearly in half, east and west, by a fjord called Somes Sound. Caroline's friend's house was on the western half of the island.

Nervously Frank drove through Somesville, at the head of the sound. This turned out to be no more than a scattering of white houses, on snowy lawns on either side of the road. He looked for something like a village commercial center but did not find one.

Now he was getting quite nervous. Just the idea of seeing her. He didn't know how to approach her. In his uncertainty he drove past the right turn that headed to her friend's place, and continued on to a town called Southwest Harbor. He wanted to eat something, also to think things over.

In the only cafe still open he ordered a sandwich and espresso. He didn't want to catch her unawares; that could be a bad shock. On the other hand there didn't seem any other way to do it. Sitting in the cafe drinking espresso (heavenly after the battery acid), he ate his sandwich and tried to think. They were the same thoughts he had been thinking the whole drive. He would have to surprise her; hopefully he could immediately explain why he was there— the possible danger she was in—so that she did not jump to the conclusion that he was somehow stalking her. They could talk; he could see what she wanted to do, perhaps even help her move somewhere else, if that's what she wanted. Although in that case...

Well, but he had run through all these thoughts a thousand times during the drive. All the scenarios led to a break point beyond which it was hard to imagine. He had to go to work on Monday. Or he should. And so...

He finished his lunch and walked around a little. Southwest Harbor's harbor was a small bay surrounded by forested hills, and filled with working boats and working docks, also a small Coast Guard station out on the point to the left. It was quiet, icy, empty of people: picturesque, but in a good way. A working harbor.

He would have to risk dropping in on her. The wand said he was clean. Edgardo's friend had said his van was clean. He had driven all night, he was five miles away from her. Surely the decision had already been made!

So he got back in his van, and drove back up the road, then took a left and followed a winding road through bare trees. Past an iced-over pond on the right, then another one on the left, this one a lake that was narrow and long, extending south for miles, a white flatness at the bottom of a classic U-shaped glacial slot. Soon after that, a left turn onto a gravel road.

He drove slower than ever, under a dense network of overarching branches. Houses to the left were fronting the long frozen lake. Caroline's friend's place was on the right, where it would overlook a second arm of the lake. The map showed a Y-shaped lake, with the long arm straight, and the other shorter arm curving into it about halfway down.

Her friend's house had no number in its driveway, but by the numbers before and after it, he deduced that it had to be the one. He turned around in a driveway, idled back up the road.

The place had a short gravel curve of driveway, with no cars in it. At the end of the driveway to the left stood a house, while to the right was a detached garage. Both were dark green with white trim. A car could have been hidden in the garage. Ah; the house number was there on the side of the garage.

He didn't want to drive into the driveway. On the other hand it must look odd, him idling out on the road, looking in—if there was anyone there to see.

He idled down the road farther, back in the direction of the paved road. Then he parked on the side at a wide spot, cursing under his breath. He got out and walked quickly down the road and up the driveway to the house in question.

He stopped between the house and the garage, under a big bare-limbed tree. The snow was crushed down to ice shards on the flagstones between the house and garage, as if someone had walked all over them and then there had been a thaw. No one was visible through the kitchen window. He was afraid to knock on the kitchen door. He stepped around the side of the house, looking in the windows running down that side. Inside was a big room, beyond it a sun porch facing the lake. The lake was down a slope from the house. There was a narrow path down, flanked by stone-walled terraces filled with snow and black weeds. Down on the water at the bottom of the path was a little white dock, anchored by a tiny white boathouse.

The door of the boathouse swung open from inside.

"Caroline?" Frank called down.

Silence. Then: "Frank?"

She peeked around the edge of the little boathouse, looking up for him with just the startled unhappy expression he had feared he would cause—

Then she almost ran up the path. "Frank, what is it?" she exclaimed as she hurried up. "What are you doing here?"

He found he was already halfway down the path. They met between two blueberry bushes, him with a hand up as if in warning, but she crashed through that and embraced him—held him—hugged him. They clung to each other.

Frank had not allowed himself to think of this part (but he had anyway): what it meant to hold her. How much he had wanted to see her.

She pushed back from him, looking past him up to the house. "Why are you here? What's going on? How did you find me?"

"I needed to warn you about that," Frank said. "At least I thought I should. My friend at NSF, the one who helped me with the election disk you gave us? He has a friend who was looking into who your ex is, and what he's doing now, you know, because they wanted to follow up on the election thing. So he wanted to talk to you about that, and my friend told him that you had disappeared, and this guy said that he knew where you probably were."

"Oh my God." Her hand flew to her mouth. Another body response common to all. She peered around him again up the driveway.

"So, I wanted to see if he was right," Frank continued, "and I wanted to warn you if he was. And I wanted to see you, anyway."

"Yes." They held hands, then hugged again. Squeezed hard. Frank felt the fear and isolation in her.

"So." He pulled back and looked at her. "Maybe you should move."

"Yeah. I guess so. Possibly. But—well, first tell me everything you can. Especially about how this person found me. Here, come on up. Let's get inside." She led him by the hand, back up the garden path to the house.

She entered it by way of the sun porch door. The sun porch was separated from the living room by diamond-paned windows above a wainscoting. An old vacation home, Frank saw, handmade, scrupulously clean, with old furniture, and paintings on every wall that appeared to be the work of a single enthusiast. The view of the lake seemed the main attraction to Frank.

Caroline gestured around her. "I first visited my friend Mary here when we were six."

"Man."

"But we haven't been in touch for years, and Ed never knew about her. I never told him. In fact, I can't quite imagine how your friend's friend tracked down the association."

"He said you called a number of an old roommate, and this was her place."

She frowned. "That's true."

"So, that's how he tracked this place down. And if he could, so could your ex, presumably. And besides," he added sharply, surprising them both, "why did you tell me that he was your boss?"

Silence as she stared at him. He explained: "My friend's friend said you were actually your husband's boss. So I wanted to know."

She glanced away, mouth tight for just an instant.

"Come on," she said, and led him through the living room to the kitchen.

There she opened the refrigerator and got out a pitcher of iced tea. "Have a seat," she said, indicating the kitchen table.

"Maybe I should move my van into the driveway," Frank remembered. "I didn't want to shock you by driving in, and I left it out on the road."

"That was nice. Yeah, go move it in. At least for now."

He did so, his mind racing. It was definitely foolish of her to remain exposed like this. Probably they should be leaving immediately.

He reentered the kitchen to find her sitting at the table before two glasses of iced tea, looking down at the lake. His Caroline. He sat down across from her, took a drink.

She looked at him across the table. "I was not Ed's boss," she said. "He was reassigned to another program. When I first came to the office, I was part of his team. I was working for him. But when the futures market program was established I was put in charge of it, and I reported to some people outside our office. Ed kept doing his own surveillance, and his group used what we were documenting, when they thought it would help them. That's the way it was when you and I met. Then he moved again, like I told you, over to Homeland Security."

She took a sip of her drink, met his eye again. "I never lied to you, Frank. I never have and I never will. I've had enough of that kind of thing. More than you'll ever know. I can't stand it anymore."

"Good," Frank said, feeling awkward. "But tell me—I mean, this is another thing I've really wondered about, that I've never remembered to ask you—what were you doing on that boat during the big flood, on the Potomac?"

Surprised, she said, "That's Ed's boat. I was going up to get him off Roosevelt Island."

"That was quite a time to be out on the river."

"Yes, it was. But he was helping some folks at the marina get their boats off, and we had already taken a few down to below Alexandria, and on one of the trips he stayed behind to help free up a boat, while I ferried one of the groups downstream. So it was kind of back and forth."

"Ah." Frank put a hand onto the table, reaching toward her. "I'm sorry," he said. "I didn't know what to think. You know—we never have had much time. Whenever we've gotten together, there's been more to say than time to say it."

She smiled. "Too busy with other stuff." And she put her hand on his.

He turned his palm up, and they intertwined fingers, squeezed hands. This was a whole different category of questions and answers. Do you still love me? Yes, I still love you. Do you still want me? Yes, I still want you. Yes. All that he had felt briefly before, during that hard hug on the garden path, was confirmed.

Frank took a deep breath. A flow of calmness spread from his held hand up his arm and then through the rest of him. Most of him.

"It's true," he said. "We've never had enough time. But now we do, so—tell me more. Tell me everything."

"Okay. But you too."

"Sure."

But then they sat there, and it seemed too artificial just to begin their life histories or whatever. They let their hands do the talking for a while instead. They drank tea. She began to talk a little about coming to this place when she was a girl. Then about being a jock, as she put it—how Frank loved that—and how that had gotten her into various kinds of trouble, somehow. "Maybe it was a matter of liking the wrong kind of guys. Guys who are jocks are not always nice. There's a certain percentage of assholes, and I could never tell in time." Reading detective stories when she was a girl. Nancy Drew and Sue Grafton and Sara Paretsky, all of them leading her down the garden path toward intelligence, first at the CIA ("I wish I had never left"), then to a promotion, or what had seemed like a promotion, over to Homeland Security. That was where she had met Ed. The way at first he had seemed so calm, so capable, and in just the areas she was then getting interested in. The intriguing parts of spook work. The way it had let her be outdoors, or at least out and about—at first. Like a kind of sport. "Ah yeah," Frank put in, thinking of the fun of tracking animals. "I did jobs like that too, sometimes. I wanted that too."

Then the ways things had changed, and gone wrong, in both work and marriage. How bad it had gotten. Here she grew vague and seemed to suppress some agitation or grimness. She kept looking out the window, as did Frank. A car passed and they both were too distracted by it to go on.

"Anyway, then you and I got stuck in the elevator," she resumed. She stopped, thinking about that perhaps; shook her head, looked out the kitchen window at the driveway again. "Let's get out of here," she said abruptly. "I don't like . . . Why don't we go for a drive in your van? I can show you some of the island, and I can get some time to think things through. I can't think here right now. It's giving me the creeps that you're here, I mean in the sense of . . . And we can put your van someplace else, if I decide to come back here. You know. Just in case. I actually have my car parked down at the other end of the lake. I've been sailing down to it when I want to drive somewhere."

"Sailing?"

"Iceboating."

"Ah. Okay," Frank said. They got up. "But—do you think we even ought to come back here?"

She frowned. He could see she was getting irritated or upset. His arrival had messed up what she had thought was a good thing. Her refuge. "I'm not sure," she said uneasily. "I don't think Ed will ever be able to find that one call I made to Mary. I made it from a pay phone I've never used before or since."

"But—if he's searching for something? For an old connection?"

"Yes, I know." She gave him an odd look. "I don't know. Let's get going. I can think about it better when I get away from here."

He saw that it was as he had feared; to her, his arrival was simply bad news. He wondered for a second if she had planned ever to contact him again.

They walked up the driveway to Frank's van, and he drove them back toward Somesville, following her instructions. She looked into all the cars going past them the other way. They drove around the head of the sound, then east through more forests, past more lakes.

Eventually she had him park at a feature called Bubble Rock, which turned out to be a big glacial erratic, perched improbably on the side of a polished granite dome. Frank looked at the rocky slopes rising to both sides of the road, amazed; he had never seen granite on the East Coast before. It was as if a little patch of the Sierra Nevada had been detached by a god and cast over to the Atlantic. The granite was slightly pinker than in the Sierra, but otherwise much the same.

"Let's go up the Goat Trail," she said. "You'll like it, and I need to do something."

She led him along the road until it reached a frozen lake just under the South Bubble, then crossed the road and stood facing the steep granite slope flanking this long lake.

"That's Jordan Pond, and this is Pemetic Mountain," gesturing at the slope above them. "And somewhere here is the start of the Goat Trail." She walked back and forth, scanning the broken jumble of steep rock looming over them. A very unlikely spot to begin a trail. The pink-gray granite was blackened with lichen, had the same faulted structure as any granite wall shaved by a glacier. In this case the ice resting on it had been a mile thick.

"My friend's father was really into the trails on the island, and he took us out and told us all about them," Caroline said. "Ah ha." She pointed at a rusted iron rod protruding from a big slab of rock, about head high. She started up past it, using her hands for balance and the occasional extra pull up. "This was the first one, he said. It's more of a marked route than a real trail. It's not on the maps anymore. See, there's the next trail duck." Pointing above.

"Ah yeah." Frank followed, watching her. This was his Caroline. She climbed with a sure touch. They had never done anything normal together before. She had talked about being a bicyclist, going for runs. This slope was easy but steep, and in places icy. A jock. Suddenly he felt the Caroline surge that had been there waiting in him all along.

Then the dark rock reared up into a wall of broken battlements thirty or forty feet high, one atop the next. Caroline led the way up through breaks in these walls, following a route marked by small stacks of flat rocks. In one of these gullies the bottom of the crack was filled with big flat stones set on top of each other in a rough but obvious staircase; this was as much of a trail as Frank had yet seen. "Mary's father wouldn't even step on those stones," Caroline said, and laughed. "He said it would be like stepping on a painting or something. A work of art. We used to laugh so much at him."

"I should think the guy who made the trail would like it to be used."

"Yes, that's what we said."

As they ascended they saw three or four more of these little staircases, always making a hard section easier. After an hour or so the slope laid back in a graceful curve, and they were on the rounded top of the hill. Pemetic Mountain, said a wooden sign on a post stuck into a giant pile of stones. 1,247 feet.

The top was an extensive flat ridge, running south toward the ocean. Its knobby bare rock was interspersed with low bushes and sandy patches. Lichen of several different colors spotted the bedrock and the big erratics left on the ridge by the ice—some granite, others schist. Exposed rock showed glacial scouring and some remaining glacial polish. It resembled any such knob in the Sierra, although the vegetation was a bit more lush. But the air had a distinct salt tang, and off to the south was the vast plate of the ocean, blue as could be, starting just a couple miles away at the foot of the ridge. Amazing. Forested islands dotted the water offshore; wisps of fog lay farther out to sea. To the immediate right and left rose other mountaintops, all rounded to the same whaleback shape. The peaks to both east and west were higher than this one, and the biggest one, to the east, had a road running up its side, and a number of radio towers poking up through its summit forest. The ice cap had carved deep slots between the peaks, working down into fault lines in the granite between each dome. Behind them, to the north, lay the forested low hills of Maine, trees green over snowy ground.

"Beautiful," Frank said. "It's mountains and ocean both. I can't believe it."

Caroline gave him a hug. "I was hoping you would like it."

"Oh yes. I didn't know the East Coast had such a place as this."

"There's nowhere else quite like it," she said.

They hugged for so long it threatened to become something else; then they separated and wandered the peak plateau for a while. It was cold in the wind, and Caroline shivered and suggested they return. "There's a real trail down the northeast side, the Ravine Trail. It goes down a little cut in the granite."

"Okay."

They headed off the northeast shoulder of the hill, and were quickly down into scrubby trees. Here the ice had hit the rock head-on, and the enormous pressures had formed the characteristic upstream side of a drumlin: smooth, rounded, polished, any flaw stripped open. And exposed to air for no more than ten thousand years; thus there was hardly any soil on this slope, which meant all the trees on it were miniaturized. They hiked down a good trail through this krummholz like giants.

It was a familiar experience for Frank, and yet this time he was following the lithe and graceful figure of his lover or girlfriend or he didn't know what, descending neatly before him, like a tree goddess. Some kind of happiness or joy or desire began to seep under his worry. Surely it had been a good idea to come here. He had had to do it; he couldn't have not done it.

The trail led them into the top of a narrow couloir in the granite, a flaw from which all loose rock had been plucked. Cedar beams were set crosswise in the bottom of this ravine, forming big solid stairs, somewhat snowed over. The sidewalls were covered with lichen, moss, ice. When they came out of the bottom of the couloir, the stairboxes underfoot were replaced by a long staircase of immense rectangular granite blocks.

"This is more like the usual trail on the east side," Caroline said, pointing at these monstrous field stones. "For a while, the thing they liked to do was make granite staircases, running up every fault line they could find. Sometimes there'll be four or five hundred stairs in a row."

"You're kidding."

"No. Every peak on the east side has three or four trails like that running up them, sometimes right next to each other. The redundancy didn't bother them at all."

"So they really were works of art."

"Yes. But the National Park didn't get it, and when they took over they closed a lot of the trails and took them off the maps. But since the trails have these big staircases in them, they last whether they're maintained or not. Mary's dad collected old maps, and was part of a group that went around finding the old trails. Now the park is restoring some of them."

"I've never seen anything like it."

"I don't think there is anything like it. Even here they only did this for a few years. It was like a fad. But a fad in granite never goes away."

Frank laughed. "It looks like something the Incas might have done."

"It does, doesn't it?" She stopped and looked back up the snowy stone steps, splotchy here with pale green lichen.

"I can see why you would want to stay here," Frank said cautiously when they started again.

"Yes. I love it."

"But..."

"I think I'm okay," she said.

For a while they went back and forth on this, saying much the same things they had said at the house. Whether Ed would look at her subjects, whether he would be able to find Mary...

Finally Frank shrugged. "You don't want to leave here."

"It's true," she said. "I like it here. And I *feel* hidden."

"But now you know better. Someone looked for you and they found you. That's got to be the main thing."

"I guess," she muttered.

They came to the road they had parked beside. They walked back to his van and she had him drive south, down the shore of Jordan Pond.

"Some of my first memories are from here," she said, looking out the window at the lake. "We came almost every summer. I always loved it. That lasted for several years, I'd guess, but then her parents got divorced and I stopped seeing her, and so I stopped coming."

"Ah."

"So, we did start college together and roomed that first year, but to tell the truth, I hadn't thought of her for years. But when I was thinking about how to really get away, if I ever wanted to, I remembered it. I never talked to Ed about Mary, and I just made the one call to her here from a pay phone."

"What did you say to her?"

"I gave her the gist of the situation. She was willing to let me stay."

"That's good. Unless, you know... I just don't know. I mean, you tell me just how dangerous these guys are. Some shots were fired that night in the park, after you left. My friends were the ones who started it, but your ex and his friends definitely shot back. And so, given that..."

Now she looked appalled. "I didn't know."

"Yeah. I also... I threw a rock at your ex," he added lamely.

"You what?"

"I threw my hand axe at him. I saw a look on his face I didn't like, and I just did it." And in fact the stone was below in the glove compartment of his van.

She squeezed his hand. Her face had the grim inward expression it took on whenever she was thinking about her ex. "I know that look," she muttered. "I hate it too." And then: "I'm sorry I've gotten you into this."

"No. Anyway, I missed him. Luckily. But he saw the rock go by his head, or felt it. He took off running down the Metro stairs. So he definitely knows something is up." Frank didn't mention going by their apartment afterward and ringing the doorbell; he was already embarrassed enough about the hand axe. "So, what I'm still worried about is if he starts looking, and, you know, happens to replicate what my friend's friend did."

"I know." She sighed. "I guess I'm hoping that he's not all that intent on me anymore. I have him chipped, and he's always in D.C., at the office, moving from room to room. I've got him covered in a number of ways—a spot cam on our apartment entry, and things like that, and he seems to be following his ordinary routine."

"Even so—he could be doing that while sending some of his team here to check things out."

She thought about it. Sighed a big sigh. "I hate to leave here when there might not be a reason to."

Frank said nothing; his presence was itself proof of a reason. Thus his appearance had indeed been a bad thing. The transitive law definitely applied to emotions.

She had directed him through some turns, and now they were driving around the head of Somes Sound again, back toward her place. As he slowed through Somesville, he said, "Where should we put my van?"

She ran her hands through her short curls, thinking it over. "Let's put it down where my car is. I'm parked at the south end of Long Pond, at the pump house there. First drop me off at the house, then drive down there, and I'll sail down on the iceboat and pick you up."

So he drove to her camp and dropped her off at the house, feeling nervous as he did so. Then he followed her instructions, back toward Southwest Harbor, then west through the forest again, on a winding small road. He only had a rough sense of where he was, but then he was driving down an incline, and the smooth white surface of Long Pond appeared through the trees. The southern end of its long arm was walled on both sides by steep granite slopes, six or seven hundred feet high: a pure glacial U, floored by a lake.

He parked in the little parking lot by the pump house and got out. The wind from the north slammed him in the face. Far up the lake he saw a tiny sail appear as if out of the rock wall to the left. It looked like a big windsurfing sail. Faster than he would have thought possible it grew larger, and the iceboat swept up to the shore, Caroline at the tiller, turning it in a neat curlicue at the end, to lose speed and drift backward to shore.

"Amazing," Frank said.

"Here, wait—park your van up in those trees, just past the stop sign up there."

Frank did so and then returned to the craft, stepped in and stowed his daypack before the mast. The iceboat was a wooden triangular contraption, obviously handmade, more like a big soapbox-derby car than a boat. Three heavy struts extended from the cockpit box, one ahead and two sideways and back from the cockpit. It was an odd-looking thing, but the mast and sails seemed to have been scavenged from an ordinary sloop, and Caroline was obviously familiar with it. Her face was flushed with the wind, and she looked pleased in a way Frank had never seen before. She pulled the sail taut and twisted the tiller, which set the angles of the big metal skates out at the ends of the rear struts, and with a clatter they gained speed and were off in a chorus of scraping.

The iceboat did not heel in the wind, but when gusts struck it merely squeaked and slid along even faster, the skates making a loud clattery hiss. When a really strong gust hit, the craft rocketed forward with a palpable jolt. Frank's eyes watered heavily under the assault of the wind. He ducked when Caroline told him to, their heads together as the boom swung over them as part of a big curving tack. To get up the narrow lake against the wind they would have to tack a lot; the craft did not appear able to hold too close to the wind.

As they worked their way north, Caroline explained that Mary's grandfather had built the iceboat out of wood left over from when he had built the garage. "He built everything there, even some of the furniture. He dug out the cellar, built the chimney, the terraces, the dock and rowboats...." Mary's father had told them about this; Caroline had met the grandfather only once, when she was very young.

"This last month I've been feeling like he's still around the place, like a ghost, but in the best kind of way. The first night I got here the electricity wasn't on and there was no sound at all. I never realized how used to noise we've gotten. That there's always some kind of sound, even if it's only the refrigerator."

"Usually it's a lot more than that," Frank said, thinking of how D.C. sounded from his treehouse.

"Yes. But this time it was completely quiet. I began to hear myself breathing. I could even hear my heart beat. And then there was a loon on the lake. It was so beautiful. And I thought of Mary's grandfather building everything, and it seemed like he was there. Not a voice, just part of the house somehow. It was comforting."

"Good for him," Frank said. He liked the sound of such a moment, also the fact that she had noticed it. It occurred to him again how little he knew her. She was watching the ice ahead of the boat, holding the boom line and the tiller in place, making small adjustments, splayed in the cockpit as if holding a kind of dance position with the wind. And there they were barreling across the frozen surface of the lake, the ice blazing in a low tarnished sun that was smeared out in long bars of translucid cloud—the wind frigid, and flying through him as if the gusts were stabs of feeling for her—for the way she was capable, the way she liked it out here. He had thought she would be like this, but they had spent so little time together he could not be sure. But now he was seeing it. His Caroline, real in the sunlight and the wind. A gust of wind was a surge of feeling.

She brought the iceboat around again, east to west, and continued the smooth curve west, as they were now shooting into the channel that began the other arm of the lake's Y. Here the north wind was somewhat blocked by the peninsula separating the two arms of the lake, and the iceboat slid along with less speed and noise. Then another curve, and they were headed into the wind again, on the short arm of the Y, running up to a little island she called

Rum Island, which turned out to be just a round bump of snow and trees in the middle of a narrow part of the lake.

As they were about to pass Rum Island, something beeped in Caroline's jacket pocket. "Shit!" she said, and snatched out a small device, like a handheld GPS or a cell phone. She steered with a knee while she held it up to her face to see it in the sunlight. She cursed again. "Someone's at camp."

She swerved, keeping Rum Island between the boat and Mary's place. As they approached the island she turned into the wind and let loose the sail, so that they skidded into a tiny cove and onto a gravel beach no bigger than the iceboat itself. They stepped over the side onto icy gravel, and tied the boat to a tree, then made their way to the island's other side. The trees on the island hooted and creaked like the Sierras in a storm, a million pine needles whooshing their great chorale. It was strange to see the lake surface perfectly still and white under the slaps of such a hard blow.

Across that white expanse, the green house and its little white boathouse were the size of postage stamps. Caroline had binoculars in the boat, however, and through them the house's lake side was quite distinct; and through its big windows there was movement.

"Someone inside."

"Yes."

They crouched behind a big schist erratic. Caroline took the binoculars back from him and balanced them on the rock, then bent over and looked through them for a long time. "It looks like Andy and George," she said in a low voice, as if they might overhear. "Uh oh—get down," and she pulled him down behind the boulder. "There's a couple more up by the house, with some kind of scope. Can those IR glasses you use for the animals see heat this far away?"

"Yes," Frank said. He had often used IR when tracking the ferals in Rock Creek. He took the binoculars back from her and looked around the side of the boulder near the ground, with only one lens exposed.

There they were—looking out toward the island—then hustling down the garden path and onto the ice itself, their long dark overcoats flapping in the wind. "Jesus," he said, "they're coming over here to check! They must have seen our heat."

"Damn it," she said. "Let's go, then."

They ran back over the little island to the beach. A hard kick from Caroline to the hull of the iceboat and it was off the gravel and ready to sail. Push it around, get in and take off, waiting helplessly for the craft to gain speed, which it did with an icy scratching that grew louder as they slid out from the island's wind shadow and skidded south.

"You saw four of them?" Frank asked.

"Yes."

Skating downwind did not feel as fast as crossing the lake had, but then they passed the end of the peninsula, and Caroline steered the craft in another broad curve, and as she did it picked up speed until it shot across the ice, into the gap leading to the longer stretch of the lake. Looking back, Frank saw the men crossing the lake. They saw him; one of them took a phone from his jacket pocket and held it to his ear. Back at the house, tiny now, he saw the two others running around the back of the house.

Then the point of the peninsula blocked the view.

"The ones still at the house went for the driveway," he said. "They're going to drive around the lake, I bet. Do you think they can get to the southern end of the lake before we do?"

"Depends on the wind," Caroline said. "Also, they might stop at Pond's End, for a second at least, to take a look and see if we're coming up to that end."

"But it wouldn't make sense for us to do that."

"Unless we had parked there. But they'll only stop a second, because they'll be able to see us. You can see all the way down the lake. So they'll see which way we're going."

"And then?"

"I think we can beat them. They'll have to circle around on the roads. If the wind holds, I'm sure we can beat them."

The craft emerged from the channel onto the long stretch of the lake, where the wind was even stronger. Looking through the binoculars as best he could given the chatter, Frank saw a dark van stop at the far end of the pond, then, after a few moments' pause, drive on.

He had made the same drive himself a couple of hours before, and it seemed to him it had taken about fifteen minutes, maybe twenty, to get to the south end of the pond by way of the small roads through the woods. But he hadn't been hurrying. At full speed it might take only half that.

But now the iceboat had the full force of the north wind behind it, funneling down the steep granite walls to both sides—and the gusts felt stronger than ever, even though they were running straight downwind. The boat only touched the ice along the edges of the metal runners, screeching their banshee trio. Caroline's attention was fixed on the sail, her body hunched at the tiller and line, feeling the wind like a telegraph operator. Frank didn't disturb her, but only sat on the gunwale opposite to the sail, as she had told him to do. The stretch of the lake they had to sail looked a couple of miles long. In a sailboat they would have been in trouble. On the ice, however, they zipped along as if in a catamaran's dream, almost frictionless despite the loud noise of what friction was left. Frank guessed they were going about twenty miles an hour, maybe twenty-five, maybe thirty; it was hard to tell. Fast enough: down a granite wind tunnel, perfectly shaped to their need for speed. The dwarf trees on the steep granite slopes to each side bounced and whistled, the sun was almost blocked by the western cliff, blazing in the pale streaked sky, whitening the cloud to each side of it. Caroline spared a moment to give Frank a look, and it seemed she was going to speak, then shook her head and simply gestured at the surrounding scene, mouth tight. Frustrated.

"I guess them showing up so soon suggests I tipped them off somehow," he said.

"Yes." She was looking at the sail.

"I'm sorry. I thought I needed to warn you."

Her mouth stayed tight. She said nothing.

The minutes dragged, but Frank's watch showed that only eight had passed when they came to the south end of the lake. There were a couple of big houses tucked back in the forest to the left. Caroline pulled the tiller and boom line and brought them into the beach next to the pump house, executing a bravura late turn that hooked so hard Frank was afraid the iceboat might be knocked on its side. Certainly a windsurfer or catamaran would have gone down like a bowling pin. But there was nothing for the iceboat to do but groan and scrape and spin, into the wind and past it, then screeching back, then stopping, then drifting back onto the beach.

"Hurry," Caroline said, and jumped out and ran up to Frank's van.

Frank followed. "What about the boat?"

She grimaced. "We have to leave it!" Then, when they were in his van: "I'll call Mary when I can get a clean line and tell her where it is. I'd hate for Harold's boat to be lost because of this *shit*." Her voice was suddenly vicious.

Then she was all business, giving Frank directions; they got out to a paved road and turned right, and Frank accelerated as fast as he dared on the still frozen road, which was often in shadow, and seemed a good candidate for black ice. When they came to a T-stop she had him turn right. "My car's right there, the black Honda. I'm going to take off."

"Where?"

"I've got a place. I've got to hurry, I don't want them to see me at the bridge. You should head directly for the bridge and get off the island. Go back home."

"Okay," Frank said. He could feel himself entering one of his indecision fugues, and was grateful she had such a strong sense of what they should do. "Look, I'm sorry about this. I thought I had to warn you."

"I know. It's not your fault. None of this is your fault. It was good of you to try to help. I know why you did it." And she leaned over and gave him a quick peck of a kiss before she got out.

"I was pretty sure my van is clean," Frank said. "And my stuff too. We checked all of it out."

"They may have you under other kinds of surveillance. Satellite cameras, or people just tailing you."

"Satellite cameras? Is that possible?"

"Of course." Annoyed that he could be so ignorant.

Frank shrugged, thinking it over. He would have to ask Edgardo. Right now he was glad she was giving him directions.

She came around the van and leaned in on his side. Frank could see she was angry.

"You'll be able to come back here someday," he said.

"I hope so."

"You know," he said, "instead of holing up somewhere, you could stay with people who would keep you hidden, and cover for you."

"Like Anne Frank?"

Startled, Frank said, "Well, I guess so."

She shook her head. "I couldn't stand it. And I wouldn't want to put anyone else to the trouble."

"Well, but what about me? I'm staying with the Khembalis in almost that way already. They're very helpful, and their place is packed with people."

Again she shook her head. "I've got a Plan C, and it's down in that area. Once I get into that I can contact you again."

"If we can figure out a clean system."

"Yes. I'll work on that. We can always set up a dead drop."

"My friends from the park live all over the city—"

"I've got a plan!" she said sharply.

"Okay." He shook his head, swallowed; tasted blood at the back of his throat.

"What?" she said.

"Nothing," he said automatically.

"Something," she said, and reached in to touch the side of his head. "Tell me what you just thought. Tell me quick, I've got to go, but I didn't like that look!"

He told her about it as briefly as he could. Taste of blood. Inability to make decisions. Maybe it was sounding like he was making excuses for coming up to warn her. She was frowning. When he was done, she shook her head.

"Frank? Go see a doctor."

"I know."

"Don't say that! I want you to promise me. Make the appointment, and then go see the doctor."

"Okay. I will."

"All right, now I've got to go. I think they've got you chipped. Be careful and go right back home. I'll be in touch."

"How?"

She grimaced. "Just go!"

A phrase which haunted him as he made the long drive south. Back to home; back to work; back to Diane. Just go!

He could not seem to come to grips with what happened. The island was dreamlike in the way it was so vivid and surreal, but detached from any obvious meaning. Heavily symbolic of something that could nevertheless not be decoded. They had hugged so hard, and yet had never really kissed; they had climbed together up a rock wall, they had iceboated on a wild wind, and yet in the end she had been angry, perhaps with him, and holding back from saying things, it had seemed. He wasn't sure.

Mile after mile winged by, minute after minute; on and on they went, by the tens, then the hundreds. And as night fell, and his world reduced to a pattern of white and red lights, both moving and still, with glowing green signs and their white lettering providing name after name, his feel for his location on the globe became entirely theoretical to him, and everything grew stranger and stranger. Some kind of fugue state, the same thoughts over and over. Obsession without compulsion. Headlights in the rearview mirror; who could tell if they were from the same vehicle or not?

It became hard to believe there was anything outside the lit strip of the highway. Once Kenzo had shown him a USGS map of the United States that had displayed the human population as raised areas, and on that map the 95 corridor had been like an immense Himalaya, from Atlanta to Boston, rising from both directions to the Everest that was New York. And yet driving right down the spine of this great density of his species he could see nothing but the walls of trees lining both sides of the endless slot. He might as well have been driving south though Siberia, or over the face of some empty forest planet, tracking some great circle route that was only going to bring him back where he had started. The forest hid so much.

DESPITE THE REESTABLISHED GULF STREAM, the jet stream still snaked up and down the Northern Hemisphere under its own pressures, and now a strong cold front rode it south from Hudson Bay and arrived just in time to strike the inauguration. When the day dawned, temperatures in the capital region hovered around zero degrees Fahrenheit, with clear sunny skies and a north wind averaging fifteen miles an hour. Everyone out of doors had to bundle up, so it was a slow process at all the security checkpoints. The audience settled onto the cold aluminum risers set on the east side of the Capitol, and Phil Chase and his entourage stepped onto the dais, tucked discreetly behind its walls of protective glass. The cold air and Phil's happy, relaxed demeanor reminded Charlie of the Kennedy inauguration, and images of JFK and Earl Warren and Robert Frost filled his mind as he felt Joe kicking him in the back. He had only been a few years older than Joe when he had seen that one on TV. Thus the generations span the years, and now his boy was huddled against him, heavy as a rock, dragging him down but keeping him warm. "Dad, let's go to the zoo! Wanna go to the zoo!"

"Okay, Joe, but after this, okay? This is history!"

"His story?"

Phil stood looking out at the crowd after the oath of office was administered by the Chief Justice, a man about ten years younger than he was. With a wave of his gloved hand he smiled his beautiful smile.

"Fellow Americans," he said, pacing his speech to the reverb of the loudspeakers, "you have entrusted me with the job of president during a difficult time. The crisis we face now, of abrupt climate change and crippling damage to the biosphere, is a very dangerous one, to be sure. But we are not at war with anyone, and in fact we face a challenge that all humanity has to meet together. On this podium, Franklin Roosevelt said, 'This generation has a rendezvous with destiny.' Now it's true again. We are the generation that has to deal with the profound destruction that will be caused by the global warming that has already been set in motion. The potential disruption of the natural order is so great that scientists warn of a mass extinction event. Losses on that scale would endanger all humanity, and so we cannot fail to address the threat. The lives of our children, and all their descendants, depend on us doing so.

"So, like FDR and his generation, we have to face the great challenge of our time. We have to use our government to organize a total social response to the problem. That took courage then, and we will need courage now. In the years since we used our government to help get us out of the Great Depression, it has sometimes been fashionable to belittle the American government as some kind of foreign burden laid on us. That attitude is nothing more than an attack on American history, deliberately designed to shift power away from the American people. I want us to remember how Abraham Lincoln said it: 'that government of the people, by the people, and for the people shall not perish from this Earth.' This is the crucial concept of American democracy—that government expresses what the majority of us would like to do as a society. It's us. We do it to us and for us. I believe this reminder is so important that I intend to add the defining phrase 'of the people, by the people, and for the people' every time I use the word 'government,' and I intend to do all I can to make that phrase be a true description. It will make me even more long-winded than I was before, but I am willing to pay that price, and you are going to have to pay it with me.

"So, this winter, with your approval and support, I intend to instruct my team in the executive branch of government of the people, by the people, and for the people, to initiate a series of federal actions and changes designed to meet the problem of global climate change head-on. We will deal with it as a society working together, and working with the rest of the world. It's a global project, and so I will go to the United Nations and tell them that the United States is ready to join the international effort. We will also help the underdeveloped world to develop using clean technology, so that all the good aspects of development will not be drowned in its bad side effects—often literally drowned. In our own country, meanwhile, we will do all it takes to shift to clean technologies as quickly as possible."

Phil paused to survey the crowd. "My, it's cold out here today! You can feel right now, right down to the bone, that what I am saying is true. We're out in the cold, and we need to change the way we do things. And it's not just a technological problem, having to do with our machinery alone. The devastation of the biosphere is also a result of there being too many human beings for the planet to support over the long haul. If the human population continues to increase as it has risen in the past, all progress we might make will be overwhelmed.

"But what is very striking to observe is that everywhere on this Earth where good standards of justice prevail, the rate of reproduction is about at the replacement rate. While wherever justice, and the full array of rights as described in the UN Declaration of Human Rights, is somehow denied to some portion of the population, especially to women and children, the rate of reproduction either balloons to unsustainably rapid growth rates, or crashes outright. Now you can argue all you want about why this correlation exists, but the correlation itself is striking and undeniable. So this is one of those situations in which what we do for good in one area, helps us again in another. It is a positive feedback loop with the most profound implications. Consider: for the sake of climate stabilization, there must be population stabilization; and for there to be population stabilization, *justice must prevail.* Every person on the planet must live with the full array of human rights that all nations have already ascribed to when signing the UN Charter. When we achieve that, at that point, and at that point only, we will begin to reproduce at a sustainable rate.

"To help that to happen, I intend to make sure that the United States joins the global justice project *fully, unequivocally,* and *without any double standards.* This means accepting the jurisdiction of the International Criminal Court, and the jurisdiction of the World Court in the Hague. It means abiding by all the clauses of the UN Charter and the Geneva Conventions, which after all we have already signed. It means supporting UN peacekeeping forces, and supporting the general concept of the UN as the body through which international conflicts get resolved. It means supporting the World Health Organization in all its reproductive rights and population reduction efforts. It means supporting women's education and women's rights everywhere, even in cultures where men's tyrannies are claimed to be some sort of tradition. All these commitments on our part will be crucial if we are serious about building a sustainable world. There are three legs to this effort, folks: technology, environment, and social justice. None of the three can be neglected.

"So, some of what we do may look a little unconventional at first. And it may look more than a little threatening to those few who have been trying, in effect, to buy our government of the people, by the people, and for the people, and use it to line their own pockets while the world goes smash. But you know what? Those people need to change too. They're out in the cold the same as the rest of us. So we will proceed, and hope those opposed come to see the good in it.

"Ultimately we will be exploring all peaceful means to initiate positive changes in our systems, in order to hand on to the generations to come a world that is as beautiful and bountiful as the one we were born into. We are only the temporary stewards of a mighty trust, which includes the lives of all the future generations to come. We are responsible to our children and theirs. What we do now will reveal much about our character and our values as a people. We have to rise to the occasion, and I think we can and will. I am going to throw myself into the effort wholeheartedly and with a feeling of high excitement, as if beginning a long journey over stormy seas."

"Good," Charlie said into his phone. "He's still saying the right stuff."

"Heck yes," Roy replied in his ear. "But you know the old saying: an ounce of law is worth a pound of rhetoric." Roy had made up this saying, and trotted it out as often as possible. He was seated on the opposite side of the viewing stands from Charlie and Joe, and Charlie thought he could just spot him talking into his cell phone across the way, but with all the hats and mufflers and ski masks bundling the heads of the audience, he could not be sure. Roy continued, "We'll see if we can wag the dog or not. Things bog down in this town."

"I think the dog will wag us," Charlie said. "I think we are the dog. We're the dog of the people, by the people and for the people."

"We'll see." As chief of staff, Roy had already worked so hard on the transition that he had, Charlie feared, lost all sight of the big picture: "Everything depends on how the start goes."

Charlie said, "A good start would help. But whatever happens, we have to persevere. Right, Joe?"

"Go Phil! Hey, Dad? It's cold."

The transition team had concocted its "first sixty days"—a gigantic master list of Things To Do, parceled out among the many agencies of the executive branch. Each agency had its own transition team and its own list, which usually began with a status report. Many units had been deliberately disabled by previous administrations, so that they would require a complete retooling to be able to function. In others, change at the top would rally the efforts of the remaining permanent staff, made up of professional technocrats. Each agency had to be evaluated for these problems and qualities, and the amount of attention given to them adjusted accordingly.

For Charlie, this meant working full-time, as he had agreed back in November. Everyone else was up to speed and beyond, and he felt an obligation to match them. Up before sunrise, therefore, groggy in the cold dark of the depths of winter, when (Frank said) hominids living this far north had used to go into a dream state very close to hibernation. Get Joe up, or at least transferred sleeping into his stroller. Quick walk with Anna down to the Metro station in Bethesda—companionable, as if they were still in bed together, or sharing a dream; Charlie could almost fall back asleep on such a walk. Then descend with her into the Earth, dimly lit and yet still lighter than the predawn world above. Slump in a bright vinyl seat and snooze against Anna to Metro Center, where she changed trains and they went up in elevators to the sidewalk, to have a last brisk walk together, Joe often awake and babbling, down G Street to the White House. There pass through security, more quickly each time, and down to the daycare center, where Joe bounced impatiently in his stroller until he could clamber over the side and plow off into the fun. He was always one of the first kids there and one of the last to leave, and that was saying a lot. But he did not remark on this, and did not seem to mind. He was still nice to the other kids. Indeed the various teachers all told Charlie how well he got along with the other kids.

Charlie found these reports depressing. He could see with his own eyes the beginning and end of Joe's days in daycare, but there weren't as many kids there at those times. And he remembered Gymboree, indeed had been traumatized by certain incidents at Gymboree.

Now, as everyone pointed out, Joe was calm to the point of detachment. Serene. In his own space. In the daycare he looked somewhat like he would have during a quiet moment on the floor of their living room at home; perhaps a bit more wary. It worried Charlie more than he could say. Anna would not understand the nature of his concern, and aside from her…he might have mentioned it to Roy during one of their phone calls, back in the old days. But Roy had no time and was obsessed, and there was no one else with whom to share the feeling that Joe had changed and was not himself. That wasn't something you could say.

Sometimes he brought it up with Anna obliquely, as a question, and she agreed that Joe was different than he had been before his fever, but she seemed to regard it as within the normal range of childhood changes, and mostly a function of learning to talk. Growing up. Her theory was that as Joe learned to talk he got less and less frustrated, that his earlier tempestuousness had been frustration at not being able to communicate what he was thinking.

But this theory presupposed that the earlier Joe had been inarticulate, and in possession of thoughts he had wanted to communicate to the world but couldn't; and that did not match Charlie's experience. In his opinion, Joe had always communicated exactly whatever he was feeling or thinking. Even before he had had language, his thoughts had still been perfectly explicit, though not linguistic. They had been precise feelings, and Joe had expressed them precisely, and with well-nigh operatic virtuosity.

In any case, now it was different. To Charlie, radically different. Anna didn't see that, and it would upset her if Charlie could persuade her to see it, so he did not try. He wasn't even sure what it was he would be trying to convey. He didn't *really* believe that the real Joe had gone away as a result of the Khembalis' ceremony for him. When Charlie had made the request, his rather vague notion had been that what such a ceremony would dispel would be the Khembalis' interest in Joe, and their belief that he harbored the spirit of one of their reincarnated lamas. Altering the Khembalis' attitude toward Joe would then change Joe himself, but in minor ways—ways that Charlie now found he had not fully imagined, for how exactly had he thought that Joe was "not himself," beyond being feverish, and maybe a bit subdued, a bit cautious and fearful? Had that really been the result of the Khembalis' regard? And if their regard were to change, why exactly would Joe go back to the way he was before—feisty, bold, full of himself?

Perhaps he wouldn't. It had not worked out that way, and now Charlie's ideas seemed flawed to him. Now he had to try to figure out just exactly what it was he had wanted, what he thought had happened in the ceremony, and what he thought was happening now.

It was a hard thing to get at, made harder by the intensity of his new schedule. He only saw Joe for a couple of hours a day, during their commutes, and their time in the Metro cars was confined, with both of them asleep on many a morning's ride in, and both of them tired and distracted by the day's events on the way home. Charlie would sit Joe beside him, or on his lap, and they would talk, and Joe was pretty similar to his old self, babbling away at things outside the window or in his stroller, or referring to events earlier in his day, telling semicoherent stories. It was hard to be sure what he was talking about most of the time, although toys and teachers and the other kids were clear enough, and formed the basis of most of his conversation.

But then they would walk home and enter the house, and life with Anna and Nick, and often that was the last they would have to do with each other until bedtime. So—who knew? It was not like the old days, with the vast stretches of the day, the week, the season, extending before and behind them in a perpetual association not unlike the lives of Siamese twins. Charlie now saw only fragmentary evidence. It was hard to be sure of anything.

Nevertheless. He saw what he saw. Joe was not the same. And so, trapped at the back of his mind (but always there) was the fear that he had somehow misunderstood and asked for the wrong thing for his son—and gotten it.

As the winter deepened it became more and more expensive to warm the entire house. The price of heating oil became a political issue, but President Chase tried to keep the focus on the alternative sources they needed to develop. At the Quiblers', Anna programmed the house's thermostat to choreograph their evenings, so that they congregated in the kitchen and living room in the early evenings, and then bumped the heat upstairs in the hour before bedtime to augment whatever heat had gathered there from below. It worked fairly well, following and reinforcing what they would have done anyway. But one exceptionally cold night in early February the power went out, and everything was suddenly different.

Anna had a supply of flashlights and candles in a cabinet in the dining room, and quickly she banged her way to them and got some candles lit in every room. She turned on a battery-powered radio, and Nick twiddled the dial trying to find some news. While Charlie was building up the fire in the fireplace, they listened to a crackly distant voice that said a cold front like one from the winter before had dropped temperatures across New York, Pennsylvania, and New Jersey by up to sixty degrees in twenty minutes, presumably causing a surge in demand or a malfunction at some point in the grid, thus crashing the system.

"I'm glad we all got home in time," Anna said. "We could have been in the Metro somewhere."

They could hear sirens beginning to oscillate through the air of the city. The Metro had an emergency generating system, Charlie thought, but no doubt the streets were clotted with cars, as they could see was true out on Wisconsin, just visible from their front window. When Charlie stepped outside to get more firewood from their screened-in porch, he smelled the smell of a power outage, unexpectedly familiar from the winter before: exhaust of burned generator fuel, smoke of green firewood.

Inside the boys were clamoring for marshmallows. Anna had unearthed a bag of them at the back of a kitchen cabinet. Anna passed on trying one, to Joe's amazement, and went to the kitchen to whip up a late salad, keeping the refrigerator door open for as short a time as possible, wondering as she did so how quickly an unopened refrigerator would lose its chill. She resolved to buy a couple of thermometers to find out. The information might come in useful.

Back in the living room, Charlie had finished lighting all the candles in the house, a profligacy that created a fine glow, especially when they were set around the room where the shadows from the fire congregated the most. Carrying one upstairs, Anna watched the shadows shift and flicker with her steps, and wondered if they would be warm enough up there that night; the bedrooms felt colder than the inside of the refrigerator had. She wondered briefly if a refrigerator would work to keep things from freezing in a subzero house.

"We should maybe sleep on the couches down here," she said when she was back in the living room. "Do we have enough firewood to keep a fire going all night?"

"I think so," Charlie said. "If the wood will burn."

Last winter after the cold snap, there had been a period when firewood had been deemed cheaper heat than oil or gas, and all the cured firewood had been quickly bought and burned. This year green wood was almost all that was available, and it burned very poorly, as Charlie was now finding out. He threw in a paraffin-and-sawdust log from time to time, and used his massive wrought-iron fire tongs to lift the heavy recalcitrant logs over the fake ones to dry them out and keep things going.

"Remind me to buy dry wood next time."

Anna took her bowl back into the kitchen. Water was still running, but it wouldn't for long. She filled her pots, and a couple of five-gallon plastic jugs they had in the basement. These too would freeze eventually, unless she put them near the fire. They needed a better blackout routine, she saw. She took them out to the living room and saw the boys settling in. This must be how it had been, she thought, for generations on end; everyone huddling together at night for warmth. Probably she would have to work from home the next day, though her laptop battery was depleted. She wished laptop batteries lasted longer.

"Remind me to check the freezer in the morning. I want to see if things have started to thaw."

"If you open it, it will lose its cool."

"Unless the kitchen is colder than the freezer. I've been wondering about that."

"Maybe we should just leave the freezer door open then."

"Maybe we can get the fire going in it!"

They laughed at this, but Anna still felt uneasy.

They built a city on the coffee table using Joe's blocks, then read by candlelight. Charlie and Nick hauled an old double mattress that they called the tigers' bed up from the basement, and they laid it right before the fire, where Joe used it as a trampoline which looked like it was going to slingshot him right into the feeble blaze.

When everything was arranged, Charlie read aloud some pages from *The Once and Future King,* about what it was like to be a goose migrating over the Norwegian Sea—a passage that had Anna and the boys entranced. Finally they put out the candles, and fell asleep—

Only to awaken all together, surprised and disoriented, when the power came back on. It was 2 a.m., and beyond the reach of the smoldering gray coals the house was very cold, but fully lit, and buzzing with the sounds of its various machines. Anna and Charlie got up to turn the lights off. The boys were already asleep again by the time they got back downstairs.

The next day, things were back to normal, more or less, though the air was still smoky. Everyone wanted to tell stories about where they had been when the power went off, and what had happened to them.

"It was actually kind of nice," Charlie said the next night at dinner. "A little adventure."

Anna had to agree, though she was still uneasy. "It wouldn't have been if the power were still off."

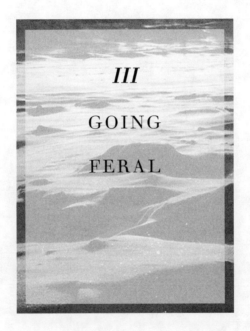

III

GOING

FERAL

"Again foul weather shall not change my mind,
But in the shade I will believe what in the sun I loved."

—*Thoreau*

A gainst the pressure at the front of one's thoughts must be held the power of cognition, as a shield. Cognition that could see its own weak points, and attempt to work around them.

Examination of the relevant literature, however, revealed that there were cognitive illusions that were as strong or even stronger than optical illusions. This was an instructive analogy, because there were optical illusions in which one's sight was fooled no matter how fully one understood the illusion and its effect, and tried to compensate for it. Spin a disk with certain black-and-white patterns on it, and colors appear undeniably to the eye. Stand at the bottom of a cliff and it will appear to be about a thousand feet tall, no matter its real height; mountaineers called this foreshortening, and Frank knew it could not be avoided. From the bottom of El Capitan, one looked up three thousand feet, and it looked like about a thousand. In Klein Scheidegg one looked up the north face of the Eiger, and it looked about a thousand feet tall. You could not alter that even by focusing on the strangely compact details of the face's upper surface. In Thun, twenty miles away, you could look south across the Thunersee and see that the north face of the Eiger was a stupendous face, six thousand feet tall and looking every inch of it. But if you returned to Klein Scheidegg, so would the foreshortening. You could not make the adjustment.

There were many cognitive errors just like those optical errors. The human mind had grown on the savannah, and there were kinds of thinking not natural to it. Calculating probabilities, thinking about statistical effects; the cognitive scientists had cooked up any number of logic problems, and tested great numbers of subjects with them, and even working with statisticians as their subjects they could find the huge majority prone to some fairly basic cognitive errors, which they had given names like anchoring, ease of representation, the law of small numbers, the fallacy of near certainty, asymmetric similarity, trust in analogy, neglect of base rates, and so on.

One test that had caught even Frank, despite his vigilance, was the three-box game. Three boxes, all closed, one ten-dollar bill hidden in one of them;

the experimenter knows which. Subject chooses one box, at that point left closed. Experimenter opens one of the other two boxes, always an empty one. Subject then offered a chance to either stick with his first choice, or switch to the other closed box. Which should he do?

Frank had decided it didn't matter; fifty-fifty either way. He thought it through.

But each box at the start had a one-third chance of being the one. When subject chooses one, the other two have two-thirds of a chance of being right. After experimenter opens one of those two boxes, always empty, those two boxes still have two-thirds of a chance, now concentrated in the remaining unchosen box, while the subject's original choice still had its original one-third chance. So one should always change one's choice!

Shit. Well, put it that way, it was undeniable. Though it still seemed wrong. But this was the point. Human cognition had all kinds of blind spots. One analyst of the studies had concluded by saying that we simulate in our actions what we wish had already happened. We act, in short, by projecting our desires.

Well—but of course. Wasn't that the point?

But clearly it could lead to error. The question was, could one's desires be defined in such a way as to suggest actions that were truly going to help make them come to pass in one of those futures still truly possible, given the conditions of the present?

And could that be done if there was a numb spot behind one's nose—a pressure on one's thoughts—a suspension of one's ability to decide anything?

And could these cognitive errors exist for society as a whole, as well as for an individual? Some spoke of "cognitive mapping" when they discussed taking social action—a concept that had been transferred from geography to politics, and even to epistemology, as far as Frank could tell. One mapped the unimaginable immensity of postmodern civilization (or, reality) not by knowing all of it, which was impossible, but by marking routes through it. So that one was not like the GPS or the radar system, but rather the traffic controller, or the pilot.

At that point it became clear even mapping was an analogy. Anna would not think much of it. But everyone needed a set of operating procedures to navigate the day. A totalizing theory forming the justification for a rubric for the daily decisions. The science of that particular Wednesday. Using flawed equipment (the brain, civilization) to optimize results. Most adaptive practices. Robustness.

Something from ecology, from Aldo Leopold: What's good is what's good for the land.

Something from Rudra (although he said from the Dalai Lama, or the Buddha): Try to do good for other people. Your happiness lies there.

Try it and see. Make the experiment and analyze it. Try again. Act on your desires.

So what do you really want?

And can you really decide?

ONE DAY WHEN FRANK WOKE UP in the garden shed with Rudra, it took him a while to remember where he was—long enough that when he sat up he was actively relieved to be Frank Vanderwal, or anybody.

Then he had trouble figuring out which pants to put on, something he had never considered before in his life; and then he realized he did not want to go to work, although he had to. Was this unusual? He wasn't sure.

As he munched on a PowerBar and waited for his bedside coffee machine to provide, he clicked on his laptop, and after the portentous chord announced the beginning of his cyber-day, he went to Emersonfortheday.com.

"Hey, Rudra, are you awake?"

"Always."

"Listen to this. It's Emerson, talking about our parcellated mind theory:

"It is the largest part of a man that is not inventoried. He has many enumerable parts: he is social, professional, political, sectarian, literary, and is this or that set and corporation. But after the most exhausting census has been made, there remains as much more which no tongue can tell. And this remainder is that which interests. Far the best part of every mind is not that which he knows, but that which hovers in gleams, suggestions, tantalizing, unpossessed, before him. This dancing chorus of thoughts and hopes is the quarry of his future, is his possibility."

"Maybe so," Rudra said. "But whole sight is good too. Being one."

"But isn't it interesting he talks about it in the same terms."

"It is common knowledge. Anyone knows that."

"I guess. I think Emerson knows a lot of things I don't know."

He was a man who had spent time in the forest, too. Frank liked to see the signs of this: "The man who rambles in the woods seems to be the first man that ever entered a grove, his sensations and his world are so novel and strange." That was right; Frank knew that feeling. Hikes in the winter forest, so surreal—Emerson knew about them. He had seen the woods at twilight. "Never was a more brilliant show of colored landscape than yesterday afternoon; incredibly excellent topaz and ruby at four o'clock; cold and shabby at six." The quick strangeness of the world, how it came on you all of a sudden— now, for Frank, the feeling started on waking in the morning. Coming up blank, the primal man, the first man ever to wake. Strange indeed, not to know who or what you were.

Often these days he felt he should be moving back out into the park, and living in his treehouse. That would mean leaving the Khembalis, however, and that was bad. But on the other hand, it would in some ways be a relief. He had been living with them for almost a year now, hard to believe but it was true, and they were so crowded. They could use all the extra space they could get. Besides, it felt like time to get back outdoors and into the wind again. Spring was coming, spring and all.

But there was Rudra to consider. As his roommate, Frank was part of his care. He was old, frail, sleeping a lot. Frank was his companion and his friend, his English teacher and his Tibetan student. Moving out would inevitably disrupt that situation.

He read on for a while, then realized he was hungry, and that in poking around and thinking about Emerson and Thoreau, and cognitive blind spots, he had been reading for over an hour. Rudra had gotten up and slipped out. "Aack!" Time to get up! Seize the day!

Up and out then. Another day. He had to consult with Edgardo about the Caroline situation. Best get something to eat first. But—from where?

He couldn't decide.

A minute or two later, angrily, and before even actually getting up, he grabbed his cell phone and made the call. He called his doctor's office, and found that, regarding a question like this, the doctor couldn't see him for a week.

That was fine with Frank. He had made the decision and made the call. Caroline would have no reason to reproach him, and he could go back to the way things were. Not that something didn't have to be done. It was getting ridiculous. It was a—an obstacle. A disability. An injury, not just to his brain, but *to his thinking*.

That very afternoon, the urgency in him about Caroline being so sharp and recurrent, he made arrangements to go out on a run with Edgardo. It was an afternoon so cold that no one but Kenzo would have gone out with them, and he was away at a conference, so after they cleared themselves with the wand (which Frank now questioned as fully reliable indicators), off they went.

The two of them ran side by side through the streets of Arlington, bundled up in nearly Arctic running gear, their heavy wool caps rolled up just far enough to expose their ears' bottom halves, which allowed sound into the eardrums so they could hear each other over the noise of traffic without shouting or completely freezing their ears. Very soon they would be moving with Diane over to the Old Executive Offices, right next door to the White House; this would be one of their last runs on this route. But it was such a lame route that neither would miss it.

Frank explained what had happened in Maine, in short rhythmic phrases synchronized with his stride. It was such a relief to be able to tell somebody about it. Almost a physical relief. One *vented,* as they said.

"So how the heck did they follow me?" he demanded at the end of his tale. "I thought your friend said I was clean."

"He thought you were," Edgardo said. "And it isn't certain you were followed. It could have been a coincidence."

Frank shook his head.

"Well, there may be other ways you are chipped, or they may indeed have just followed you physically. We'll work on that, but the question now becomes what has she done."

"She said she has a Plan C that no one can trace. And she said it would get her down in this area. That she'd get in touch with me. I don't know how that will work. Anyway now I'm wondering if we can, you know, root these guys out. Maybe sic the president on them."

"Well," Edgardo said, elongating the word for about a hundred yards. "These kinds of black operations are designed to be insulated, you know. To keep those above from responsibility for them."

"But surely if there was a problem, if you really tried to hunt things down from above? Following the money trail, for instance?"

"Maybe. Black budgets are everywhere. Have you asked Charlie?"

"No."

"Maybe you should, if you feel comfortable doing that. Phil Chase has a million things on his plate. It might take someone like Charlie to get his attention."

Frank nodded. "Well, whatever happens, we need to stop those guys."

"We?"

"I mean, they need to be stopped. And no one else is doing it. And, I don't know—maybe you and your friends from your DARPA days, or wherever, might be able to make a start. You've already made the start, I mean, and could carry it forward from there."

"Well," Edgardo said. "I shouldn't speak to that."

Frank focused on the run. They were down to the river path now, and he could see the Potomac was frozen over again, looking like a discolored white sheet that had been pulled over the river's surface and then tacked down roughly at the banks. The sight reminded him of Long Pond, and the shock of seeing those men striding across the ice toward them; his pulse jumped, but his hands and feet got colder. The tip of his nose, still a bit numb at the best of times, was even number than usual. He squeezed and tugged it to get some feeling and blood flow.

"Nose still numb?"

"Yes."

Edgardo broke into the song "Comfortably Numb": "I—I, have become, comfortably numb," then scat singing the famous guitar solo, "Da daaaa, da da da da da-da-daaaaaa," exaggerating Gilmour's bent notes. "Okay! Okay, okay, Is there anybody *in there?*" Abruptly he broke off. "Well, I will go talk to my friend whom you met. He's into this stuff and he has an interest. His group is still looking at the election problem, for sure."

"Do you think I could meet him again? To explore some strategies?" And ask a bunch of questions, he didn't say.

"Maybe. Let me talk to him. It may be pointless to meet. It depends. I'll check. Meanwhile you should try your other options."

"I don't know that I have any."

"Are you still having trouble making decisions?"

"Yes."

"Go see your doctor, then."

"I did! I mean, I've got an appointment. The time has almost come."

Edgardo laughed.

"Please," Frank said. "I'm trying. I made the call."

But in fact, when the time came for his doctor's appointment, he went in unhappily. Surely, he thought obstinately, deciding to go to the doctor meant he was well enough to decide things!

So he felt ridiculous as he described the problem to the doctor, a young guy who looked rather dubious. Frank felt his account was sketchy at best, as he very seldom tasted blood at the back of his throat anymore. But he could not complain merely of feeling indecisive, so he emphasized the tasting a little more than the most recent data would truly support, which made him feel even more foolish. He hated visiting the doctor at any time, so why was he there just to exaggerate an occasional symptom? Maybe his decision-making capability was damaged after all! Which meant it was good to have come in. And yet here he was making things up. Although he was only trying to physicalize the problem, he told himself. To describe real symptoms.

In any case, the doctor offered no opinion, but only gave him a referral to an ear nose and throat guy. It was the same one Frank had seen immediately after his accident. Frank steeled himself, called again (two decisions?) and found that here the next appointment available was a month away. Happily he wrote down the date and and forgot about it.

Or would have; except now he was cast back into the daily reality of struggling to figure out what to do. Hoping every morning that Emerson or Thoreau would tell him. So he didn't really forget about the appointment, but it was scheduled and he didn't have to go for a long time, so he could be happy. Happy until the next faint taste of old blood slid down the back of his throat, like the bitterness of fear itself, and he would check and see the day was getting nearer with a mix of relief and dread.

Once he noticed the date when talking with Anna, because she said something about not making it through the winter in terms of several necessary commodities that people had taken to hoarding. She had gotten into studying hoarding in the social science literature. Hoarding, Anna said, represented a breakdown in the social contract which even their economy's capacity for overproduction in many items could not compensate for.

"It's another case of prisoner's dilemma," Frank said. "Everyone's choosing the 'always defect' option as being the safest. Or the one in which you rely least on others."

"Maybe."

Anna was not one for analogies. She was as literal-minded a person as Frank had ever met; it was always good to remember that she had started her scientific training as a chemist. Metaphors bounced off of her like spears off bulletproof glass. If she wanted to understand hoarding, then she googled "hoarding," and when she saw links to mathematical studies of the economics and social dynamics of "hoarding in shortage societies," those were the ones she clicked on, even if they tended to be old work from the socialist and post-socialist literature. Those studies had had a lot of data to work with, sadly, and she found their modeling interesting, and spoke to Frank of things like choice rubrics in variable information states, which she thought he might be able to formalize as algorithms.

"It's called 'always defect,' " Frank insisted.

"Okay, but then look at what that *leads to*."

"All right."

Clearly Anna was incensed at how unreasonable people were being. To her it was a matter of being rational, of being logical. "Why don't they just do the math?" she demanded.

A rhetorical question, Frank judged. Though he wished he could answer it, rhetorically or not, in a way that did not depress him. His investigations into cognition studies were not exactly encouraging. Logic was to cognition as geometry was to landscape.

After this conversation, Frank recalled her saying "end of the winter" as if that were near, and he checked his desk calendar—the date for his ENT appointment was circled there, and not too far away—and suddenly he real-ized that in America, when it came to health care, the most important product of them all, they always operated in a shortage society.

In any case, he went to the doctor when the day came. Ear, nose, and throat—but what about *brain*? He read *Walden* in the waiting room, was ushered into an examination room to wait and read some more, then five minutes of ques-tions and inspections, and the diagnosis was made: he needed to see another specialist. A neurologist, in fact, who would have to take a look at some scans, possibly CT, PET, SPECT, MRI; the brain guy would make the calls. The ENT guy would give him a referral, he said, and Frank would have to see where they could fit him in. Scans; the reading and analysis of the brain guy; then perhaps a re-examination by the ENT. How long would it all take? Try it and see. They hurried things up in scheduling when there were questions about the brain, but only so much could be done; there were a lot of other people out there with equally serious problems, or worse ones.

So, Frank thought as he went back to work in his office. You could buy DVD players for thirty dollars and flat-screen TVs for a hundred, also a mil-lion other consumer items that would help you to experience vicariously the lives that your work and wages did not give you time to live (that T-shirt seen on Connecticut Avenue, "Medieval Peasants Worked Less Than You Do")—everything was cheap, in overproduction—except you lived in a permanent shortage of doctors, artificially maintained. Despite the high cost of medical insurance (if you could get it) you had to wait weeks or months on tests to find out how your body was sick or injured, when such events befell you. Even though it was possible to measure statistically how much health care a given population was going to need, and provide it accordingly.

But there was nothing for it but to think about other things, when he could; and when not, to bide his time and try to work, like everyone else.

It had been every kind of winter so far, warmer, drier, stormier, colder. Bad for agriculture, but good for conversation. In the first week of March, a cold front swept south and knocked them back into full winter lockdown, the river frozen, the city frozen, every Metro vent steaming frost, which then froze and fell to the ground as white dust. The whole city was frosted, and with all the steam curling out of the ground, looked as if it had been built atop a giant hot spring. Bad Washington. When the sun came out everything glittered whitely, then prismatically when the melting began, then went gray when low stratus clouds obscured the sun.

For Frank this was another ascent into what he thought of as high latitude or high altitude: a return to the high country one way or another, because weather *was* landscape, in that however the land lay underfoot, it was the weather that gave you a sense of where you were.

If it was below zero, then you were in the arctic. You found yourself on the cold hill's side, in a dreamscape as profound as any imaginable. One recalled in the body itself that the million-year ballooning of the brain, the final expansion with its burst into language and art and culture, had occurred in the depths of an ice age, when it had been like this all the time. No wonder the mind lit up like a fuse in such air!

And so Frank got out his snowshoes and gaiters and ski poles, and drove over to Rock Creek Park and went out for hikes, just as he had the winter before. And though this year there was not that sense of discovery in the activity, it was certainly just as cold, or almost. Wind barreling down the great ravine from the north—the icy new rip in the canyon, looking from its rim just as blasted by the great flood as the day the waters had receded.

The park was emptier this year, however. Or maybe it was just that there was no one at Site 21. But many of the other sites were empty as well. Maybe it was just that during weeks this cold, people simply found shelter. That had happened the previous winter as well. In theory one could sleep out in temperatures like this, if one had the right gear and the right expertise, but it took a great deal of time and energy to accomplish, and would still be somewhat dangerous; it would have to become one's main activity. And no doubt some people were doing it; but most had found refuge in the coffee shops by day and the shelters and feral houses by night, waiting out the coldest part of the winter indoors. As Frank had done, when he had been taken in by the Khembalis.

Leaving, in these most frigid days, the animals. He saw the aurochs once; and a Canada lynx (I call it the Concord lynx, Thoreau said), as still as a statue of itself; and four or five foxes in their winter white. And a moose, a porcupine, coyote, and scads of white-tailed deer; also rabbits. These last two were the obvious food species for what predators there were. Most of the exotic ferals were gone, either recaptured or dead. Although once he spotted what he thought was a snow leopard; and people said the jaguar was still at large.

As were the frisbee guys. One Saturday Frank heard them before he saw them—hoots over a rise to the north—Spencer's distinctive yowl, which meant a long putt had gone in. Cheered by the sound, Frank poled around the point in the ravine wall, snowshoes sinking deep in the drifts there, and suddenly there they were, running on little plastic showshoes, without poles, and throwing red, pink, and orange frisbees, which blazed through the air like beacons from another universe.

"Hi guys!" Frank called.

"Frank!" they cried. "Come on!"

"You bet," Frank said. He left his poles and daypack under a tree at Site 18, and borrowed one of Robert's disks.

Off they went. Quickly it became clear to Frank that when the snow was as hard as it was, running on snowshoes was about as efficient as walking on them. One tended to leap out of each step before the snowshoe had sunk all the way in, thus floating a bit higher than otherwise.

Then he threw a drive straight into a tree trunk, and broke the disk in half. Robert just laughed, and Spencer tossed him a spare. The guys did not over-value any individual disk. They were like golf balls, made to be lost.

Work as hard as they did, and you would sweat—just barely—after which, when you stopped, sweat would chill you. As soon as they were done, there-fore, Frank found out when they thought they would play snow golf again, then bid farewell and hustled away, back to his daypack and poles. A steady hike then, to warm back up: plunging poles in to pull him uphill, to brace him downhill; little glissades, tricky traverses, yeoman ups; quickly he was warm again and feeling strong and somehow full, the joy of the frisbee buzzing through the rest of the afternoon. The joy of the hunt and the run and the cold.

He walked by his tree, looked up at it longingly. He wanted to move back out there. But he wanted to stay with Rudra too. And Caroline's ex might be keeping watch out here. The thought made him stop and look around. No one in sight. He would have to wand his tree to see if there was anything there. The floorboards of the treehouse were visible, at least if you knew where to look, and of course Frank did, so it was hard for him to judge how obvious they were to others. Wherever he went in the park, if his tree was in sight, he could see various bits of the little black triangle that was his true home.

The following Monday he made sure to arrange a run with Edgardo again. The need to speak securely was going to drive them to new levels of fitness.

As they trailed Kenzo and Bob down the narrow path next to Route 66, he said, "So did you ever hear anything back from your friend?"

"Yes. A little. I was going to tell you."

"What?"

"He said, the problem with taking the top-down approach is the operation might be legal, and also legally secret, such that even the president might have trouble finding out about it."

"You're kidding."

"No. He said that most presidents want it that way, so they aren't breaking the law by knowing, if the operation chooses to do something illegal for the higher good. So, Chase might have to order a powerful group right under his command to seek something like this out."

"Jesus. Are there any such powerful groups?"

"Oh sure. He would have his choice of three or four. But this presumes that you could get him that interested in the matter. The thing you have to re-member is, a president has a lot on his plate. He has a staff to filter it all and prioritize what gets to him, so there are levels to get through. So, these people we're interested in know that, and they trust he would never go after something this little."

"Something as little as stolen presidential elections?"

"Well, maybe, but how much would he want to know about that, when he just won?"

They paced on while Frank tried to digest this.

"So did your friend have any other ideas?"

"Yes. He said, it might be possible to get these people embroiled in some kind of trouble with an agency that is less black than they are. Some kind of turf battle or the like."

"Ahhh..."

Quickly Frank began to see possibilities. While at NSF, Diane had been fighting other agencies all over the place, usually David-and-Goliath type actions, as most of NSF's natural rivals in the federal bureaucracy were far bigger than it. And size mattered in the Feds, as elsewhere, because it meant money. This little gang of security thugs Frank had tangled with were surely treading on some other more legitimate agency's turf. Possibly they had even started in some agency and gone rambo without the knowledge of their superiors.

"That's a good idea. Did they have any specific suggestions?"

"He did, and he was going to work up some more. It turns out he has reasons to dislike these guys beyond the destruction-of-democracy stuff."

"Oh good."

"Yes. It is best never to rely on people standing on principle."

"So true," Frank said grimly.

This set off Edgardo's raucous laugh and his little running prance of cynical delight. "Ah yes, you are learning! You are beginning to see! My friend said he will give me a menu of options soon."

"I hope it's real soon. Because *my* friend's out there enacting her Plan C, and I'm worried. I mean, she's a data analyst, when you get right down to it. She isn't any kind of field spook. What if her Plan C is as bad as her Plan B was?"

"That would be bad. But my friend has been looking into that too. I asked him to, and he did, and he said he can't see any sign of her. She seems to be really off the net this time."

"That's good. But her ex might know more than your friend. And she said she'd be around here somewhere."

"Yes. Well, I'll go see my friend as soon as I can. I have to follow our protocol though, unless it's an emergency. We only usually talk once a week."

"I understand," Frank said, then wondered if he did.

WITH CHASE NOW IN OFFICE the new administration's activity level was manic but focused. Among many more noted relocations, Diane and all the rest of the science advisor's team moved into their new offices in the Old Executive Building, just to the west of the White House and within the White House security barrier.

So Frank gave up his office at NSF, which had served as the living room and office in his parcellated house. As he moved out he felt a bit stunned, even dismayed. He had to admit that the set of habits that had been that modular house was now completely demolished. He followed Diane to their new building, wondering if he had made the right decision to go with her. Of course his real home now was the Khembali embassy's garden shed. He was not really homeless. Maybe it was a bad thing not to have rented a place somewhere. If he had kept looking he could have found something.

Then Diane convened a week's worth of meetings with all the agencies and departments she wanted to deal with frequently, and during that week he saw that being inside the White House compound was a good thing, and that he needed to be there for Diane. She needed the help; there were literally scores of agencies that had to be gathered into the effort they had in mind, and many of them had upper managements appointed during the years of executive opposition to climate mitigation. Even after the long winter, not all of them were convinced they needed to change. "They're being actively passive-aggressive," Diane said with a wry grin. "War of the agencies, big-time."

"Such trivial crap they're freaking about," Frank complained. He was amazed it didn't bother her more. "EPA trying to keep USGS from interpreting pesticide levels they're finding, because interpretation is EPA's job? Energy and Navy fighting over who gets to do new nuclear? It's always turf battles."

She waved them all away with a hand, seemingly unannoyed. "Turf battles matter in Washington, I'm sorry to say. We're going to have to get things done using these people. Chase has to make a lot of appointments fast for us to have any chance of doing that. And we'll have to be scrupulous in keeping to the boundaries. It's no time to be changing the bureaucracy too much; we've got bigger fish to fry. I plan to try to keep all these folks happy about their power base holding fast, but just get them on board to help the cause."

It made sense when she put it that way, and after that he understood better her manner with the old-guard technocracy they were so often dealing with. She was always conciliatory and unassuming, asking questions, then laying out her ideas as more questions rather than commands, and always confining herself to whatever that particular agency was specifically involved in.

"Not that that's what I always do," Diane said, when Frank once made this observation to her. She looked ashamed.

"What do you mean?" Frank asked quickly.

"Well, I had a bad meeting with the deputy secretary of Energy, Holderlin. He's a holdover, and he was trying to disparage the alternatives program. So I got him fired."

"You did?"

"I guess so. I sent a note over to the president describing the problem I was having, and the next thing I knew he was out."

"Do people know that's how it happened?"

"I think so."

"Well—good!"

She laughed ruefully. "I've had that thought myself. But it's a strange feeling."

"Get used to it. We probably need a whole bunch of people fired. You're the one who always calls it the war of the agencies."

"Yes, but I never had the power to get people in other agencies fired before."

To change the subject to something that would make her more comfortable, Frank said, "I'm having some luck getting the military interested. They're the eight-hundred-pound gorilla in this zoo. If they were to come down definitively on the side of our efforts, as being a critical aspect of national defense, then these other agencies would either get on board or become irrelevant."

"Yes, maybe," Diane said. "But what *they* are you talking about? The Joint Chiefs?"

"Well, to an extent. Although I've been starting with people I know, like General Wracke. Also meeting some of the chief scientists. They're not much in the decision-making loop, but they might be easier to convince about the science. I show them the Marshall Report they did internally, rating climate change as more of a defense threat than terrorism. It seems to help."

"Can you make a copy of that for distribution?"

"Yes. It would also make sense to reach out to all the scientists in government, and ask them to get behind the National Academy statement on the climate for starters, then help us to work on the agencies they're involved with."

"Sure. But they don't decide, and there's management who will be against us no matter what their scientists say, because that's why they were appointed in the first place."

"There's where your firing one of them may have an effect." Frank grinned and Diane made a face.

"Okay, fine," she said. "Maybe it's time to talk to Energy then. If they're scared that they'll lose their funding, that's the moment to strike."

"Which means we should be talking to the OMB?"

"Yes. We definitely need the OMB on our side. That should be possible, if Chase has appointed the right people to head it."

"And then the appropriations committees."

"The best chance there is to talk to their staffs, and to win some new seats in the midterm election. For Chase's first two years, it'll be a bit uphill when it comes to Congress."

"At least he's got the Senate."

"Yes, but really you need both."

"Hm."

Frank saw it anew: hundreds of parts to the federal government, each part holding a piece of the jigsaw puzzle, jockeying to determine what kind of picture they all made together. War of the agencies, the Hobbesian struggle of all against all—it needed to be changed to some kind of dance. Made coherent. Lased.

In his truncated time off it was hard to get many hours in with Nick anymore, as Nick was often busy with other people in FOG, including a youth group, as well as with all his other activities at school and home. They still held to a meeting at the zoo every third Saturday morning, more or less, starting with an hour at the tiger enclosure, taking notes and photos, then doing a cold-certification course, or walking up to the beaver pond to see what they might see. But that time quickly passed, and then Nick was off. Frank missed their longer days out together, but it wasn't something that he could press about. His friendship with the Quiblers was unusual enough as it was to make him feel awkward, and he didn't want them wondering if he had some kind of peculiar thing going on about Nick—really the last thing that would occur to him, although he enjoyed the boy's company greatly. He was a funny kid.

More likely a suspicion was that Frank might have some kind of a thing for Anna, because there was some truth to it. Although it was not something he would ever express or reveal in any way, it was only just a sort of heightened admiration for a friend, an admiration that included an awareness of the friend's nice figure and her passionate feelings about things, and most of all, her quick and sharp mind. An awareness of just how smart she was. Indeed, here was the one realm in which Frank felt he must know Anna better than Charlie did—in effect, Charlie didn't know enough to know just how smart Anna was. It was like it had been for Frank when trying to evaluate Chessman as a chess player. Once while waiting for Nick to get ready, Frank had posed the three-box problem to Anna, and she had repeated his scenario carefully, and squinted, and then said "I guess you'd want to change to that other box, then?" and he had laughed and put out his hands and bowed like the kids on *Saturday Night Live*. And this was just the smallest kind of indicator of her quickness—of a quality of thought Frank would have to characterize as boldly methodical.

Charlie only grinned at the exchange and said, "She does that kind of thing all the time." He would never see the style of her thought well enough to know how to admire it. Indeed what he called her quibbling was often his own inability to see a thrust right to the heart of a problem he had not noticed. She had married a man who was blind in exactly the area she was most dashing.

Well, there were no total relationships. Maybe what he felt for Anna was just what friendship was with certain co-workers of the opposite sex. Nietzsche had declared friendship between men and women to be impossible, but he had written many stupid things among his brilliant insights, and had had terrible relationships with women and then gone insane. Surely on the savannah there would have been all sorts of friendships between the sexes. On the savannah things might have been a little more flexible at the borders.

But he did not want Charlie to misunderstand, and so all this was just a matter of thoughts. Trying to figure things out. Feelings and behaviors. Sociobiology was like a green light cast over their naked faces. Sometimes he classed these among the thoughts that made him worry about his mentation.

At work now, however, he missed Anna very much. He tried to focus on the various problems on his master list of Things To Do, and about twice a day he would have gone over to ask her a question about something or other. But not anymore. Now he forged on with what was in effect Diane's list of Things To Do, compiled by them all. Frank focused on the solar-power front in particular, as being the crux of the problem. If solar did not step in immediately, they were going to have to commission and build a whole lot of new nuclear power plants. Or else they would go ahead and burn the 530 gigatons of carbon that would raise the atmospheric level of CO_2 to five hundred parts per million, frying the planet.

Put like that, the priority on solar power went pretty high. Which made it baffling to see how little money had been invested in it in the past three decades. But what was done was done. And looking forward, it was a little encouraging, even gratifying, to see results beginning to come out of the experiments he had funded in the previous two years, because some of the new prototypes were looking pretty good. There were new photovoltaics at 42 percent efficiencies now. This was getting closer and closer to the holy grail. And at the largest scales, the Stirling engines were doing almost as well, at even less expense.

Really, with results like that, it was now only a matter of money, and time, and they could be there. Clean power.

Sometimes he even skipped to the other items on the list.

Among the really big-ticket items when it came to carbon emissions, transportation and agriculture ranked up there with power generation. Here again, the expense of changing out such a big and fundamental technology would be very high—until one compared it to the cost of not changing.

This was the case that Diane wanted to make to the reinsurance companies, and the UN, and everyone else. Say it cost a trillion dollars to install clean energy generators and change out the transport fleet. Weigh that against the financial benefit to civilization of continuing with approximately the sea level it now enjoyed, the weather, the biosphere support, etc.; also the difficult-to-calculate-in-dollars but undoubtedly huge benefit of avoiding a great deal of human suffering. Not to mention a mass extinction event for the rest of the biosphere, which might threaten their very survival.

Wouldn't it pencil out? It seemed like it would have to. Indeed, if it didn't pencil out, maybe there was something wrong with the accounting system.

Compare these costs to the U.S. military budget. Two trillion dollars would not be more than three or four years of the Pentagon's budget. This gave Frank a shock—that the military was so expensive, sure, but also that they could shift to clean power and transport so cheaply relative to the total economy. Electricity now cost about six cents a kilowatt hour, and they spoke of clean energy costing up to ten—and then said it couldn't be done? For financial reasons? "It wouldn't take much of a carbon-ceiling regulation to make it pencil out immediately," Frank said to Diane when they were talking on the phone. "Companies like Southern California Edison must be begging for a strict emissions cap. They'll make a killing when that happens. They'll be raking it in."

"True."

"I wonder what would happen if the reinsurance companies refused to insure oil companies that didn't get with the cap program right now?"

"Good idea." She sighed. "Boy, if only we could sic them on the World Bank and the IMF too."

"Maybe we can. Phil Chase is president now."

"So maybe we can! Hey, it's two already—have you had lunch?"

In his office, Frank smiled. "No, you wanna?"

"Yes. Give me five minutes."

"Meet you at the elevator."

So they had lunch, and among other things talked over the move to the White House, and what it meant. The danger of becoming an advisory body only, of having no budget to *do* things—as against the potential advantage of being able to tell all the federal agencies, and to an extent the whole government, what to do.

Diane said, "My guess is Chase is still trying to work out what's really possible. He's talked quite a line but now push has come to shove, and it's a big machine he's got to move. I've gotten a whole string of questions about the technical agencies, and just today I got an e-mail asking me to submit a thorough analysis of all the particulars of the New Deal—what he called the scientific aspects of the New Deal. I have no idea what he means."

Nevertheless, she had looked into it. There had been five New Deals, she said. Each had been a distinct project, with different goals and results. She listed them with a pen on the back of a napkin:

1) Hundred Days, 1933
2) Social Security, 1935
3) Keynesian stimulation 1938 (this package, she explained, had been enacted partly to re-prime the pump, partly to restore what the Supreme Court had blocked from New Deal 2)
4) the defense buildup of 1940–41, and
5) the G.I. Bill of Rights of 1944

"Number five was entirely FDR's idea, by the way. Nothing's ever done more for ordinary Americans, the analysis said. It was what made the postwar middle class, and the baby boom."

"Encouraging," Frank said, studying the list.

"Very. Granted, this all took twelve years, but still. It doesn't even count the international stuff, like getting us prepared for the war, or winning it. Or starting the UN!"

"Impressive," Frank said. "Let's hope Chase can do as well."

Here Diane looked doubtful. "One thing seems pretty clear already," she confessed. "He's too busy with other stuff for me to be able to make many of our arguments to him in person. I mean, I've barely met him yet."

"*That's* not good." Frank was surprised to hear this.

"Well, he's pretty good at replying to his e-mail. And his people get back to me when I send along questions or requests."

"Maybe that's where I should ask Charlie for help. He might be able to influence the decision about how to allocate Chase's meeting time."

"That would be good."

It seemed to Frank, watching her and thinking about other kinds of things, that she appeared to have forgotten his abrupt cancellation of their post–North Atlantic date. Or—since no one ever really forgot things like that—to have let it go. Forgiven, if not forgotten—all he could expect, of course. Maybe it had only been a little weird. In any case a relief, after his experiences with Marta, who neither forgot nor forgave.

Which reminded him that he had to talk to Marta sometime soon about Small Delivery Systems' Russian experiment. Damn.

As always, the thought of having to communicate with his ex-partner filled Frank with a combination of dread and a perverse kind of anticipation, which came in part from trying to guess how it would go wrong this time. For go wrong it would. He and Marta had always had a stormy relationship, and Frank had come to suspect that all Marta's intimate relationships were stormy. Certainly her relations with her ex-husband had been inflamed, which had been one of the reasons she and Frank too had come to a nasty end. Marta had needed to keep her name off the paperwork on the house she and Frank had bought together, in order to keep it clear of the divorce and bankruptcy morass created by Marta's always soon-to-be ex. This absence of her name had created the possibility for Frank later to sign a third mortgage, in effect taking all their equity out of the place and losing it in a surefire biotech that had guttered out.

A very bad idea. One of a string of bad decisions that Frank had made in those years, many clustered around Marta. There had to be some kind of nostalgia for bad times involved in Frank's desire to talk to her. In any case he had to call her, because she was his contact with the Russian lichen project, and he needed to know more about how that was going. Given the ongoing opacity of Russian government and science—the weird mix of Kremlinocracy and nouveau-capitalist corporate secrecy—a (semi)reliable informant was crucial if he was going to learn anything solid. So the call had to be made. Or rather the visit. Because he wanted to see the new facility too. NSF had rented the very same building once occupied by Torrey Pines Generique, and the committee involved had offered contracts to an array of very good people in the relevant sciences, including Yann and Marta. The geosciences were hot these days, and the new head of the institute had called a conference to discuss various proposals for new action. Frank was unsurprised to see that Yann and Marta were on the program. He called down to the travel office to have them book a flight for him.

FOR THE QUIBLERS AS FOR THE REST of the capital's residents, the winter's blackouts had developed their own routines, with the inconveniences balanced by the seldom-indulged pleasures of the situation: fire in the fireplace, candles, blankets, blocks, and books. Anna had taken up knitting again, so when the power went out she helped get things settled and then got under a comforter and clicked away. Charlie read aloud to them. He and Anna discussed whether they should get satellite cell phones, so they could stay in contact if they happened to get caught out somewhere when the next one hit. The blackouts were getting more frequent; it was widely debated whether they were caused by overdemand, mechanical failure, sabotage, computer viruses, corporate rigging, or the cold drought, but no one could deny they were becoming regular occurrences. And sometimes they lasted for two days.

On this particular dark evening, after Anna had gone to the appropriate drawer and cabinets and got out their blackout gear, there came a knock at their door, very unusual. So much so that Nick said, "Frank must be here!"

And so he was.

He stamped in looking freeze-dried, put the back of his hand to their cheeks and had them shrieking. "Is it okay?" he asked Charlie uncertainly.

"Oh sure, sure, what do you mean?"

"I don't know."

It seemed to Charlie almost as if Frank's thinking had been chilled on the hike over; his words were slow, his manner distracted. He had been out snowshoeing in Rock Creek Park, he said, checking on his homeless friends, and had decided afterward to drop by.

"Good for you. Have some tea with us."

"Thanks."

Nick and Joe were delighted. Frank brought a new element to the power-free evening with his hint of mystery and strangeness. "Tiger man!" Joe exclaimed. Nick talked with him about the animals at the zoo, and still at large in the park. Joe plucked the appropriate plastic animals out of his big box as they spoke, lining them up in a parade on the floor for their inspection. "Tiger tiger tiger!" he said, pleasing Charlie very much; lately he had been showing a preference for zebras and dolphins and hippos.

Frank and Nick were saying that there were very few feral animals still at large, and almost all the holdouts were either arctic or mountain species. The other exotics had all come in from the cold, or died.

Charlie noticed Nick smoothly change the subject: "What about your friends?"

The human ferals, Frank said, were still pretty easy to find. "My own group is kind of scattered, but in general I think there'll be more and more people like them as time goes on. Housing is just too expensive. If you can arrange some other way, it makes sense in a lot of ways."

"You wouldn't have to worry about blackouts," Charlie remarked.

Later, when the boys were asleep, Frank hunkered down by the fire, holding his hands to it and staring into the flames.

"Charlie," he said hesitantly, "has anyone on Chase's staff been looking into the election, and that talk that went around about irregularities in some of the votes?"

"No one I know of."

"I'm surprised."

"Well, it's kind of a Satchel Paige moment."

"What does that mean?" Anna said.

"Don't look back—something might be gaining on you."

Frank nodded. "But what if something *is* gaining on you?"

"I think that was Satchel's point. But what do you mean?"

"What if there was a group that tried to fix the election, but failed?"

Charlie was surprised. "Then good."

"But what if they're still out there?"

"I'm sure they are. It's a spooky world these days."

Frank glanced quickly at Charlie, then nodded, the corners of his mouth tight. "A spooky world indeed."

"You mean spooks," Anna clarified.

Frank nodded, eyes still on the fire. "There's seventeen intelligence agencies in the federal government now. And some of them are not fully under anyone's control anymore."

"Whoah. How do you mean?"

"You know. Black agencies. Black agencies so black they've disappeared, like black holes."

"Disappeared?" Charlie said.

"No oversight. No connections. I don't think even the president knows about them. I don't think anyone knows about them, except the people in them."

"But how would they get funding?"

Anna laughed at that, but Frank frowned. "I don't know. I suppose they have access to some kind of slush fund."

"So, whoever was responsible for those funds would know."

"They might only know . . . maybe they're being run by people who have discretionary funds, so those people know, but they're in the groups, or leading them. Forming them . . . I don't know. You know more about that kind of stuff than I do. But surely there's money sloshing around that certain people have access to? Especially in intelligence?"

Charlie nodded. "Forty billion per year on intelligence. Black program money could get subdivided. I've heard of that happening before."

"Well . . ." Frank paused, as if weighing his words carefully. "They are a danger to the republic."

"Whoah." Charlie had never heard Frank say such a thing.

Frank shrugged. "Sorry, but it's true. If we mean to be a constitutional government, then we're going to have to root some of these groups out. Because they are a danger to democracy and open government as we're used to thinking of it. They're trying to move all the important stuff into the shadows."

"And so . . ."

"So I'm wondering if you could direct Chase's attention to them. Make him aware of them, and urge him to root them out."

"Do you think he could?"

"I should hope so!" Frank looked disturbed at the question. "I mean, if he followed the money, made his secretaries and agency heads account for all of it fully—maybe sicced the OMB on all the black money to find out who was using it, and for what . . . couldn't you?"

"I'm not sure," Charlie admitted. "Maybe you could."

"The Pentagon can't account for its outlays," Anna pointed out grimly, knitting like one of the women under the guillotine, *click click click!* "They have a percentage gone missing that is bigger than NSF's entire budget."

"Gone missing?"

"Unaccounted for. Unaccountable. I call that gone missing." Anna's disapproval was like dry ice, smoking with cold. Freeze all the excess carbon dioxide in the atmosphere into one big cake of dry ice and drape it around Anna's shoulders, in the few moments when she was professionally contemptuous.

"But if it were done by a competent team," Frank persisted, "without any turned people on it, and presidential backing to look into everything?"

Charlie still was dubious, but he said, "In theory that would work. Legally it should work."

"But?"

"Well, but the government, you know. It's big. It has lots of nooks and crannies. Like what you're talking about—black programs that have been fire-walled so many times, there are blacks within blacks, superblacks, superblack blacks. With black accounts and dedicated political contributions, so that the money is socked away in Switzerland, or Wal-Mart. . . ."

"Jesus. There are government programs with that kind of funding?"

Charlie shrugged. "Maybe."

Frank was staring at him, startled, even perhaps frightened. "In that case, we could all be in big trouble."

Anna was shaking her head. "A complete audit would find even that. It would include all accounts of every federal employee or unit, and also what they're doing with every hour of their work time. It's a fairly simple spread-sheet, for God's sake."

"But it could be faked so easily," Charlie objected.

"Well, you have to have some way to check the data."

"But there are hundreds of thousands of employees."

"I guess you'd have to use a statistically valid sampling method."

"But that's just the kind of method you can hide your black programs out of the reach of!"

"Hmm." Now Anna was frowning too. She was also sending curious glances Frank's way. This was a pretty un-Frank-like inquiry, in both content and style. "Well, maybe you'd have to be comprehensive with the intelligence and security agencies in particular. Account for everything in those."

Charlie said, "So, that being the case, they probably aren't tucked there. They're probably in Commerce or the Coast Guard or the Treasury. Which by itself is huge. Like, you know, the bank."

Frank said, "So maybe it isn't possible."

Charlie and Anna did not reply; each was thinking it over.

Frank sighed. "Maybe if we found a specific problem, and then told the president about it? Or, whoever could best put a stop to it? Wouldn't that *be* the president?"

Charlie said, "I should think the president would always be best at that kind of thing. But there are a lot of demands on his time."

"Everyone keeps saying that. But this could be important. Even, you know . . . crucial."

"Then I would hope it would get attended to. Maybe there's a unit de-signed to do it. In the Secret Service or something."

Frank nodded. "Maybe you could talk to him, then. When you think it's a good time. Because I know where to start the hunt."

Charlie and Anna glanced at each other, saw that neither knew what he was talking about.

"What do you mean?" Charlie said.

"I've run across some stuff," Frank said, adjusting a log in the fire.

Then the power flickered and hummed back on, and after a while Frank made his excuses and took off, still looking distant and thoughtful.

"What was that all about?" Charlie said.

"I don't know," Anna replied. "But I'm wondering if he found that woman in the elevator."

Anna had been pleased when Diane asked her to join the Presidential Science Advisor's staff, but it only took her a short period of reflection to decide against accepting the offer.

She knew she was right to do so, but explaining why to Diane and Frank had been a little tricky. She couldn't just come out and say "I prefer doing things to advising people to do things," or "I like science more than politics." It wouldn't have been polite, and besides, she wasn't sure that was the real reason anyway. So all she could do was claim an abiding interest in her work at NSF, which was true. It was always best when your lies were true.

"But you're the one who has been finding all these programs that knit together the federal agencies," Frank said. "You'd be perfect to help in a project like this. You could maybe come over on loan for a year or so."

This confirmed Anna's suspicion that it was Frank's idea to invite her over to the White House. Very nice of him, she liked that very much—but she said, "I can keep doing that from here, and still run my division too."

"Maybe."

Frank frowned, almost said something, stopped. Anna could not guess what it might have been. Some personal appeal? He looked a bit flushed. But maybe he was abashed at the thought of how little time he now had to give to his work on biological algorithms, his actual field. With this move he had shifted almost entirely to policy—to administration. To politics, in a word.

Of course maybe their circumstances called for a shift from science to policy, as an emergency measure, so to speak. Also an application of science *to* policy, which she knew was what Frank had in mind. Anna knew it was very common among scientists to be science snobs, and hold that no work in the world was as good and worthy as scientific research. Anna did not want to fall prey to that error even though she felt it pretty strongly herself, or at least, felt that she was better at science than at any of the mushier stuff. Correcting for that bias adequately was one part of the confusion of her feelings about all this. She would make lists sometimes of arguments pro and con, of qualities and their relative values, attempting to quantify and thus clarify her feelings.

In any case she held to her refusal, and to her job at NSF. And as she sat in the Metro on the way home, she thought somewhat grimly that it was too bad that Charlie hadn't stuck to his guns too, and refused his new job offer like she had. Because here she was going home early again, to pick up Nick from school and take him to his piano lessons.

Of course Charlie's situation had been different: he had been faced with a case of "come back or lose your job." Still—if he had held—how much easier life would have been for her. Not that she ever shirked any work at all, but it would have been easier for the boys too. Not so much Nick, but Joe. She was intensely worried about Joe going into the White House daycare center. Was he ready for that? Would it make him even stranger—stranger and more difficult, to put it plainly—than he already was? Or would it normalize him? Was he perhaps autistic? Or just fractious? And why was he fractious? And what would be the effect on him (and on the other children) of confining him in a single room or group or situation for an entire day? Even Charlie, with all his energy and flexibility, had not been able to keep up with Joe's demand for the new. She was afraid that in daycare, he and everyone around him would go mad.

Not that she put it exactly that way to herself. In her conscious mind she focused on incremental changes, specific worries, without moving on to larger and vaguer concepts. The conscious mind wasn't the whole story, as she knew from her troubled sleep, but that was what she could actually think about and work on directing, and so she did.

This was one of many differences between her and Charlie, most of which were accentuated when they both worked at home. This was a bad system for other reasons, because it meant Joe was around too, scheming for attention when she was attempting to work or think, but sometimes it just had to be done, as when the Metro was down for the supposedly last round of flood repairs. And there she would be, at the computer, staring at the spreadsheet on the screen, entering data on pesticides in stream water as part of a project to measure their effects on amphibians, endless lists of chemical and product names collated from a wide range of studies, so that quantities had to be normed and reformatted and analyzed, meaning a whole flurry of highly specific technical e-mails from colleagues to be dealt with—questions, comments, criticisms concerning details of math or chemistry or statistical methodology, working in the parts per billion range—

And at the same time Charlie would be audible from the floor below, trying to amuse Joe while holding a simultaneous headphone conversation with his friend Roy, shouting out things like, "Roy these are not IDIOTS you're dealing with here, you can't just LIE to them! WHAT? Okay well maybe you can lie to THEM, but make it a smart lie. Put it at the level of myth, these are like Punch and Judy figures, and your people want to be doing the punching! Sledgehammer them in the forehead with this stuff! JOE! STOP THAT!"

And so on. Sledgehammer them in the forehead? Really, Anna couldn't bear to listen.

But now this was Charlie's work, full-time and more—meaning, as in the old days, evenings too. Of course Anna spent a lot of evenings working, but for Charlie it was something he had not done since Joe had arrived. Endless phone conversations now, how much help could these be? Of course there was the new administration's first sixty days to execute successfully, accounting for much of this rush, but Anna doubted that very much would come of that. How could it? The system was simply slower than that. You could only do things at the speed they could be done.

So, whereas before she had most often come home to find the house in an uproar, Charlie cooking operatically while Joe banged pots and Nick read under the lamp in his corner of the couch, with the dinner soon to be on the table, now she often got home to find Nick sitting there like an owl, reading in the dark, and no one else home at all—and her heart would go out to him, all alone at seven p.m., at age twelve—

"You'll go blind," she would say.

"Mom," he would object happily.

—and she would kiss his head and turn on his light and barge around banging her toes as she turned on the other lights and went out to the kitchen to rustle something up before she starved—and sometimes there would be nothing in the fridge or the cupboards that she could cook or eat, and grumpily she would throw on her daypack and tell Nick to answer the phone, if she did not need him to come along and carry extra bags, and would walk down the street to the Giant grocery store, still grumpy at first but then enjoying the walk—

And then at the grocery store there would be no meat on the shelves, and few fresh veggies, fewer fruits. She would have to forget about her list and troll the aisles for something palatable, amazed once again at the sight of so many empty shelves—she had thought like everyone else that it would be a temporary thing—then getting angry at people for their selfish hoarding instincts. Before this winter—ever since the flood, really—people had hoarded some of the essentials, but now it had spread far beyond toilet paper and bottled water, to almost every shelf in the store. But particularly to all the foods she most liked to eat. It had gotten so bad that once, when in her hurry she had driven the car, she got back in and drove over to the smaller grocery store on Woodson, and they didn't have any eggplant either, though she craved it. So she got zucchini instead, and back home, late, starving, made chicken soup.

All this distracted her as she worked over the data in her biostatistical studies, but it also caused her to continue to think about the situation. She had chosen to stay at NSF because she felt she could do more there, and that NSF still had a crucial part to play in the larger effort. It was a small agency but it was central, in that it coordinated basic scientific research—really the heart of all their solutions. So she continued to do her work there, organizing the grant evaluation process and running the division. And when she could she kept working on the FCCSET program she had discovered, which Diane was going to try to get OMB to get Chase to reinstate—that kind of coordination of all the federal departments and agencies into overarching project architectures was a development with huge potential. But there had to be other things she could do too. She talked to Alyssa and the others in her office about it, she talked to Diane and Edgardo, she talked to Drepung, and then to Sucandra.

Sucandra she found particularly interesting. He was the one who had been her Cognizant Program Manager, so to speak, at the Khembalung Institute for Higher Studies, and he had been the single most disconcerting person she had ever talked to about the underlying purposes of science, being a doctor himself (but of Tibetan medicine) as well as a kind of Buddhist teacher, or even mentor to her, if there could be such a thing—as well as her Tibetan tutor, which she liked the best as being the most straightforward of their interactions. But in that context she mentioned to him once her attempt to balance her scientific work with something larger, amorphous though it might be.

He said to her: "Look to China."

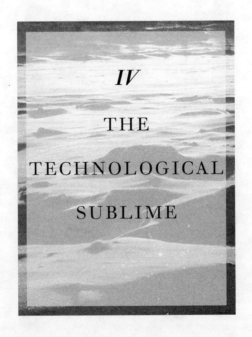

IV

THE

TECHNOLOGICAL

SUBLIME

The formalized "shortage economics" Anna had found had been pioneered by one Janos Kornai, a Hungarian economist who had lived through the socialist era in Soviet-controlled Eastern Europe. His work focused on the period 1945 to 1989, when most of his data had been generated. Anna found certain parallels to their current situation interesting, particularly those having to do with the hoarding response.

One day when she was visiting with Frank and Edgardo after a task force meeting in the Old Executive Offices, she showed some of what she had found to them. Edgardo happily pored over the relevant pages of the book she had brought along, chuckling at the graphs and charts. "Wait, I want to Xerox this page." He was the happiest broadcaster of bad news imaginable, and indeed had recently confessed that he was the one who had started the tradition of taping especially bad news to the walls of the copy room called the Department of Unfortunate Statistics over at NSF—a revelation that was no surprise to his two friends.

"See?" Anna said, pointing to the top of the diagram he was looking at now. "It's a decision tree, designed to map what a consumer does when faced with shortages."

"A shopping algorithm," Frank said with a short laugh.

"And have we made these choices?" Edgardo asked.

"You tell me. Shortages start because of excess demand—a disequilibrium which leads to a seller's market, which creates what Kornai calls suction."

"As in, this situation sucks," Edgardo said.

"Yes. So the shelves empty, because people buy when they can. Then the queuing starts. It can be either a physical line in a store, or a waiting list. So for any given item for sale, there are three possibilities. It's either available immediately, or available after a queue, or not available.

That's the first split in the tree. If it isn't available at all, then the next choice comes. The shopper either makes a forced substitution, like apples for artichokes, or else searches harder for the original item, or else postpones the purchase until the item is available, which Kornai also calls 'forced saving'—or else abandons the purchasing intent entirely."

"I like this term 'investment tension,' " Edgardo said, reading ahead on the page. "When there aren't enough machines to make what people want. But that's surely not what we have now."

"Are you sure?" Frank said, paging through the paper. "What if there's a shortage of energy?"

"It should work the same," Anna said. "So see, in a 'shortage economy' you get shortages that are general, frequent, intensive, or chronic. The classical socialist systems had all these. Although Kornai points out that in capitalism you have chronic shortages in health care and urban housing. And now we have intensive shortages too, during the blackouts. No matter what the product or service is, you get consumers who have a 'notional demand,' which is what they would buy if they could, and then 'completely adjusted demand,' which is what they really intend to buy knowing all the constraints, using what he calls 'expectation theory.' Between those you have 'partially adjusted demand,' where the consumer is in ignorance of what's possible, or in denial about the situation, and still not completely adjusted. So the move from notional demand to completely adjusted demand is marked by failure, frustration, dire rumors, forced choices, and so on down his list. Finally the adjustment is complete, and the buyer has abandoned certain intentions, and might even forget them if asked. Kornai compares that moment to workers in capitalism who stop looking for work, and so aren't counted as unemployed."

"I know some of those," Frank said. He read aloud, " 'A curious state of equilibrium can arise,' " and laughed. "So you just give up on your desires! It's almost Buddhist."

"I don't know." Anna frowned. " 'Forced adjustment equilibrium'? That doesn't sound to me like what the Khembalis are talking about."

"No. Although they are making a forced adjustment," Frank mused.

"And they would probably agree we are forced to adjust to reality, if we want equilibrium."

"Listen to this," Edgardo said, and read: " 'The less certain the prospect of obtaining goods, the more intensively buyers have to hoard.' Oh dear, oh my; here we are in a partially adjusted demand, not in equilibrium at all, and we don't have what he calls monetary overhang, or even a gray or black market, to take care of some of our excess demand."

"So, not much adjustment at all," Frank noted.

"I've seen examples of all these behaviors already at the grocery store," Anna said. "The frustrating thing is that we have adequate production but excessive demand, which is the hoarding instinct. People don't trust that there will be enough."

"Maybe thinking globally, they are right," Edgardo pointed out.

"But see here," Anna went on, "how he says that socialism is a seller's market, while capitalism is a buyer's market? What I've been wondering is, why shouldn't capitalism want to be a seller's market too? I mean, it seems like sellers would want it, and since sellers control most of the capital, wouldn't capital want a seller's market if it could get it? So that, if there were some real shortages, real at first, or just temporarily real, wouldn't capitalists maybe seize on those, and try to keep the sense that shortages are out there waiting, maybe even create a few more, so that the whole system tips from a buyer's market to a seller's market, even when production was actually adequate if only people trusted it? Wouldn't profits go up?"

"Prices would go up," Edgardo said. "That's inflation. Then again, inflation always hurts the big guys less than the little guys, because they have enough to do better at differential accumulation. And it's differential accumulation that counts. As long as you're doing better than the system at large, you're fine."

"Still," Frank said. "The occasional false shortage, Anna is saying. Or just stimulating a fear. Creating bogeymen, pretending we're at war, all that. To keep us anxious."

"To keep us hoarding!" Anna insisted.

Edgardo laughed. "Sure! Like health care and housing!"

Frank said, "So we've got all the toys and none of the necessities."

"That's backwards, isn't it," Anna said.

"It's insane," Frank said.

Edgardo was grinning. "I told you, we're stupid! We're going to have a tough time getting out of this mess, we are so stupid!"

A GAIN FRANK FLEW OUT TO SAN DIEGO. Descending
the escalator from the airport's glassed-in pedestrian walkway, he marveled that everything was the same as always; the only sign of winter was a
certain brazen quality to the light, so that the sea was a slate color, and the
cliffs of Point Loma a glowing apricot. Gorgeous Mediterranean coast of the
Pacific. His heart's home.

He had not bothered to make hotel reservations. Rent a van and that was
that—no way was Mr. Optimodal, Son of Alpine Man, going to pay hundreds
of dollars a night for the dubious pleasure of being trapped indoors at sunset!
The light at dusk over the Pacific was too precious and superb to miss in such
a thoughtless way. And the Mediterranean climate meant every night was
good for sleeping out, or at the very least, for leaving the windows of the van
open to the sea breezes. The salt-and-eucalyptus air, the cool warmth, it was
all otherworldly in its sensuous caress. His home planet.

During the day he dropped by his storage locker in Encinitas and got some
stuff, and that night he parked the van on La Jolla Farms Road and walked out
onto the bluff between Scripps and Black's Canyons. This squarish plateau,
owned by UCSD, was a complete coastal mesa left entirely empty—a very rare
thing at this point. In fact it might have been the only undeveloped coastal
mesa left between Mexico and Camp Pendleton. And its sea cliff was the tallest
coastal cliff in all of southern California, some 350 feet high, towering directly
over the water so that it seemed taller. A freak of both nature and history, in
short, and one of Frank's favorite places. He wasn't the first to have felt that
way; there were graves on it that had given carbon-14 dates around seven
thousand years before present, the oldest archeological site in mainland southern California.

It occurred to him as he walked out to the edge of the cliff that on the night he had lost his apartment and first gone out into Rock Creek Park, he had been expecting something like this: instant urban wilderness, entirely empty, overlooking the world. To bang into the bros in the claustrophobic forest had come as quite a shock.

At the cliff's edge itself there were small scallops in the sandstone that were like little hidden rooms. He had slept in them when a student, camping out for the fun of it. He recognized the scallop farthest south as his regular spot. It had been twenty-five years since the last time he had slept there. He wondered what that kid would think to see him here now.

He slept there again, fitfully, and in the gray wet dawn hiked up to the rented van and dropped off his sleeping bag and ground pad, then continued up to campus and the huge new gym called RIMAC. His faculty card got him entry into the spotless men's rooms, where he showered and shaved, then walked down to Revelle College for a catch-up session at the department office. A good effort now would save him all kinds of punitive work when he finally made it back.

After that he bought an outdoor breakfast at the espresso stand overlooking the women's softball diamond, and watched the team warm up as he ate. Oh my. How he loved American jock women. These classics of the type threw the ball around the horn like people who fully understood the simple joys of throwing something at something. The softballs were like intrusions from some more Euclidean universe, a little example of the technological sublime in which rocks like his hand axe had become Ideas of Order. When the gals whipped them around the pure white spheres did not illustrate gravity or the wind, as frisbees did, but rather a point drawing a line. Whack! Whack! God that shortstop had an arm. Frank supposed it was perverted to be sitting there regarding women's softball practice as some kind of erotic dance, but oh well, he couldn't help it; it was a very sexy thing.

After that he walked down La Jolla Shores Road to the Visualization Center at Scripps. This was a room located at the top of a wooden tower six stories tall, one room to each floor. Two or three of the bottom floors were occupied by a single computer, a superpowerful behemoth like something out of a 1950s movie; it was rather mind-boggling to consider the capacities of that much hardware now. They must have entered the kingdom of petaflops.

The top room was the visualizing center per se, consisting of a 3-D wrap-around movie theater that literally covered three walls. Two young women in shorts, graduate students of the professor who had invited Frank to drop by, greeted him and tapped up their show, placing Frank in the central viewing spot and giving him 3-D glasses. When the room went dark, the screen disappeared and Frank found himself standing on the rumpled black floor of the Atlantic, just south of the sill that ran like a range of hills between Iceland and Scotland, and looking north, into the flow at the two-thousand-meter level. Small temperature differences were portrayed in false color that extended across the entire spectrum, all the colors transparent, so that the air appeared to have become flowing banners of red, orange, yellow, green, blue, and indigo. The main flow was about chest high on Frank. Like standing in a lava lamp, one of the techs suggested, although Frank had been thinking he was flying in a rainbow that had gone through a shredder. The pace of the flow was speeded up, the techs told him, but it was still a stately waving of flat bands of red and their penumbral oranges, ribboning south through the blues and blue-greens, undulating like a snake, and then rolling smoothly over a blue and purple layer and down, as if passing over a weir.

"That was five years ago," one of the grad students said. "Watch now, this is last year this time—"

The flow got thinner, slower, thinner. A yellow sheet, roiling under a green blanket in a midnight-blue room. Then the yellow thinned to nothing. Green and blue pulsed gently back and forth, like kelp swinging in a moon swell, in a sea of deep purple.

"Wow," Frank said. "The stall."

"That's right," the woman at the computer said. "But now:"

The image lightened; tendrils of yellow appeared, then orange; then ribbons of red appeared, coalesced in a broad band. "It's about ninety percent what they first measured at the sill."

"Wow," Frank said. "Everyone should see this. For one thing, it's so spacy."

"Well, we can make DVDs, but it's never the same as, you know, what you have here. Standing right in the middle of it."

"No. Definitely not." For a time he stood and luxuriated in the wash of colors running past and through him. It looked kind of like a super-slo-mo screening of the hyperspace travel at the end of *2001: A Space Odyssey*. The underside of the Gulf Stream, flowing through his head. "Very pretty," he finally said, rousing himself. "Say thanks to Mark for getting me down to see this."

Then it was less than a mile's walk back up the road (though he was the only person walking it), and he was north of the university, at the old Torrey Pines Generique facility, now the National Science Foundation's Regional Research Center in Climate and Earth Sciences, RRCCES, which of course they were pronouncing "recess," with appropriate comparisons to Google's giant employee utopia in Mountain View—"They've got the playground, but we've got recess."

Inside, the reception room was much the same. The labs themselves were still under construction. His first meeting was in one of these, with Yann Pierzinski.

Frank had always liked Yann, and that was easier than ever now that he knew Yann and Marta were just friends and not a couple. His earlier notion that they were a couple had not really made sense to him, not that any couple made sense, but his new understanding of Yann, as Marta's housemate and some kind of gay genius, like Da Vinci or Wittgenstein, did make sense, maybe only because Yann was odd. Creative people *were* different—unless of course they weren't. Yann was, and in a strangely attractive way; it was as if Frank, or anybody, could see the appeal Yann would have to his partner.

So, now they discussed the latest concerning the new institute, comparing it to the Max Planck Institutes that had been its model. It was an intriguing array of sciences and technologies being asked to collaborate here; the scientists ranged from the most theoretical of theorists to the most lab-bound of experimentalists. In this gathering, as one of the only first-rank mathematicians working on the algorithms of gene expression, and one with actual field experience in designing and releasing an engineered organism into the wild, Yann was going to be a central figure. The full application of modern biotechnology to climate mitigation; it got interesting to think about.

Yann's specialty was Frank's too, and to the extent Frank had been on Yann's doctoral committee, and had employed him for a while, he knew what Yann was up to. But during the two years Frank had been away Yann had been hard at work, and he was now far off into new developments, to the point where he was certainly one of the field's current leaders, and as such, getting pretty hard to understand. It took some explaining from him to bring Frank up to speed, and speed was the operative word here: Yann had a tendency to revert to a childhood speech defect called speed-talking, which emerged whenever he got excited or lost his sense of himself. So it was a very rapid and tumbling tutorial that Yann now gave him, and Frank struggled just to follow him, leaping out there on the horizon of his mind's eye.

Great fun, in fact: a huge pleasure to be able to follow him at all, to immerse himself in this mode of thinking which used to be his normal medium. And extremely interesting too, in what it seemed might follow from it, in real-world applications. For there was a point at which the proteins Yann had been studying had their own kind of decision tree; in Yann's algorithm it looked like a choice, like a protein's free will, unless it was random. Frank pointed this out to Yann, wondering what Yann had been thinking when he wrote that part of the equation. "If you could force or influence the protein to always make the same choice," he suggested, "or even simply predict it..." They might get the specific protein they ultimately wanted. They would have called for a particular protein to come out from the vasty deep of a particular gene, and it would have come when they called for it.

"Yes," Yann agreed, "I guess maybe. I hadn't thought about it that way." This kind of obliviousness had always been characteristic of Yann. "But maybe so. You'd have to try some trials. Take the palindrome codons and repeat them maybe, see if they make the same choice in the operation if that's the only codon you have there?"

Frank made a note of it. It sounded like some pretty good lab work would be needed. "You've got Leo Mulhouse back here, right?"

Yann brightened. "Yeah, we do."

"Why don't we go ask him what he thinks?"

So they went to see Leo, which was also a kind of flashback for Frank, in that it was so like the last time he had seen him. Same people, same building—had all that out in D.C. really happened? Were they only dreaming of a different world here, in which promising human health projects were properly funded?

But after a while he saw it wasn't the same Leo. As with the lab, Leo looked outwardly the same, but had changed inside. He was less optimistic, more guarded. Less naive, Frank thought. Almost certainly he had gone through a very stressed job hunt, in a tight job market. That could change you all right. Mark you for life sometimes.

Now Leo looked at Yann's protein diagrams, which illustrated his model for how the palindromic codons at the start of the KLD gene expressed, and nodded uncertainly. "So, basically you're saying repeat the codons and see if that forces the expression?"

Frank intervened. "Also, maybe focus on this group here, because if it works like Yann thinks, then you should get palindromes of that too..."

"Yeah, that would be a nice result." The prospect of such a clearly delineated experiment brought back an echo of Leo's old enthusiasm. "That would be very clean," he said. "If that would work—man. I mean, there would still be the insertion problem, but, you know, NIH is really interested in solving that one..."

Getting any of their engineered genes into living human bodies, where they could supersede damaged or defective DNA, had proven to be one of the serious stoppers to a really powerful gene therapy. Attaching the altered genes to viruses that infected the subject was still the best method they had, but it had so many downsides that in many cases it couldn't be used. So literally scores or even hundreds of potential therapies, or call them outright cures, remained ideas only, because of this particular stumbling block. It vexed the entire field; it was, ultimately, the reason that venture capital had mostly gone away, in search of quicker and more certain returns. And if it wasn't solved, it could mean that gene therapy would never be achieved at all.

To Frank's surprise, it was Yann who now said, "There's some cool new stuff about insertion at Johns Hopkins. They've been working on metallic nanorods. The rods are a couple hundred nanometers long, half nickel and half gold. You attach your altered DNA to the nickel side, and some transferrin protein to the gold, and when they touch cell walls they bind to receptors in pits, and get gooed into vesicles, and those migrate inside the cell. Then the DNA detaches and goes into the nucleus, and there it is. Your altered gene is delivered and expressing in there. Doing its function."

"Really?" Leo said. He and his Torrey Pines Generique lab had been forced to look at a lot of options on this front, and none had worked. "What about the metals?"

"They just stay in the cell. They're too small to matter. They're trying out platinum and silver and other metals too, and they can do a three-metal nanorod that includes a molecule that helps get the thing out of the vesicles faster. They want a fourth one to attach a molecule that wants into the nucleus. And the nickel ones are magnetic, so they've tried using magnetic fields to direct the nanorods to particular areas of the body."

"Wow. Now that would be cool."

And on it went. Leo was clearly very interested. He seemed to be suggesting in his manner that insertion was the last remaining problem. If this were true, Frank thought . . . for a while he was lost in a consideration of the possibilities.

Leo followed Yann better than Frank had. Frank was used to thinking of Leo as a lab man, but then again, lab work was applying theory to experiments, so Leo was in his element. He wasn't just a tech. Although he was obviously confident of his ability to work the lab as such, to design experiments expressly for his machinery and schedule. Sometimes he stopped and looked around at all the new machinery as if he were in the dream of a boy on Christmas— everything he ever wanted, enough to make him suspicious, afraid he might wake up any second. Cautious enthusiasm, if there could be such a thing. Frank felt a pang of envy: the tangible work that a scientist could do in a lab was a very different thing from the amorphous, not to say entirely illusory, work that was consuming him in D.C. Was he even doing science at all, compared to these guys? Had he not somehow fallen off the wagon? And once you fell off, the wagon rolled on; again and again as the minutes passed he could barely follow what they were saying!

Then Marta walked in the room and he couldn't have followed them even if they had been reciting the periodic table or their ABCs. That was the effect she had on him.

And she knew it; and did all she could to press home the effect. "Oh hi, Frank," she said with a microsecond pause discernible only to him, after which she merrily joined the other two, pushing the outside of the discussion envelope, where Frank was certain to be most uncomprehending.

Irritating, yes. But then again this was stuff he wanted to know. So he worked on focusing on what Yann was saying. It was Yann who would be leading the way, and emphasizing this truth with his attentiveness was the best way Frank had of sticking it back to Marta, anyway.

So they jostled each other like kids sticking elbows into ribs, as Yann invented the proteomic calculus right before their eyes, and Leo went deep into some of the possible experiments they might run to refine their manipulation of the biochemistry of cell wall permeability.

A very complicated and heady hour. RRCCES was off to a good start, Frank concluded at the end of this session, despite his sore ribs. Combine the efforts of this place with UCSD and the rest of the San Diego biotech complex, not to mention the rest of the world, and the syncretic result could be something quite extraordinary. Some newly powerful biotech, which they would then have to define and aim somehow.

Which was where the work at the White House would come in. There had to be some place where people actually discussed what to do with the advances science continually made. Somewhere there had to be a way to prioritize, a way that didn't have to do with immediate profit possibilities for outside investors. If it took ten more years of unprofitable research to lift them into a realm of really robust health care, leading to long, healthy lives, shouldn't there be some place in their huge economy to fund that?

Yes.

Which was why he did not have to feel superfluous, or on the wrong track, or that he was wasting his time, or fooling around. As Marta was implying with all her little digs.

But then she said, offhandedly, and almost as if trying to be rude, "We're going to go out to dinner to celebrate the lab getting back together. Do you want to join us?"

Surprised, Frank said, "Yeah, sure."

Ah God—those two words committed him to an awkward evening, nowhere near as serene as eating tacos on the edge of Black's Cliffs would have been. Decisions—why be so fast with them? Why be so wrong? Now he would be pricked and elbowed by Marta's every glance and word, all night long.

And yet nevertheless he was glad to be with them, slave as he was to *Homo sapiens'* universal sociability. And also, to tell the truth, he was feeling under some kind of new dispensation with Marta: not that she had forgiven him, because she never would, but that she had at least become less angry.

As him with her.

Mixed feelings, mixed drinks; mixed signals. They ate in Del Mar, in one of the restaurants near the train station, on the beach. The restaurant's patio and its main room were both flooded with sunset, the light both direct and reflective, bouncing off the ocean and the ceilings and the walls and the mirrors until the room was as hyperilluminated as a stage set, and everyone in it as vivid and distinct as a movie star. Air filled with the clangor of voices and cutlery, punctuating the low roar of the incoming surf—air thick with salt mist, the glorious tang of Frank's home ground. Perhaps only Frank came from a place that allowed him to see just how gorgeous all this was.

Then again, now that he thought of it, Marta and Yann were just returning from a year in Atlanta, a year that could have been permanent. And they too looked a little heady with the scene.

And there was an extra charge in this restaurant, perhaps—some kind of poignant undercurrent to the celebrating, as if they were drinking champagne on a sinking liner. Because for this row of restaurants it was certainly the end time. This beach was going to go under, along with every other beach in the world. And what would happen to the beach cultures of the world when the beaches were gone? They too would go. A way of life, vanished.

Places like this first. Someone mentioned that high tides had waves running into the patio wall, a waist-high thing with a stairway cut through it to get to the beach. Frank nursed his margarita and listened to the others talk, and felt Marta's elbow both metaphorically and sometimes literally in his ribs. He could feel her heat, and was aware of her kinetically, just as he had been years before when they had first started going out, meeting in situations just like this, drinks after work, and she the wild woman of the lab, expert at the bench or out in the waves. Passionate.

After dinner they went out for a walk on the beach. Del Mar's was almost the only beach in North County left with enough sand for a walk; development meant all the southern California beaches had lost their sources of sand, but enough was left here to provide a fine white promenade for the sunset crowd. Surfers, shrieking kids in bathing suits, sandcastle engineers, runners, couples, and groups on parade. Frank had played all these parts in his time. All there together in the horizontal light.

They came to the mouth of the Del Mar River, and turned back. Marta walked beside Frank. Leo and Yann were chattering before them. They fell behind a little bit farther.

"Happy to be back?" Frank ventured.

"Oh God yes. You have *no idea,*" and all of a sudden she collared him and gave him a quick rough hug, intended to hurt. He knew her so well that he could interpret this gratitude precisely. He knew also that she had had a couple of margaritas and was feeling the effects. Although just to be back in San Diego was doubtless the biggest part of her mood, the boisterous high spirits he remembered so well. She had been a very physical person.

"I can guess," Frank said.

"Of course," she said, gesturing at the sea grumbling on and on to their right. "So—how are you doing out there, Frank? Why are you still there and not back here too?"

"Well..." How much to tell? His decision gears crunched to a halt with a palpable shudder. "I'm interested in the work. I moved over to the Presidential Science Advisor's office."

"I heard about that. What will you do there?"

"Oh, you know. Be an advisor to the advisor."

"Diane Chang?"

"That's right."

"She seems to be doing some good stuff."

"Yes, I think so."

"Well, that's good...." But still: "I bet you wish you could do that from here." Gesturing again at the sea. "Won't you have to come back to UCSD pretty soon?"

"Eventually, sure. But the department and the administration are happy to have someone out there, I think."

"Sure, I can see that."

She considered it as they walked along behind the other two. "But—but what about the rest of it? What about *girls*, Frank, have you got a *girl*friend?"

Oh God. Stumped. No idea what to reveal or how. And he had only a second before she would know something was up—

"Ah ha!" she cried, and crashed her shoulder into him, like she used to—just like Francesca Taolini had in Boston, so familiar and intimate, but in this case real, in that Marta really did know him. "You *do* have one! Come on, tell me, tell me!"

"Well yes, kind of."

"*Kind of.* Yes? And? Who is it?"

She had not the slightest idea that it might be Diane Chang, despite him having said he was following her from NSF to the White House. But of course—people didn't think that way. And it was not something Frank had told anyone about, except maybe Rudra. It was not even really true.

But what then could he say? I have two sort-of girlfriends? My boss, whom I work for and who is older than I am and whom I have never kissed or said anything even slightly romantic to, but love very much, then also a spook who has disappeared, gone undercover, a jock gal who likes the outdoors (like you) and with whom I have had some cosmic outdoor sex (like we used to have), but who is now off-radar and incommunicado, I have no idea where? Whom I'm scared for and am desperate to see?

Oh, and along with that I'm also still freaked out by my instant attraction to an MIT star who thinks I am a professional cheater, and yes I still find you all too attractive, and remember all too well the passionate sex we used to have when we were together, and wish you weren't so angry at me, and indeed can see and feel right now that you're maybe finally giving up on that, and aren't as angry as you were in Atlanta....

He too had had a couple of margaritas in the restaurant.

"Well? Come on, Frank! Tell me."

"Well, it isn't really anything quite like that."

"Like *what*! What do you *mean*?"

"I've been busy."

She laughed. "You mean you're too busy to call them back afterward? That's what *too busy* means to me."

"Hey."

She crowed her laugh and Yann and Leo looked over their shoulders to see what was going on. "It's all right," Marta called, "Frank is just telling me how he neglects his girlfriend!"

"Am not," Frank explained to them. Yann and Leo saw this was not their conversation and turned back to their own.

"I bet you do though," she went on, chortling. "You did me."

"I did not."

"You did too."

"Did not."

"Did too."

Frank shrugged. Here they were again.

"You wouldn't even go dancing with me."

"But I don't know how to dance," he said. "And we still went anyway, all the time." Except when you wanted to go by yourself to meet new guys and maybe disappear with them for the night.

"Yeah right. So come on, who is it? And why are you so busy anyway? What do you do besides work?"

"I run, I climb, I play frisbee golf, I go for walks—"

"Go for *walks*?"

"—snowshoeing, tracking animals—"

"Tracking *animals*?" Now she had gotten to the snorting phase of her laughter.

"Yes. We follow the animals that escaped from the National Zoo, and do feral rescue and the like. It's interesting."

She snorted again. She was thinking like the Californian she was: there were no such things as *animals*.

"I go ice-skating, I'm going to start kayaking again when the river thaws. I stay busy, believe me."

"When the river *thaws*. But big deal, so what! You're never too busy for *company*."

"I guess."

"So. Okay."

She saw that he wasn't going to say anything to her about it. She elbowed him again, and let it pass. She caught them up to the others.

The sun was almost down now, and the ocean had taken on the rich glassy sheen that it often did at that hour, the waves greenly translucent.

"Have you been out surfing yet?" he asked.

"Yeah, sure. What about you?"

"Not on this trip."

They came back to their restaurant, went through to the parking lot, stood in a knot to say good-byes.

"Yann and I are going to go dancing," Marta said to Frank. "Do you want to come along?"

"Too busy," Frank said promptly, and grinned as she cried out and punched him on the arm.

"Oh come on, you're out here visiting! You don't have any work at all."

"Okay," he said. Dancing, after all, was on his paleolithic list of Things To

Do. "What is it, some kind of rave again? Do I have to blast my mind with ecstasy to get with the beat?"

"*Rave.* That isn't even a word anymore. It's just a band at the Belly-Up."

"A rave band," Yann confirmed.

Frank nodded. "Of course." That was Marta's thing.

"Come on," Marta said. "It only means you'll know how to do it. No swing or tango. Just bop up and down and groove. You could use it, if you're so busy out there."

"Okay," he said.

Leo had already driven off. He was outside Marta's sphere of influence.

So he followed Yann and Marta up the Coast Highway to Solana Beach, and turned inland to the Belly-Up, a big old Quonset hut by the train tracks that had hosted concerts and dances and raves for many years now.

This night's bill appeared to Frank to be catering to the gay and lesbian crowd, or maybe that was just what the Belly-Up audience always looked like these days. Although the band was a mostly butch all-girl acid reggae kind of thing, with perhaps a score of people on the little stage, and a few hundred bopping on the dance floor. So he could join Yann and Marta both on the dance floor, and start dancing (that curious moment when the rules of movement changed, when one *began* to dance) and then it was *bop rave bop rave bop,* in the heavy beat and the flashing lights, easy to lose one's mind in, which was always good, dionysiac release into shamanic transcendence, except when it involved losing his sense of all that had gone on between him and Marta (Yann was somewhere nearby) and also his sense of just how dangerous it would be to regard her only as a sexy woman dancing with him, seemingly oblivious to him but always right there and deep in the rhythm, and occasionally giving him a light bang with hip or shoulder. (In the old days these bumps would have come from pubic bone as well.) He had always loved the way she moved. But they had a history together, he struggled to remember. A really bad history. And he was already overcommitted and overentangled in this realm, it would be crazy and worse to have anything more to do with Marta in that way. He had gotten her back to San Diego as a way to make up for taking their money out of their house without telling her, and that was that—they were even! No more entanglements needed or wanted!

Although he did want her. Damn those softball players anyway.

"Here eat this," she shouted in his ear, and showed him a pill between her forefinger and thumb. Ecstasy, no doubt, as in the old days.

"No!"

"Yes!"

The paleolithics had gotten stupendously stoned, he recalled, in the midst of their dionysiac raves. Some of their petroglyphs made this perfectly clear, .depicting people flying out of their own heads as birds and rockets. He remembered the feeling of peace and well-being this particular drug used to give him when he danced on it; and let her shove the pill in between his teeth. Nipped her fingers as she did. Leap before you look.

He danced with his back to her, and felt her butt bumping his as he looked at the other dancers. Quite a radical scene for good old San Diego, which Frank still thought of as a sun-and-sports monoculture, a vanilla Beach Boys throwback of a place, hopelessly out of it in cultural terms. Maybe one had to stay out in the water all the time for that to be true anymore. Although in fact the surf culture was also crazed. Certainly it was true that in the Belly-Up of the beast, in the cacophonous sweaty strobed space of the rave, there were plenty of alternative lifestyles being enacted right before his very eyes. Most provocatively in fact. Some very serious kissing and other acts, dance as simulated standing sex, heck actual standing sex if you were at all loose with the definition. A very bad context in which to keep only pure thoughts about his bouncing surfer-scientist ex, who always had been a party gal, and who was now looking like someone who did not remember very well the bad parts of their past together. That was not what dancing was about.

Maybe there was such a thing as being too forgiven.

Random thoughts began to bounce to their own rave in his head. Oh dear he was feeling the buzz. Could one get away with *just one night of sex* without consequences? Go out to Black's Cliffs, for instance, and then later pretend it was just an aberration or had not happened at all? Marta had certainly done that before. It was pretty much a *modus vivendi* for her. But practical problems—she had rented a house with Yann again, Yann would know: bad. He didn't have a hotel room to go to, and didn't want Marta to know that—bad. So—no place to go, even though the cliffs would have been *so* nice, a trysting place of spectacular memory, in fact he had gone out there with two or three different women through those undergraduate years, among them some of the nicest of all the women he had ever met. It had been so nice, it would be so nice, it was all jostling in his head, Caroline, Diane, the dance, two young beauties nearby, groping each other in the crush of bouncing bodies, oh my, it was having an effect on him—an unusually vivid effect. Not since a well-remembered dance in a bar on the Colorado River during spring break of 1973 had he gotten an erection while on a dance floor dancing. It was not the effect ecstasy usually had on him. He really must be feeling it, Marta and her vibe, and her butt. And yes, that was her pubic bone too.

Maybe that was the cause of the erection. He turned to her again, and naturally now when she bumped against him she hit something else, and felt it, and grinned.

They had to shout in each other's ears to be able to hear each other within the surround sound of the crunchingly loud bass line.

"I guess you liked the tab!"

"I don't remember ecstasy doing this!"

She laughed. "They mix in Viagra now!" she shouted in his ear.

"Oh shit!"

"Yann's friends make them, they're great!"

"What the fuck, Marta!"

"Yeah well?"

"No way! You're kidding me!"

Angry, even fearful, he stopped dancing and stared at her bopping in front of him. "I don't like it! It's making me feel sick!"

"You'll get used to it!"

"No! No! I'm gonna go, I'll see you later!"

"Okay go then!"

She looked surprised, but not horribly displeased. Amused at him. Maybe it really was just the new dance drug. Maybe it was revenge. Or an experiment. Or that for Marta there would still be a lot of potential partners there, for dancing or anything else, so it didn't matter what he did. Who knew San Diego could be so depraved? People were totally making out right in front of his eyes. There were so many doing it they had a kind of privacy in numbers.

"See you then!" Marta said in his ear, and gave him a swift sweaty hug and a kiss, already looking around for Yann or whomever. Happy, he thought— maybe even happy at becoming free from her anger at him—or happy at her last little tweak of revenge. Happy to see him go! Maybe all the prurient thoughts about the two of them together had been his only and not hers. And the pill just the new dance pill.

He pondered this as he walked through the dark gravel parking lot to his rented van, cooled swiftly by his sweat and the salty night air, his erection like a rock in his pants. She didn't care!

The erection was not a comfortable feeling, not a natural feeling, not a sexual feeling. Normally Frank was as happy as the next guy to have an erection, meaning very happy, but this was ridiculous. He was drugged by drugs, it had no connection to his feelings—he might as well be at the doctor's, undergoing some horrible diagnostic! People were so stupid. Talk about technology replacing the natural pleasures, this really took the cake!

He cursed Marta viciously as he drove. Marine layer gusting in, lit by the city from underneath, then out over the sea darker, lit only by moonlight from above. Marta, angry at him: would he miss that when it was gone? A feeling was a relationship. Then again, now he was angry at her. There was something pressing on his brain, even more than the usual; a headache was coming on, the likes of which he had never felt before. A migraine, perhaps, and at the same time as a drug-induced hard-on that hurt. It was like priapism—maybe it was priapism! The side-effects warnings on the TV ads mentioned this ever so quickly, but it was a serious danger. Terrible permanent damage could result. Shit—he was going to have to go find an ER somewhere and confess all. Tell the truth that he hadn't known he was taking it, and get laughed at as a liar.

He cursed again, drove up the long hill of Torrey Pines, past their new facility and UCSD. Park on La Jolla Farms Road and walk out onto the bluff in the dark, his stuff in a daypack.

He had spent some sexy nights out here, he thought as he throbbed. Oh well. Now he just wanted to be free of it. Just embrace the cliff and make love to Mother Earth. But it hurt and his head pounded and he was afraid. It felt as if an orgasm would blow out every little sac, or shoot his spine right out of him while his head exploded. Horror movie images—damn Marta anyway. What a horrible drug thus to ruin one of the best feelings of all. Some guys must be so desperate. But of course. Everyone desperate for love, so now you could buy it, of course, but it hurt. Would he have to give up and go to the ER and explain—have to feel the needles stuck in there to drain him?

Abruptly he got up and downclimbed over the lip of his little scallop, out onto the cliff. Now he was hanging there in space, and could slip and die at any moment. Not a good move really. Fear, real fear, stuck him like a stab in the ribs, and his blood rushed everywhere in him, hot and fast. Suddenly the sandstone was as if lit from within. His left foot was on a gritty hold, and slipping slightly. He grasped a shrub that had sent a branch over the lip, wondered if it would hold his weight. It was terrible climbing rock, gritty and weak, and suddenly he was angry as well as afraid. Sound of the surf cracking below— 350 feet below. Hanging by a shrub on Black's Cliffs. He set his feet and pulled smoothly back up onto the scallop, a desperately graceful little move.

And the blood had indeed evacuated his poor penis. Detumescence, a new pleasure, never before experienced as such. Blessed relief. Even his head felt a little better. And he had worked his will over a powerful drug, and over Marta too. Hopefully he had survived undamaged. Little sacs, all overfull; he was going to be sore, he could tell. It felt like last winter's brush with penile frostbite.

Scared back to normality. Not a smart move. The margaritas might be implicated in that one. Leap before you look, sure—but not really.

He took a deep breath, feeling foolish in multiple ways. Well, no one knew the full extent of his folly. And he was back in his scallop. He could sit on his sleeping bag, breathe deeply, shake his head shuddering, like someone casting off a nightmare.

So much for Marta. She could not have cured him of his momentary lust for her any more effectively than if she had given him the exact antidote for it. Homeopathic poison; just her style. He recalled the last time he had taken mescaline, back in the days he had slept out here, throwing up and thinking it was stupid to poison oneself to get high. But that was what life with Marta had been. He liked her in some ways, he liked her energy and her wit, but there had always been so much he didn't like about her. And any excess of her good qualities quickly became so obnoxious.

He wanted his Caroline. Somewhere out east she also was alone, and thinking of him. He knew it was true at least some of the time. How he wanted to *talk* to her! Cell phone to cell phone—surely they could both get one, on some account unknown to her ex? He needed to talk to her!

Like he could always talk to Diane.

Slowly the susurrus of surf calmed him, and then, as his body finally relaxed, it helped to make him sleepy. For a long time he just sat there. In D.C. it was three a.m. Diane and Caroline. His own personal D. C. He was jetlagged. San Diego—or really this campus, these very cliffs—this beautiful place... this was his home. The ocean made him happy. The ground here was good. Just to be here, to feel the air, to feel the thump of the breaking waves, to hear their perpetual grumble and hiss, grumble and hiss, crack grumble and hiss... To breathe it. Salt air fuzzy in the moonlight. The brilliant galaxy of light that was La Jolla, outlining its point. Ah, if only he knew what to do.

A T FIRST PHIL CHASE wanted to call his blog "The Fireside Chat," but then someone pointed out to him that he was already doing those on talk radio, so he changed the name to "Cut to the Chase." He wrote his entries late at night in bed before falling asleep, and hit send without even a spell check, so that his staff got some horrible jolts with their morning coffee, even though Phil had clearly stated right at the top of the home page that these were his private personal musings only, blogged to put the electorate in touch with his thinking as a citizen, and no reflection of formal policies of his administration. No impact whatsoever on anything at all—just the president's blog.

CUT TO THE CHASE
Posted 11:53 PM:

We Americans don't want to be in a state of denial about our relationship to the world and its problems. If we're five percent of the world's population and we're burning one quarter of the carbon being burned every year, we need to know that, and we need to think about why it's happening and what it means. It's not a trivial thing and we can't just deny it. It's a kind of obesity.

There are different kinds of denial. One is sticking your head in the sand. You manage not to know anything. Like that public service ad where there's a bunch of ostriches down on a big beach, and all the big ones have their heads in the sand, and some of the little ones do too, but a lot of the little ones are running around, and they see a giant wave is coming in and they start yelling down the holes to the big ones, *There's a wave coming!* and one of the big ones pulls his head out and says *Don't worry, just stick your head in like this,* and the little ones look at each other and figure that if that's what their parents are doing it must be okay, so they stick their heads in the sand too—and in the last frame you see that all the holes in the sand are windows made of little TVs and computer screens. That kind of says it all. And there you are seeing it on TV.

But there are other kinds of denial that are worse yet. There's a response that says I'll never admit I'm wrong and if it comes to a choice between admitting I'm wrong or destroying the whole world, then bring it on. This is the Götterdämmerung, in which the doomed gods decide to tear down the world as they lose the big battle. The god-damning of the world. It's a term sometimes used to describe what Hitler did in the last months of World War Two, after it was clear Germany was going to lose the war.

Of course people are offended by any comparison to the actions of Adolf Hitler. But consider how many species have died already, and how many more might die if we keep doing what we're doing. It may not be genocide, but it is ugly. Species-cide. As if nothing else matters but us, and specifically the subset of us that agrees with everything we say. When you take a look at our own Rapture culture, these people pretending to expect the end of the world anytime now, you see that we have our own Götterdämmerung advocates, all very holy of course, as the world destroyers always are. And it's an ugly thing. Countries can go crazy, we've seen it happen more than once. And empires always go crazy.

But right now we need to stay sane. We don't want the United States of America to be hauled before the World Court on a charge of attempted Götterdämmerung. We can't let that happen, because THIS IS AMERICA, land of the free and home of the brave—the country made of people from all the other countries—the grand experiment that all world history has so far been conducting! So if we blow it, if America blows it, then all world history might be judged a failure so far. We don't want that. We don't want to go from being the hope of the world to convicted in the World Court of attempted Götterdämmerung.

5,392,691 responses

BACK IN D.C. IT WAS STILL SO COLD that the idea that he could have been surfing the day before struck Frank as ludicrous. Crossing the continent in March was like changing planets. It was a bigger world than they thought.

It was so many planets at once. The Hyperniño had left California, following the Pacific's oceanic heat shift to the west, which signaled the onset of a La Niña, predicted to be devastating to Southeast Asia. Now all of California was fully in the drought that had begun in the northern half of the state several years before. The East Coast, meanwhile, was in a kind of cold drought, which included occasional dumps of snow that had the consistency of styrofoam. Like the snow in Antarctica, Charlie's colleague Wade said in a phone call. Frank called Wade fairly often now, finding him to be the best contact person on the Antarctic situation. Every once in a while, at the end of a call, they would talk for a minute or two about personal matters, which was interesting, as they had never met. But somehow something had come up, perhaps Wade describing his plans for a coming week, and after that they both seemed to like talking to someone they had never met about these kinds of things. Wade too had a girlfriend whom he saw all too infrequently. He described himself as a desert rat, who endured the polar cold for the chance to see this woman.

At the embassy, only the older Khembalis were used to cold. The younger ones were tropical creatures, and walked around blue-lipped; those of Rudra's generation never seemed to notice the cold at all. They left their arms bare in really frigid temperatures.

Rudra often was reading in bed when Frank came in, or looking at picture books. Then one day Qang brought him a laptop, and he chuckled as he tapped away at it, looking at photo collections of various sorts, including pornographic. Other times Frank found him humming to himself, or asleep with a book still swaying on his chest.

When he was up and about, he was slower than ever. When Frank and he went for walks, they always got the wheelchair out from under the stairs; it was as if this was the way they had always done it.

Frank said, "Listen to this: 'If he had the earth for his pasture and the sea for his pond, he would be a pauper still. He only is rich who owns the day. There is no king, rich man, fairy or demon who possesses such power as that.' "

Rudra said, "Emerson?"

"Right." They had begun a game in which Rudra tried to guess which of the two New Englanders Frank was reading from. He did pretty well at it.

"Good man. Means, go for a walk?"

It was too much like a dog begging to get out. "Sure."

And so out they would go, Rudra bundled in down jacket and blankets against the cold he claimed not to notice, Frank in a suitable selection from his cold-weather gear. They had a route now that took them north to the Potomac under a line of tall oaks flanking Irving and Fillmore Streets. This brought them to the river at the mouth of Windy Run, which was often free of ice, and thus a temporary water hole frequented by deer, foxes, beaver, and muskrats. They looked for these regulars, and any unusual visiting animals, and then the wind would force them to turn their backs and head downstream for a bit, on a rough old asphalt sidewalk, after which they could angle up 24th Street, and thus back to the house. The walk took about an hour, and sometimes they would stop by the river for another hour. Once as they turned to go Frank saw a flash of dark flank, and had the impression it might have been some kind of antelope. It would have been the first time in Virginia he had seen a feral exotic, and as such worthy of calling in to Nancy for entry into the GIS. But he wasn't sure, so he let it go.

The quiet neighborhood between Rock Creek Park and Connecticut Avenue was looking more withdrawn than ever. It had always been empty-seeming compared to most of D.C., but now three or four houses had burned and not been rebuilt, and others were still boarded up from the time of the great flood. At night these dark houses gave the whole place an eerie cast.

Some of the dark houses gleamed at the cracks or smoked from the chimneys, and if after a dusk hike in the ravine Frank was hungry, or wanted company, he would call up Spencer and see if he was in any of these places. Once when Spencer answered they established that he was inside the very house Frank was looking at.

In Frank went, uncertain at first. But he was a familiar face now, so without further ado he helped to hold a big pot over the fire, ate broiled steak, and ended up banging on the bottom of an empty trash can while Spencer percussed his chair and sang. Robert and Robin showed up, ate, sang duets to Robert on guitar, then pressed Spencer and Frank to go out and play a round of night golf.

It was full moon that night, and once they got going, Frank saw that they didn't need to see to play their course. They had played it so many times that they knew every possible shot, so that when they threw they could feel in their bodies where the frisbee was going to land, could run to that spot and nine times out of ten pick it up. Although on that night they did lose one of Robert's, and spent a few minutes looking for it before Spencer cried, as he always did in this situation, "LO AND BEHOLD," and they were off again.

Socks and shoes got wet with melted snow. No snowshoes tonight, and so he leaped through drifts and abandoned his feet to their soggy fate. On a climbing expedition it would have meant disaster. But in the city it was okay. There was even a certain pleasure in throwing caution to the wind and crashing through great piles of snow, snow which ranged from powder to concrete.

Then in one leap he hooked a foot and crashed down onto a deer's layby, panicking the creature, who scrambled under him. Frank tried to leap away too, slipped and fell back on the doe; for a second he felt under him the warm quivering flank of the animal, like a woman trying to shrug off a fur coat. His shout of surprise seemed to catapult them both out of the hole in different directions, and the guys laughed at him. But as he ran on he could still feel in his body that sudden intimacy, the kinetic jolt: a sudden collision with a woman of another species!

Power outages were particularly hard on the few feral exotics still out in this second winter. The heated shelters in Rock Creek Park were still operating, and they all had generators for long blackouts, but the generators made noise, and belched out their noxious exhaust, and none of the animals liked them, even the humans. On the other hand, the deep cold of these early spring nights could kill, so many animals hunkered down in the shelters when the worst cold hit, but they were not happy. It would have been better simply to be enclosed, Frank sometimes felt; or rather it was much the same thing, as they were chained to the shelters by the cold. So many different animals together in one space—it was so beautiful and unnatural, it never failed to strike Frank.

Such gatherings gave the zoo's zoologists a chance to do all kinds of things with the ferals, so the FOG volunteers who were cold-certified were welcomed to help. With Frank's help, Nick was now the youngest cold-certified member of FOG, which seemed to please him in his quiet way. Certainly Frank was pleased—though he also tried to be there whenever Nick was out on FOG business in extreme cold, to make sure nothing went wrong. Hard cold was dangerous, as everyone had learned by now. The tabloids were rife with stories of people freezing in their cars at traffic lights, or on their front doorsteps trying to find the right key, or even in their own beds at night when an electric blanket failed. There were also regular Darwin Award winners out there, feeding the tabloids' insatiable hunger for stupid disaster. Frank wondered if a time would come when people got enough disaster in their own lives that they would no longer feel a need to vampire onto others' disasters. But it did not seem to have happened yet.

Frank and Nick got back into a pattern in which Frank dropped by on Saturday mornings and off they would go, sipping from the steaming travel cups of coffee and hot chocolate Anna had provided. They started at the shelter at Fort de Russey, slipping in from the north. On this morning they spotted, among the usual crowd of deer and beaver, a tapir that was on the zoo's wanted list.

They called it in and waited uneasily for the zoo staff to arrive with the dart guns and nets and slings. They had a bad history together on this front, having lost a gibbon that fell to its death after Frank hit it with a trank dart. Neither mentioned this now, but they spoke little until the staffers arrived and one of them shot the tapir. At that the other animals bolted, and the humans approached. The big RFID chip was inserted under the tapir's thick skin. The animal's vital signs seemed good. Then they decided to take it in anyway. Too many tapirs had died. Nick and Frank helped hoist the animal onto a gurney big enough for all of them to get a hand on. They carried the unconscious beast through the snow like its pallbearers. From a distant ridge, the aurochs looked down on the procession.

After that, the two of them hiked down the streambed to the zoo itself. Rock Creek had frozen solid, and was slippery underfoot wherever it was flat. Often the ice was stacked in piles, or whipped into a frothy frozen meringue. The raw walls of the flood-ripped gorge were in a freeze-thaw cycle that left frozen spills of yellow mud splayed over the ribbon of creek ice.

Then it was up and into the zoo parking lot. The zoo itself was just waking up in the magnesium light of morning, steam frost rising from the nostrils of animals and the exhaust vents of heating systems; it looked like a hot springs in winter. There were more animals than people. Compared to Rock Creek it was crowded, however, and a good place to relax in the sun, and down another hot chocolate.

The tigers were just out, lying under one of their powerful space heaters. They wouldn't leave it until the sun struck them, so it was better now to visit the snow leopards, who loved this sort of weather, and indeed were creatures who could go feral in this biome and climate. There were people in FOG advocating this release, along with that of some of the other winterized predator species, as a way of getting a handle on the city's deer infestation. But others at the zoo objected on grounds of human (and pet) safety, and it didn't look like it would happen anytime soon. The zoo got enough grief already for its support of the feral idea; advocating predators would make things crazy.

After lunch they would hitch a ride from a staffer back up to Frank's van, or snowshoe back to it. If the day got over the freezing mark, the forest would become a dripping rainbow world, tiny spots of color prisming everywhere.

Then back to the Quiblers, where Nick would have homework, or tennis with Charlie. On some days Frank would stay for lunch. Then Charlie would see him off: "So—what are you going to do now?"

"Well, I don't know. I could..."

Long pause as he thought it over.

"Not good enough, Frank. Let's hear you choose."

"Okay then! I'm going to help the Khembalis move stuff out to their farm!" Right off the top of his head. "So there."

"That's more like it. When are you going to see the doctor again?"

Glumly: "Monday."

"That's good. You need to find out what you've got going on there."

"Yes." Unenthusiastically.

"Let us know what you find out, and if there's anything we can do to help out. If you have to like have your sinuses rotorootered, or your nose broken again to get it right or whatever."

"I will."

It still felt strange to Frank to have his health issues known to the Quiblers. But he had been trying to pursue a course of open exchange of (some) information with Anna, and apparently whatever she learned, Charlie would too, and even Nick to an extent. Frank hadn't known it would be like that, but did not want to complain, or even to change. He was getting used to it. And it was good Charlie had asked, because otherwise he might not have been able to figure out what to do. The pressure was becoming like a kind of wall.

So: off to Khembali House, to fill his van with a load of stuff for the farm. Out there in the snowy countryside the construction of the new compound was coming along. Enough Khembalis had gotten licensed in the various trades that they could do almost all the work legally on their own. The whole operation ran like some big family or baseball team, everyone pitching in and getting things done, the labor therefore outside the money economy. It was impressive what could be done that way.

Frank still had his eye on the big knot of trees that stood on the high point of the farm. These were mostly chestnut oaks. They were like his treehouse tree but much bigger, forming a canopy together that covered most of an acre. It seemed to him that the interlaced heavy inner branches formed a perfect foundation or framework for a full Swiss Family extravaganza, and Padma and Sucandra liked the idea. So there was that to be considered and planned for too. Spring was about to spring, and there were materials and helpers on hand. No time like the present! Leap before you look!—but maybe peek first.

All the various scans that Frank's doctors had ordered had been taken, at an increasing pace as they seemed to find things calling for some speed; and now it was time to meet with the brain guy.

This was an M.D. who did neurology, also brain and face surgery. So just in ordinary terms a very imposing figure, and in paleolithic terms, a shaman healer of the rarest kind, being one who actually accomplished cures. Awesome: scarier than any witch doctor. Whenever the technological sublime was obvious, the fear in it came to the fore.

The doctor's office was ordinary enough, and him too. He was about Frank's age, balding, scrubbed very clean, ultra-close-shaven, hands perfectly manicured. Used to the sight of the bros' hands, and Rudra's hands, Frank could scarcely believe how perfect this man's hands were. Very important tools. They gave him a faintly wax-figurish look.

"Have a seat," he said, gesturing at the chair across his desk from him.

When Frank was seated, he described what he had found in Frank's data. "We're seeing a chronic subdural hematoma," he said, pointing to a light spot in an array of spots that roughly made the shape of a brain section—Frank's brain. The CT scan and the MRI both showed evidence of this hematoma, the doctor went on, and pretty clearly it was a result of the trauma Frank had suffered. "Lots of blood vessels were broken. Most were outside the dura. That's the sack that holds your brain."

Frank nodded.

"But there are veins called bridging veins, between the dura and the surface of the brain. Some of them broke, and appear to be leaking blood."

"But when I taste it?"

"That must be from encapsulated blood in scar tissue on the outside of the dura, here." He pointed at the MRI. "Your immune system is trying to chip away at that over time, and sometimes when you swing your head hard, or raise your pulse, there might be leaking from that encapsulation into the sinus, and then down the back of your throat. That's what you're tasting. But the subdural hematoma is inside the dura, here. It may be putting a bit of pressure on your frontal cortex, on the right side. Have you been noticing any differences in what you think or feel?"

"Well, yes," Frank said, thankful and fearful all at once. "That's really what brought me in. I can't make decisions."

"Ah. That's interesting. How bad is it?"

"It varies. Sometimes any decision seems really hard, even trivial ones. Occasionally they seem impossible. Other times it's no big deal."

"Any depression about that? Are you depressed?"

"No. I mean, I have a lot going on right now. But I often feel pretty great. But—confused. And concerned. Worried about being indecisive. And—afraid I'll do something—I don't know. Stupid, or—dangerous. Wrong, or dangerous. I don't trust my judgment." And I have reasons not to.

"Uh huh," the doctor was writing all this down on Frank's chart. Oh great. Confessing to his health insurance company. Not a good idea. Perhaps a bad decision right here and now, in this room. A sample of what he was capable of.

"Any changes in your sense of taste?"

"No. I can't say I've noticed any."

"And when you taste that blood taste, does it correlate with periods of decisiveness or indecisiveness?"

"I don't know. That's an interesting thought, though."

"You should keep a symptom calendar. Dedicate a calendar to just that, put it by your bed and rate your day for decisiveness. From one to ten is the typical scale. Then also, mark any unusual tastes or other phenomena—dizziness, headaches, strange thoughts or moods, that kind of thing. Moods can be typified and scaled too."

Frank was beginning to like this guy. Now he would become his own experiment, an experiment in consciousness. He would observe his own thoughts, in a quantified meditation. Rudra would get a kick out of that; Frank could hear his deep laugh already. "Good idea," he said to the doctor, hearing the way Rudra would say it. "I'll try that. Oh, I've forgotten to mention this—I still can't feel anything right under my nose, and kind of behind it. It's numb. It feels like a nerve must have been, I don't know."

"Oh yeah? Well—" Looking at the scans. "Maybe something off the nine nerve. The glossopharyngeal nerve is back there where we're seeing the encapsulation."

"Will I get the feeling back?"

"You either will or you won't," the doctor said. All of them had said that; it must be the standard line on nerve damage, like the line about the president having so much on his plate. People liked to say the same things.

"And the hematoma?"

"Well, it's been a while since your injury, so it's probably pretty stable. It's hypodense. We could follow it with serial scans, and it's possible it could resolve itself."

"And if it doesn't?"

"We could drain it. It's not a big operation, because of the location. I can go in through the nose. It looks like it would be straightforward," checking out the images again. "Of course, there's always some risk with neurosurgery. We'd have to go into that in detail, if you wanted to move forward with it."

"Sure. But do you think I should?"

He shrugged. "It's up to you. The cognitive problems you're reporting are fairly common for pressure on that part of the brain. It seems that some components of decision making are located in those sulci. They have to do with the emotional components of risk assessment and the like."

"I've read some of the literature," Frank said.

"Oh yes? Well, then, you know what can happen. There are some pretty unusual cases. It can be debilitating, as you know. Some cases of very bad decision making, accompanied by little or no affect. But your hematoma is not so big. It would be pretty straightforward to drain it, and get rid of the encapsulated clot too."

"And would I then experience changes in my thinking?"

"Yes, it's possible. Usually that's the point, so patients like it, or are relieved. Some get agitated by the perception of difference."

"Does it go away, or do they get used to it?"

"Well, either, or both. Or neither. I don't really know about that part of it. We focus on draining the hematoma and removing that pressure."

It will or it won't. "So if I'm not in too much distress, maybe I ought not to mess with it?" Frank said. He did not want to be looking forward to brain surgery; even clearing out his sinuses sounded pretty dire to him.

The doctor smiled ever so slightly, understanding him perfectly. "You certainly don't want to take it lightly. However, there is a mass of blood in there, and often the first sign of it swelling more is a change in thinking or feeling, or a bad headache. Some people don't want to risk that. And problems in decision making can be pretty debilitating. So, some people preempt any problems and choose to have the surgery."

"Jeez," Frank said, "this is just the kind of decision I can't make anymore!"

The doctor laughed briefly, but his look was sympathetic. "It would be a hard call no matter what. Why don't you give it a set period of time and see how you feel about it? Make some lists of pros and cons, mark on your symptom calendar how you feel about it for ten days running, stuff like that. See if one course of action is consistently supported over time."

Frank sighed. Possibly he could construct an algorithm that would make this decision for him, by indicating the most robust course of action. Some kind of aid. Because it was a decision that he could not avoid; it was his call only. And doing nothing was a decision too. But possibly the wrong one. So he had to decide, he had to consciously decide. Possibly it was the most important decision he had before him right now.

"Okay," he said. "I'll try that."

BACK AT WORK, FRANK TRIED to concentrate. He simply couldn't do it. Or he concentrated, but it was on the word *hematoma*. *Chronic subdural hematoma*. There's pressure on my brain. He thought, I can concentrate just fine, I can do it for hours at a time. I just can't decide.

He closed his eyes, poked at his Things To Do list with a pen. That was what it had come to. Well, actually he had bundled three things to do in a military category, and now he realized he should have poked the GO TO THE PENTAGON item on the list, because Diane had told him to and he had made appointments, and today was the day. So there hadn't been any choice to be made. Check the calendar first to avoid such tortures.

1) *Navy,* 2) *Air Force,* 3) *Army Corps of Engineers,* the list said. Secretary of the Navy's office first: chief nuclear officer, happy to meet with the president's science advisor's advisor, Diane had said. Lunch at the Pentagon.

The Pentagon had its own Metro stop, just west of the Potomac. Frank came up out of the ground and walked the short distance to the steps leading up to the big doors of the place. These faced the river. From them it was impossible to see how big the Pentagon was; it looked like any plain concrete building, wide but not tall.

Inside there was a waiting room. He went through a metal detector, as at an airport, was nodded onward by a military policeman. At the desk beyond another MP took his driver's license and checked his name against a list on his computer, then used a little spherical camera on top of the computer to take a picture of him. The MP took the photo from a printer and affixed it to a new ID badge, under a bar code, Frank's name, and his host's name. Frank took the badge from the man and clipped it to his shirt, waited in the waiting room. There was a table with promotional brochures, touting each of the services and its missions, also the last two wars.

The Navy's chief nuclear officer was a Captain Ernest Gamble. He had been a physics professor at Annapolis. Cool and professional in style.

They walked down a very long hallway. Gamble took him up some stairs to an interior window, where the pentagonal inner park stood in the sunlight. Then it was onward, down another very long hallway. "They used to have little golf carts for the halls," Gamble explained, "but people kept running them into things. It takes a long time to get repairs done here. The joke is, it took eighteen months to build the Pentagon, and ten years to remodel it."

They passed a small shopping mall, which Frank was surprised to see there inside the Pentagon itself, and finally came to a restaurant, likewise deep inside the building. Sat down, ordered, went to a salad bar and loaded up. As they ate, they discussed the Navy's nuclear energy capabilities. Ever since Admiral Hyman Rickover had taken over the nuclear fleet in the 1950s, the Navy's nuclear program had been held to the highest possible safety standards, and had a spotless record, with not a single (unclassified) accident releasing more than fifty rads.

"What about classified accidents?"

"I wouldn't know about those," Gamble deadpanned.

In any case, the Navy had had no reactor accidents, and a half-century's experience with design and operation. They discussed whether the Navy could lead the way in designing, maybe even overseeing, a number of federally funded "National Security Nuclear Plants." That might avoid the cost-cutting disasters that free-market nuclear energy inevitably led to. It would also excuse the new power plants from those environmental regulations the military already had exemptions from. Overall those exemptions were a bad idea, but in this case, maybe not.

In effect, pursuing this plan would nationalize part of the country's energy supply, Gamble pointed out. A bit of a Hugo Chavez move, he suggested, which would enrage the *Wall Street Journal* editorial page and its ilk. Between that and the environmental objections, there would be no lack of opponents to such a plan.

But the Navy, Frank suggested, had no reason to fear critics of any stripe. They did what Congress and the president asked them to do.

Gamble concurred. Then, without saying so outright, he conveyed to Frank the impression that the Navy brain trust might be happy to be tasked with some of the nation's energy security. These days, global military strategy and technology had combined in a way that made navies indispensable but unglamorous; they functioned like giant water taxis for the other services. Ambition to do more was common in the secretary's office, and over at Annapolis.

"Great," Frank said. While listening to this artful description, vague but suggestive, something had occurred to him: "When there are blackouts, could the nuclear fleet serve as emergency generators?"

"Well, yes, if I understand you. They've done things like that before, doing emergency relief in Africa and Southeast Asia. Hook into the grid and power a town or a district."

"How big a town?"

"The ships range from a few to several megawatt range. I think a Roosevelt-class aircraft carrier could power a town of a hundred thousand, maybe more."

"I'd like to get the totals on that."

Then lunch was over and it was time for 2) *Air Force*. A new aide appeared and escorted him around two bends of the Pentagon, to the Air Force hall. The walls here were decorated with giant oil paintings of various kinds of aircraft. Many of the gleaming planes were portrayed engaged in aerial dogfights, the enemy planes going down under curved pillars of smoke and flames. It was like being in a war-crazed teenager's bedroom.

The Air Force's chief scientist was an academic, appointed for a two-year stint. Frank asked him about the possibility of the Air Force getting involved in space-based solar power, and the rapid deployment thereof. The chief scientist was optimistic about this. Solar collectors doing photovoltaic in orbit, beaming the power down in microwaves to Earth, there to be captured by power plants, which became capture-and-transfer centers, rather than generating plants per se. Have to avoid frying too many birds and bees with the microwaves, not unlike the wind turbine problem in that regard, otherwise pretty straightforward, technically, and with the potential to be exceptionally, almost amazingly, clean.

But?

"You would need a big honking booster to lift all that hardware into space," the chief scientist said. Maybe something that had horizontal takeoffs and landings both, some kind of ramjet thing. In any case a major new booster, like the old Saturn rocket, so foolishly canceled at the end of Apollo, but modernized by all that a half-century's improvements in materials and design could give it. A good booster could make the shuttle look like the weird and dangerous contraption it had always been.

"Much progress on that, then?" Frank asked.

The matter had been studied, and some starts made, but it could not be said to be going full speed yet. Even though it was a crucial part of a full clean energy solution.

"What have people been thinking this last decade or two?" Frank wondered once. "Why not do the obvious things?"

The chief scientist shrugged; a rhetorical question, obviously. Only Edgardo would bother to shout out *Because we are stupid!*

Frank said, "Could the Air Force itself commission a big booster, as a defense priority?"

"Well, it's supposed to be NASA's thing. And there's lots of people nervous about what they call militarizing space."

"Can NASA do it?"

Another shrug, very expressive. NASA was tricky, small, often very messed up. Maybe the Air Force could partner with them, try to help without being too intrusive.

"Even fund it," Frank suggested.

But of course that brought up the problem of "reprogrammed funds," as General Wracke had described to him the year before. Really something like that could only be Congress's call. Again. But the Air Force would be willing to advocate such a thing to Congress, sure. They would serve as called on.

So. Frank thanked the man and was escorted around to the Army hall, for his 3) *Army Corps of Engineers* meeting.

But here it turned out General Wracke had been called away unexpectedly, so his escort led him back to the waiting room, the only place where he could exit the building.

Back onto the Metro (and who had built that?), he tried to work it out. Navy helps Energy, Air Force helps NASA, Army Corps of Engineers helps all the land-based infrastructure, including carbon sequestration and shoreline stabilization. Together with all the other mitigation efforts, they would be terraforming the Earth. It was, after all, a matter of national defense. Defense of all the nations, but never mind. Republic in danger; the military should be involved. Especially given their budget. A military as big as all the other militaries on the planet, working for a country that had explicitly renounced any imperial ambitions or world police responsibilities, which it wanted to cede over to the UN as a globalized world project. That meant there was now a gigantic budget and productive capacity, extending into the private sector in the form of the military's many contractors, that did not have all that much to do. It was an instantaneous investment overhang. Maybe it could be devoted to the mitigation project. The Swiss Army did work like that. Frank wondered if the FCCSET program could be used to coordinate all these federal efforts, perhaps out of the OMB. Construct an overarching mission architecture.

He wondered if the FBI could be sicced on black-black programs that had taken off on their own and hidden within the greater intelligence and security morass.

It was hard to imagine how all this would work, but Frank felt that here he was baffled not by his own cognitive problems, but by the sheer size and complexity of the federal government, and of the problem. In any case one thing was clear: there was serious money being disbursed out of the Pentagon. If they were interested in trying to help with this, it could be an incredible resource.

In the private sphere, meanwhile, it was time to find and talk to big pools of accumulated capital. As, for instance, the reinsurance companies, with total assets in the ten-trillion-dollar range. Next item on the list. If he could only keep this busy, there would be no need to decide anything. Or to wonder where Caroline was and why she hadn't contacted him yet.

The reinsurance companies had underwritten most of the previous year's North Atlantic salt fleet, so they were already acquainted with the huge costs of such projects, but also were the world's experts in the even bigger costs of ignoring problems. They had been the one who ultimately had paid for the long winter, and they had their cost-benefit algorithms. And they were already well acquainted with the concept of robust decision making—something very desirable to them, as being less destructive to their business over the long haul.

Diane had invited representatives of the four big reinsurance companies to meet with her global-warming task force. About twenty people filled the conference room in the Old Executive Offices, including Anna, over for the day from NSF.

After Diane welcomed them, she got to the point in her usual style, and invited Kenzo to share what was known about the situation in the North Atlantic and more globally. Kenzo waved at his PowerPoint slides like a pops orchestra conductor. Then one of the reinsurance nat cat (natural catastrophe) guys from Swiss Re gave a talk which made it clear that in insurance terms, sea-level rise was the worst impact of all. A quarter of humanity lived on the coastlines of the world. About a fifth of the total human infrastructure was at risk, he said, if sea level rose even two meters; and this was the current best guess as to what might happen in the coming decade. And if the breakup of the West Antarctic Ice Sheet went all the way, they were facing a rise of seven meters.

It was something you could be aware of without quite comprehending. They sat around the table pondering it.

Frank seized his pen, squeezed it as if it were his recalcitrant brain. "I've been looking at some numbers," he said haltingly. "Postulating, for a second, that we have developed really significant clean energy generation, then, observe, the amount of water displaced by the detached Antarctic ice so far is on the order of forty thousand cubic kilometers. Now, there are a number of these basins in the Sahara Desert and all across central Asia, and in the basin and range country of North America. Also in southern Africa. In effect, the current position of the continents and the trade wind patterns have desiccated all land surfaces around the thirtieth latitudes north and south, and in the south that doesn't mean much, but in the north it means a huge land area dried out. All those basins together have a theoretical capacity of about sixty thousand cubic kilometers."

He looked up from his laptop briefly, and it was as he had expected; they were looking at him like he was a bug. He shrugged and looked back at the PowerPoint, and forged on:

"So, you could pump a lot of the excess sea water into these empty basins in the thirties, and perhaps stabilize the ocean's sea level proper."

"Holy moly," Kenzo said in the silence after it was clear Frank was done. "You'd alter the climate in those regions tremendously if you did that."

"No doubt," Frank said. "But you know, since the climate is going haywire anyway, it's kind of like, so what? In the context of everything else, will we even be able to distinguish what this would do from all the rest?"

Kenzo laughed.

"Well," Frank said defensively to the silent room, "I thought I'd at least run the numbers."

"It would take an awful lot of power to pump that much water inland," Anna said.

"I have *no idea* what kind of climate alteration you would get if you did that," Kenzo said happily.

Frank said, "Did the Salton Sea change anything downwind of it?"

"Well, but we're talking like a thousand Salton Seas here," Kenzo said. He was still bug-eyed at the idea; he had never even imagined curating such a change, and he was looking at Frank as if to say, Why didn't you mention something this cool out on our runs? "It would be a real test of our modeling programs," he said, looking even happier. Almost giddy: "It might change everything!" he exclaimed.

"And yet," Frank said. "People might judge those changes to be preferable to displacing a quarter of the world's population. Remember what happened to New Orleans. We couldn't afford to have ten thousand of those, could we?"

"If you had the unlimited power you're talking about," Anna said suddenly, "why couldn't you just pump the equivalent of the displaced water back up onto the Antarctic polar plateau? Let it freeze back up there, near where it came from?"

Again the room was silent.

"Now there's an idea," Diane said. She was smiling. "But Frank, where are these dry basins again?"

Frank brought that slide back up on the PowerPoint. The basins, if all of them were entirely filled, could take about twenty percent of the predicted rise in sea level if the whole WAIS came off. It would take about thirty terawatts to move the water. The cost in carbon for that much energy would be ten gigatons, not good, but only a fraction of the overall carbon budget at this point. Clean energy would be better for doing it, of course. What effects on local climates and ecologies would be caused by the introduction of so many big new lakes was, as Kenzo had said, impossible to calculate.

"Those are some very dry countries," Diane said after perusing Frank's map. "Dry and poor. I can imagine, if they were offered compensation to take the water and make new lakes, some of them might decide to roll the dice and take the environmental risk, because net effects might end up being positive. It might make opportunities for them that aren't there now. There's not much going on in the Takla Makan these days, that I know of."

The Swiss Re executive returned to Anna's comment, suggesting that the system might be able go through proof of concept in Antarctica, after which, if it worked, countries signing on would have a better idea of what they were in for. Antarctic operations would incur extra costs, to keep pumps and pipelines heated; on the other hand, the environmental impacts were likely to be minimal, and population relocation not an issue at all. Maybe they could even relocate the excess ocean water entirely on the Antarctic polar cap. That would mean shifting water that floated away from the West Antarctic Ice Sheet up to the top of the Eastern Antarctic Ice Sheet.

"Of course if we're going to talk about stupendous amounts of new free energy," Anna pointed out, "you could do all sorts of things. You could desalinate the sea water at the pumps or at their outlets, and make them fresh water lakes in the thirties, so you wouldn't have Salton Sea problems. You'd have reservoirs of drinking and irrigation water, you could replenish groundwater, and build with salt bricks, and so on."

Diane nodded. "True."

"But we don't have stupendous new sources of clean energy," Anna said.

Good photovoltaics existed, Frank reminded her doggedly. Also a good Stirling engine; good wind power; and extremely promising ocean energy-to-electricity systems.

That was all very well, Diane agreed. That was promising. But there remained the capital investment problem, and the other transitional costs associated with changing over to any of these clean renewables. Who was going to pay for it?

It was the trillion-dollar question.

Here the reinsurance people took center stage. They had paid for the salting of the North Atlantic by using their reserves, then upping their premiums. Their reserves were huge, as they had to be to meet their obligations to the many insurance companies paying them for reinsurance. But swapping out the power generation system was two magnitudes larger a problem, more or less, than the salt fleet had been, and it was impossible to front that kind of money—almost impossible to imagine collecting it in any way.

"Well, but it's only four years of the American military budget," Frank pointed out.

People shrugged, as if to say, but still—that was a lot.

"It's going to take legislation," Diane said. "Private investment can't do it. Can't or won't."

General agreement, although the reinsurance guys looked unhappy. "It would be good if it made sense in market terms," the Swiss Re executive said.

This led them to a discussion of macroeconomics, but even there, they kept coming back to the idea of major public works. No matter what kind of economic ideology you brought to the table, the world they had set up was resolutely Keynesian—meaning a mixed economy in which government and business existed in an uneasy interaction. Public works projects were sometimes crucial to the process, especially in emergencies, but that meant legislating economic activity, and so they needed to have the political understanding and support it would take to do that. If so, they could legislate investment, and then in effect print the money to pay for it. That was standard Keynesian practice, a kind of pump-priming used by governments ever since the third New Deal of 1938, as Diane told them now, with World War II itself an even bigger example.

Other economic stimuli might also complement this old standby. Edgardo had done some studies here, and it could all be handed to Chase as a kind of program, a mission architecture. A list of Things To Do.

After that, they heard a report from the Russian environmental office. The altered tree lichens they had distributed in Siberia the previous summer were surviving the winter there like any ordinary lichen. Dispersal had been widespread, uptake on trees rapid, as the engineers at Small Delivery Systems had hoped for.

The only problem the Russian could see was that it was possible, at least in theory, that the lichen dispersal would become too successful. What they were seeing now led them to think they might have overseeded, or actually overdispersed. Since most of what they had dispersed had survived, by next summer the Siberian forest around the site would reap whatever the winds and the Russians had sown. In the lab it was proving to grow more like algal blooms encased in mushrooms than like ordinary lichens. "Fast lichen, we call it," the Russian said. "We didn't think it was possible, but we see it happening."

All that was very interesting, but when Frank got back in his office, he found that his computer wouldn't turn on. And when the techs arrived to check it out, they went pale, and isolated the machine quickly, then carried the whole thing away. "That's one bad virus," one of them said. "Very dangerous."

"So was I hacked in particular?" Frank asked.

"We usually see that one when someone has been targeted. A real poke in the eye. Did you back up your disks?"

"Well..."

"You better have. That's a complete loss there."

"A hard-drive crash?"

"A hard-drive bombing. You'll have to file and report, and they'll be adding you to the case file. Someone did this to you on purpose."

Frank felt a chill.

CHARLIE'S DAYTIME OUTINGS WITH JOE had to happen on the weekends now. Even though they were past the First Sixty Days and had had a pretty good run with them, they were trying to keep the momentum going, and things kept popping up to derail the plans, sometimes intentional problems created by the opposition, sometimes neutral matters created by the sheer size and complexity of the system. Roy was pushing so hard that sometimes he even almost lost his cool. Charlie had never seen that, and would have thought it impossible, at least on the professional level. In personal matters, Roy and Andrea had gone through a spectacular in-office breakup, and during that time Charlie had endured some long and bitter rants from Roy. But when it came to business, Roy had always prided himself on staying calm. Calmness at speed was his signature style, as with certain surfing stars. And even now he persisted with that style, or tried to; but the workload was so huge it was hard to keep the calmness along with the pace. They were far past the time when he and Charlie were able to chat about things like they used to. Now their phone conversations went something like:

"Charlie it's Roy have you met with IPCC?"

"No, we're both scheduled to meet with the World Bank on Friday."

"Can you meet them and the Bank team at six today instead?"

"I was going to go home at five."

"Six then?"

"Well if you think—"

"Good okay more soon bye."

"Bye."—said to the empty connection.

Charlie stared at his cell phone and cursed. He cursed Roy, Phil, Congress, the World Bank, the Republican Party, the world, and the universe. Because it was nobody's fault.

He hit the cell phone button for the daycare.

He was going to have to carve time for an in-person talk with Roy, a talk about what he could and couldn't do. That would be an unusual meeting. Even though Charlie was now at the White House fifty hours a week, he still never saw Roy in person; Roy was always somewhere else. They spoke on the phone even when one of them was in the West Wing and the other in the Old Executive Offices, less than a hundred yards away. For a second Charlie couldn't even remember what Roy looked like.

So; call to arrange for "extended stay" for Joe, a development his teachers were used to. Another exception to the supposed schedule. Because they needed the World Bank executing Phil's program; in the war of the agencies, now fully engaged, the World Bank and the International Monetary Fund were among the most mulish of their passive-aggressive opponents. Phil had the power to hire and fire the upper echelons in both agencies, which was good leverage, but it would be better to do something less drastic, to keep the midlevels from shattering. This meeting with the Intergovernmental Panel on Climate Change, a UN organization, might be a good venue for exerting some pressure. The IPCC had spent many years advocating action on the climate front, and all the while they had been flatly ignored by the World Bank. If there was now a face-off, a great reckoning in a little room, then it could get interesting.

But the meeting, held across the street in the World Bank's headquarters, was a disappointment. These two groups came from such different world-views that it was only an illusion they were speaking the same language; for the most part they used different vocabularies, and when by chance they used the same words, they meant different things by them. They were aware at some level of this underlying conflict, but could not address it; and so everyone was tense, with old grievances unsayable and yet fully present.

The World Bank guys said something about nothing getting cheaper than oil for the next fifty years, ignoring what the IPCC guys had just finished saying about the devastating effects fifty more years of oil burning would have. They had not heard that, apparently. They defended having invested 94 percent of the World Bank's energy investments in oil exploration as necessary, given the world's dependence on oil—apparently unaware of the circular aspect of their argument. And, being economists, they were still exteriorizing costs without even noticing it or acknowledging such exteriorization had been conclusively demonstrated to falsify accounts of profit and loss. It was as if the world were not real—as if the actual physical world, reported on by scientists and witnessed by all, could be ignored, and because their entirely fictitious numbers therefore added up, no one could complain.

Charlie gritted his teeth as he listened and took notes. This was science versus capitalism, yet again. The IPCC guys spoke for science and said the obvious things, pointing out the physical constraints of the planet, the carbon load now in the atmosphere altering everything, and the resultant need for heavy investment in clean replacement technologies by all concerned, including the World Bank, as one of the great drivers of globalization. But they had said it before to no avail, and so it was happening again. The World Bank guys talked about rates of return and the burden on investors, and the unacceptable doubling of the price of a kilowatt hour. Everyone there had said all of this before, with the same lack of communication and absence of concrete results.

Charlie saw that the meeting was useless. He thought of Joe, over at the daycare. He had never stayed there long enough even to see what they did all day long. Guilt stuck him like a sliver. In a crowd of strangers, fourteen hours a day. The Bank guy was going on about differential costs, "and that's why it's going to be oil for the next twenty, thirty, maybe even fifty years," he concluded. "None of the alternatives are competitive."

Charlie's pencil tip snapped. "Competitive for *what*?" he demanded.

He had not spoken until that point, and now the edge in his voice stopped the discussion. Everyone was staring at him. He stared back at the World Bank guys.

"Damage from carbon dioxide emission costs about $35 a ton, but in your model no one pays it. The carbon that British Petroleum burns per year, by sale and operation, runs up a damage bill of fifty billion dollars. BP reported a profit of twenty billion, so actually it's thirty billion in the red, every year. Shell reported a profit of twenty-three billion, but if you added the damage cost it would be eight billion in the red. These companies should be bankrupt. You support their exteriorizing of costs, so your accounting is bullshit. You're helping to bring on the biggest catastrophe in human history. If the oil companies burn the five hundred gigatons of carbon that you are describing as inevitable because of your financial shell games, then two-thirds of the species on the planet will be endangered, including humans. But you keep talking about fiscal discipline and competitive edges in profit differentials. It's the stupidest head-in-the-sand response possible."

The World Bank guys flinched at this. "Well," one of them said, "we don't see it that way."

Charlie said, "That's the trouble. You see it the way the banking industry sees it, and they make money by manipulating money irrespective of effects in the real world. You've spent a trillion dollars of American taxpayers' money over the lifetime of the Bank, and there's nothing to show for it. You go into poor countries and force them to sell their assets to foreign investors and to switch from subsistence agriculture to cash crops, then when the prices of those crops collapse you call this nicely competitive on the world market. The local populations starve and you then insist on austerity measures even though your actions have shattered their economy. You order them to cut their social services so they can pay off their debts to you and to your financial community investors, and you devalue their real assets and then buy them on the cheap and sell them elsewhere for more. The assets of that country have been strip-mined and now belong to international finance. That's your idea of development. You were intended to be the Marshall Plan, and instead you've been the United Fruit Company."

One of the World Bank guys muttered, "But tell us what you really think," while putting his papers in his briefcase. His companion snickered, and this gave him courage to continue: "I'm not gonna stay and listen to this," he said.

"That's fine," Charlie said. "You can leave now and get a head start on looking for a new job."

The man blinked hostilely at him. But he did not otherwise move.

Charlie stared at him for a while, working to collect himself. He lowered his voice and spoke as calmly as he could manage. He outlined the basics of the new mission architecture, including the role that the World Bank was now to play; but he couldn't handle going into detail with people who were now furious at him, and in truth had never been listening. It was time for what Frank called limited discussion. So Charlie wrapped it up, then gave them a few copies of the mission architecture outline, thick books that had been bound just that week. "Your part of the plan is here in concept. Take it back and talk it over with your people, and come to us with your plan to enact it. We look forward to hearing your ideas. I've got you scheduled for a meeting on the sixth of next month, and I'll expect your report then." Although, since we will be decapitating your organization, it won't be you guys doing the reporting, he didn't add.

And he gathered his papers and left the room.

Well, shit. What a waste of everyone's time.

He had been sweating, and now out on the street he chilled. His hands were shaking. He had lost it. It was amazing how angry he had gotten. Phil had told him to go in and kick ass, but it did no good to yell at people like that. It had been unprofessional; out of control; counterproductive. Only senators got to rave like that. Staffers, no.

Well, what was done was done. Now it was time to pick up Joe and go home. Anna wouldn't believe what he had done. In fact, he realized, he would not be able to tell her about it, not in full; she would be too appalled. She would say "Oh Charlie" and he would be ashamed of himself.

But at least it was time to get Joe. At this point he had been at daycare for twelve hours exactly. "Damn it," Charlie said viciously, all of a sudden as angry as he had been in the meeting; and then, glad that he had shouted at them. Years of repressed anger at the fatuous destructiveness of the World Bank and the system they worked for had been released all at once; the wonder was he had been as polite as he had. The anger still boiled in him uselessly, caustic to his own poor gut.

Joe, however, seemed unconcerned by his long day. "Hi Dad!" he said brightly from the blocks and trucks corner, where he had the undivided attention of a young woman who reminded Charlie of their old Gymboree friend Asta. "We're playing chess!"

"Wow," Charlie said, startled; but by the girl's sweet grin, and the chess pieces strewn about the board and the floor, he saw that it was Joe's version of chess, and the mayhem had been severe. "That's really good, Joe! But now I'm here and it's time, so can we help clean up and go?"

"Okay Dad."

On the Metro ride home, Joe seemed tired but happy. "We had Cheerios for snack."

"Oh good, you like Cheerios. Are you still hungry?"

"No, I'm good. Are you hungry, Dad?"

"Well, yes, a little bit."

"Wanna cracker?" And he produced a worn fragment of a Wheat Thin from his pants pocket, dusted with lint.

"Thanks, Joe, that's nice. Sure, I'll take it." He took the cracker and ate it. "Beggars can't be choosers."

"Beggars?"

"People who don't have anything. People who ask you for money."

"Money?"

"You know, money. The stuff people pay for things with, when they buy them."

"Buy them?"

"Come on Joe. Please. It's hard to explain what money is. Dollars. Quarters. Beggars are people who don't have much money and they don't have much of a way to get money. All they've got is the World Bank ripping their hearts out and eating their lives. So, the saying means, when you're like a beggar, you can't be too picky about choosing things when they're offered to you."

"What about Han? Is she too picky?"

"Well, I don't know. Who's Han?"

"Han is the morning teacher. She doesn't like bagels."

"I see! Well, that sounds too picky to me."

"Right," Joe said. "You get what you get."

"That's true," Charlie said.

"You *get* what you *get* and you *don't* throw a *fit*!" Joe declared, and beamed. Obviously this was a saying often repeated at the daycare. A mantra of sorts.

"That's very true," Charlie said. "Although to tell you the truth, I did just throw a fit."

"Oh well." Joe was observing the people getting on at the UDC stop, and Charlie looked up too. Students and workers, all going home late. "These things happen," Joe said. He sat leaning against Charlie, his body relaxed, murmuring something to the tiny plastic soldier grasped in his fist, looking at the people in their bright-pink-seated car.

Then they were at the Bethesda stop, and off and up the long escalator to the street, and walking down Wisconsin together with the cars roaring by.

"Dad, let's go in and get a cookie! Cookie!"

It was that block's Starbucks, one of Joe's favorite places.

"Oh Joe, we've got to get home, Mom and Nick are waiting to see us, they miss us."

"Sure Dad. Whatever you say Dad."

"Please, Joe! Don't say that!"

"Okay Dad."

Charlie shook his head as they walked on, his throat tight. He clutched Joe's hand and let Joe swing their arms up and down.

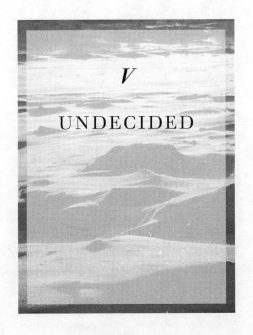

V

UNDECIDED

*P*leasure is a brain mechanism. It's a product of natural selection, so it must help to make us more adaptive. Sexual attraction is an index of likely sexual pleasure.

Frank stopped in his reading. Was that true?

The introduction to this book claimed the collected sociobiological papers in it studied female sexual attractiveness exclusively because there were more data about it. Yeah right. Also, female sexual attractiveness was easier to see and describe and quantify, as it had more to do with physical qualities than with abstract attributes such as status or prowess or sense of humor. Yeah right! What about the fact that the authors of the articles were all male? Would Hrdy agree with any of these justifications? Or would she laugh outright?

Evolutionary psychology studies the adaptations made to solve the information-processing problems our ancestors faced over the last couple million years. The problems? Find food; select habitat; stay safe; choose a mate. Obviously the brain must solve diverse problems in different domains. No general-purpose brain mechanism to solve all problems, just as no general-purpose organ to solve all physiological problems. Food choice very different from mate choice, for instance.

Was this true? Was not consciousness itself precisely the general-purpose brain mechanism this guy claimed did not exist? Maybe it was like blood, circulating among the organs. Or the whole person as a gestalt decision maker. One decision after another.

Anyway, mate choice: or rather, males choosing females. Sexual attraction had something to do with it. (Was this true?) Potential mates vary in mate value. Mate value could be defined as how much the mate increases reproductive success of the male making the choice. (Was this true?) Reproductive success potential can be determined by a number of variables. Information about some of these variables was available in specific observable characteristics of female bodies. Men were therefore always watching very closely. (This was true.)

Reproductive variables: age, hormonal status, fecundity, birth history.

A nubile female was one having begun ovulation, but never yet pregnant. Primitive population menarche average start, 12.4 years; first births at 16.8 years; peak fertility between 20 and 24 years; last births at around 40 years. In the early environment in which they evolved, women almost always were married by nubility (were they sure?). The biological fathers of women's children were likely to be their husbands. Women started reproducing shortly after nubility, one child every three or four years, each child nursed intensively for a few years, which suppressed conception.

A male who married a nubile female had the maximum opportunity to father her offspring during her most fecund years, and would monopolize those years from their start, thus presumably not be investing in other men's children.

If mate selection had been for the short term only, maximal fecundity would be preferred to nubility, because chance of pregnancy was better at that point. Sexual attraction to nubility rather than maximal fecundity indicates it was more a wife detector than a short-term, one-time mother detector.

Was this true?

In the early environment, female reproductive time lasted about 26 years, from 16 to 42, but this included average of 6 years of pregnancy, and 18 years of lactation. Thus females were pregnant or nursing for 24 of the relevant 26 years, or 92 percent of reproductive life. So, between first average birth age (17) and last conception age (39), average woman was nonpregnant and nonlactating for two years; thus 26 ovulations total. Say three days of fecundity per cycle, thus females were capable of conceiving on only 78 of 8,030 days, or one percent of the time. Thus only about one in a hundred random copulations could potentially result in conception.

Did this make sense? It seemed to Frank that several parts of an algorithm had been crunched into one calculation, distorting all findings. Numbers for numbers' sake: specifics following an averaging was one sign, "random copulations" another, because there were no such things; but that was the only way they could get the figure to be as low as one percent.

In any case, following the argument, a nubile woman before first pregnancy was more fecund than a fully fecund woman in her early twenties, if one were considering her lifetime potential. And so nubility cues were *fertility cues*, as males considered their whole futures as fathers. (But did they?) Thus natural selection assigned maximum sexual attractiveness to nubility cues. And this attraction to nubility rather than fecundity indicated monogamous tendencies; male wants long-term cohabitation, with its certainty about parentage for as many offspring as possible.

And what were nubility cues? Skin texture, muscle tone, stretch marks, breast shape, facial configuration, and waist-to-hip ratio. All these indexed female age and parity. Female sexual attractiveness varied inversely with WHR, which was lowest at nubility; higher when both younger and older. Etc. Even the face was a reliable physical indicator. (Frank laughed.) Selection showed a preference for average features. This was asserted because students in a test were asked to choose a preferred composite; the "beautiful composite," as created by both male and female subjects, had a shorter bottom half of the face than average, typical of a twelve-year-old girl; full lips in vertical dimension, but smaller mouth than true average. Higher cheekbones than true average, larger eyes relative to face size; thinner jaw; shorter distances between nose and mouth, and between mouth and chin. High cheekbones and relatively short lower face and gracile jaw indicated youth, low testosterone/estrogen ratio, and nullipara. Bilateral symmetry was preferred. Deviation in hard tissue reduced sexual attractiveness more than the same amount of deviation in say nose form, which could have resulted from minor mishap indicating little about design quality. Ah, Francesca Taolini's beautiful crooked nose, explained at last!

As was "masticatory efficiency." This was the one that had gotten Frank and Anna laughing so hard, that day when Frank had first run across the study. Sexy chewing.

In the early environment, total body fat and health were probably correlated, so fat, what little could be accumulated, was good. Now that was reversed, and thinner meant both younger and healthier. Two possible readings, therefore, EE and modern. Which might explain why all women looked good to Frank, each in her own way. He was adaptable, he was optimodal, he was the paleolithic postmodern!

Were women evaluating men as mates in exactly the same way? Yes; but not exactly. A woman always knew her children were biologically hers. Mate choice thus could focus on different criteria than in effect capturing all of a mate's fecundity. Here is where the sociobiologist Hrdy had led the way, by examining and theorizing female choice.

Patriarchy could thus be seen as a group attempt by men to be more sure of parentage, by controlling access. Men becoming jailers, men going beyond monogamy to an imprisoning polygamy, as an extension of the original adaptive logic—but an extension that was an obvious reductio ad absurdum, ending in the seraglio. Patriarchy did not eliminate male competition for mates; on the contrary, because of the reductio ad absurdum, male competition became more necessary than ever. And the more force available, the more intense the competition. Thus patriarchy as a solution to the parentage problem led to hatred, war, misogyny, gynophobia, harems, male control of reproductive rights, including anti-abortion laws (those photos of a dozen fat men grinning as they signed a law on a stage) and, ultimately, taken all in all, patriarchy led directly to the general very nonadaptive insanity that they lived in now.

Was that true? Did sociobiology show how and why they had gone crazy as a species? Could they, using that knowledge, work backwards to sanity? Had there ever been sanity? Could they create sanity for the first time, by understanding all the insanities that had come before? By looking at adaptation and its accidental by-products, and its peacock exaggerations past the point of true function?

And could Frank figure out what he should do about his own mating issues? It brought on a kind of nausea to be so undecided.

MOST OF THE KHEMBALIS still in the D.C. area were now moving out to their farm in Maryland. The compound was nearly finished, and although a thin layer of hard snow still lay on most of the ground, spring was springing, and they were beginning to clear the area they wanted to cultivate with crops. They rented a giant rototiller, and a little tractor of their own was on its way. Sucandra was excited. "I always wanted to be a farmer," he said. "I dreamed about it for years, when we were in prison. Now we are going to try what crops will thrive here." He gestured: "It looks just like it did in my dream."

"When the ground thaws," Frank suggested.

"Spring is coming. It's almost the equinox."

"But growing season here starts late, doesn't it?"

"Not compared to Tibet."

"Ah."

Sucandra said, "Will you move out here with us, and build your tree-house?"

"I don't know. I need to talk it over with Rudra."

"He says he wants to. Qang wonders if he should stay closer to hospital."

"Ah. What's wrong with him, do they know?"

Sucandra shrugged. "Old. Worn out."

"I suppose."

"He will not stay much longer in that body."

Frank was startled. "Has he got something, you know—progressive?"

Sucandra smiled. "Life is progressive."

"Yes." But he's only eighty-one, Frank didn't say. That might be far beyond the average life span for Tibetans. He felt a kind of tightness in him.

"I don't know what I'll do," he said at last. "I mean, I'll stay where he is.

So—maybe for now I'll just work on the treehouse, and stay in Arlington with him. If that's okay."

"That would be fine, of course. Thank you for thinking of it that way."

Disturbed, Frank went up the hill to the copse of trees at the high point.

He walked around in the grove, trying to concentrate. They were beautiful trees, big, old, intertwined into a canopy shading the hilltop. Snow filled every crevice of the bark on their north sides. If only they lived as long as trees. He went back to his van and got his climbing and window-washing gear, and trudged back up the hill. It was sunny but cold, a stiff west wind blowing. He knew that up in the branches it would be colder still. He wasn't really in the mood to climb a tree, and you needed to be in the mood. It was more dangerous than most rock climbing.

But, however, here he was. Time to amp up and ramp up, as they used to say in the window-washing business—often before smoking huge reefers and downing extra-tall cups of 7-Eleven coffee, admittedly—but the point still held. One needed to get psyched and pay attention. Crampons, linesman's harness, strap around, kick in, deep breath. Up, up, up!

Eyes streaming in the cold wind. Blink several times to clear vision. Through the heavy lowest branches, up to the level under the canopy, where big branches from different trees intertwined. In the wind he could see the independent motion of all the branches. Hard to imagine, offhand, what that might mean in terms of a treehouse. If an extensive treehouse were to rest on branches from more than one tree, wouldn't it vibrate or bounce at cross-purposes, rather than sway all of a piece, as his little Rock Creek treehouse did? An interference pattern, on the other hand, might be like living in a perpetual earthquake. Not good. What was needed was a big central room, set firmly on one big trunk in the middle, with the other rooms set independently on branches of their own—yes—much like the Swiss Family treehouse at Disneyland. He had heard it was the Tarzan treehouse now, but he wasn't willing to accept that. Anyway the design was sound. He saw the potential branches, made a first sketch on a little pocket notebook page, hanging there. It could be good.

And yet he wasn't looking forward to it.

Then he saw that the smallest branches around him were studded with tiny green buds. They were the particular light vivid green that was still new to Frank, that he had never seen in his life until the previous spring, out in Rock Creek Park: deciduous bud green. An East Coast phenomenon. The color of spring. Ah yes: spring! Could spring ever be far behind? The so-called blocked moments, the times of stasis, were never really still at all. Change was constant, whether you could see it or not. Best then to focus on the new green buds, bursting out everywhere.

Thoreau said the same, the next morning. Frank read it aloud: "March fans it, April christens it, and May puts on its jacket and trousers. It never grows up, but is ever springing, bud following close upon leaf, and when winter comes it is not annihilated, but creeps on mole-like under the snow, showing its face occasionally by fuming springs and watercourses."

Rudra nodded. "Henry sees things. 'The flower opens, and lo! another year.' "

Thoughts of spring came to Frank often in the days that followed, partly because of the green now all over town, and partly because Chase kept referring to his first sixty days as a new spring. It struck Frank again when he went with Diane and Edgardo over to the White House to witness the dedication of the new solar projects. Phil had ordered that photovoltaic panels be put in place (be put back in place, as Carter had done it in his time) to power the White House. When there was some debate as to which system should be installed, he had instructed them to put in three or four different systems, to make a kind of test.

The purple-blue of the photovoltaic panels was like another kind of spring color, popping out in the snowy flowerbeds. Phil made a little speech, after which he was to be driven to Norfolk naval station; he had already had the Secret Service swap out his transport fleet, so now instead of a line of black SUVs pulling through the security gate, it was a line of black bulletproof Priuses. These looked so small that everyone laughed; they resembled the miniature cars that Shriners drove in parades. Chase laughed hardest of all, jumping out and directing the traffic so that the little cars made a circle around him. As he waved good-bye to the crowd, Frank noticed that he wore two wedding bands, one on his left ring finger, the other on the little finger of his right hand.

The White House demonstration project was only a tiny part of the solar power debate raging through NSF, the Department of Energy, and, Frank supposed, the world at large. Sudden effort to find the holy grail. It looked like desperation, and to a certain extent it was. But it was also that volatile time that came early in the history of any new technology, when decisions about many of the basic structures and methods emerged from a general confusion.

The small scale of this test was not going to be fair to Stirling engines in competition with photovoltaic. PV panels could be scaled to any size, which made them best for home use, while the external heat engine required a group of mirrors big enough to heat the heating element fully and drive the pistons to maximum output. It was a system meant for power plants. So the test here was only a PR thing. Still, not a bad idea. To see the systems creating electricity, even on cloudy days, was suddenly to understand that they had the means for the world's deliverance already at hand. Paradoxically, the units on the south lawn shifted the attention from technology to finance. Now Chase was talking about tax credits for home installations that were big enough that the cost of a system would be the equivalent of about three years of electricity bills. A subsidy like that would make a huge difference. The cost to the federal budget would be about a tenth the cost of the last war. The main problem then would be manufacturing enough silicon.

One of the workmen scaling the southwest corner of the White House was having trouble, even though belayed from the roof. Frank shook his head, thinking: I could do better than that. Cutter and his friends could do better than that.

Kayaking was fun. The ice had broken up, and Frank, Charlie, and Drepung had joined a program at the Georgetown boathouse which gave them a couple of lessons, and then renting privileges for Charlie and Drepung; Frank had an old blue kayak of his own. Now their routine was to try to meet every other weekend to paddle around, playing on the slight riffles in the Potomac upstream from the Key Bridge. These riffles, however small compared to the drops at Great Falls, nevertheless involved an immense flow of water, and were fun to struggle up and shoot down. They could practice on them until they were good enough for Great Falls, Frank would say. Great Falls had a variety of white-water runs on the Maryland side, spanning a wide range of difficulties. Charlie and Drepung would nod at this information while glancing at each other, in full solidarity to resist any such improvement.

Drepung, it seemed to Charlie, was doing well, despite all the bustle at the embassy; in high spirits because of the move to the farm, and Phil taking office, and probably just the sheer fact of spring. He was young, the cherry blossoms were blossoming, and the Wizards were in the playoffs. He had an iPod that he had programmed with everything from the Dixie Chicks to the Diamond Sutra. Charlie often saw him bopping up their sidewalk in his oversized running shoes, snapping his fingers to some iPodded beat or other, not fast or slow, but in the groove. The bopper with the Betty Boop face, his gaze curiously fresh, direct, warm, open—a kind of hail, or greeting, even a challenge—a look unusual in D.C., the world capital of insincere sincerity.

Now Drepung paddled by and said, "I know that you said that when Phil Chase said to us, *I'll see what I can do,* he was only using the usual Washington code for 'No.' But I am thinking now that maybe he meant it literally."

"Could be," Charlie opined cautiously. "What makes you think so?"

"Well, because he has apparently called up the State Department, and told someone in the South Asia division to get hold of us and set up a meeting with him. There's even some of the China people to be included in this meeting."

"Chinese people?"

"No, China people. State Department foreign service people who specialize in China. Sridar has been trying to set up such a meeting with them for months and months, but with no success. And now we have a date and an agenda of topics. And all because of this request from President Chase."

"Amazing how that happens."

"Yes, isn't it? We are going to see what we can do!"

Later that spring, when the time came to move to Maryland, Frank drove Rudra out there in his van. Everything they had had in the garden shed barely covered the floor of the van's rear. This was pleasing, but leaving their garden shed was not. As Frank closed and locked the door for the last time, he felt a pang of nostalgia. Another life gone. Some feelings were like vague clouds passing through one, others were as specific as the prick of acupuncture needles.

As they drove up the George Washington Parkway he still felt uneasy about leaving, and he thought maybe Rudra did too. He had left the garden shed without a look back, but now he was staring silently out at the Potomac. Very hard to tell what he might be thinking. Which was true of everyone of course.

The farm was bristling with people. They had built the treehouse in the hilltop grove, using Frank's design but augmenting it in several ways. Once, right after they had begun to build it, he had tried to help in the actual construction of the thing, but when he saw some of the Khembali carpenters pulling out a beam that he had nailed in, he had realized that he had to leave the carpentry to them. They had built the thing at speed, not out of bamboo but out of wood, and in a very heavy *dzong* or hill fortress style, each room so varnished and painted with the traditional Tibetan colors for trim that they perched in the branches like giant toychests—rather wonderful, but not at all like the airy structures of the Disneyland masterpiece Frank had been conceptualizing. Frank wasn't sure that he liked their version.

The overall design, however, had held. There was a grand central room, like a cottage that the biggest tree had grown through and uplifted thirty feet, so that now it hung in the middle of the copse. This circular room had an open balcony or patio all the way around it, and from this round patio several railed staircases and catwalks led over branches or across open space, out and up to smaller rooms, about a dozen of them.

Sucandra arrived and pointed out one of the lowest and outmost of the hanging rooms, on the river side of the hill: that one, he said, was to be Frank and Rudra's. The roommates nodded solemnly; it would do. It definitely would do.

Late that day, having moved in, they looked back into the grove from their doorway and its own little balcony, and saw all the other rooms, their windows lit like lanterns in the dusk. On the inside their room was small. Even so their belongings looked rather meager, stacked in cardboard boxes in one corner. Sucandra and Padma and Qang all stood in the doorway, looking concerned. They had not believed Rudra's assurances that the broad circular staircase and the narrow catwalk out the low branch would present no problems to him. Frank didn't know whether to believe him either, but so far the old man had ascended and descended with only the help of the railing and some sulfurous muttering. And if problems arose, there was a kind of giant dumbwaiter or open lift next to the trunk, in which he could travel up and down. Even now they were using it to bring up their furniture—two single beds, a table and a couple of chairs, two small chests. Once all that was moved in the room looked larger than before, and more normal.

So. Here they were. Rudra sat before the window, looking down at the river. He had his laptop on the table, and he seemed content. "Very nice outlook," he said, pointing out. "Nice to have such a view."

"Yes," Frank said, thinking of his treehouse in Rock Creek. Rudra would have enjoyed that. It might have been possible to lash the old man to Miss Piggy and then haul him up using the winch. He couldn't have weighed more than a hundred pounds.

But here they were. And in fact the view was much more extensive than Rock Creek's had been. The sweep of the Potomac was now a glassy silver green, with bronze highlights under the far bank. Very nice. The expansion of space over the river, the big open band of sky over it, struck Frank with a kind of physical relief, a long ahhhhhhh. This was what you never got in the forest, this kind of open spaciousness. No wonder forest people loved their rivers— not just great roads for them, but the place of the sky and the stars!

In the days that followed, Frank woke at dawn to look out at this prospect, and saw at different times on the water highlights of yellow or rose or pink, and once it was a clean sheet of gold. These fine dawns were about the only time Frank saw the view; the rest of the day he was gone. Perhaps for that reason, he woke early, usually at first light. A mist would often be rolling over the glass, wisping up on puffs of wind. On windy mornings, waves would push upstream like a tide, although here they were above the tidal surge, and seeing only the wind chop. Sometimes it was enough to create little whitecaps, and their room would bounce and sway gently, in a way very unlike his old treehouse. There he had been on a vertical trunk, here a horizontal branch; it made a big difference.

In their new room Rudra did not talk as much as he had in Arlington. He slept a lot. But sometimes he would be sitting up in bed, humming or reading when Frank came home, or looking at his laptop screen, and then they would chat as before.

"Nice day?"

"Yes."

"More salt in ocean?"

"Yes, precisely. What about you?"

"Oh, very nice day. Sun on water flicker so nicely. And some tantric websites, yum."

"It's like you're back in Shambhala then."

"No *like*. This *is* Shambhala."

"So, it follows you around? It's a kind of, what, a phase space, or a magnetic field around you, or something like that?"

"Buddhafield, I think you mean. No, Shambhala is not like that. The buddhafield is always there, yes. But that can be wherever you make one. Shambhala is a particular place. The first hidden valley. But the valley moves from time to time. We performed the ceremony that asked if it should be here. The spirits said yes."

"Were you the, the what do you call it?"

"The voice? Oracle? No. I'm not strong enough anymore. Retired, like I told you. But Qang did well. Guru Rimpoche came to her and spoke. Khembalung is drowned for good, he said. Shambhala is now right here," waving down at the river.

"Wow," Frank said. As if on cue, when he looked out their window he saw the light of the rising moon, squiggling over the river in big liquid S's. Suddenly it had a mysterious beauty.

Another time Frank was out on the river with Drepung and Charlie. They had kayaked out from the boathouse at the mouth of Rock Creek. Rock Creek where it debouched into the Potomac was still a very undistinguished little channel, raw from the great flood, all sand and sandstone and mangled trees.

On this day there was practically no downstream flow in the great river, and they were able to paddle straight across to Roosevelt Island and poke into the many little overhangs there, to look up the slope of the island park through forest. White-tailed deer, white-tailed deer; it was disturbing to Frank to see what a population boom there was in this species, a kind of epidemic. The native predators that were now returning, and the occasional exotic feral (the jaguar?) were nowhere near numerous enough to cull the flock. Big rabbits, as everyone called them. One had to remember they were wild creatures, big mammals, therefore to be loved. That vivid embrace with the doe. It was an old mistake not to value the common wildlife. They did that with people and look at the result.

So: deer; the occasional porcupine; foxes; once a bobcat; and birds. They were almost back to the old depopulate forest from the time before the flood. Frank found this depressing. He grew almost to hate the sight of the deer, as they were in some sense the cohort of humans, part of humanity's own overpopulation surge. Then again, having them around beat a forest entirely empty; and from time to time he would catch a glimpse of something *other*. Brindled fur, striped flank, flash of color like a golden tamarind monkey; these and other brief signs of hidden life appeared. Because of the road bridges, Roosevelt Island was not really an island after all, but a sort of big wilderness peninsula. In that sense Teddy Roosevelt had the greatest D.C. monument of them all.

But on this day, as they were paddling back from the upstream tip of the island to the boathouse, Frank felt cold water gushing over his feet, thighs, and butt, all at once—catastrophic leak! "Hey!" he shouted, and then he had to hurry to wiggle out of the kayak's skirt and into the river. It really was coming in fast. Nothing for it but to start swimming, Charlie and Drepung there by his side, full of concern, and close enough that Frank was able to hold on to Charlie's stern end with one hand, and grasp the sunken bow of his kayak in the other, and kick to keep his position as the link between the two as Charlie dug in and paddled them back across the river to their dock. Cold but not frigid. Suddenly swimming! As if in San Diego. But the river water tasted silty.

Back on the dock they hauled Frank's kayak up and turned it over to drain it and inspect the bottom. Up near the very front, the hull had split along the midline, gaping wide enough to let in the water that had sunk it. "Factory defect," Frank said with quick disapproval. "Look, it split a seam. It must have been a bad melt job. I'll have to give the kayak company some grief about a defect like that."

"I should say so!" Charlie exclaimed. "Are you okay?"

"Sure. I'm just wet. I'll go get a change of clothes from my car." And Frank rolled the kayak back over, noting that neither Charlie or Drepung seemed aware that this kayak, like most, was a single cast piece of plastic, with no seam on the keel to delaminate. They took his explanation at face value, it appeared.

Which was a relief to him, as it would have been hard to find any way to explain why someone would want to melt a weakness into his kayak, a flaw that would crack under the pressure of his paddling. He was having a hard time with that himself.

He opened his van and got out a change of clothes, looking around at the interior of the van curiously, feeling more and more worried—worried and angry both. Someone trying to harass him—to intimidate him—but why? What reaction did they want to induce from him, if any? And how could he counter them without falling into that particular reaction?

Caroline's ex—that face, sneering over the shoulder as he descended into the Metro. And Frank had thrown the hand axe at him. Suddenly the feeling came over Frank, in a wave, that he would throw it again if he had the chance. He wanted the chance. He realized he was furious and trying not to feel that. Also scared—mainly for Caroline, but for himself too. Who knew what this asshole would do?

He changed clothes in his van, made the short drive up Rock Creek Parkway to the zoo, parked off Broad Branch and walked through the green trees out to Connecticut Avenue and the Delhi Dabai. He found himself inside, seated at a corner table looking at a menu, and realized he had not decided a single move since leaving the boathouse. It had been automatic pilot; but now he had a menu to choose from, and he couldn't. Decision trees. The automatic pilot was gone. Something hot and angry; just order the curry like always. Indigestion before he had even started eating. Off again through the early evening. The days were getting longer, the temperature balmy. Twilight spent at the overlook, checking out the salt lick at the bottom of the ravine. Big bodies in the infrared. Most were white-tailed deer, but not all. Ethiopian antelope; ibex; hedgehog. Rock Creek was still the epicenter of the feral population.

Back in his van he found the engine wouldn't start. Startled, he cursed, jumped out, looked under the hood.

The battery cables had been cut.

He tried to collect his thoughts. He looked up and down the dark streets. The van had been parked more or less at random, and locked. No way to get the hood up without getting inside the van; no way of getting into the van without a key. Well, dealers had master keys. Presumably spooks did too.

This must mean that Edward Cooper knew who he was. Knew that he was Caroline's helper, and no doubt presumed to be more; the man who had thrown a rock at his head, etc. Had him chipped or at least his van.

The hair on the back of Frank's neck prickled. His feet were cold. He looked around casually as he called AAA on his FOG phone and waited for a tow. When the guy in the tow truck took a look under the hood, he said "Ha." He took out his toolbox, installed a replacement cable. Frank thanked him, signed, got in the driver's seat; the engine coughed and started. Back out to the Khembalis' farm. He didn't know what else to do.

That night as he turned the matter over in his mind, he began to get both angrier and more frightened. If they had found him, did that mean they had found Caroline too? And if so what would they do? Where would they stop? What was their point?

And *where was Caroline?*

He had to talk to Edgardo again.

So he did, out on their lunch run the very next day. They ran down the Mall toward the Lincoln Memorial. It was a good running route, almost like a track: two miles from the Capitol to the Lincoln Memorial, on grass or decomposed granite all the way. There were other runners in the White House compound, and sometimes they went out with some OMB guys, but Edgardo and Frank now usually ran by themselves. It wasn't the same without Kenzo and Bob and the others, but it was what they had, and it gave them the chance to talk.

They had run a chip wand over each other before taking off, and after they got going Frank described what was happening.

"My computer crash could have been them too. Maybe they were erasing signs that they had broken into my system."

"Maybe," Edgardo was shaking his head back and forth like Stevie Wonder, his lips pursed unhappily. "I agree, if they are the ones vandalizing your stuff, then they must have found out you're the one who helped Caroline get away. But I'm wondering how they did that, if they did."

"And if they've managed to relocate Caroline as well."

"That doesn't follow," Edgardo pointed out. "You're not trying to hide, and she is."

"I know. I'm just wondering. I'm worried. Because I don't know how they found me."

They pounded on a few paces thinking about it.

"Do you have no way of getting in contact with her?"

"No."

"You need that. That should be a normal part of the repertory. Next time she contacts you, you have to tell her you need a dead drop, or a dedicated cell phone, or some other way to get in touch with her."

"I said that up on Mount Desert Island, believe me."

"She was reluctant?"

"I guess. She said she would get in touch with me. But that was four months ago."

"Hmm."

More running. Now they had been out long enough that Frank had begun to sweat.

Edgardo said, "I wonder. You said she said she is surveiling her ex. So I wonder if you can use that surveillance of hers, and tap into it to get a message to her."

"Like . . . pin a message to his door, and hope she'll see it and read it on camera before he gets home?"

"Well, something like that. You could show up at his doorstep, hold up a sign, then off you go. Your gal can stop her video, if she's got one there, and read what you've said."

"What if he's got a camera on his place too?"

"Well, yes, but would he watch himself like that? I'm not sure too many people take things that far."

"I guess not. Anyway it's an idea. Even if he saw it too, he wouldn't know any more than he did before. I'll think about it."

"Good. You might also go back up and check that place in Maine, especially if nothing else works. If she liked it as much as she said she did, maybe she's gone back there, or stayed all along. Sometimes being close to where you were, but not too close, is the best place to hide."

"Interesting," Frank said. "I'd have to be sure not to lead him back to her though."

"Yes."

A few more strides. Frank shook his head, snorted unhappily. "It's too complicated, this surveillance stuff. I hate it. I just want to be able to call her."

"You need a dead drop system. They're easy to set up, even within the current tech."

"Yeah, but I need to find her first."

"Yeah yeah. You need to change vans too, if that's really how they followed you north. My friend still doesn't believe that."

"Yeah well they just found it again. I should get rid of it."

"Wait till you need to get clear, then buy an old one for cash. Or just go without a car."

"I need a car! I need a van, actually. God damn it."

"Let's just run. That's all the going round and round we need right now."

"Okay. Sorry. Thanks."

"No problem. We will figure something out and prevail. The world and your love life deserve no less."

"Shit."

"Did you schedule a time for that nasal surgery yet?"

"No! Let's just run!"

THE FEELING OF HELPLESSNESS and indecision grew in him until he couldn't sleep at night. You had to decide to sleep a night through. In one of the long cold insomniac hours, listening unhappily to Rudra's uneven snore, he realized he had to do something about finding Caroline, no matter how futile it might be, just to give himself some small release from the anxiety of the situation. So the next night, after Rudra fell asleep, he drove to Bethesda, and at three a.m. parked and got out, and walked quickly up the empty streets to the apartment building that Caroline and her ex had lived in before her disappearance.

All empty. Streetlight across the street from the building; a dim doorway light illuminating the steps of the building. If Caroline had the place under surveillance then she would presumably have some kind of motion sensor on her camera or her data. If she saw him in that doorway, she would know that he wanted her to contact him. He was afraid that there might also be a security camera of some kind on the building, perhaps monitored by Caroline's ex. It would make sense, if you were in that line of work and thinking along those lines. Well, shit. She definitely was surveiling the building, her ex only possibly. It had to be tried.

He walked deliberately up to the steps of the place, looked at the address panel as if seeking a name. Shaking his head slightly, he looked out at the street and the buildings across the street, said "call me," feeling awkward. Then off again into the night. Lots of people had to come to that door, and some would be lost, or just looking randomly at things. It was the best he could do. He couldn't decide whether it was adequate or not. When he tried to figure out what to do he felt sick to his stomach.

He went to work the next day wondering if she would see him. Wondering where she was and what she was thinking. Wondering how she could stay away from him so long. He wouldn't have done it to her.

At work they were getting things done while still settling into the Old Executive Offices. Diane and the others were obviously pleased to be there. It still amazed Frank that physical proximity mattered in questions of influence and power within the executive branch. It was as clear a sign of their primate nature as any he could think of, as it made no sense given current technology. But some previous president had kicked his science advisor out of the Old Executive Offices, and so Phil Chase's immediate order that it return to the fourth floor of the old monstrosity, and take up one whole wing, had been an excellent sign. And there was even a practical sense in which it was useful, in that once inside the security barrier of the White House compound they were free to walk next door any time they wanted, to consult in person with the president's various staffers, or even with the man himself, if it should come to that.

Their new building was officially named after Eisenhower, but in practice always referred to by its older name, the Old Executive Offices. It was spectacularly ugly on the outside, disfigured by many pairs of nonfunctional pillars, some rising from ground level to the third floor, others filling embrasures on the upper stories, and all blackened as if by one of London's coal smogs. Frank had never seen anything like it.

Inside it was merely a very old musty office complex, retrofitted for modern conveniences a few too many years before, and otherwise about as moldy and dim as the outside of the hulk might suggest. In physical terms it was a real step down for those coming from the light-filled tower that NSF occupied in Arlington, but the political coup for science meant no complaints. All they really needed were rooms with electrical outlets and high-speed internet access, and these they had. And it had to be admitted that it was an interesting thing to look out one's window and see the business side of the White House right there across a little concrete gap. The seat of power itself; and thus a sign that Phil Chase understood the importance of science in their current crisis. Which was an encouragement to them to throw themselves into things even more intently than before.

So, at least, Diane seemed to take it. She had commandeered one of the offices with a window facing the White House, and set her desk in such a way that she saw it when she looked to her right. She did not actually see Phil Chase, he was so busy, but he sent e-mail questions on a regular basis, and Charlie Quibler and the rest of his staffers concerned with environmental questions were always dropping by.

Her main conference room was across the hall from her office, and as soon as it was properly outfitted, she convened the climate group to discuss their next moves.

Frank took notes doggedly, trying to stay focused. It looked like the Arctic ice would not break up this summer, which would set a base for an even thicker layer next winter. This meant that the northern extension of the Gulf Stream would probably be salty for the next few seasons, which meant the Gulf Stream's petawatt per year of heat would again be transferred twenty degrees of latitude north, and this in turn would bring heat back to the Arctic, and contribute again to the ongoing overall warming that despite the harsh winters in the eastern half of North America and in Europe was still dominating world weather. To Frank it was beginning to look like a lose-lose situation, in that no matter what they did, things were likely to degrade. It was a war of feedback loops, and very difficult to model. Kenzo pointed to the graphs on his last slide and simply shrugged. "I don't know," he said. "Nobody knows. There are too many factors in play now. Cloud action by itself is enough to confound most of the models. The one thing I can say for sure is that we need to reduce carbon emissions as soon as possible. We're in damage control mode at best, until we get to clean energy and transport. The sea water pH change alone is a huge problem, because if the ocean food chain collapses because of that, well, then..."

"Can that danger be quantified?" Diane asked.

"Sure, they are trying. Lots of the finest seashells are dissolved by what we're seeing already, but it may be that more resilient ones will bloom to fill the niche. So we have some parameters, but it's all pretty loose. What's clear is that if the plankton and the coral reefs both die, the oceans could go catastrophic. A major mass extinction, and there's no recovering from that. Not in less than several million years."

Unlike his pronouncements on the weather, Kenzo exhibited none of his usual happy air, of an impresario with a particularly spectacular circus. This stuff could not possibly be interpreted as some kind of fun, too-interesting-to-be-lamented event; this was simply bad, even dire. To see Kenzo actually being grave startled Frank, even frightened him. Kenzo Hayakawa, making a dire warning? Could there be a worse sign?

And yet there were ongoing matters to attend to, new things to try. The springtime reports from Siberia indicated that the altered lichens the Russians had released the previous summer were continuing to grow faster than predicted. "Like pond scum," as one of the Russian scientists reported. This was very unlike the pace of growth and dispersion for ordinary lichens, and seemed to confirm the suggestion that the bioengineered version was behaving more like an algae or a fungus than like the symbiosis of the two typically did. That was interesting, perhaps ominous; Kenzo thought it could cause a major carbon drawdown from the atmosphere if it continued. "Unless it kills the whole Siberian forest, and then who knows? Maybe instead of gray goo, we die by green goo, eh?"

"Please, Kenzo."

On other fronts the news was just as ambiguous. Vicious infighting at the

Department of Energy, the nuclear folks still doing their best to forestall the alternatives crowd; Diane was trying to convince the president to order Energy to develop clean energy ASAP—first finding bridge technologies, moving away from what they had now while still using it—then the next real thing, the next iteration on the way to a completely sustainable technology. Diane thought it would take two or three major iterations. Lots of federal agencies would have to be entrained to this effort, of course, but DOE was crucial, given that energy was at the heart of their problem. But all this would depend on who Phil appointed to be the new Energy Secretary. If that person were on board with the program, off they would all go; if opposed, more war of the agencies. One could only hope that Phil would not tie down his people in such a self-defeating way. But campaign debts were owed, and Big Oil had a lot of people still in positions of great power. And Phil had not yet appointed his Energy Secretary.

After a meeting running over the list of possible candidates for this crucial cabinet position, Diane came by Frank's new office, which had no living-room feel whatsoever—in fact it looked like he had been condemned to clerk in some bureaucratic hell, right next to Bob Cratchit or Bartelby the Scrivener.

Even Diane seemed to notice this, to the point of saying "It's a pretty weird old facility."

"Yes. I don't think I'll ever like it like I did NSF."

"That turned out pretty well, in terms of the building. Although that too was a political exile."

"So Anna told me."

"Want to go out and hunt for a new coffee place?"

"Sure."

Frank got his windbreaker from its hook and they left the building and then the compound. Just south of the White House was the Ellipse, and then the Washington Monument, towering over the scene like an enormous sundial on an English lawn. The buildings around the White House included the Treasury, the World Bank, and any number of other massive white buildings, filling the blocks so that every street was as if walled. These big expanses of granite and concrete and marble were very bad in human terms; even Arlington was better.

But there were many coffee shops and delis tucked into the ground floor spaces, and so the two of them hiked around in an oblong pattern, looking at the possibilities and chatting. Nothing looked appealing, and finally Diane suggested one of the little National Park tourist kiosks out on the Mall itself. They were already east of the White House, and when they came out on the great open expanse into the low sun they could see much of official Washington, with the Capitol and the Washington Monument towering over everything else. That was the dominant impression Frank had of downtown at this point; the feel of it was determined principally by the height limit, which held all private buildings to a maximum of twelve stories, well under the height of the Washington Monument. The downtown was as if sheered off by a knife at that height, an unusual sight in a modern city, giving it a strangely nineteenth-century look, as for instance Paris right before the arrival of the Eiffel Tower. Once away from the federal district, this invisible ceiling gave things a more human scale than the skyscraper downtowns of other cities, and Frank liked that quality, even though the result was squat or unwieldy.

Diane nodded as he tried to express these mixed feelings. She pointed out the lion statues surrounding Ulysses S. Grant in front of the Capitol: "See, they're Disney lions!"

"Like the ones on the Connecticut Avenue bridge."

"I wonder which came first, Disney or these guys?"

"These must have, right?"

"I don't know. Disney lions have looked the same at least since *Dumbo*."

"Maybe Disney came here and saw these."

Within a week or so they had worked up a new traditional walk together. One afternoon as they drank their coffee, Diane suggested they return to work by way of a pass through the National Gallery annex; and there they found a Frederic Church exhibit. "Hey!" Frank said, and then had to lie a little bit, explaining that he had learned about Church on Mount Desert Island, long ago. As they walked through he remembered his intense time on the island, which he now saw through the eyes of the painter who had invented rusticating. His paintings were superb, far better than Bierstadt or Homer or any other American landscape artist Frank had ever seen. Church had been able to put an almost photorealist technique in the service of a Transcendentalist eye; it was the visionary, sacred landscape of Emerson and Thoreau, right there on the walls of the National Gallery. "My God," Frank said more than once. This was also the time of Darwin and Humboldt; indeed the wall-sized "Heart of the Andes," fifteen feet high and twenty wide, stood there like some stupendous Power-Point slide illustrating all of natural selection at once, both data and theory.

"My—God."

"It's like the IMAX movie of its time," Diane said.

In the rooms beyond they saw Church travel and grow old, and become almost hallucinogenic in his coloring, like Galen Rowell after he discovered Fujichrome. These were the best landscape paintings Frank had ever seen. A giant close-up of the water leaping off the lip of Niagara Falls; the Parthenon at sunset; waves striking the Maine coast; every scene leaped off the wall, and Frank goggled at them. Diane laughed at him, but he could not restrain himself. How had he never been exposed to such an artist as this? What was American education anyway, that they could all grow up and not be steeped in Emerson and Thoreau and Audubon and Church? It was like inheriting billions and then forgetting it.

Then Diane put her hand to his arm and directed him out of the gallery and back toward their new office. Back into the blackened old building, if not arm in arm, then shoulder to shoulder.

Their meeting that evening had to do with the latest from Antarctica, compiled by NSF's Antarctic division from the austral summer just past.

Much of the research had been devoted to trying to determine how much of the West Antarctic Ice Sheet might come off, and how fast it would happen. The abstract of the summary made it clear that the several big ice streams that ran like immense glaciers through more stationary parts of the ice sheet had accelerated yet again, beyond even the earlier two accelerations documented in previous decades. The first acceleration had followed the rapid detachment of the two big floating ice shelves, the Ross and the Weddell. Their absence had destabilized the grounding line of the WAIS, which rested on land that was a bit below sea level, and so was susceptible at the edges to the lifting of tides and tearing of currents. As the ice margins tore away and followed the ice shelves out to sea, that exposed more grounded ice to the same tides and currents.

What they had found this last summer was that all Antarctic temperatures, in air, water, and ice, had risen, and this was allowing melt water on the surface of the WAIS to run down holes and cracks, where it froze and split the ice around it further. When this "water wedging" reached all the way through the ice it poured down and pooled underneath, thus floating the broken ice a bit and lubricating its slide into the sea.

Why the ice streams moved so much faster than the surrounding ice was still not fully understood, but some were now postulating under-ice watersheds, where melt water was flowing downstream, carrying the ice over it along. This would explain why the ice streams were now acting more like rivers than glaciers. There were different hydrodynamics resulting in different speeds.

Diane interrupted the two glaciologists making the report before they got too deep into the mysteries of their calling. "So what kind of sea-level rise are we looking at?" she asked. "How much, and when?"

The glaciologists and the NOAA people looked around at each other, then made a kind of collective shrug. Frank grinned to see it.

"It's difficult to say," one finally ventured. "It depends so much on stuff we don't know."

"Give me parameters then, and your best bets."

"Well, I don't know, I'm definitely getting out of my comfort zone here, but I'd say as much as half of the ice sheet could detach in the next several years. That would be down the middle on the Ross Sea side, where there's a big trough under Ice Stream B. All that could flood and the ice get tugged away. Here, and here," red-lighting the map like a kid waving a penlight, "are under-ice ranges connecting the Peninsular Range and the Transantarctics, and those create catchment basins which will probably anchor a good bit of these regions," making big red circles. Having made his ignorance disclaimer, he was now carving the map like a geography teacher. Diane ignored this discrepancy, as did everyone else; it was understood that they were now guessing, and that his red circles were not data, but rather him thinking aloud.

"So—that implies what, a couple-few meters of sea-level rise?"

"A couple."

"So, okay. That's pretty bad. Time scales, again?"

"Hard to say? Maybe—if these rates hold—thirty years? Fifty?"

"Okay. Well . . ." Diane looked around the room. "Any thoughts?"

"We can't afford a sea-level rise that high."

"Better get used to it! It's not like we can stop it."

They turned with renewed interest to Frank's suggestion of flooding the world's desertified lake basins. The discussion went over the parts of an informal NSF study which suggested that big salt lakes would indeed cause clouds and precipitation downwind, so that watersheds to the east would receive more water. Local weather patterns would change with the general rise in humidity, but as they were changing anyway, the changes might be hard to distinguish from the background. Ultimate effects impossible to predict. Frank noted how many studies were coming to that conclusion. Like all of them, when it came to weather. It was like nerve damage.

They looked at each other. Maybe, someone suggested, if that's what it takes to save the seacoasts from flooding, the global community would compensate the new lakes' host nations for whatever environmental damage was assessed. Possibly a sea water market could be established along with the carbon market; possibly they could be linked. Surely the most prosperous quarter of humanity could find ways to compensate the people, often poor, who would be negatively impacted by the creation of these reservoirs.

Frank said, "We've tried some back-of-the-envelope numbers, estimating the capital worth of the major port cities and other coastal development, and got figures like five hundred trillion dollars."

General Wracke, an active member of Diane's advisory group, put his hands together reverently. "A half a quadrillion dollars," he said, grinning. "That's a lot of construction funding."

"Yes. On the other hand, for comparison purposes, the infrastructural value of property in the superdry basins of Africa, Asia, and the American basin and range comes to well under ten billion, unless you throw in Salt Lake City, which actually has a legal limit on the books as to how high the Great Salt Lake is allowed to rise, that isn't much higher than it is now. Anyway, in global terms, statistically, there's nothing out there in those basins. Statistically insignificant populations to displace, possibility of building new settlements by new water. Local weather deranged, but it is already. So . . ."

The general nodded and asked about pumping water back up onto the Eastern Antarctic Ice Sheet, which was very high and stable. Some of the NSF report was devoted to this question. The pumped sea water would freeze and then sit unconformably as a kind of salty ice cap on the fresh ice cap. Every cubic kilometer of sea water placed up there would reduce sea level by that same amount, without the radical changes implied by creating new salt seas all across the thirties north and south. Could only pump half of the year using solar power.

The energy requirements needed to enact the lift and transfer remained a stumbling block; they would have to build many powerful clean energy systems. But they had to do that anyway, as several of them pointed out. The easy oil would soon be gone, and burning the oil and coal that was left would cook the world. So if some combination of sunlight, wind, wave, tide, currents, nuclear, and geothermal power could be harnessed, this would not only replace the burning of fossil fuels, which was imperative anyway, but possibly save sea level as well.

Some there advocated nuclear for the power they needed, others called for fusion. But others held fast for the clean renewables. The advocates of tidal power asserted that new technologies were already available and ready to be ramped up, technologies almost as simple as Archimedes' screw in concept, relying on turbines and pumps made of glassy metals that would be impervious to sea water corrosion. Anchor these units in place and the ocean would flow through them and power would be generated. It was only a matter of making the necessary investment and they would be there.

"But where's the money going to come from?" someone asked.

"The military budgets of the world equal about a trillion dollars a year," Frank noted, "half of that coming from the United States. Maybe we can't afford to throw that work away anymore. Maybe the money could be reallocated. And we do need a really big manufacturing capacity here. What if the entire military-industrial complex, funded by these enormous budgets, were redirected to the projects we are outlining? How long would it take for the global effects to be measurable?"

Dream on, someone muttered.

Others thought it over, or punched numbers into their handhelds, testing out possibilities. Of course redirecting the military budgets of the world was "unrealistic." But it was worth bringing it up, Frank judged, to suggest the size of the world's industrial capacity. What could be done if humanity were not trapped in its own institutions? "To wrest Freedom from the grasp of Necessity," Frank said. "Who said that?"

People in the meeting were beginning to look at him strangely again. Dream on, oh desperate fool, their looks said. But it wasn't just him who was desperate.

"You're beginning to sound like the Khembalis," Anna said. But she liked that, she was pleased by that. And if Anna approved, Frank felt he must in some sense be on the right track.

By the time they were done with that meeting it was late, the wind barreling through the empty streets of the federal district.

"What about dinner?" Diane said to Frank when they had a moment in private, and Frank nodded. She said, "I still don't know any restaurants around here, but we can look."

"Maybe over toward the Capitol. For some reason the whole area around George Washington University is pretty dead this late at night, I don't know why."

"Let's see what we find."

And off they went, on another date in the nation's capital.

It was a fun date. They found a Greek restaurant, and sat across a little table and talked over the meeting and the day and everything else. Frank drank a glass of retsina, a glass of ouzo, and a cup of Greek coffee, all while wolfing down dolmades, sliced octopus arms in oil, and moussaka. He laughed a lot. Looking across the table at Diane's round face, so vivacious and intelligent, so charismatic and powerful, he thought: I love this woman.

He could not think about the feeling. He shied away from the thought and just felt it. Everything else at the moment was unreal, or at least nonpresent. He focused on the present in the way Rudra was always encouraging him to do. The advantages of such a focus were evident in a certain calmness that spread through him, a feeling that might have been happiness. Or maybe it was the food, the alcohol, the caffeine. The tastes and looks and sounds. Her face. Were those what happiness consisted of? A smile, a glance, as the old man had said—what ample borrowers of eternity they are!

Afterward they walked back to the compound, and Frank walked her to her car in the underground parking lot.

"Good night, that was nice."

"Yes it was." She looked up and Frank leaned over, their lips met in a perfect little kiss, and off he went.

He drove to the Khembali farm with his heart all aflutter. He didn't know what he thought. Rudra was asleep and he was glad, and then sorry. He tried to sleep and could not sleep. Finally he sat up and turned on his laptop.

Thoreau was a solitary. He fell in love with his brother's girlfriend, and proposed to her after his brother had proposed to her and been turned down. Henry too was turned down. There were rumors the girl's father did not think the Thoreaus were good enough. But if she had insisted . . . Anyway Henry became a solitary. "There was a match found for me at last. I fell in love with a shrub oak."

That night the website had something from his journal:

I spend a considerable portion of my time observing the habits of the wild animals, my brute neighbors. By their various movements and migrations they fetch the year about to me. Very significant are the flight of the geese and the migration of suckers, etc., etc. But when I consider that the nobler animals have been exterminated here,—the cougar, panther, lynx, wolverine, wolf, bear, moose, deer, the beaver, the turkey, etc., etc.,—I cannot but feel as if I lived in a tamed, and, as it were, emasculated country. Would not the motions of those larger and wilder animals have been more significant still? Is it not a maimed and imperfect nature that I am conversant with? As if I were to study a tribe of Indians that had lost all its warriors. When I think what were the various sounds and notes, the migrations and works, and changes of fur and plumage which ushered in the spring and marked the other seasons of the year, I am reminded that this my life in nature, this particular round of natural phenomena which I call a year, is lamentably incomplete. I list to a concert in which so many parts are wanting. The whole civilized country is to some extent turned into a city, and I am that citizen whom I pity. All the great trees and beasts, fishes and fowl are gone.

From his journal, March 23, 1856; he had been thirty-eight years old. What would he think now, after another century and a half of destruction and loss? Maybe he would not have been surprised. He had seen it already started. Frank groaned.

"What wrong?"

"Oh nothing. Sorry I woke you."

"I was not sleeping. I don't sleep much."

"You sounded like you were sleeping."

"No."

"Maybe you were dreaming."

"No. What wrong?"

"I was thinking about all the animals that are in trouble. In danger of extinction. Thoreau was writing about the predators being wiped out."

"Ah well. You still see animals in park?"

"Yes, but mostly just deer now."

"Ah well."

Rudra fell back asleep. After a while Frank drifted into uneasy dreams. Then he was awake again and thinking about Diane. He wasn't going to fall asleep; it was four. He got up and made his way out of the treehouse and across the farm to his van. Back into the city, down Connecticut from the already-crowded Beltway. Left on Brandywine, park on Linnean, get out and cross Broad Branch, and thus out into Rock Creek Park.

He hiked around the rim of the new gorge, and saw nothing but a single deer. He hiked up to Fort de Russey, back down on the eastern wild way, and saw nothing but a trio of deer, standing upslope like wary statues. He decided as he watched them that he would be the predator—that he would scare these creatures, and at the same time test his ability, and see how long he could keep them in sight, not as a stalker, but a predator in pursuit. He set the timer on his wristwatch to zero, clicked it and took off after them, up the open forest floor with its black soil underfoot, sprinting hard. They bolted over the nearest ridge, he flew up to it—no deer to be seen! Empty forest! But where had they—he stopped his watch. 4.82 seconds. He barked a laugh and stood there for a while, panting.

When he started walking again he headed toward Site 21, to see if the guys were there and check in with his treehouse.

Except from a distance he saw that something was wrong with it. He ran to it, trying to understand the gap in the air. When he got to it he saw it had been cut down.

He inspected the trunk. Cut by a chain saw, a smallish one it seemed by the sweep of the cut marks. The tree had fallen across Rock Creek; you could have used the trunk as a bridge over the stream. Maybe someone had needed a bridge. But no. You could cross the creek almost anywhere.

The treehouse itself was part of the wreckage on the other bank. At some point last year he had removed all of his gear except for the winch.

He crossed the creek on his boulder path, took a look; the winch was now gone. Only the plywood sheets and two-by-fours were left, all now horribly askew, with some of the plywood loose on the ground.

He sat down next to these fragments. They were just sticks. He was never going to have lived in this treehouse again. So it didn't matter.

Edward Cooper had probably done this, or had it done. Of course it might have been total strangers, looking to scavenge whatever the treehouse might have held, like for instance the winch. Surely this Cooper would have left the winch as part of his revenge, as mockery. But maybe not. He didn't really know. There seemed to be a pattern—computer, kayak, van. His stuff and his life. It looked like deliberate action.

He didn't know what to do.

ONE SATURDAY THE QUIBLERS got to a project they had been planning for some time, which was the installation of garden beds in the backyard. No more suburban lawn wasting their yard space!

And indeed it was a great pleasure to Charlie to cut big rectangles of turf out of the backyard and wheelbarrow these out to the street for disposal by the composting trucks. He was sick of mowing that yard. There was some old lumber stacked at the back of the garage, and now he and Nick laid lengths of it down in the remaining lawn to serve as borders. Then they transferred many wheelbarrow loads of expensive amended soil from the pile in the driveway where the dump trunk had left it, around the house to the rectangles, dodging Joe at many points along the way. The resulting raised beds were loamy and black and looked highly productive and artificial. The grass in between the beds was going to be difficult to cut, Charlie realized, and he envisioned transitioning entirely to mulch between the beds as the seasons went by, leaving only a decorative border of grass around the beds.

Nick and Anna were now working the soil in, and planting their first vegetables. It was full spring now, middle of May, steamy and green, and so they planted the usual summer vegetables: tomatoes, zucchini, strawberries, peppers, pumpkins, melons, basil, eggplant, cilantro, cucumbers.

Nick stood looking down at a broccoli plant, small and delicate between his feet. "So where will the broccoli come out?" he asked Charlie.

Charlie stared at the plant. It looked like an ornamental. "I don't know," he confessed, feeling a little stab of fear. They didn't know anything.

Nick rolled his eyes. "Well, if we're lucky they won't show up at all."

"Come on now. Broccoli is good for you."

One of their agreements was that they would plant vegetables that Nick and Joe liked to eat, which was a severe constraint, but one they had agreed to, because it was not exclusive; they were planting for Anna and Charlie too. But for the boys it was mostly down to potatoes, an entire bed of them, and carrots. Joe would eat some other vegetables, but Nick would not, and so he was put in charge of the carrot bed. These were to be planted from seed, and apparently the soil had to be specially amended. Sandy soil was best, and white cloth laid over the soil during the germination was recommended—by Drepung, anyway, who was serving as their consultant on this project.

"Although it shouldn't be me," he kept saying, "I don't know anything about gardening really, it's all Qang at our place, you should have her over to do things like plant carrot seed. I think that one is tricky. She would do a fire puja and everything."

Still, he helped them to get it planted and covered, on his hands and knees digging happily, and showing worms to Joe. After the planting it was mostly a matter of watering and weeding. Also removing snails and slugs. Joe carried these carefully to the back of their lot, where they could start life over in the weeds bordering the lawn.

"Don't overwater," Charlie advised Nick. "You don't want to drown things in their beds. You have to be precise in how much you water them. I estimate about say this much, if you want to be accurate."

"Do you mean accurate or precise?" Anna asked from the new flower bed.

"No quibbling allowed."

"I'm not quibbling! It's an important distinction."

"Hello, what do you mean? Accurate and precise mean the precisely same thing!"

"They do not."

"What do you mean," Charlie was giggling at her now, "how so?"

"Accuracy," she said, "means how close an estimate is to the true value. So if you estimate something is five percent and it turns out to be eight percent, then you weren't very accurate."

"This is statistics."

"Yes, it is. And precision refers to how broad your estimate is. Like, if you estimate something is between five and eight percent, then you aren't being very precise, but if you say a range is between 4.9 and 5.1 percent, then it's a more precise estimate."

"I see," Charlie said, nodding solemnly.

"Quit it! It's a very important distinction!"

"Of course it is. I wasn't laughing at that."

"At what then?"

"At you!"

"But why?"

"Oh, no reason."

"It is a real distinction," Nick pointed out to Charlie.

"Oh of course, of course!"

So this then became one of the recurrent motifs of the Quiblers on patrol, a distinction applicable, once you agreed it existed, to an amazing number of situations. Cell-phone call to fine-tune the grocery list, with one of them in the store and one at home; get some potatoes. How many? Get about half a dozen potatoes. Was that being accurate or precise? Or when someone was re-marking that Nick was a very precise person, Charlie quipped, "He's not pre-cise, he's accurate." And so on.

On the way back to the garden-supply store, to get more plants and stakes and other supplies, Charlie said, "I wonder how many cubic feet of compost we need if we want to cover all four of the beds, let's see, they're six by twelve, say a foot deep in compost, make it simple...."

"Mom can tell you."

"No that's all right, I'm working on it—"

"Two hundred and eighty-eight cubic feet," Anna said, while driving.

"I told you she would."

"It isn't fair," Charlie said, still looking at his fingers. "She uses all these tricks from when she was in math club."

"Come on," Anna said.

Nick was helpless with laughter. "Yeah, right, Dad—she uses all these clever fiendish tricks—like *multiplication,*" and he and Anna laughed all the way to the store.

Unfortunately their new spring quickly became the hottest and driest on record in the Potomac watershed, and soon, it having been a dry winter on the whole, the region had to resort to water rationing. Between that and the mos-quitoes, everyone began to reminisce with affection about the long winter, and wonder if it had been such a good idea to restart the Gulf Stream, since cold winters were so much preferable to drought. Crops were dying, the rivers falling low, streams drying out entirely, fish populations dying with them; it was bad. A bit of snow and cold temperatures would have been easy in com-parison. You could always throw on more clothes when it got cold, but in this heat!

But of course now they didn't have a choice.

The Quiblers did what they could to micro-irrigate their crops, and they had enough water to water such a small garden; but many of the plants died anyway. "We're only going to have about a fifty percent survival rate, if that!"

"Is that being accurate or being precise?"

"I hope neither!"

Anna was going to websites like safeclimate.net or fightglobalwarming.com and comparing how they rated when she entered their household statistics on a carbon-burning chart. She was interested in the different methods they were using. Some accepted general descriptions as answers, others wanted the fig-ures from your heating and electric bill, your car's odometer and its real miles per gallon. Your actual air travel miles; charts of distances between major flying destinations were given. "The air travel is killer," Anna muttered. "I thought it was a really energy-efficient way to travel."

Giving her numbers to play with was like giving catnip to the cats, and Charlie watched her affectionately, but with a little bit of worry, as she speed-typed around on a spreadsheet she had adapted from the chart. Despite their garden's contribution to their food supply, which she estimated at less than two percent of their caloric intake, and the flex schedule for power that they had signed up for with their power provider, still they were burning about 75 metric tons of carbon a year. Equivalent to eight football fields of Brazilian rain forest, the site said. Per year.

"You just can't get a good number in a suburban home with a car and all," she said, annoyed. "And if you fly at all."

"It's true." Charlie stared over her shoulder at her spreadsheet. "I don't see what else we can do here either, given the infrastructure."

"I know. But I wish there was a way. Nick! Turn that light off, please!"

"Mom, you're the one who told me to turn it on."

"That's when you were using it. Now you're not."

"Mom."

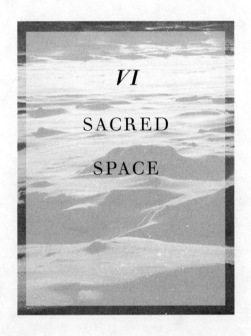

VI

SACRED

SPACE

B eing Argentine, he was angry. Not that all Argentines were angry but many were, and rightfully so, after all the mistakes and crimes, but especially after the dirty war and its dirty resolution—a general amnesty for everybody for everything, for anything, even the foulest crimes. In other words repression of the past and of even the idea of justice, and of course the return of the repressed is a guaranteed thing, and always a nightmare, a breakout of monsters.

So Edgardo Alfonso had left Argentina behind, like so many other children of the desaparecidos, unable to live among the torturers and murderers both known and unknown who were free to walk the streets of Buenos Aires and ride the trams, who stared at Edgardo over the edges of their newspapers which held on their backsides the articles Edgardo had written identifying and denouncing them. He had had to leave to remain sane.

So of course he was at the Kennedy Center to see an evening of Argentinean tango, Bocca's troupe out on Bocca's farewell world tour, where the maestro would dance with a ladder and handstand his way to heaven for one last time, to Piazzolla's "Soledad." Edgardo cared nothing for dance per se, and despised tango the dance the way certain Scottish acquaintances winced at the sound of bagpipes; but Edgardo was a Piazzollista, and so he had to go. It was not often one got a chance to hear Astor Piazzolla's music played live, and of course it would never be the same now that Astor was gone, but the proof of the strength of his composing was in how these new pickup bands backing the dance troupes would play their accompaniments to the dancers, tangos for the most part made of the utterly clichéd waltzes, two-steps, ballads, and church music that had been cobbled together to make old-style tango, and then they would start a piece by Astor and the whole universe would suddenly become bigger—deeper, darker, more tragic. A single phrase on the bandoneon and all of Buenos Aires would appear in the mind at once. The feeling was as accurate as if music possessed a kind of *acupuncture that could strike particular nerves of the memory and immediately evoke it all.*

The audience at the Kennedy Center was full of Latin Americans, and they watched the dancers against the black backdrop closely. Bocca was a good choreographer and the dances were insistent on being interesting— men with men, women with women, little fights, melodramas, clever sex— but all the while the band was hidden behind the black curtain at the back, and Edgardo began to get angry yet again, this time that someone would conceal performing musicians for so long. The itch of their absence bit into him and he began to hate the skillful dancers, he wanted to boo them off the stage, he even wondered for a second if the music had been prerecorded and this tour was being done on the cheap, like the Bolshoi in Europe in 1985.

Finally however they pulled back the curtain, and there was the band: bandoneon, violin, piano, bass, electric guitar. Edgardo already knew they were a very tight group, playing good versions of the Piazzolla songs, faithful to the original, and intense. Tight band, incandescent music—it was strange now to observe how young they were, and to see the odd contortions they had to make in order to get those sounds; strange but wonderful; music at last, the ultimate point of the evening. Huge relief.

They had been revealed in order to play "Adios Nonino," of course, Piazzolla's good-bye to his dead father, his most famous song out of the three thousand in his catalog, and even if not the best, or rather not Edgardo's favorite, which was "Mumuki" for sure, still it was the one with the most personal history. Edgardo's father had been disappeared. God knew what had happened to him, Edgardo resisted thinking about this as being part of the poison, part of the torture echoing down through the years and the generations, one of the many reasons torture was the worst evil of all, and, when the state used and condoned it, the death of a nation's sense of itself. This was why Edgardo had had to leave, also because his mother still met every Thursday afternoon in the Plaza de Mayo in Buenos Aires with all the other mothers and wives of the desaparecidos gathered in their white scarves, symbolic of their lost children's diapers, to remind Argentina and the world (and in Buenos Aires these two were the same) of the crimes that still needed to be remembered, and the criminals who still must face justice. It was more than Edgardo could face on a weekly basis. Now even in his nice apartment east of Dupont Circle he had to keep the blinds shut on Sunday mornings so as not to see the dressed-up, good, kindly Americans, mostly black, walking down the street to the corner church, so as not to start again the train of thought that would lead him to memories and the anger.

He had to look away or it would kill him. His health was poor. He had to run at least fifty miles a week to keep himself from dying of anger. If he didn't he couldn't sleep and quickly his blood pressure ballooned dangerously high. You could run a lot of anger out of you. For the rest, you needed Piazzolla.

His own father had taken him to see Piazzolla at the Teatro Odeon, in 1973, shortly before he had been disappeared. Piazzolla had five years before disbanded his great quintet and gone to Europe with Amelita, gone through the melodramas of that relationship and its breakup and a succession of bands trying to find a Europop sound, trying electronica and string quartets and getting angrier and angrier at the results (though they were pretty good, Edgardo felt), so that when he came back to Buenos Aires for the summer of 73–74 and regathered the old quintet (with the madman Tarantino sitting in on piano) he was not the same confident composer, devoted to destroying tango and rebuilding it from the ground up for the sake of his modernist musical ambitions, but a darker and more baffled man, an exile who was home again, but determined to forge on no matter what. But now more willing to admit the tango in him, Edgardo's father had explained, he was willing to admit his genius was Argentinean as well as transcendental. He could now submit to tango, fuse with it. And his audience was much changed as well, they no longer took Piazzolla for granted or thought he was a crazy egoist who had gone mad. With the quintet dispersed they had finally understood they had been seeing and hearing something new in the world, not just a genius but a great soul, and of course at that point, now that they had understood, it was gone.

But then it had come back. Maybe only for one night, everyone thought it was only for one night, everyone knew all of a sudden that life itself was a fragile and evanescent thing and no band lasted long, and so the atmosphere in the theater had been absolutely electric, the audience's attentiveness quivering and hallucinatory, the fierce applause like thanks in a church, as if finally you could do the right thing in a church and clap madly and cheer and whistle to show your appreciation of God's incredible work. At the end of the show they had leaped to their feet and gone mad with joy and regret, and looking around him young Edgardo had understood that adults were still as full of feeling as he was, that they did not "grow up" in any important respect and that he would never lose the huge feelings surging in him. An awesome sight, never to be forgotten. Perhaps it was his first real memory.

Now, here, on this night in Washington, D.C., the capital of everything and nothing, the dancers were dancing on the stage and the young band at the back was charging lustily through one of Piazzolla's angriest and happiest tunes, the furiously fast "Michelangelo 70." Beautiful. Astor had understood how to deal with the tragedy of Buenos Aires better than anyone, and Edgardo had never ceased to apply his lesson: you had to attack sadness and depression head-on, in a fury, you had to dance through it in a state of utmost energy, and then it would lead you out the other side to some kind of balance, even to that high humor that the racing tumble of bandoneon notes so often expressed, that joy that ought to be basic but in this world had to be achieved or as it were dragged out of some future better time: life ought to be joy, someday it would be joy, therefore on this night we celebrate that joy in anticipation and so capture an echo of it in advance of the fact, a kind of ricochet. That this was the best they could do in this supposedly advanced age of the world was funny in an awful way. And there weren't that many things that were both real and funny, so there you had to hang your hat, on how funny it was that they could be as gods in a world more beautiful and just than humanity could now imagine, and yet instead were torturers on a planet where half the people lived in extreme immiseration while the other half killed in fear of being thrust into that immiseration, and were always willing to look the other way, to avoid seeing the genocide and speciescide and biospherecide they were committing, all unnecessarily, out of fear and greed. Hilarious! One had to laugh!

During intermission the beautifully dressed people filled the halls outside and gulped down little plastic flutes of wine as fast as they could. The sound of three thousand voices all talking at once in a big enclosed space was perhaps the most beautiful music of all. That was always true, but on this night there was a lot of Spanish being spoken, so it was even more true than usual. A bouncing glossolalia. This was how the apostles had sounded when the tongues of fire had descended on them, all trying to express directly in scat singing the epiphany of the world's glory. One of Piazzolla's bandoneon lines even seemed to bounce through the talk. No doubt one appeal of that thin nasal tone was how human it sounded, like the voice of a lover with a cold.

And all the faces. Edgardo was on the balcony with his elbows resting on the railing, looking down at the crowd below, all the hair so perfect, the raven blaze of light on glossy black tresses, the colorful clothes, the strong faces so full of the character of Latin America. This was what they looked like, they had nothing to be ashamed of in this world, where indeed could you find handsomer faces.

His friend Umberto stood down there near the door, holding two wine flutes. When he looked up and met Edgardo's eye, Edgardo raised his chin in acknowledgment. Umberto jerked his head a fraction to the side, indicating a meeting; Edgardo nodded once.

In the second half the band was kept in view throughout the dances, and Edgardo was happier. Now the black curtain was his own eyelids, he could close them and ignore the dancers who were in any case making their limitations known, and only listen to the Piazzolla. The second half had four songs by Astor out of the eight, same as the first; this was typical in tango shows passing through the States on tour, sticking to the maestro to be sure of blowing away the audiences. In one case a touring troupe's leader had had some kind of a problem with Piazzolla, perhaps political in nature but probably mainly personal, the maestro could be withering, and so to avoid printing Piazzolla's name even though he was playing his music, this leader had printed no composers' names at all in the program book, a maneuver which had made Edgardo furious, although he had wanted to hear the music too much to able to walk out on the performance, because the band had been excellent, with four bandoneonists to re-create the effect Astor had made by himself. A better band even than on this night, though these young people were good, especially the young woman sawing away at her bass, amazing what a difference that made. And they were going to finish with the "Four Seasons of Buenos Aires," a suite of four pieces, one for each season, on the model of Vivaldi.

These were among Piazzolla's masterpieces, and Edgardo loved them all. Through all the years in Washington he had played the one that was appropriate to the season in the southern hemisphere, over and over, to keep himself properly oriented, or rather australized. Thus when Phil Chase had won the election he had been playing "Primavera Porteño" at high volume, because it was November, spring in Buenos Aires, and also perhaps on that night it marked a different kind of spring in the American political world, a much-needed birth of a new dispensation. Piazzolla had captured perfectly that magical budding sensation of springtime, the whole world quick with life and dancing.

Now it was baking summer in the world capital, a dry sauna with the rain gone, and at home he was playing "Invierno Porteño" to express the chill raw world to the south, and now the band was doing a very creditable job of it themselves, even the bandoneon player, who seemed suddenly possessed. And in the coda the pianist plinked the final falling trios of single notes in a perfect little ritard. Could be a lover walking away forever; could be the end of winter and thus the passing of another precious year. The two dancers sank to the floor in a knot—very nice, but not Edgardo's image of it. He closed his eyes again and listened to the band rip into "Primavera Porteño," the last one in the sequence. He bobbed and tapped his feet, eyes closed, uncaring about the people around him, let them think what they like, the whole audience should be on its feet at this moment.

Which they were during the ovation afterward, a nice thing to be part of, a Latin thing, lots of shouting and whistling in the applause, at least for an audience at the Kennedy Center. There was even a group above him to the right shouting "As-tor—As-tor—As-tor!" which Edgardo joined with the utmost happiness, bellowing the name up at the group of enthusiasts and waving in appreciation. He had never gotten the chance to chant Astor's name in a cheer before, and it felt right, it felt good in his mouth. He wondered if they did that in Buenos Aires now, or if it was only something that would happen in Europe, or here—Astor the perpetual exile, even in death. Well, but now he was a hero in Argentinean music, and the reason these tours were popular, that and the possibility of seeing some choreographed nudity and sex on stage, which of course was also a bit of a draw. But you could see more sex by accident on the internet in a night than tango would give you your whole life, unless you believed in sublimation— which Edgardo did. The return of the repressed was a volcanic thing, a matter of stupendous force blasting into the world. The giants unleashed. As America had yet to learn, alas, to its great confusion. It had repressed the reality of the rest of the world, and now the rest of the world was coming back.

Show over. All the people mingling as they made their exit. Outside it was still stifling. More Spanish in the gorgeous choir of the languages. Edgardo walked aimlessly in the crowd going north, then stopped briefly below the strange statue located on the lawn there, which appeared to portray a dying Quixote shooting a last arrow over his shoulder, roughly in the direction of the Saudi Arabian embassy. An allegory for the futility of fighting Big Oil, perhaps. Anyway there was Umberto approaching him, lighting a cigarette and coughing, and together they strolled down the grass to the railing overlooking the river.

They leaned with their elbows on the rail and watched obsidian sheets of water glide past.

They conversed in Spanish:

"So?"

"We're still looking into ways of isolating these guys."

"Is she still helping?"

"Yes, she's the decoy while we try to cut these guys out. She's playing the shell game with them."

"And you think Cooper is the leader?"

"Not sure about that. He may have a stovepipe that goes pretty high. That's one of the things we're still trying to determine."

"But he's part of ARDA?"

"Yes."

"And where did they relocate that most exciting program?"

"There's a working group, suspended between Homeland Security and the National Security Council. ARDA prime."

Edgardo laughed. He danced a little tango step while singing the bitter wild riff at the start of "Primavera Porteño." "They are so fucking stupid, my friend! Could it get any more byzantine?"

"That's the point. It's a work of art."

"It's a fucking shambles. They must be scared out of their wits, granting they ever had any wits, which I don't. I mean if they get caught . . ."

"It will be hard to catch them outright. I think the best we can do is cut them out. But if they see that coming, they will fight."

"I'm sure. Is all of ARDA in on it?"

"No, I don't think so."

"That's good. I know some of those guys from my time at DARPA. I liked them. Some of them, anyway."

"I know. I'm sure the ones you liked are all innocent of this."

"Right." Edgardo laughed. "Well, fuck them. What should I tell Frank?"

"Tell him to hang in there."

"Do you think it would be okay to tip him that his girlfriend is still involved in a root canal?"

"I don't know." Umberto sucked on his cigarette, blew out a long plume of white smoke. "Not if you think he'll do anything different."

A LL FRANK COULD THINK ABOUT NOW was how he could get in touch with Caroline. Apparently showing up in her surveillance of her ex had not worked; there was no way of telling why. Surely she had motion checkers to flag intrusions or appearances or changes that she needed to check. That was the way surveillance cameras worked; you couldn't just film real time and watch it later, there was never the time for that. And so . . .

Something must be wrong.

He could go to Mount Desert Island. He thought there was a good chance that Edgardo was right about her staying up there. It was a big island, and she had obviously loved it; her idea of what hiding out meant was tied to that place. And if she kept a distance from her friend's camp, kept to herself somewhere else on the island, her ex would assume she had bolted elsewhere (unless he didn't) and she would be able to lie low.

But in that case, how would Frank find her?

What would she have to have? What would she not stop doing? Shopping for food? Getting espressos? Bicycling?

He wasn't really sure; he didn't know her well enough to say. She had said there was great mountain biking to be had on the gravel carriage roads that wound around the granite knobs on the eastern half of the island, on which you could bike with no one seeing you, except for other bikers. Did that mean he should go up and rent a mountain bike and ride around on this network, or hang out at the backwoods intersections of these gravel roads, and wait for her to pass by accident? No. It took a long time to drive up there and back. If you couldn't fly you had to drive. But there was so much else going on down in D.C., and even elsewhere around the world; he needed to go to San Diego again, he needed to visit London, it would be good to see that site in Siberia, even get to Antarctica and visit Wade if he could.

On the other hand, his tree had been cut down, his battery cables cut, his kayak wrecked, his computer destroyed. He had to deal with it somehow. It was in his face and in his thoughts. He had to do something.

But instead of doing something, he sat in the garden at the farm, and weeded. He woke up at dawn to find Rudra at the window, looking out at the river. Quicksilver slick under gray mist streamers. Trees on the far bank looking like ghosts.

He helped Rudra with his morning English lessons. Rudra was working from a primer prepared under the tutelage of the Dalai Lama, and used to teach the Tibetan-speaking children their English:

" 'There are good anchors to reality and bad anchors to reality. Try to avoid the bad ones.' Ha!" Rudra snorted. "Thanks for such wisdom, oh High Holiness! Look, he even calls them the Four Bad D's. It's like the Chinese, they are always Four Thises and Six Thats."

"The Eight Noble Truths?" Frank said.

"Bah. That's Chinese Buddhism."

"Interesting. And what exactly are the Four Bad D's?"

"Debt, depression, disease, death."

"Whoah. Those are four bad D's, all right. Are there four good D's?"

"Children, health, work, love."

"Man you are a sociobiologist. Could you add habits, maybe?"

"No. Number very important. Only room for four."

Frank laughed. "But it's such a good anchor. It's what allows you to love your life. You love your habits the way you love your home. As a kind of gravity that includes other emotions. Even hate."

Rudra shrugged. "I am an exile."

"Me too."

Rudra looked at him. "You can move back to your home?"

"Yes."

"Then you are not an exile. You are just not at home."

"I guess that's right."

"Why would you not move home if you could?"

"Work?" Frank said.

But it was a good question.

That night, as they were falling asleep in the ever-so-slightly-rocking dark of their suspended room, the wind rustling the leaves of the grove, Frank came back to the morning's conversation.

"I've been thinking about good correlations. We need a numbered list of those. My good correlation is the one between living as close to a prehistoric life as you can, and being happy, and becoming more healthy, and reducing your consumption and therefore your impact on the planet. That's a very good correlation. Then Phil Chase had another one at his inaugural. He talked about how social justice and women's rights correlate with a steady-state replacement rate for the population, which would mean the end of rapid population growth, and thus reduce our load on the planet. That's another very good correlation. So, I'm thinking of calling them the Two Good Correlations."

"Two is not enough."

"What?"

"Two is not a big enough number for this kind of thing. There is never the Two This or the Two That. You need at least three, maybe more."

"But I only know two."

"You must think of some more."

"Okay, sure." Frank was falling asleep. "You have to help me though. The question will be, what's the third good correlation?"

"That's easy."

"What?"

"You think about it."

For some reason no one was hanging out at Site 21 these days. Maybe the heat and the mosquitoes. Back at the farm Frank yanked weeds out of the garden rows. He cut the grass of the lawn with a hand scythe, swinging it like a golf club, viciously driving shot after shot out to some distant green. At night in the dining room he ate at the end of a table, reading, bathed in a sea of Tibetan voices. Sometimes he would talk to Padma or Sucandra, then go to bed and read his laptop for a while. He missed the bros and their rowdy assholery. It occurred to him one night in the dining hall that not only was bad company better than no company, there were times when bad company was better than good company. But it was a different life now.

At work, Frank was passing along some great projects for Diane to propose to the president. The converter that could be put in all new cars so that they could run on eighty-five percent ethanol could in a different form be added to already existing cars, like smog-control devices had been. Legislating that as a requirement would immediately change their fuel needs, and overwhelm their limited ability to make ethanol, but Brazil had shown it could be ramped up pretty fast. And there were advances on that front coming out of RRCCES, another offshoot of Eleanor's work, carried forward by other colleagues of hers, in which an engineered enzyme allowed them to get away from corn and start to use wood chips for their ethanol feed stock, and might soon allow them to use grass; that biotech accomplishment was another kind of holy grail.

Burning ethanol still released carbon to the atmosphere, of course, but the difference was that this was carbon that had only recently been drawn down from the atmosphere by plant growth, and when they grew more feedstock, carbon would be drawn down again, so that it was almost a closed loop, with human transport as part of the cycle. As opposed to releasing the fossil carbon that had been so nicely sequestered under the ground in the form of oil and coal.

On that front too there were interesting developments. Clean coal had, up until this point, only meant burning coal and capturing the particulate load released to the atmosphere. That was called clean, but it was a strange issue, because the particulates were probably lofting into the high atmosphere and reflecting sunlight away, creating at least part of the so-called "global dimming," meaning the lower levels of sunlight that had been reaching the surface of the Earth in the last few decades compared to when it had first been measured. So that cleaning up coal burning in that way might actually let more light through and add to the global warming overall.

As for the carbon dioxide released when coal was burned, that had not been a part of what they had been calling clean coal. But now their prototype plant's blueprint included a complete plan for burning coal and capturing both carbon dioxide and particulates before release. None of the elements were speculative; all existed already and could be combined. It would be expensive; it would mean that each coal-burning power plant would become a complicated and expensive factory. But so what? It could be argued that this was only another advantage for the manufacturers of such plants. Public utilities, private investors, ultimately it didn't matter; it had to be done, it had to be paid for, someone would get paid when society made the payment. It was simply work to be done.

Meanwhile, on another front, captured carbon dioxide was being injected into depleted oil wells. Compressed and frozen, the dry ice was put under pressure until it flowed down old oil pipes and filled the pores of rock that had been drained of its oil. They were doing it in Canada, off Norway in the North Sea, and they were now starting to do it in Texas. Putting the carbon dioxide down there both sequestered it nicely, for thousands of years at least, and also put more pressure on the remaining oil deposits, making them easier to pump up. Because even if they stopped burning oil, they still needed it as the feedstock for plastics and pesticides. They would still be wearing it and eating it; they would just stop burning it.

All these projects were pouring into NSF and Energy and many other federal agencies and being screened by Diane's committee and placed into the mission architecture that indicated what they needed all up and down the structure of their new technology. There were very few weak points or question marks in this architecture! They could swap out power and transport in less than ten years!

But even if they stabilized carbon emissions immediately, even if they were to stop burning carbon entirely, which was a theoretical possibility only, for the sake of calculation, global temperatures would continue to rise for many years. The continuity effect, as they called it, and a nasty problem to contemplate. It was an open question whether temperatures even in the best case scenario would rise enough to cross the threshhold to further positive feedbacks that would cause it to rise even more. Models were not at all precise on this subject.

So they had to continue to discuss the ocean problems, among many others. In one meeting, Diane asked Frank about the Sample Basin Study that was looking into flooding dry lake basins, and Frank called up an e-mail from the P.I.

Frank said, "China likes the idea. They say they've already done similar things, at Three Gorges of course, but also at four more dams like Three Gorges. Those are mostly for hydroelectric and flood control, and they're seeing climate effects downwind, but they feel they've got experience with the process, and say they would be willing to take more. And the biggest basins on Earth are all theirs."

"But, salt water?"

"Any lake helps cloud formation, so they would be hydrating the deserts downwind by precipitating out."

"Still, it's hard to imagine them sacrificing that much land."

"True. But clearly there's going to be something like carbon cap credits set up. Some kind of sea water credits, given to countries for taking up sea water. Maybe even combine it with carbon trading, so that taking up sea water earns carbon credits. Or funding for desalination plants on the basin's new shorelines. Or whatever. Some kind of compensation."

Diane said, "I suppose we could arrange a treaty with them."

Later they worked on the Antarctic aspect of the plan. The dry basins of the world didn't have enough capacity to keep sea level in place anyway, so they needed to push the Antarctic idea too. If that ended up working, then in theory the Eastern Antarctic Ice Sheet would be able to handle all possible excess, and the dry basins up north would only be filled if the net effects of doing so looked good to the host country.

"Sounds good. But it's a lot of water."

That night Frank walked out of the security gate on 17th Street, at the south end of the Old Executive Offices, and across the street there was a woman standing as if waiting for the light to change. His heart pounded in his chest like a child trying to escape. He stared—was it really her?

She nodded, jerked her head sideways: *follow me.* She walked up to G Street and Frank did too, on the other side of the street. His pulse was flying. An amazing physical response—well, but she had been out of touch and now there she was, her face so vivid, so distinctly hers, leaping out of reality into his mind. Oh my, oh my. She must have seen his jump through her surveillance camera, or heard his mental call. So often telepathy seemed real. Or maybe she had been discovered, and forced to go on the run again. In need of his help. It could be anything.

A red light stopped him. She had stopped too, and was not crossing with the green to him. Apparently they were to walk in parallel for a while, west on G Street. It was a long light. If you felt each second fully, a lifetime would become an infinity. Maybe that was the point of being in love, or the reward. Oh my. He could feel the knock of his heart in the back of his nose. He followed her down G Street, past the Watergate complex, and across the Parkway, through the boating center parking lot, down into the trees at the mouth of Rock Creek, where finally they could converge, could crash into each other's arms and hug each other hard, hard, hard. Ah God, his partner in exile, his fellow refugee from reality, here at last, as real as a rock in his hands.

"What's up?" he said, his voice rough, out of his control. Only now did he feel just how scared he had been for her. "I've been scared!" he complained. "Look—I *have* to have a way to get in touch with you, I just *have to*. We *have* to have a drop box or something, some way to do it. I can't stand it when we don't. I can't stand it anymore!"

She pulled back, surprised at his vehemence. "Sorry. I've been working out my routines, figuring out what I can do and what I can't. They're still after me, and I wasn't totally sure I could stay off their radar, and so—I didn't want to get you caught up in anything."

"I already *am* caught up in it. I am fully caught up in it!"

"Okay, okay. I know. But I had to make sure we were both clear. And usually you're not. They know about that Khembalung embassy house, and their place in Maryland too."

"I know! They know all that! What about now? Am I clear?"

She took a wand out of her pocket, ran it over him. "Right now you are. It happens most often right when you leave work. The chips are mostly in stuff you leave at your other places. But I had to see you. I *needed* to see you."

"Well good." Then he saw on her face how she felt, and his spirits ballooned: at this first flash of reciprocation, the feeling blazed up in him again. Love was like a laser beam bouncing between two mirrors. She smiled at the look on his face, then they embraced and started to kiss, and Frank was swept away in a great wave of passion, like a wave catching him up in the ocean. Off they went in it, but it was more than passion, something bigger and more coherent, a feeling *for her,* his Caroline—an overwhelming feeling. "Oh my," he said over her shoulder.

She laughed, trembling in his arms. They hugged again, harder than ever. He was in love and she was in love and they were in love with each other. Kissing was a kind of orgasm of the feelings. He was breathing heavily, and she was too—heart pounding, blood pulsing. Frank ran a hand through her hair, feeling the tight curl, the thick springiness of it. She tilted her head back into the palm of his hand, giving herself to him.

They were in a dark knot of trees. They sat on the previous year's mat of leaves, burrowed into them as they kissed. A lot of time was lost then, it rushed past or did not happen. Her muscles were hard and her soft spots were soft. She murmured, she hummed, she moved without volition against him.

After a while she laughed again, shook her head as if to clear it. "Let's go somewhere and talk," she said. "We're not that well hidden here."

"True." In fact the Rock Creek Parkway, above them through the trees, was busy with cars, and in the other direction they could see a few of the lights of the Georgetown riverfront, blinking through branches.

When they were standing again she took his face in both hands and squeezed it. "I *need* you, Frank."

"I knee woo too," he said, lips squeezed vertically.

She laughed and let his face go. "Come on, let's go get a drink," she said. "I've got to tell you some stuff."

They walked up to the footbridge over Rock Creek, then along the promenade fronting the Potomac. Down into a sunken concrete plaza, set between office buildings, where there was a row of tables outside a bar. They floated down the steps hand in hand and sat at one of them.

After they ordered (she a bloody mary, he white wine), she pressed a forefinger into the top of his thigh. "But look—another reason I had to see you— I needed to tell you, I'm pretty sure that Ed is on to who you are. I think he's tracking you."

"He's been doing more than that," Frank said. "That's why I wanted to find you. I've been getting harassed these last few weeks." He told her all that had happened, watching her mouth tighten at the corners as he described each incident. By the time he was done her mouth was turned down like an eagle's.

"I wondered about that. That's him all right," she said bitterly. "That's him all over."

Frank nodded. "I was pretty sure."

He had never seen her look so grim. It was frightening, in more ways than one; you would not want her angry at you.

They sat there for a few moments. Their drinks arrived and they sipped at them.

"And so . . . ?" Frank said.

After another pause, she said slowly, "I guess I think you've got to disappear, like I did. Come with me and disappear for a bit. My Plan C is working out really well. I'm in the area here, and I have a solid cover identity, with a bank account and apartment lease and car and everything. I don't think he can possibly find any of it. At this point I'm the one surveiling him, and I can see that he's still looking, but he's lost my trail."

"But he's tracking the people you were surveiling," Frank supposed.

"I think that's right."

"And so, he's figured out I must be the one who helped you get away?"

"Well—judging by what he's doing to you, I think he might still not be quite sure about it. He may be kind of testing you, to see if you'll jump. To see if you react like you know it's him. And if you did, then he'd know for sure. Also, you might then lead him to me."

"So—but that means if I disappear, then he'll be sure I'm the one. Because I'll have jumped, like he was looking for."

"Yes. But he must be pretty sure anyway, that's the thing. And then he won't be able to find you. Which is good, because I'm just—I'm afraid what he might do."

Frank was too, but he did not want to admit it. "Well, but I can't—"

"I've got an ID all ready for you. It's got a good legend and a deep cover. It's just as solid as mine."

"But I can't leave," Frank objected. "I mean, I have my job to do. I can't leave that right now." And your fucking ex can't make me, he didn't say.

She frowned, hesitated. Maybe her ex was worse than Frank had thought. Although what did that mean? Surely he wouldn't—wouldn't—

She shook her head, as if to clear it and think things through. "If there was someone at your work that you could explain the situation to, that you trusted? Maybe you could set up a system and send your work in to them, and like that."

"A lot of it is done in meetings now. I don't think that would work."

"But . . ." She scowled. "I don't like him knowing where you are!"

"I know. But, you know." Frank felt confused, balked—caught. He was moving into his zone of confusion, beginning to blank out at the end of trains of thought—"I have to keep doing my job," he heard himself say. "Maybe I could just make a strong effort to keep off the radar when I'm away from work. You know—show up for work out of the blue, be there in the office, but with everyone else, all day, in a high-security environment. Then disappear out of the office at the end of the day, and he won't be able to find where. Maybe I could do that."

"Maybe. That's a lot of exposure to get away from every day."

"I know, but—I have to."

She was shaking her head unhappily—

"It's okay," he said. "I can do it. I mean it. The White House compound is a secure environment. So when I'm where they know where I am, I'll have security. When I don't have security, they won't know where I am. I'd rather do it that way than stop everything I'm doing!"

"Well, that's what I had to do!"

"Yes, but you had to, because of the election and everything." Because you were married to him.

She was eagle-mouthed again. "But look," she said, "you're in on that too, okay? Thanks to me. I'm sorry about that, but it's true, and you can't just ignore it. That would be like I was being, when you showed up and I didn't want to leave camp." She sipped at her drink, thinking things over. At last she shook her head unhappily. "I'm afraid of what he might do."

"Well, but to you too," Frank said. "Maybe you should go back up to Mount Desert Island. I was thinking if you stayed away from your friend's place, it would be a good place to hide."

She shook her head more vehemently. "I can't do that."

"Why not?"

"I've got stuff I've gotta do here." She glanced at him, hesitated, took another drink. She frowned, thinking things over again. Their knees were pressed together, and their hands had found each other on their own and were clutched together, as if to protest any plan their owners might make that would separate them.

"I really think you should come with me," she said. "Get off the grid entirely."

Frank struggled for thought.

"I can't," he said at last.

She grimaced. She seemed to be getting irritated with him, the pressure of her hand's grip almost painful.

Worse yet, she let go of him, straightened up. She was somehow becoming estranged, withdrawing from him. Even angry at him. An invitation to be with her, all the time— "Listen," Frank said anxiously, "don't be mad at me. Tell me how we're going to keep in touch now. We *have* to have a way. I have to."

"Okay, yeah, sure."

But she was upset by his refusal to go with her, and distracted. "We can always do a dead drop," she said as she continued to frown over other things. "It's simple. Pick a hidden spot where we leave notes, and only check the spot when you're positive you're clean, say once a week."

"Twice a week."

"If I can." Her mouth was still pursed unhappily. She shook her head. "It's better to have a regular time that you're sure you can meet, and keep to that schedule."

"Okay, once a week. And where?"

"*I* don't know." She seemed to be getting more frustrated the more she thought about things.

"How about where we were making out, back there in the trees?" Frank suggested, trying to press past her mood. "Do you know where that was, can you find it again?"

She gave him a very sharp look, it reminded him of Marta. Women weak at geography—he hadn't meant it that way. Although there were women who didn't have a clue.

"Of course," she said. "Down there by the mouth of the creek. But—it should be a place where we can tuck notes out of the rain, and be sure we can find them and all."

"Okay, well, we can go back out there and bury a plastic bag in the leaves under a tree."

She nodded unenthusiastically. She was still distracted.

"Are you sure you don't want to go back up to Mount Desert Island?" Frank asked.

"Of course I do!" she snapped. "But I can't, okay? I've got stuff I've got to do around here."

"What? Maybe I can help."

"You can't help! Especially not if you stay exposed in your job and all!"

"But I have to do that."

"Well. There you are then."

He nodded, hesitantly. He didn't understand, and wasn't sure how to proceed. "Shall we go back out there and pick a spot?"

"No. There's a pair of roots there with a hole between them. I felt it under me, it was under my head. You can put something in that gap, and I'll find it. I need to get going." She checked her watch, looked around, stood abruptly; her metal chair screeched over the concrete.

"Caroline—"

"*Be careful*," she said, leaning down to stare him right in the face. She brought her hand up between their faces to point a finger at his nose, and he saw it was quivering. "I mean it. You're going to have to be really careful. I can see why you want to keep going to work, but this is no game we're caught in."

"I know that! But we're stuck with it. Don't be mad at me. *Please.* There's just things we both still have to do."

"I know." Her mouth was still a tight line, but now at least she was looking him in the eye. "Okay. Let's do the dead drop, every week. I'll check on Saturdays, you check Wednesdays."

"Okay. I'll leave something there for this Saturday, and you get it and leave something for Wednesday."

"Okay. But if I can't, check the next week. But I'll try." And with a peck to the top of his head she was off into the dark of Georgetown.

Frank sat there, feeling stunned. A little drunk. He didn't know what to think. He was confused, and for a moment overwhelmed, feeling the indecision fall hard on him. When you feel love, elation, worry, fear, and puzzlement, all at once, and all at equally full volume, they seem to cancel each other out, creating a vacuum, or rather a plenum. He felt Carolined.

"Fuck," he said half-aloud. It had been that way from the moment they met, actually; only now it was intensified, fully present in his mind, still felt in his body. Abruptly he finished his drink and took off into the dark. Over the creek's footbridge, back to the spot where they had kissed.

One of the trees on the river side of their impromptu layby had the two big roots she had referred to, growing out in a fork and then plunging down into the rich loamy earth and reuniting, leaving a leaf-filled pocket. He tore one of the clear plastic credit card holders out of his wallet, took a receipt from his pocket and wrote on the back:

I LOVE YOU I'LL LOOK EVERY WEDNESDAY WRITE ME

Then he put it in the sleeve and buried it under leaves shoved into the hole. Topped it all with leaves and hoped she would find it, hoped she would use it and write him. It seemed like she would. They had kissed so passionately, right here on this very spot, no more than an hour or so before. Why now this edge of discord between them?

Well, that seemed pretty clear: her desire for him to disappear with her. Obviously she felt it was important, and that he might even be in danger if he didn't join her. But he couldn't join her.

That feeling was in itself interesting, now that he thought of it. Was that a sign of decisiveness, or just being balky? Had he had any choice? Maybe one would never go into hiding unless there were no other choice. This was probably one cause of Caroline's irritation; she had to hide, while he didn't. Although maybe he did and just didn't know it.

Big sigh. He didn't know. For a second he lost his train of thought and didn't know anything. What had just happened? He looked down on the bed of leaves they had lain on. Caroline! he cried in his mind, and groaned aloud.

H E WAS SITTING WITH RUDRA at the little table under their window, both of them looking at laptops and tapping away, the room itself slightly swaying on a wind from the west. After the heat of the day, the cool fragrance coming off the river was a balm. Moonlight broke and squiggled whitely on the black sweep of the water. Frank was reading Thoreau and at one point he laughed and read aloud to Rudra:

> "We hug the earth—how rarely we mount! Methinks we might elevate ourselves a little more. We might climb a tree, at least. I found my account in climbing a tree once. It was a tall white pine, on the top of a hill; and though I got well pitched, I was well paid for it, for I discovered new mountains on the horizon which I had never seen before—so much more of the earth and the heavens. I might have walked about the foot of the tree for three score years and ten, and yet I certainly should never have seen them."

Rudra nodded. "Henry likes the same things you do," he observed.
"It's true."
"A treehouse is a good idea," Rudra said, looking out the windows at the dark river.
"It is, isn't it?"
Frank read on for a while, then: "Here, listen to this, he might as well be at the table with us:

> "I live so much in my habitual thoughts that I forget there is any outside to the globe, and am surprised when I behold it as now—yonder hills and river in the moonlight, the monsters. Yet it is salutary to deal with the surface of things. What are these rivers and hills, these hieroglyphics which my eyes

behold? There is something invigorating in this air, which I am peculiarly sensible is a real wind, blowing from over the surface of a planet. I look out at my eyes, I come to my window, and I feel and breathe the fresh air. It is a fact equally glorious with the most inward experience. Why have we ever slandered the outward?"

"What say, speak bad?" Rudra asked. "About this?" He waved at their view. "Maybe that is your third good correlation. The outer and the inner."

"I want something more specific."

"Maybe he means we should stop reading, and look at the river."

"Ah yes. True."

And they did.

But the next night, when Frank drove into the farm's parking lot after work, late, and got out of his van and headed for the treehouse, Qang came out of the big farmhouse and hurried over to intercept him.

"Frank, sorry—can you come in here, please?"

"Sure, what's up?"

"Rimpoche Rudra Cakrin has died."

"*What?*"

"Rudra died this day, after you left."

"Oh no. Oh no."

"Yes. I am afraid so." She held his arm, watched him closely.

"Where is he? I mean—"

"We have his body in the prayer room."

"Oh no."

The enormity of it began to hit him. "Oh, no," he said again helplessly.

"Please," she said. "Be calm. Rudra must not be disturbed now."

"What?" So he had misheard—

"This is an important time for his spirit. We here must be quiet, and let him focus on his work in the bardo. What say—help him on his way, by saying the proper prayers."

Frank felt himself lose his balance a little bit. Gone weak at the knees—yet another physiological reaction shared by all. Shock of bad news, knees went weak. "Oh no," he said. She was so calm about it. Standing there talking about helping Rudra through the first hours of the afterlife—suddenly he realized he was living with aliens. They didn't even look human.

He went over and sat down on the front steps of the house. Everything still scrubbed, new paint, Tibetan colors. Qang was saying something, but he didn't hear it.

After a while, it was Drepung sitting beside him. Briefly he put an arm around Frank's shoulders and squeezed, then they just sat there side by side. Minutes passed; ten minutes, maybe fifteen.

"He was a friend," Frank explained. "He was my friend."

"Yes. He was my teacher."

"When—when did you meet him?"

"I was ten."

Drepung explained some of Rudra's role in Khembalung, some of his personal history. Frank glanced up once and saw that tears had rolled down Drepung's broad cheeks as he spoke, even though his voice and manner were calm. This was a comfort to Frank.

"Tell me what happens now," he said when Drepung was silent.

Drepung then explained their funeral customs. "We will say the first prayers for a day and a half. Then later there will be other ceremonies, at the proper intervals. Rudra was an important guru, so there will be quite a few of these. The big one will be after forty days, as with anyone, and then one last one at forty-nine days."

Eventually they got up and clomped up the central stairs of the treehouse, winding around the trunk of one of the main trees. Then down the catwalk to their room.

Others had already been there. Presumably this was where Rudra had died. The sight of the empty and sheetless bed cast another wave of grief through Frank. He sat down in the chair by the window, looked down at the river flowing by. He thought that if they had not left their garden shed, maybe Rudra would not have died.

Well, that made no sense. But Frank saw immediately that he could not continue to stay there. It would make him too sad. Then again (remembering his conversation with Caroline) moving out would help his evasion of Cooper anyway. He was free to go and do the necessary things.

In the days that followed, Frank moved his stuff out of the Khembali treehouse back into his van, now the last remaining room of his modular house, compromised though it might be. He usually parked it in the farm's little parking lot, just to be near Drepung and Sucandra and Padma; he found that nearness comforting, and he did not want them to think that he had abandoned them or gone crazy or anything. "You need the room," he kept saying about the treehouse. "I like it better now to be in my van." They accepted that and put four people in the room.

As the days passed they went through one or the other of the various stages of Rudra's passage through the bardo—Frank lost track of the details, but he tried to remember the last funeral's date, said to be the most important one for those who wished to honor the memory of that particular incarnation.

He was at a loss for what to do when not at work. The Old Executive Offices, though much closer to the centers of national power, were nowhere near as comfortable to spend time in as the NSF building had been. It was not possible to sleep there, for instance, without security noticing and dropping by to check on him. Meanwhile his van was probably still GPSed and would be one of the ways that Edward Cooper was keeping track of him. He needed it for a bedroom and to get out to the Khembalis, and yet he wanted to be able to drop off the grid every day when he left work.

He didn't know. Show up to work, work, disappear, then show up again the next day. This was important, given the things that were happening.

What would happen if he got Edgardo's help to take all the transponders out of his van?

But that would alert Cooper that Frank knew the chips were there and had removed them. It was better the way it was, perhaps, so that he could find them and remove them when he really had to, and then travel off-grid. He might need the van if Caroline went back to Mount Desert Island and he wanted to drive up to see her. In general it was an advantage. That was what Edgardo had meant.

He didn't know what to do. He couldn't figure it out, and he had no place to stay. What to do, how to live. Always a question, but never more so than now. He could do this, he could do that. Anyone could; no one had to.

Do the duty of the day. (Emerson.)

The easiest thing was to work as long as possible. It was a kind of default mode, and he needed that now. The fewer decisions the better. He needed a job that filled all the waking hours of the day, and he had that. But now Opti-modal was not optimum, and he didn't really want to go to the farm, and his treehouse was gone. His home had washed away in the flood of events. All he had left was his van, and his van was chipped.

Out of habit he went back out to Site 21. Summer was fully upon them, and all the leaves were green. But the site was empty these days, and Sleepy Hollow had been dismantled.

He sat there at the picnic table wondering what to do.

Spencer and Robin and Robert came charging in, and Frank leaped up to join them. "Thank God," he said, hugging each in turn; they always did that, but this time it mattered.

They ran the course in an ecstasy, as usual, but for Frank there was an extra element, of release and forgetfulness. Just to run, just to throw, life crashing through the greenery everywhere around them. They ran in a swirl of becoming. Everyone died sometime; but it was life that mattered.

Afterward Frank sat down with Spencer near the chuckling creek, brown and foamy. "I'm wondering if I could join your fregans," he said.

"Well, sure," Spencer said, looking surprised. "But I thought you lived with the Khembalis?"

"Yes. But my friend there died, and I—I need to get away. There are some issues. I'm under a weird kind of surveillance, and I want to get away from that. So, I'm wondering if you would mind, maybe—I don't know. Introduc-ing me to some people or whatever. Like those times we went to a dinner."

"Sure," Spencer said. "That happens every night. No problem at all."

"Thanks."

"So you're doing something classified then?"

"I don't know."

Spencer laughed. "Well, it doesn't matter. Life outdoors is a value in itself. You'll like it, you'll see."

So he went with Spencer, on foot, to the house of choice for that evening—a boarded-up monster, not a residential house but a half-block apartment complex that had been wrecked in the flood and never renovated. There were a lot of these, and the ferals and fregans now had maps and lists, locks and keys and codes and phones. Every few nights they moved to a new place, within a larger community, most of whom were also moving around. Spencer started calling Frank on his FOG phone to let him know where they would be that night, and Frank started leaving work at more or less the normal time, using a wand Edgardo gave him to see that he was clear, then meeting Spencer in the park, running a frisbee round, then walking somewhere in Northwest to the rendezvous of the night. Once or twice Frank joined the dumpster-diving teams, and was interested to learn that most restaurant dumpsters were now locked shut. But this was to satisfy insurance-company liability concerns more than to keep people from the food, because for every dumpster they visited they had either the key or the combination, provided by kitchen workers who were either sympathetic or living the life themselves. And so they would go into the parking lots and workspaces behind the city's finest, and set a look-out, and then unlock the dumpster and remove the useful food, which often was set carefully in one corner by the kitchen help, but in any case was obvious.

It wasn't even that smelly of an operation, Frank learned (although some-times it was); and then they would hustle off with backpacks full of half-frozen steaks or big bags of lettuce, or potatoes, really almost all the raw materials of the wonderful meals all the restaurants had not made and could preserve no longer, and by the time they got to the meeting house, its kitchen would be powered up by a generator in the backyard, or the fireplace would be ablaze with a big fire, and cooks would be working on a meal that would feed thirty or forty people through the course of the evening.

Frank floated through all this like a jellyfish. He let the tide of humanity shove him along. This way or that. Billow on the current. He was grunioning in the shallows of the city.

Then it came time for the last of Rudra's major funerals. Frank was sur-prised to see the date on his watch. Well, that was interesting. Forty-nine days had passed and he hadn't quite noticed. Now it was the day.

He didn't know what to do.

He didn't want to go. He didn't want to admit Rudra was dead, he didn't want to feel those feelings again. He didn't want to think that Rudra was alive but in some horrible netherworld, where he was having to negotiate all kinds of terrors in order to get to the start of some putative next life. It was absurd. He didn't want any of it to be real.

He sat there at his desk in his office, paralyzed by indecision. He *could not decide.*

A call came on his FOG phone.

It was Nick Quibler. "Frank, are you okay? Did you forget that it's the day for Rudra's funeral?"

Nick did not sound accusatory, or worried, or anything. Nick was good at not sounding emotional. Teenage flatness of affect.

"Oh yeah," he said to the boy, trying to sound normal. "I did forget. Thanks for calling. I'll be right over. But don't let them delay anything on my account."

"I don't think they could even if they wanted to," Nick said. "It's a pretty strict schedule, as far as I can tell." He had taken an interest in the supposed sequence of events Rudra had been experiencing during these forty-nine days in the bardo, reading the *Tibetan Book of the Dead* and telling Frank too many of the details, all too like one of his video games. Suddenly it all seemed to Frank like a cruel hoax, a giant fiction meant to comfort the bereaved. People who died were dead and gone. Their soul had been in their brains and their brains decomposed and the electrical activity was gone. And then they were gone too, except to the extent they were in other people's minds.

Well, fair enough. He was going to the funeral now. He had decided. Or Nick had decided.

Suddenly he understood that he had been sitting there about to miss it. He was so incapacitated that he had almost missed a friend's funeral. Would have missed it, if not for a call from another friend. Before leaving he grabbed up the phone and called up the neurologist's office. "I have a referral from Dr. Mandelaris for elective surgery," he explained. "I'd like to schedule that now please. I've decided to do it."

EVERY SUMMER CHARLIE FLEW BACK to California to spend a week in the Sierra Nevada, backpacking with a group of old friends. Most of them were high school friends, and some of them had gone to UC San Diego together, many years before. That they and Frank Vanderwal had been undergraduates at UCSD at the same time had come up at dinner one night at the Quiblers' the previous winter, causing a moment of surprise, then a shrug. Possibly they had been in classes together—they couldn't remember. The subject had been dropped, as just one of those coincidences that often cropped up in Washington, D.C. So many people came from somewhere else that sometimes the elsewheres were the same.

This coincidence, however, was certainly a factor in Charlie inviting Frank to join the group for this summer's trip. Perhaps it played a part in Frank's acceptance as well; it was hard for Charlie to tell. Frank's usual reticence had recently scaled new heights.

The invitation had been Anna's idea. Frank was having an operation on his nose, she said, and if he didn't go away afterward he would not stop working. He did not particularly like the move from NSF to the White House, she felt, but he certainly worked very long hours there. And since Rudra's death, he had seemed to her lonely.

This was all news to Charlie, despite his kayaking expeditions with Frank—although anyone could see that the death of Rudra Cakrin had shaken him. When he showed up for the forty-nine-day ceremony, quite late—most of the gazillion prayers over, in fact—he had been obviously distressed. He had arrived in time for the part where everyone there took bites out of little cakes they had been given, then turned the remaining pieces back in, to help sustain Rudra's spirit—a beautiful idea—but Frank had eaten his piece entirely, having failed to understand. It was always a shock to see someone one re-garded as unemotional suddenly become distraught.

So, soon after that Frank had had the surgery to correct problems behind his nose resulting from his accident. "No big deal," he described it, but Anna just shook her head at that.

"It's right next to his brain," she told Charlie.

They all visited him in the hospital, and he said he was fine, that it had gone well, he had been told. And yes, he would like to join the backpacking trip, thanks. It would be good to get away. Would he be okay to go to high al-titude? Charlie wondered. He said he would be.

After that everyone got busy with summer daycamp and swim lessons for Nick, the White House for Charlie and Joe, NSF for Anna; and they did not see Frank again for a couple weeks, until suddenly the time for the Sierra trip was upon them.

Charlie's California friends were fine with the idea of an added member of the trip, which they had done from time to time before, and they were looking forward to meeting him.

"He's kind of quiet," Charlie warned them.

This annual trek had been problematized for Charlie on the home front ever since Nick's birth, him being the stay-at-home parent, and Joe's arrival had made things more than twice as bad. Two consecutive summers had passed without Charlie being able to make the trip. Anna had seen how despondent he had gotten on the days when his friends were hiking in the high Sierra without him, and she was the one who had suggested he just make what-ever kid coverage arrangement it would take, and go. Gratefully Charlie had jumped up and kissed her, and between some logistical help on the Nick sum-mer daycamp front from their old Gymboree friend Asta, and extended White House daycare for Joe, he found they had coverage for both boys for the same several hours a day, which meant Anna could continue to work almost full-time. This was crucial; the loss of even a couple of hours of work a day caused her brow to furrow vertically and her mouth to set in a this-is-not-good ex-pression very particular to work delays.

Charlie knew the look well, but tried not to see it as the departure time ap-proached.

"This will be good for Frank," he would say. "That was a good idea you had."

"It'll be good for you too," Anna would reply; or she would not reply at all and just give him a look.

Actually she would have been completely fine with him going, Charlie thought, if it were not that she still seemed to have some residual worries about Joe. When Charlie realized this by hearing her make some non sequitur that skipped from the one subject to the other, he was surprised; he had thought he was the only one still worrying about Joe. He had assumed Anna would have had her mind put fully at ease by the disappearance of the fever. That had always been the focus of her concern, as opposed to the matters of mood and behavior which had been bothering Charlie.

Now, however, as the time for the mountain trip got closer and closer, he could see on Anna's face all her expressions of worry, visible in quick flashes when they discussed things, or when she was tired. Charlie could read a great deal on Anna's face. He didn't know if this was just the ordinary result of long familiarity or if she was particularly expressive, but certainly her worried looks were very nuanced, and, he had to say, beautiful. Perhaps it was just because they were so legible to him. You could see that life *meant something* when she was worrying over it; her thoughts flickered over her face like flames over burning coals, as if one were watching some dreamily fine silent-screen actress, able to express anything with looks alone. To read her was to love her. She might be, as Charlie thought she was, slightly crazy about work, but even that was part of what he loved, as just another manifestation of how much she cared about things. One could not care more and remain sane. Mostly sane.

But Anna had never admitted, or even apparently seen, the Khembali connection to the various changes in Joe. To her there was no such thing as a metaphysical illness, because there was no such thing as metaphysics. And there was no such thing as psychosomatic illness in a three-year-old, because a toddler was not old enough to have problems, as his Gymboree friend Cecelia had put it.

So it had to be a fever. Or so she must have been subconsciously reasoning. Charlie had to intuit or deduce most of this from the kinds of apprehension he saw in her. He wondered what would happen if Anna were the one on hand when Joe went into one of his little trances, or said "*Namaste*" to a snowman. He wondered if she knew Joe's daytime behavior well enough to notice the myriad tiny shifts that had occurred in his daily moods since the election-day party at the Khembalis'.

Well, of course she did; but whether she would admit some of these changes were connected to the Khembalis was another matter.

Maybe it was better that she couldn't be convinced. Charlie himself did not want to think there was anything real to this line of thought. It was one of his own forms of worry, perhaps—trying to find some explanation other than undiagnosed disease or mental problem. Even if the alternative explanation might in some ways be worse. Because it disturbed him, even occasionally freaked him out. He could only think about it glancingly, in brief bursts, and then quickly jump to something else. It was too weird to be true.

But there were more things in heaven and earth, etc.; and without question there were very intelligent people in his life who believed in this stuff, and acted on those beliefs. That in itself made it real, or something with real effects. If Anna had the Khembalis over for dinner while Charlie was gone, maybe she would see this. Even if the only "real" part of it was that the Khembalis believed something was going on, that was enough, potentially, to make for trouble.

In any case, the trouble would not come to a head while he was out in the Sierras. He would only be gone a week, and Joe had been much the same, week to week, all that winter and spring and through the summer so far.

So Charlie made his preparations for the trip without talking openly to Anna about Joe, and without meeting her eye when she was tired. She too avoided the topic.

It was harder with Joe: "When you going Dad?" he would shout on occasion. "How long? What you gonna do? Hiking? Can I go?" And then when Charlie explained that he couldn't, he would shrug. "Oh my." And make a little face. "See you when you back Dad."

It was heartbreaking.

On the morning of Charlie's departure, Joe patted him on the arm. "Bye Da. Be *careful*," saying it just like Charlie always said it, as a half-exasperated reminder, just as Charlie's father had always said it to him, as if the default plan were to do something reckless, so that one had to be reminded.

Anna clutched him to her. "Be careful. Have fun."

"I will. I love you."

"I love you too. Be careful."

Charlie and Frank flew from Dulles to Ontario together, making a plane change in Dallas.

Frank had had his operation eighteen days before. "So what was it like?" Charlie asked him.

"Oh, you know. They put you out."

"For how long?"

"A few hours I think."

"And after that?"

"Felt fine."

Although, Charlie saw, he seemed to have even less to say than before. So on the second leg of the trip, with Frank sitting beside him looking out the window of the plane, and every page of that day's *Post* read, Charlie fell asleep.

It was too bad about the operation. Charlie was in an agony of apprehension about it, but as Joe lay there on the hospital bed he looked up at his father and tried to reassure him. "It be all right Da." They had attached wires to his skull, connecting him to a bulky machine by the bed, but most of his hair was still unshaved, and under the mesh cap his expression was resolute. He squeezed Charlie's hand, then let go and clenched his fists by his sides, preparing himself, mouth pursed. The doctor on the far side of the bed nodded; time for delivery of the treatment. Joe saw this, and to give himself courage began to sing one of his wordless marching tunes, "Da, da da da, da!" The doctor flicked a switch on the machine and instantaneously Joe sizzled to a small black crisp on the bed.

Charlie jerked upright with a gasp.

"You okay?" Frank said.

Charlie shuddered, fought to dispel the image. He was clutching the seat arms hard.

"Bad dream," he got out. He hauled himself up in his seat and took some deep breaths. "Just a little nightmare. I'm fine."

But the image stuck with him, like the taste of poison. Very obvious symbolism, of course, in the crass way dreams sometimes had—image of a fear he had in him, expressed visually, sure—but so brutal, so ugly! He felt betrayed by his own mind. He could hardly believe himself capable of imagining such a thing. Where did such monsters come from?

He recalled a friend who had once mentioned he was taking St. John's wort in order to combat nightmares. At the time Charlie had thought it a bit silly; the moment you woke up from dreams you knew they were not real, so how bad could a nightmare be?

Now he knew, and finally he felt for his old friend Gene.

So when his old friends and roommates Dave and Vince picked them up at the Ontario airport and they drove north in Dave's van, Charlie and Frank were both a bit subdued. They sat in the middle seats of the van and let Dave and Vince do most of the talking up front. These two were more than willing to fill the hours of the drive with tales of the previous year's work in criminal defense and urology. Occasionally Vince would turn around in the passenger seat and demand some words from Charlie, and Charlie would reply, working to shake off the trauma of the dream and get into the good mood that he knew he should be experiencing. They were off to the mountains—the southern end of the Sierra Nevada was appearing ahead to their left already, the weird desert ranges above Death Valley were off to their right. They were entering Owens Valley, one of the greatest of mountain valleys! It was typically one of the high points of their trips, but this time he wasn't quite into it yet.

In Independence they met the van bringing down the two northern members of their group, Jeff and Troy, and they all wandered the little grocery store there, buying forgotten necessities or delicacies, happy at the sudden reunion of all these companions from their shared youth—a reunion with their own youthful selves, it seemed. Even Charlie felt that, and slowly managed to push the horrible dream away from his conscious awareness and his mood, to forget it. It was, in the end, only a dream.

Frank meanwhile was an easy presence, cruising the tight aisles of the rustic store peering at things, comfortable with all their talk of gear and food and trailhead firewood. Charlie was pleased to see that although he was still very quiet, a tiny little smile was creasing his features as he looked at displays of beef jerky and cigarette lighters and postcards. He looked relaxed. He knew this place.

Out in the parking lot, the mountains to east and west hemmed in the evening sky, and told them they were already in the Sierras—or, to be more precise, in the space the Sierras defined, which very much included Owens Valley. To the east, the dry White Mountains were dusty orange in the sunset; to the west, the huge escarpment of the Sierra loomed over them like a stupendous serrated wall. Together the two ranges created a sense of the valley as a great roofless room.

The room could have been an exhibit in a museum, illustrating what California had looked like a century before. Around then, Los Angeles had stolen the valley's water, as described in the movie *Chinatown* and elsewhere. Ironically, this had done the place a tremendous favor, by forestalling subsequent development and making it a sort of time capsule.

They drove the two cars out to the trailhead. The great escarpment fell directly from the crest of the Sierra to the floor of Owens Valley, the whole plunge of ten thousand feet right there before them—one of the biggest escarpments on the face of the planet. It formed a very complex wall, with major undulations, twists and turns, peaks and dips, buttressing ridges, and gigantic outlier masses. Every low point in the crest made for a potential pass into the back country, and many not-so-low points had also been used as cross-country passes. One of the games that Charlie's group of friends had fallen into over the years was that of trying to cross the crest in as many places as they could. This year they were going in over Taboose Pass, "before we get too old for it," as they said to Frank.

Taboose was one of what Troy had named the Four Bad Passes (Frank smiled to hear this). They were bad because their trailheads were all on the floor of Owens Valley, and thus about five thousand feet above sea level, while the passes on the crest, usually about ten miles away from the trailheads, were all well over eleven thousand feet high. Thus six thousand vertical feet, usually hiked on the first day, when their packs were heaviest. They had once ascended Baxter Pass, and once come down Shepherd's Pass; only Sawmill and Taboose remained, and this year they were going to do Taboose, said to be the hardest of them all. 5,300 feet to 11,360, in seven miles.

They drove to a little car campground by Taboose Creek and found it empty, which increased their good cheer. The creek itself was almost completely dry—a bad sign, as it drained one of the larger east-side canyons. There was no snow at all to be seen up on the crest of the range, nor over on the White Mountains. Frank stuck his hand in the creek and nodded to himself. "Glacier blood," he said.

"They'll have to rename them the Brown Mountains," Troy said. He was full of news of the drought that had been afflicting most of the Sierra for the last few years—a drought that was worse the farther north one went. Troy went into the Sierras a lot, and had seen the damage himself. "You won't believe it," he told Charlie ominously.

They partied through the sunset around a picnic table crowded with gear and beer and munchies. One of the range's characteristic lenticular clouds formed like a spaceship over the crest and turned pale orange and pink as the evening lengthened. Taboose Pass itself was visible above them, a huge U in the crest. Clearly the early native peoples would have had no problem identifying it as a pass over the range, and Troy told them of what he had read about the archeological finds in the area of the pass while Vince barbequed filet mignon and red bell peppers on a thick old iron grate.

Frank prodded the grate curiously. "I guess these things are the same everywhere," he said.

They ate dinner, drank, caught up on the year, reminisced about previous trips. Charlie was pleased to see Vince ask Frank some questions about his work, which Frank answered briefly if politely. He did not want to talk about that, Charlie could see; but he seemed content. When they were done eating he walked up the creekside on his own, looking around as he went.

Charlie relaxed in the presence of his old friends. Vince regaled them with ever-stranger tales of the L.A. legal system, and they laughed and threw a frisbee around, half-blind in the dusk. Frank came out of the darkness to join them for that. He turned out to be very accurate with a frisbee.

Then as it got late they slipped into their sleeping bags, promising they would make an early start, even, given the severity of the ascent facing them, an actual early start, with alarms set, as opposed to their more usual legendary early start, which did not depend on alarms and could take until eleven or noon.

So they woke, groaning, to alarms before dawn, and packed in a hurry while eating breakfast; then drove up the last gravel road to a tiny trailhead parking lot, hacked into the last possible spot before the escarpment made its abrupt jump off the valley floor. They were going to be hiking up the interior sides of a steep and deep granite ravine, but the trail began by running on top of a lateral moraine which had been left behind by the ravine's Ice Age glacier. The ice had been gone for ten thousand years but the moraine was still perfect, as smooth-walled as if bulldozers had made it.

The trail led them onto the granite buttress flanking the ravine on its right, and they rose quickly, and could see better and better just how steep the escarpment was. Polished granite overhead marked how high the glacier had run in the ravine. The ice had carved a trough in hard orange granite.

After about an hour the trail contoured into the gorge and ran beside the dry creekbed. Now the stupendous orange battlements of the side walls of the ravine rose vertically to each side, constricting their view of anything except the sky above and a shrinking wedge of valley floor behind them and below.

None of the escarpment canyons they had been in before matched this one for chiseled immensity and steepness.

Troy often talked as he hiked, muttering mostly to himself, so that Charlie behind him only heard every other phrase—something about the great U of Taboose Pass being an ice field rather than just a glacier. Not much of the crest had gotten iced over even at the height of the Ice Age, he said. A substantial ice cap had covered big parts of the range, but mostly to the west of the crest. To the east there had been only these ravine glaciers. The ice had covered what were now the best hiking and camping areas, where all the lakes and ponds had been scooped out of the tops of mostly bare granite plutons. It had been a lighter glaciation than in the Alps, so the tops of the plutons had been left intact for lakes to dot, not etched away by ice until there were only cirques and horns and deep forested valleys. The Alps' heavier snowfall and higher latitude had meant all its high basins had in effect been ground away. Thus (Troy concluded triumphantly) one had the explanation for the infinite superiority of the Sierra Nevada for backpacking purposes.

And so on. Troy was their mountain man, the one whose life was focused on it most fully, and who therefore served as their navigator, gear innovator, historian, geologist, and all-around Sierra guru. He spent a lot of hiking time alone, and although happy to have his friends along, still had a tendency to hold long dialogues with himself, as he must have done when on his solo trips.

Troy's overarching thesis was that if backpacking were your criterion of judgment, the Sierra Nevada of California was an unequaled paradise, and essentially heaven on Earth. All mountain ranges were beautiful, of course, but backpacking as an activity had been invented in the Sierra by John Muir and his friends, so it worked there better than anywhere else. Name any other range and Troy would snap out the reason it would not serve as well as the Sierra; this was a game he and Charlie played from time to time.

"Alps."

"Rain, too steep, no basins, dangerous. Too many people."

"But they're beautiful right?"

"Very beautiful."

"Colorado Rockies."

"Too big, no lakes, too dry, boring."

"Canadian Rockies."

"Grizzly bears, rain, forest, too big. Not enough granite. Pretty though."

"Andes."

"Tea hut system, need guides, no lakes. I'd like to do that though."

"Himalayas."

"Too big, tea hut system. I'd like to go back though."

"Pamirs."

"Terrorists."

"Appalachians."

"Mosquitoes, people, forest, no lakes. Boring."

"Transantarctics."

"Too cold, too expensive. I'd like to see them though."

"Carpathians?"

"Too many vampires!"

And so on. Only the Sierras had all the qualities Troy deemed necessary for hiking, camping, scrambling, and contemplating mountain beauty.

No argument from Charlie—although he noticed it looked about as dry as the desert ranges to the east. It seemed they were in the rain shadow of the range even here. The Nevada ranges must have been completely baked.

All day they hiked up the great gorge. It twisted and then broadened a little, but otherwise changed little as they rose. Orange rock leaped at the dark blue sky, and the battlements seemed to vibrate in place as Charlie paused to look at them—the effect of his heart pounding in his chest. Trudge trudge trudge. It was a strange feeling, Charlie thought, to know that for the next hour you were going to be doing nothing but walking—and after that hour, you would take a break and then walk some more. Hour following hour, all day long. It was so different from the days at home that it took some getting used to. It was, in effect, a different state of consciousness; only the experience of his previous backpacking trips allowed Charlie to slip back into it so readily. Mountain time; slow down. Pay attention to the rock. Look around. Slide back into the long ruminative rhythms of thought that plodded along at their own pedestrian pace, interrupted often by close examination of the granite, or the details of the trail as it crossed the meager stream which to everyone's relief was making occasional excursions from deep beneath boulderfields. Or a brief exchange with one of the other guys, as they came in and out of a switchback, and thus came close enough to each other to talk. In general they all hiked at their own paces, and as time passed, spread out up and down the trail.

A day was a long time. The sun beat down on them from high overhead. Charlie and some of the others, Vince especially, paced themselves by singing songs. Charlie hummed or chanted one of Beethoven's many themes of resolute determination, looping them endlessly. He also found himself unusually susceptible to bad pop and TV songs from his youth; these arose spontaneously within him and then stuck like burrs, for an hour or more, no matter what he tried to replace them with—things like "Red Rubber Ball" (actually a great song) or "Meet the Flintstones"—tromping methodically uphill, muttering over and over "We'll have a gay old—we'll have a gay old—we'll have a gay old time!"

"Charlie please shut up. Now you have me doing that."

"—a three-hour tour! A three-hour tour!"

So the day passed. Sometimes it would seem to Charlie like a good allegory for life itself. You just keep hiking uphill.

Frank hiked sometimes ahead, sometimes behind. He seemed lost in his thoughts, or the view, never particularly aware of the others. Nor did he seem to notice the work of the hike. He drifted up, mouth hanging open as he looked at the ravine's great orange sidewalls.

In the late afternoon they trudged up the final stony rubble of the head-wall, and into the pass—or onto it, as it was just as huge as the view from below had suggested: a deep broad U in the crest of the range, two thousand feet lower than the peaks marking each side of the U. These peaks were over a mile apart; and the depression of the pass was also nearly a mile from east to west, which was extremely unusual for a Sierra pass; most dropped away immediately on both sides, sometimes very steeply. Not so here, where a number of little black-rimmed ponds dotted an uneven granite flat.

"It's so big!"

"It looks like the Himalayas," Frank remarked as he walked by.

Troy had dropped his pack and wandered off to the south rise of the pass, checking out the little snow ponds tucked among the rocks. Now he whooped and called them all over to him. They stood up, groaning and complaining, and rubber-legged to him.

He pointed triumphantly at a low ring of stacked granite blocks, set on a flat tuck of decomposed granite next to one of the ponds. "Check it out guys. I ran into the national park archeologist last summer, and he told me about this. It's the foundation of a Native American summer shelter. They built some kind of wicker house on this base. They've dated them as old as five thousand years up here, but the archeologist said he thought they might be twice as old as that."

"How can you tell it's not just some campers from last year?" Vince demanded in his courtroom voice. This was an old game, and Troy immediately snapped back, "Obsidian flakes in the Sierra all come from knapping arrowheads. Rates of hydration can be used to date when the flaking was done. Standard methodology, accepted by all! And—" He reached down and plucked something from the decomposed granite at Vince's feet, held it aloft triumphantly: "Obsidian flake! Proof positive! Case closed!"

"Not until you get this dated," Vince muttered, checking the ground out now like the rest of them. "There could have been an arrowhead-making class up here just last week."

"Ha ha ha. That's how you get criminals back on the streets of L.A., but it won't work here. There's obsidian everywhere you look."

And in fact there was. They were all finding it; exclaiming, shouting, crawling on hands and knees, faces inches from the granite. "Don't take any of it!" Troy warned them, just as Jeff began to fill a baggie with them. "It screws up their counts. It doesn't matter that there are thousands of pieces here. This is an archeological site on federal land. You are grotesquely breaking the law there Jeffrey. Citizen's arrest! Vincent, you're a witness to this! What do you mean, you don't see a thing?" Then he fell back into contemplating the stone ring.

"Awesome," Charlie said.

"It really gives you a sense of them. The guy said they probably spent all summer up here. They did it for hundreds of years, maybe thousands. The people from the west brought up food and seashells, and the people from the east, salt and obsidian. It really helps you to see they were just like us."

Frank was on his hands and knees to get his face down to the level of the low rock foundation, his nose inches from the lichen-covered granite, nodding as he listened to Troy. "It's beautiful drywall," he commented. "You can tell by the lichen that it's been here a long time. It looks like a Goldsworthy." Then: "This is a sacred place."

Finally they went back to their packs, put them back on their backs, and staggered down into a high little basin to the west of the pass, where scoops of sand and dwarf trees appeared among some big erratic boulders. The day's hump up the great wall had taken it out of them. When they found a flat area with enough sandy patches to serve as a camp, they sat next to their backpacks and pulled out their warm clothes and their food bags and the rest of their gear, and had just enough energy and daylight left to get water from the nearest pond, then cook and eat their meals. They groaned stiffly as they stood to make their final arrangements, and congratulated each other on the good climb. They were in their bags and on the way to sleep before the sky had gone fully dark.

Before exhaustion knocked him out, Charlie looked over and saw Frank sitting up in his sleeping bag, looking west at the electric-blue band of sky over the black peaks to the west. He seemed untired by their ascent, or the sudden rise to altitude: absorbed by the immense spaces around them. Wrapped in thought. Charlie hoped his nose was doing all right. The stars were popping out overhead, swiftly surpassing in number and brilliance any starscapes they ever saw at home. The Milky Way was like a moraine of stars. Sound of distant water clucking through a patch of meadow, the wind in the pines; black spiky horizons all around, the smooth airy gap of the pass behind. It was a blessing to feel so tired in such a place. They had made the effort it took to regather, and here they were again, in a place so sublime no one could truly remember what it was like when they were away, so that every return had a sense of surprise, as if re-entering a miracle. Every time it felt this way. It was the California that could never be taken away.

Except it could.

Charlie had, of course, read about the ongoing drought that had afflicted the Sierra for the last few years, and he was also familiar with the climate models which suggested that the Sierra would be one of those places most affected by the global rise in temperature. California's wet months had been November through April, with the rest of the year as dry as any desert. A classic Mediterranean climate. Even during the Hyperniño this pattern had tended to endure, although in El Niño conditions more rain fell in the southern half of the state and less in the northern half, with the Sierras therefore getting a bit of both. In the past, however, whatever the amount of precipitation, it had fallen on the Sierra in the form of snow; this had created a thick winter snowpack, which then took most of the summer to melt. That meant that the reservoirs in the foothills got fed a stream of melting snow at a rate that could then be dispersed out to the cities and farms. In effect the Sierra snowpack itself had been the ultimate reservoir, far bigger than what the artificial ones behind dams in the foothills could hold.

Now, however, with global temperatures higher, more of the winter precipitation came down as rain, and thus ran off immediately. The annual reservoir of snow was smaller, even in good years; and in droughts it hardly formed at all.

California was in an uproar about this. New dams were being built, including the Auburn dam, located right on an earthquake fault; and the movement to remove the Hetch Hetchy dam had been defeated, despite the fact that the next reservoir down the Tuolomne had the capacity to hold all Hetch Hetchy's water. State officials were also begging Oregon and Washington to allow a pipeline to be built to convey water south from the Columbia River. The Columbia dumped a huge amount into the Pacific, one hundred times that of the maximum flow of the Colorado River, and all of it *unused*. It was immoral, some said. But naturally the citizens of Oregon and Washington had refused to agree to the pipeline, happy at a chance to stick it to California. Only the possibility that many Californians would then move north, bringing their obese equities with them, was causing any of them to reconsider their stance. But of course clear cost-benefit analysis was not the national strong suit, so on the battle would go for the foreseeable future.

In any case, no matter what political and hydrological adjustments were made in the lowlands, the high Sierra meadows were dying.

This was a shock to witness. It had changed in the three years since Charlie had last been up. He hiked down the trail on their second morning with a sinking feeling in his stomach, able to cinch the waistbelt of his pack tighter and tighter.

They were walking down the side of a big glacial gorge to the John Muir Trail. When they reached it, they headed north on it for a short distance, going gently uphill as the trail followed the south fork of the Kings River up toward Upper Basin and Mather Pass. As they hiked, it became obvious that the high basin meadows were much too dry for early August. They were desiccated. Ponds were often pans of cracked dirt. Grass was brown. Plants were dead: trees, bushes, ground cover, grasses. Even mosses. There were no marmots to be seen, and few birds. Only the lichen seemed okay—although as Vince pointed out, it was hard to tell. "If lichen dies does it lose its color?" No one knew.

After a few of these discouraging miles they turned left and followed an entirely dry tributary uphill to the northwest, aiming at the Vennacher Needle—a prominent peak, extremely broad for a needle, as Vince pointed out. "One of those famous blunt-tipped needles. One of those spherical needles."

Up and up, over broken granite, much whiter than the orange stuff east of Taboose Pass. This was the Cartridge Pluton, Troy told them as they ascended. A very pure bubble of granite. The batholith, meaning the whole mass of the range, was composed of about twenty or thirty plutons, which were the individual bubbles of granite making up the larger mass. The Cartridge was one of the most clearly differentiated plutons, separated as it was by glacial gorges from all the plutons around it. There was no easy way to get over its curving outer ridge into Lakes Basin, the high granite area atop the mass. They were hiking up to one of these entry points now, a pass called Vennacher Col.

The eastern approach to the col got steeper as they approached it, until they were grabbing the boulders facing them to help pull themselves up. And the other side was said to be steeper! But the destination was said to be fine: a basin remote, empty of trails and people, and dotted with lakes—many lakes—and lakes so big, Charlie saw with relief as he pulled into the airy pass, that they had survived the drought and were still there. They glittered in the white granite below like patches of cobalt silk.

Far, far below; for the western side of Vennacher Col was a very steep glacial headwall—in short, a cliff. The first five hundred vertical feet of their drop lay right under their toes, an airy nothing.

Troy had warned them about this. The Sierra guidebooks all rated this side of the pass class 3. In scrambling or (gulp) climbing terms, it was the crux of their week. Normally they avoided anything harder than class 2, and now they were remembering why.

"Troy?" Vince said. "Why are we here?"

"We are here to suffer," Troy intoned.

"Bayer Aspirin, it was your idea to do this; what the fuck?"

"I came up this way with these guys once. It's not as bad as it looks."

"You think you came up it," Charlie reminded him. "It was twenty years ago and you don't remember exactly what you did."

"It had to be here."

"Is this class 2?" Vince demanded.

"This side has a little class 3 section that you see here."

"You're calling this cliff little?"

"It's mostly a class 2 cliff."

"But don't you rate terrain by the highest level of difficulty?"

"Yes."

"So this is a class 3 pass."

"Technically, yes."

"Technically? You mean in some other sense, this cliff is not a cliff?"

"That's right."

The distinction between class 2 and class 3, Charlie maintained, lay precisely in what they were witnessing now: on class 2, one used one's hands for balance, but the terrain was not very steep, so that if one fell one could not do more than crack an ankle, at most. So the scrambling was fun. Whereas class 3 indicated terrain steep enough that although one could still scramble up and down it fairly easily, a fall on it would be dangerous—perhaps fatally dangerous—making the scramble nerve-racking, even in places a little terrifying. The classic description in the Roper guidebook said of it, "like ascending a steep narrow old staircase on the outside of a tower, without banisters." But it could be much worse than that. So the distinction between class 2 and class 3 was fuzzy in regard to rock, but very precise emotionally, marking as it did the border between fun and fear.

In this case, the actual class 3 route down the cliff, as described by the guidebooks and vaguely remembered by Troy from twenty years before, was a steep incision running transversely down the face from north to south. A kind of gully; and they could see that if they could get into this gully, they would be protected. The worst that could happen then was that they might slide down the gully a ways if they slipped.

But getting into the gully from the top was the trick. The class 3 moment, in effect. And no one liked the look of it, not even Troy.

The five old friends wandered back and forth anxiously on the giant rocks of the pass, peering down at the problem and talking it over. The top of the inner wall of the slot was a sheer cliff and out of the question. The class 3 route appeared to require downclimbing a stack of huge boulders topping the outer wall of the slot.

No one was happy at the prospect of getting down the outer wall's boulder stack. With backpacks or without, it was very exposed. Charlie wanted to be happy with it, but he wasn't. Troy had come up it once, or so he said, but going up was generally easier than going down. Maybe Troy could now downclimb it; and presumably Frank could, being a climber and all. But the rest of them, no.

Charlie looked around to see what Frank might say. Finally he spotted him, sitting on the flat top of one of the pass rocks, looking out to the west. It seemed clear he didn't care one way or the other what they did. As a climber he existed in a different universe, in which class 3 was the stuff you ran down on after climbing the real thing. Real climbing *started* with class 5, and even then it only got to what climbers would call serious at 5.8 or 5.9, or 5.10 or 5.11. Looking at the boulder stack again, Charlie wondered what 5.11 would look like—or feel like to be on! Never had he felt less inclined to take up rock climbing than he did at that moment.

But Frank didn't look like he was thinking about the descent at all. He sat on his block looking down at Lakes Basin, biting off pieces of an energy bar. Charlie was impressed by his tact, if that's what it was. Because they were in a bit of a quandary, and Charlie was pretty sure that Frank could have led them into the slot, or down some other route, if he had wanted to. But it wasn't his trip; he was a guest, and so he kept his counsel.

Or maybe he was just spacing out, even to the point of being unaware there was any problem facing the rest of them. He sat staring at the view, chewing ruminatively, body relaxed. A man at peace. Charlie wandered up the narrow spine of the pass to his side.

"Nice, eh?"

"Oh, my, yes," Frank said. "Just gorgeous. What a beautiful basin."

"It really is."

"It's strange to think how few people will ever see this," Frank said. He had not volunteered even so much as this since they had met at Dulles, and Charlie crouched by his side to listen. "Maybe only a few hundred people in the history of the world have ever seen it. And if you don't see it, you can't really imagine it. So it's almost like it doesn't exist for most people. So really this basin is a kind of secret. A hidden valley that you have to search for. And even then you might never find it."

"I guess so," Charlie said. "We're lucky."

"Yes."

"How's your head feel up here?"

"Oh good. Good, sure. Interesting!"

"No post-op bleeding, or psychosis or anything?"

"No. Not as far as I can tell."

Charlie laughed. "That's as good as."

He stood and walked down the spine to where the others were continuing to discuss options.

"What about straight down from the lowest point here?" Vince demanded.

Charlie objected, "That won't work—look at the drop." He still wanted to want to try the boulder stack.

"But around that buttress down there, maybe," Dave pointed out. "Something's sure to go around it."

"Why do you say that?"

"I don't know. Because it always goes in the Sierra."

"Except when it doesn't!"

"I'm going to try it," Jeff declared, and took off before anyone had time to point out that since he was by far the most reckless among them, his ability to descend a route said very little about it as far as the rest of them were concerned.

"Don't forget your comb!" Vince said, in reference to a time when Jeff had used a plastic comb to hack steps up a vertical snowbank no one else had cared to try.

Ten minutes later, however, he was a good portion of the way down the cliff, considerably off to the left as they looked down, where the steepness of the rock angled outward, and looked quite comfy compared to where they were.

He yelled back up at them, "Piece of cake! Piece of cake!"

"Yeah right!" they all yelled.

But there he was, and he had done it so fast that they had to try it. They found some very narrow ledges hidden under the buttress, trending down and left, and by holding on to the broken white granite of the wall next to their heads, and making their way carefully along the ledges and down from ledge to ledge, they had all soon followed Jeff to the less steep bulge in the cliff, and from there each took a different route to a horrible jumble of rocks in a flat trough at the bottom.

"Wow!" Charlie said as they regathered on a big white rock among the rest, next to a little bowl of caked black dust that had once been a pool of water. "That was class 2! I was wrong. It wasn't so bad! Wasn't that class 2?" he asked of Troy and Frank.

"It probably was," Troy said.

"So you guys just discovered a class 2 route on a wall that all the guidebooks call class 3!"

"How could that happen?" Vince wondered. "Why would we be the ones to find it?"

"We were desperate," Troy said, looking back up. From below the cliff looked even steeper than it had from above.

"That's probably actually it," Charlie said. "The class ratings up here have mostly been made by climbers, and when they came up to this pass they probably saw the big slot in the face, and ran right up it without a second thought, because it's so obvious. The fact it was class 3 meant nothing to them, they didn't care one way or the other, so they rated it 3, which is right if you're only talking about the slot. They never even noticed there was a much trickier class 2 line off to the side, because they didn't need it."

Frank nodded. "Could be."

"We'll have to write to the authors of the guidebooks and see if we can get them to relist Vennacher Col as class 2! We can call the route the Jeffrey Dirretissimma."

"Very cool. You do that."

"Actually," Vince pointed out, "it was my refusal to go down the slot that caused Jeff to take the new route, and I'm the one that spotted it first, so I'm thinking it should be called the Salami Dirretissima. That has a better ring to it anyway."

That night, in a wonderful campsite next to the biggest of the Lakes Basin's lakes (none had names), their dinner party was extra cheery. They had crossed a hard pass—an impossible pass—and were now in the lap of beauty, lying around on ground pads dressed like pashas in colorful silken clothing, drinking an extra dram or two of their carefully hoarded liquor supplies, watching the sun burnish the landscape. The water copper, the granite bronze, the sky cobalt. On the northern wall of the basin a single tongue of cloud lapped up the slope like some sinuous creature, slowly turning pink. Each of them cooked his own dinner, on various kinds of tiny backpacking stoves, and in various styles of backpacking fare: Dave and Jeff sticking with the old ramen and mac-and-cheese, Vince with the weirdest freeze-dried meals currently available at REI; Troy downing a glop of his own devising, a mixture of powders from the bins of his food co-op, intensely healthy and fortified; Charlie employing the lark's-tongues-in-aspic theory of extreme tastiness, in a somewhat vain attempt to overcome the appetite suppression that often struck him at altitude. Frank appeared to favor a diet that most resembled Troy's, with bars and bags of nuts and grains supplying his meals.

After dinner the Maxfield Parrish blues of the twilight gave way to the stars, and then the Milky Way. The moon would not rise for a few hours, and in the starlight they could still see the strange tongue of low cloud, now gray, licking the north wall of the basin. The lake beside them stilled to a starry black mirror. Quickly the cold began to press on the little envelopes of warmth their clothes created, and they slid into their sleeping bags and continued to watch the tiny stove-pellet fire that Dave kept going, feeding it from time to time with the tiniest of twigs and pine needles.

The conversation wandered, and sometimes grew ribald. Dave was outlining an all-too-convincing biological basis for the so-called midlife crisis, and general confessions of inappropriate lust for young women were soon augmented by one or two individual case studies of close calls, at work or in the gym. Laughter in the dark, and some long silences too.

Voices by starlight. But it's stupid. It's just your genes making one last desperate scream when they can feel they're falling apart. Programmed cell death. Apoptosis. They want you to have more kids to up their chance of being immortal, they don't give a shit about you or your actual happiness or anything.

If you're just fooling around, if you don't mean to leave your wife and go with that person, then it's like masturbating in someone else's body.

Yuck! Jesus, yuck!

Hoots of horrified hilarity, echoing off the cliffs across the lake. That's so gross I'll never again be able to think about having an affair!

So I cured you. So now you're old. Your genes have given up.

My genes will never give up.

The little stove pellet burned out. The hikers went quiet and were soon asleep, under the great slow wheel of the stars.

The next day they explored the Lakes Basin, looking into a tributary of it called the Dumbbell Basin, and dropping to the Y-shaped Triple Falls on Cartridge Creek, before turning back up toward the head of the basin proper. It was a beautiful day, the heart of the trip, just as it was the heart of the pluton, and that pluton the heart of the Sierra itself. No trails, no people, no views out of the range. They walked on the heart of the world.

On such days some kind of freedom descended on them. Mornings were cold and clear, spent lazing around their sleeping bags and breakfast coffee.

They chatted casually, discussed the quality of their night's sleep. They asked Charlie about what it was like to work for the president: Charlie gave them his little testimonial. "He's a good guy," he told them. "He's not a normal guy, but he's a good one. He's still real. He has the gift of a happy temperament. He sees the funny side of things." Frank listened to this closely, head cocked to one side.

Once they got packed up and started, they wandered apart, or in duos, catching up on the year's news, on the wives and kids, the work and play, the world at large. Stopping frequently to marvel at the landscapes that constantly shifted in perspective around them. It was very dry, a lot of the fellfields and meadows were brown, but the lakes were still there and their borders were green as of old. The distant ridges; the towering thunderheads in the afternoons; the height of the sky itself; the thin cold air; the pace of the seconds, tocking at the back of the throat; all combined to create a sense of spaciousness unlike any they ever felt anywhere else. It was another world.

But this world kept intruding.

Their plan was to exit the basin by way of Cartridge Pass, which was south of Vennacher Col, on the same border ridge of the pluton. This pass had been the original route for the Muir Trail; the trail over it had been abandoned in 1934, after the CCC built the replacement trail over Mather Pass. Now the old trail was no longer on the maps, and Troy said the guidebooks described it as being gone. But he didn't believe it, and in yet another of his archeological quests, he wanted to see if they could relocate any signs of it. "I think what happened was that when the USGS did the ground check for their maps in 1968, they tried to find the trail over on the other side, and it's all forest and brush over there, so they couldn't pick it up, and they wrote it off. But over on this side there's nothing but rock up near the top. I don't believe much could happen to a trail up there. Anyway I want to look."

Vince said, "So this is another cross-country pass, that's what you're saying."

"Maybe."

So once again they were on the hunt. They hiked slowly uphill, separating again into their own spaces. " 'Now I know you're not the only starfish in the sea!' Starfish? How many other great American songs are about starfish, I ask you? 'Yeah, the worst is over now, the morning sun is rising like a *red, rubber ball!*' "

Then on the southeast slope of the headwall, where the maps showed the old trail had gone, their shouts rang out once more. Right where one would have hiked if one were simply following the path of least resistance up the slope, a trail appeared. As they hiked up, it became more and more evident, until high on the headwall it began to switchback up a broad talus gully that ran up between solid granite buttresses. In that gully the trail became as obvious as a

Roman road, because its bed was made of decomposed granite that had been washed into a surface and then in effect cemented there by years of rain, without any summer boots ever breaking it up. It looked like the nearly concretized paths that landscapers created with decomposed granite in the world below, but here the raw material had been left in situ and shaped by feet. People had only hiked it for some thirty or forty years—unless the Native Americans had used this pass too—and it was another obvious one, and near Taboose, so maybe they had—in which case people had hiked it for five or ten thousand years. In any case, a great trail, with the archeological component adding to the sheer physical grandeur of it.

"There are lost trails like this on an island in Maine," Frank remarked to no one in particular. He was looking around with what Charlie now thought of as his habitual hiking expression. It seemed he walked in a rapture.

The pass itself gave them long views in all directions—north back into the basin, south over the giant gap of the Muro Blanco, a granite-walled canyon. Peaks beyond in all directions.

After a leisurely lunch in the sun, they put on their packs and started down into the Muro Blanco. The lost trail held, thinning through high meadows, growing fainter as they descended, but always still there.

But here the grass was brown. This was a south-facing slope, and it almost looked like late autumn. Not quite, for autumn in the Sierra was marked by fall colors in the ground cover, including a neon scarlet that came out on slopes backlit by the sun. Now that same ground cover was simply brown. It was dead. Except for fringes of green around drying ponds, or algal mats on the exposed pond bottoms, every plant on this south-facing slope had died. It was as burnt as any range in Nevada. One of the loveliest landscapes on the planet, dead before their eyes.

They hiked at their different paces, each alone on the rocky rumpled landscape. Bench to bench, terrace to terrace, graben to graben, fellfield to fellfield, each in his own private world.

Charlie fell behind the rest, stumbling from time to time in his distress, careless of his feet as his gaze wandered from one little ecodisaster to the next. He loved these high meadows with all his heart, and the fellfields between them too. Each had been so perfect, like works of art, as if hundreds of meticulous bonsai gardeners had spent centuries clipping and arranging each watercourse and pad of moss. Every blade of grass deployed to best effect, every rock in its proper place. It had never occurred to Charlie that any of it could ever go away. And yet here it was, dead.

Desolation filled him. It pressed inside him, slowing him down, buffeting him from inside, making him stumble. Not the Sierra. Everything living that he loved in this Alpine world would go away, and then it would not be the Sierra. Suddenly he thought of Joe and a giant stab of fear pierced him like a sword, he sank back and sat on the nearest rock, felled by the feeling. Never doubt our emotions rule us, and no matter what we do, or say, or resolve, a single feeling can knock us down like a sword to the heart. A dead meadow— image of a black crisp on a bed—Charlie groaned and put his face to his knees.

He tried to pull himself back into the world. Behind him Frank was still wandering, lonely as a cloud, deep in his own space; but soon he would catch up.

Charlie took a deep breath, pulled himself together. Several more deep breaths. No one would ever know how shaken he had been by his thoughts. So much of life is a private experience.

Frank stood over him. He looked down at him with his head cocked. "You okay?"

"I'm okay. You?"

"I'm okay." He gestured around them. "Quite the drought."

"That's for sure!" Charlie shook his head violently from side to side. "It makes me sad—it makes me afraid! I mean—it looks so bad. It looks like it could be gone for good!"

"You think so?"

"Sure! Don't you?"

Frank shrugged. "There's been droughts up here before. They've found dead trees a couple hundred feet down in Lake Tahoe. Stuff like that. Signs of big droughts. It seems like it dries out up here from time to time."

"Yes. But—you know. What if it lasts a hundred years? What if it lasts a thousand years?"

"Well, sure. That would be bad. But we're doing so much to the weather. And it's pretty chaotic anyway. Hopefully it will be all right."

Charlie shrugged. This was thin comfort.

Again Frank regarded him. "Aside from that, you're okay?"

"Yeah, sure." It was so unlike Frank to ask, especially on this trip. Charlie felt an urge to continue: "I'm worried about Joe. Nothing in particular, you know. Just worried. It's hard to imagine, sometimes, how he is going to get on in this world."

"Your Joe? He'll get on fine. You don't have to worry about him."

Frank stood over Charlie, hands folded on the tops of his walking poles, looking out at the sweep of the Muro Blanco, the great canyon walled by long cliffs of white granite. At ease; distracted. Or so it seemed. As he wandered away he said over his shoulder, "Your kids will be fine."

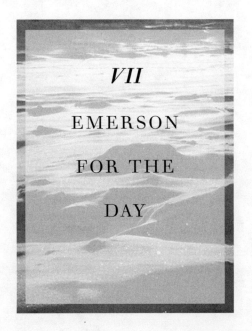

VII

EMERSON

FOR THE

DAY

"There are days which are the carnival of the year. The angels assume flesh, and repeatedly become visible. The imagination of the gods is excited and rushes on every side into forms."

—*Emerson*

Wake up Sunday morning. In the van, outside a fregan potluck house, down in Foggy Bottom. Put on clothes one would wear to give a talk: "scientist nice," meaning shirt with collar, dark walking shoes, Dockers pants.

Walk to the Optimodal that Diane found near the White House. Work out, shower and shave, then east on G Street. Find a deli open for lunch; most of them closed on weekend. Eat lunch and then continue east to the MCI Center, where the Wizards play basketball.

A building like all the others in the area, filling a whole block. This one, instead of offices and shops bordering the sidewalk, has glass doors by the dozen, and poster-holders between the doors, advertising all kinds of events. The glass doors have lines of people outside them. Many Asians, many of them in Asian attire.

Wait in line, then give an attendant a Ticketron ticket. Inside, wander down the hallway looking at the tunnel entries, checking the section numbers. Hallway lined with food stalls and souvenir stands and restrooms, as in any sports arena in the country. Beer, wine, hot dogs, pretzels, nachos. Like a basketball game, or a rock concert. Strange to see when attending a talk by the Dalai Lama. Walking in a category error. Maybe that was always true.

Plan to meet the Quiblers at their seats, a good thing; impossible to tell if one has circled ninety degrees or a hundred and eighty. Which way is north? No way to tell.

After two hundred and seventy degrees, perhaps, come to proper number and show ticket to usher, get ushered to seat. Great seats if it were basketball, in the middle, just above floor, which is now occupied by rows of chairs, slowly filling with people. Stage at the end of the floor, where one basket would be. Empty seats; presumably the Quiblers'. An hour and a half before the scheduled start. Don't want to be late for the Dalai Lama! Arena at this point nearly empty. And big. A big oval of seats, rising to a great height on all sides. Was that glassed row what they called luxury boxes? Maybe the Dalai Lama is not a sellout.

But he is. Arena fills. Quiblers show up around half an hour before the start. Shake hands with Charlie and the boys, give Anna a hug. She too dressed up a bit—as if giving a talk at a conference, yes. Looks nice. All the women in the arena look nice.

Sit and chat about the crowd and the venue and the event, the boys looking around with the same curious expression one can feel in one's own face. Watching people. Mesmerized by the sight of so many people, pouring in tunnels from concourse and taking their seats. Charlie says capacity twenty thousand, but with the section behind the stage cordoned off and left empty, more like thirteen thousand. Thirteen thousand human beings, all races, nations, and ethnicities seemingly represented. All gathered to hear one man speak. This is Washington, D.C. Capital of the world.

A big screen behind the stage. They test a video system that shows, greatly magnified on the screen, the image of an armchair on the stage, which makes the actual chair suddenly look tiny. There are two armchairs, in fact, and a carpet between them, a coffee table. Small tree in pot behind. Bouquets of flowers surround the base of a lectern, set off to one side.

People appear on stage, causing a groundswell of voices, then applause. An American woman from the Tibetan-American Friendship Society welcomes the crowd, which now packs the arena to capacity, no unoccupied seats to be seen, except in the empty section behind the screen. A Democratic congresswoman introduces the Dalai Lama, at great length and with little eloquence. Then a pause; the hall goes silent.

"What?" Joe asks, looking around bug-eyed.

A cluster of people in maroon robes walk up the steps onto the stage, and sudden applause bursts out. Everyone stands, everyone. Joe stands on his chair, then climbs into Charlie's arms. His head is then just higher than Charlie's. Now it can be seen how their faces look alike.

Dalai Lama on stage. A big swell of applause. He wears the kind of robe that leaves his arms bare. He holds his hands together, bows slightly in various directions, smiling graciously. All this is repeated hugely on the screen behind him. The face familiar from photographs. An ordinary Tibetan monk, as he always says himself.

On the stage with him appears a shorter Tibetan man in a Western three-piece suit. This man sits in the armchair on the right and watches as twenty or thirty more people ascend the stairs onto the stage. They are all dressed in colorful national or ethnic or religious costumes, Asian in look. Buddhist, one supposes, with lots of white and many splashes of brilliant color. There is a light purple they appear to favor.

They array themselves in a line facing the Dalai Lama, and the American woman who first welcomed them returns to the lectern to explain to the audience that these are representatives of all the Buddhist communities in Asia who regard the Dalai Lama as their spiritual leader. More applause.

Each representative approaches the Dalai Lama in turn, holding a white scarf. With a bow the Dalai Lama takes the scarves, bows again, often touching foreheads with the person who has approached, then puts the scarves around their necks. After a verbal exchange not broadcast to the crowd, the representatives move to one side.

Some are clearly almost overwhelmed by this interaction with the Dalai Lama. They crab toward him, or walk bent in a bow. But the Dalai Lama greets all alike with a big grin and a friendly greeting, and when they leave him they have straightened up and are more relaxed.

The last dignitary to approach is Drepung, in flowing white robes. It takes checking on the big screen to be sure of this. Yes, their Drepung. Joe is jerking up and down in Charlie's arms, pointing. Nick too is pointing.

The almost stereopticon effect of the two images, one little and three-dimensional, one huge and two-dimensional, creates a kind of hyperreality, a five-dimensional vertigo. On the screen, one can see that under his white ceremonial robes Drepung is still wearing his running shoes, now more enormous than ever. He bounces toward the Dalai Lama with a huge grin on his face, the Dalai Lama matching it watt for watt; they seem to know each other. The Dalai Lama bows as Drepung approaches, Drepung bows, they keep eye contact all the while. They meet and touch foreheads, Drepung bowing lower to make this contact, even though the Dalai Lama is not a small man. The crowd cheers. Many Asians around them are weeping. Drepung hands the Dalai Lama the white scarf he is carrying, and the Dalai Lama touches it to his forehead and puts it around Drepung's neck, Drepung bowing low to receive it. When that's done they speak for a bit in Tibetan, laughing at something. The Dalai Lama asks a question, Drepung cocks his head to the side, nods, makes some jest; laughing, the Dalai Lama turns and takes a white scarf from one of his aides standing behind, then gives it to Drepung. Drepung touches it to his forehead, then extends it over the Dalai Lama's bowed head and places it around his neck. As the Dalai Lama straightens, Drepung flicks one end of the scarf and it lands over the Dalai Lama's shoulder like a flapper's boa. The Dalai Lama laughs and vamps for a second, to audience laughter, then gestures Drepung off the stage as if shooing away a fly.

The white-scarved group also leaves the stage. The Dalai Lama sits down in the armchair to the left, across from his compatriot. He puts on a radio microphone that works well, as everyone finds out when he says in a deep voice, "Hello." Amplification in the arena is clearer than one would have thought possible.

The crowd says hello back. The Dalai Lama kicks off his sandals, leaves them on the carpet and tucks his feet up under his legs, in either a meditation pose or just a comfortable position. Bare arms make it seem he could be cold, but no doubt he is used to it and does not notice. It's hot outside anyway.

He begins to speak, but in Tibetan. Around his amplified words is silence. The airy whoosh of the building's ventilation system becomes audible: a surreal disjunction, between the absence of crowd noise and the visible presence of thirteen thousand people. All quiet, all listening intently to a man speaking a language they don't know.

Low sonorous Tibetan, unlike the sound of Chinese, or the other east Asian languages. Yes, he sounds like Rudra Cakrin. Then he pauses, and the man in the other armchair speaks in English. Ah, the translator. Presumably he is summarizing what the Dalai Lama just said. Another good headset microphone. Voices booming out of the giant black scoreboard console hanging over center court.

The translator finishes translating what was apparently an entirely conventional welcome, and the Dalai Lama starts again in Tibetan. This is going to be a long affair. Then all of a sudden the Dalai Lama switches to English. "I hope we can talk about all this in the rest of our time together. How to live in this world. How to achieve peace and balance."

His English is perfectly clear. He jokes about his inability in it, and from time to time he dives back into Tibetan, apparently to be sure of being accurate about important things. Possibly even here his attempt in English would be more interesting than the translator's more expert locutions. In any case, back and forth between languages they bounce, both getting some laughs.

The Dalai Lama talks about the situation they find themselves in, "a difficult moment in history" as he calls it, acknowledging this truth with a shrug. Reality is not easy; as a Tibetan this has been evident all his life; and yet all the more reason not to despair, or even to lose one's peace of mind. One has to focus on what one can do oneself, and then do that, he says. He says, "We are visitors on this planet. We are here for ninety or one hundred years at the very most. During that period, we must try to do something good, something useful, with our lives. Try to be at peace with yourself, and help others share that peace. If you contribute to other people's happiness, you will find the true goal, the true meaning of life."

He sounds so much like Rudra Cakrin. Suddenly it's hard to believe that such an idiosyncratic mind as Rudra Cakrin's can be gone. Many of the people here presumably do not believe it. The man speaking is agreed to be the fourteenth reincarnation of a particular mind or soul. Although in an interview published that morning in the Post, the Dalai Lama was asked when he had first recalled his previous lives, and he replied, "I have never had that experience," and then added, "I am an ordinary human being." He did not even make any particular claim to special knowledge, or expertise in anything metaphysical.

Now he says, "What happens beyond our senses we cannot know. All we can see indicates that everything is transitory."

This is not the kind of thing a religious leader is expected to say—admissions of ignorance, jokes about translation error. The whole situation feels nonreligious, more like a fireside chat than the Sermon on the Mount. Maybe the Sermon on the Mount would have felt like that too.

"Knowledge is important, but much more important is the use toward which it is put. This depends on the heart and mind of the one who uses it."

It's the argument for always-generous. Even if you only manage to love your own DNA, it exists in a diffuse extension through the biosphere. All the eukaryotes share the basic genes; all life is one. If you love yourself, or just want to survive—or maybe those are the same thing—then the love has to diffuse out into everything, just to be accurate.

To love accurately. The Dalai Lama says something about mindful consumption. We eat the world the way we breathe it. Thanks must be given, devotion must be given. One must pay attention, to do what is right for life.

These were all the things a sociobiologist would recommend, if he could talk about what ought to be as well as what is. Buddhism as the Dalai Lama's science; science as the scientist's Buddhism. Again, as when Rudra Cakrin gave his lecture at NSF, it all becomes clear.

Time passes in a flow of ideas. A couple of hours, in fact; no concessions to any suppposedly short attention spans. And the crowd is still silent and attentive. The time has gone fast somehow, and now the Dalai Lama is winding things up by answering a few questions submitted by e-mail, read by his translator from a printout.

"Last question, Rebecca Sampson, fifth grade: Why does China want Tibet so bad?"

Nervous titter from the crowd.

The Dalai Lama tilts his head to the side. "Tibet *is very beautiful," he says, in a way that makes everyone laugh. A certain tension dissipates.* "Tibet has a lot of forests. Animals, minerals—not so many vegetables." *Another surprised laugh, rustling unamplifed through the arena like wind in the trees.*

"Most of all, Tibet has room. China is a big country, but it has a lot of people. Too many people for them to care for on their own land, over the long term. And Tibet is at the roof of Asia. When you are in Tibet, no one can attack you from above! So, there are these strategic reasons. But most of them, when examined, are not very important. And I see signs that the Chinese are beginning to realize that. There are ways of accommodating everybody's desires, and so I see some progress on this matter. They are willing to talk now. It will all come in time."

Soon after that they are done. Everyone is standing and clapping. A moment of union. Thirteen thousand human beings, all thankful at once.

Say good-bye to the Quiblers. Wander with the crowd, disoriented, uncaring; it doesn't matter where you leave the building. Just get outside and figure out then where you are.

Outside. Westward on H Street. Quickly separate from the crowd that has witnessed together such an event: back among the strangers of the city. No more union. Over to G Street and west, past the White House with its fence, past the ugly Old Executive Offices, don't turn in there to work. Just look. Think about the place from the outside. From the Dalai Lama's point of view. Why had the Dalai Lama given Drepung a scarf to bless and put around his own neck? He hadn't done that with anyone else. Must ask Drepung. Some kind of power.

What was it the Dalai Lama said about compassion?

The words are gone, the feeling remains. Did he really use the word oxytocin, *did he really say* positron emission topography, *laughing with the translator as he mangled the phrase? What just happened?*

One can always just walk away. The Dalai Lama had said that for sure. Things you don't like, things you think are wrong, you can always just walk away. You will be happier. Love and compassion are necessities, not luxuries. Without them humanity cannot survive. But compassion is not just a feeling. You have to act.

HOMELESS NIGHTS IN THE CITY. Slip out the security gate at sunset and off the grid, into the interstices, following the older system of paths and alleys and rail beds that web the urban forest like animal trails. Join the ferals living outdoors, in the wind.

Frank worked from dawn until sunset on weekdays. The rest of the time he wandered the streets and the parks and the cafes. He turned in his van to the Honda place in Arlington, then paid cash to one of the fregans for a VW van with a burnt-out engine, and got Spencer to sign the papers to take ownership of it. He slept in it while he and Spencer and Robin and Robert worked at replacing its engine. It turned out Robin and Robert had VW experience, and they did not mind sitting around in a driveway after a run, fingering over a pile of parts. Apparently this was a recognized form of post-frisbee entertainment.

"The VW engine is the last piece of technology humans could actually understand. You look under the hood of a new car, it's like whoah."

"I lived in one of these for three years."

"I lost my virginity in one of these."

General laughter. Spencer sang, "I would fight for hippie chicks, I would die for hippie chicks!"

"See if you can get the fan belt slipped over that there now."

The one thing which we seek with insatiable desire is to forget ourselves, to be surprised out of our propriety, to lose our memory and to do something without knowing how or why; in short to draw a new circle. The way of life is wonderful; it is by abandonment. A man never rises so high as when he knows not whither he is going.

If that was true, then all should be well. He should be very high indeed.

Decision was a feeling. In the morning he woke up in the back of the VW van, and saw his Acheulian hand axe up there on the dashboard, and his whole life and identity leaped to him, as solid as that chunk of quartzite. Awake at dawn: now was the time to eat a little breakfast bar, read a little Emerson. So he did. No pressure there, impeding his progress through time; he flowed with perfect equanimity. "To hazard the contradiction—freedom is necessary. If you please to plant yourself on the side of Fate, and say, Fate is all; then we say, a part of Fate is the freedom of man. Forever wells up the impulse of choosing and acting."

And so it did. With a sure hand he opened the door on the day.

He got rid of his cell phone. He stopped using credit cards or checks; he got cash from the ATM in the office and he did all his e-mail there. He kept his FOG phone, but did not use it. He left the system of signs.

Most of his waking hours he was working at the Old Executive Offices. While the VW van was still stationary, when he had an hour, he took the Metro out to Ballston to see Drepung and some of the other Khembalis at their office in the NSF building. Sometimes he walked from there out to the embassy house in Arlington. Once he looked in the garden shed.

When they got the VW van running (it sounded like Laurel and Hardy's black truck) he also added visits to the farm, to see the gang, and help out in the big garden there. He never stayed long.

At the office he started working with a team from the OMB on funding proposals. They had done some macrocalculations for strategic planning purposes, and it turned out they could swap out the electricity-generating infrastructure for about three hundred billion dollars—an astonishing bargain, as one OMB guy put it. Stabilizing sea level might cost more, because the amount of water involved was simply staggering. Sustainable ag, on the other hand, was only expensive in terms of labor. If it wasn't going to be fossil fueled, it was going to be much more labor intensive. They needed more farmers, they needed intensive management grass-range ranchers. In other words they needed more cowboys, incredible though that seemed. It was suggestive, when one thought of the federal lands in the American West, and public employment possibilities. The emptying high plains—you could repopulate a region where too few people meant the end of town after town. Landscape restoration—habitat— buffalo biome—wolves and bears. Grizzly bears. Cost, about fifty billion dollars. These are such bargains! the OMB guy kept exclaiming. It doesn't take that much to prime the pump! Who knew?

A little before sunset, unless something was absolutely pressing, Frank would leave the Old Executive Offices and the security compound, and take off into the streets. Check for tails, sprint at a few strategic moments down little cross streets, to test those behind; no one could follow him without him seeing it. Sometimes he then took the Metro up to the Zoo; sometimes he walked all the way. It was only two miles, about thirty minutes' hiking. When traffic was bad the drive wouldn't be that much faster. The city felt larger than it was because when in cars there were so many delays and turns and buildings; and when walking, the distances took a bit too long. At a running pace you saw how compact it was.

Run off the map and into the forest. *In good health, the air is a cordial of incredible virtue. Crossing a bare common, in snow puddles, at twilight, under a clouded sky, without having in my thoughts any occurrence of special good fortune, I have enjoyed a perfect exhilaration. I am glad to the brink of fear.*

That was it exactly; to the brink of fear. It filled you up. The wind in your face. These Concord guys! That America's first great thinkers had been raving nature mystics was not accident, but inevitable. The land had spoken through them. They had lived outdoors in the great stony forest of New England, with its Himalayan weather. The blue of the sky, the abyss of fear behind things. A day out on the river, skinny-dipping with Ellery Channing.

One evening as he hiked past Site 21 he saw that the old gang was back, looking as if they had never been away.

"Zeno, Fedpage, Andy, Cutter!"

"Hey there! Doctor Blood! Where you been?"

"How are you guys, where *you* been?"

"We haven't been anywhere," Zeno declared.

"What!" Frank cried. "You haven't been here!"

Cutter waved a hand at two of his city park friends, sitting at the table with him. "Out and about, you know."

Andy yelled, "What do you mean where you been? Where *you* been?"

"I've been staying with some friends," Frank said.

"Yeah well—us too," Zeno growled.

"Any sight of Chessman?"

"*No.*" And stupid of you to ask.

"Are you still doing stuff with FOG?"

"With FOG! Are you kidding?"

They told him about it all together, Zeno prevailing in the end: "—and Fedpage is still pissed off at them!"

"He sure has bad luck with that federal government."

"You mean they have bad luck with him! He's a Jonah!"

"I am not a Jonah! I'm just the only one who looks up my rights in the personnel policies and then sticks up for them."

"You need to be more ignorant," Zeno instructed.

"I do! I've *got* to stop reading all this shit, but I can't." Fedpage was reading the *Post* as he said this, so the others laughed at him.

Actually, it transpired, he was still doing some work with FOG, despite his beef with them, helping Nancy to organize chipping expeditions to tag more animals. To no one's surprise, the bros had liked being given little dart guns, which shot chipped darts the size of BBs; and they liked their big hunts, when they went out in beater lines to shoot all the remaining unchipped animals they could find.

"The problem," Zeno told Frank, "is that half these animals are already chipped, and we aren't supposed to plunk them twice, but it's so tempting once you've got one in your sights."

"So you shoot anyway?"

"No, we start shooting each other!" Triumphant laughter at this. "It's like those paintball wars. Andy must have ten chips in him by now."

"That's only 'cause he shot so many people first!"

"Now there are surveillance screens in this city where he is like twelve people in one spot."

"He's a jury!"

"So don't you be trying to send us on no more secret spy missions," Andy told Frank. "We're all lit up like Christmas trees."

"Protective coloration," Frank suggested. "I should pass through you guys every night."

"Don't do that," Zeno warned. "We take this opportunity to say no to Dr. No."

"Yeah well, sorry about that guys, I meant to thank you and I know it was a long time ago now, but whenever I came out here you guys weren't here, so I didn't know."

"We've been around," Zeno said.

A silence stretched, and Frank sat on his old bench. "Why are you pissed off at FOG?" he asked Fedpage. "How exactly did you get bogarted by the evil Big Brother that is Friends of the National Zoo?"

"The Department of Parkland Security, you mean? Look, all I was saying was that we were doing regular national-park work on a volunteer basis, and that made us subject to federal liability, which means we *have* to sign their stipulated waivers or else the NPS would be left liable for any accidents, whereas with the waivers it would fall on Interior's general personnel funds, which is where you would want it if you wanted any timely compensation! But what do I know?"

Zeno said, "So get on that, Blood. We want that fixed."

"Okay. Well hey guys, I was just passing through on my way to meet the frisbees, I'm going to go join them. But it's good to see you. I'll drop on by again. I'm doing some sunset counts for FOG, and dawn patrols too, so I'll be around. Are folks hanging here much now?"

No replies, as usual. The bros never much on discussing plans.

"Well, I'll see you if I see you," Frank said.

"*I'll* join you for a FOG walk," Fedpage said darkly. "You need to hear the whole story about them."

That day's sunset was now gilding the autumn forest's dull yellows and browns. Leaves covered the surrounding hillsides to ankle depth everywhere they could see. Cutter gestured at the view with the can of beer in his hand: "Ain't it pretty? All these leaves, and nobody's gonna have to leaf-blow them away."

Fedpage did join him on a dawn patrol one morning, massaging his face to wake up. The two of them wandered slowly up the ravine, peering through the trees, pinging animals they saw with their FOG RFID readers. Fedpage talked under his breath most of the time. Perhaps obsessive-compulsive, with huge systems in his mind which made better sense to him than he could convey to other people. He was not unlike Anna in this intense regard for systems, but did not have Anna's ability to assign them their proper importance, to prioritize and see a path through a pattern, which was what made Anna so good at NSF. Without that component, or even radically lacking in it, Fedpage was living on the street and crying in his beer, always going on about lost battles over semihallucinated bureaucratic trivia. An excess of reason itself a form of madness, indeed.

You needed it all working. Otherwise things got strange. Indecisiveness was a kind of vertigo in time, a loss of balance in one's sense of movement into the future. When you weren't actually in the state it was hard to remember how it had felt. "Forever wells up the impulse of choosing." So it might seem, when all was well.

He and Fedpage came on an old man, comatose in his layby—blue-skinned, clearly in distress. The two of them kneeled over him, trying to determine if he was still alive, calling Nancy and 911 both, then wondering whether they should try to carry him out to Broad Branch Road, or instead wait where they were and be the ping for the rescue team. Fedpage babbled angrily about poor response time averages while Frank sat there wishing he knew more about medical matters, resolving (yet again) to at least take a CPR course.

He said this to Fedpage and Fedpage snorted. "Like Bill Murray in *Groundhog Day*."

Bill Murray, trying to help a stricken homeless guy. Yet another truth from that movie so full of them; if you really wanted to help other people you would have to devote years of your life to learning how.

He tried to express this to Fedpage, just to pass the time congealing around them. Fedpage nodded as he listened to the stricken man's stertorous breathing. "Maybe it's just sleep apnea we got here. What a great fucking movie. Me and Zeno were arguing about how many years that day had to go on for Bill Murray. I said it couldn't be less than ten years, because of the piano lessons and the med school and the, you know," and he was off on a long list of all of the character's accomplishments and how many hours it would take to learn these skills, and how much time he had had for them in any given version of the repeated day. "Also, when you think about it, if Bill Murray can do different things every day, and get a different response from the people around him, just how exactly is that different from any ordinary day? It ain't any different, that's what! Other people don't remember what you did the day before, they don't give a shit, they've got their own day to deal with! So in essence we're all living our own Groundhog Day, right? Every day is always just the same fucking day."

"You should be a Buddhist," Frank said. "You should talk to my Buddhist friends."

"Yeah *right*. I don't go in for that hippie shit."

"It's not hippie shit."

"Yeah it is. How would you know."

"I talk to them is how I know. I *lived* with them."

"Oh. Well. That explains it then. But it also proves my point about them being hippies. I mean you don't just *live* with people, do you."

All while the old man cradled between them gasped, or did not gasp. Eventually the rescue team arrived, and under a blistering critique from Fedpage they got the old guy out to their ambulance. There Fedpage tried to grill them on the paperwork the operation would require of all involved, but the meds waved him away and drove off.

Talking to Fedpage was like talking to Rudra Cakrin. Frank knew some strange people. Some of these people had problems.

None more so, for instance, than the blond woman from the park. Frank saw her again, one evening at Site 21 when some of them were there, and he said "Hi," and sat down next to her to ask how she was doing.

"Oh—day eighteen," she said, with a wry look.

Frank said, "Well. Eighteen's better than none."

"That's true."

"But, you know, after all this time, I still don't think we've ever been introduced. I'm Frank Vanderwal." He stuck out a hand, which she took and shook daintily, with her fingertips.

"Deirdre. Nice to meetcha, ha ha."

"Yeah, the bros aren't much on introductions. Hey Deirdre—any sign of Chessman?"

"No, I ain't seen him. I'm sure he's moved."

And on from there. She was happy to talk. Lots happened when you were homeless. It was starting to get cold again. She was staying at the UDC shelter again. The whole gang had spent most of the summer there, or over at the feral camp in Klingle Park. Lots of people were going feral in Northwest—

hundreds—it made it safer in some ways, more dangerous in others. It could be fun; it could be too fun.

"Have you ever looked into that house on Linnean?"

"Yeah, I think I know the one you mean. Bunch of kids. They don't want old drunk ladies there."

"Oh I don't know. They seemed friendly to me. All kinds of people. I think you'd be fine with them."

"I don't know. They drink a lot."

"Who doesn't?" Frank said, which made her laugh her nicotine laugh. "Well, maybe one of those church outreach groups," he added, "if that's what you're looking for. There wouldn't be any drinking there."

"Okay okay, maybe I better check out the kids after all!"

The next morning, Emerson:

"Yesterday night, at fifteen minutes after eight, my little Waldo ended his life."

Only son. Scarlet fever. Six years old.

Frank wandered the streets of the city. Strange to feel so bad for a man long dead. Reading all the ecstatic sentences one could conclude Emerson had been some kind of space cadet, soaring through some untroubled space cadet life. But it wasn't so. "To be out of the war, out of debt, out of the drought, out of the blues, out of the dentist's hands, out of the second thoughts, mortifications, and remorses that inflict such twinges and shooting pains—out of the next winter, and the high prices, and company below your ambition . . ." This was the world they all lived in. He had loved a world where death could strike down anyone at any time. A young wife—a treasured friend—even his own boy. A boy like Nick or Joe. And it was still like that now. The odds had been improved, but nothing was certain. Surgeons had drained a blood clot on his brain. Without science he would have died, or been one of those mysterious people who always fucked up, who could not conduct their lives properly. All from a pop on the nose.

Whereas now, on the other hand, he was wandering the streets of Washington, D.C., a homeless person working at the White House with burnt-out Vietnam vets for friends and a spook girlfriend he did not know how to find! Miracles of modern medicine! Well, not all of that was his fault. Some kind of fate. Followed step by step it had all made sense. It was just a situation. It could be dealt with. It could be surfed. All his people were alive, after all—except Rudra Cakrin—and there he did what he could to keep him alive in his thoughts. Rudra would have said this, Rudra would have thought that. Good idea!

Up 19th Street to Dupont and then Connecticut, into his neighborhood of restaurants, bookstores, the laundromat by UDC. Certain neighborhoods became one's own, while the great bulk of the city remained no more than various terrain to be traversed. Only a few city dwellers had London-taxi-driver knowledge of their city. He followed his routes in the great metropolis.

He seldom went to the Optimodal that Diane had found on New York Avenue. It was one of his known places when not at work, and thus to be avoided. It meant he didn't see Diane then, which was too bad, but they still did their lunch walks on most days. She was getting frustrated at the many ways things could bog down.

He went to the drop spot under the tree again, and found undisturbed the last note he had left for Caroline. He crumpled it up, left another one.

HI ARE YOU OKAY? WRITE ME

He left it and walked away.

The following week, only that note was there.

He stood there in the knot of trees. Carved into the trunk of one was a simple figure, like a cross between Kilroy and Kokopelli. The shaman, looking out at him. Autumn forest, brassy in the afternoon light. Where was she, what was she doing? Even without a clot on the brain one could feel baffled. Right here they had lain kissing. Two creatures huddled together. Something was keeping her from making the drop.

The Air Intelligence Agency. Army Intelligence and Security Command. Central Intelligence Agency. National Clandestine Service. Coast Guard Intelligence. Defense Intelligence Agency. Office of Intelligence, Department of Energy (really?). Bureau of Intelligence and Research, Department of State. Office of Intelligence Support, Department of the Treasury. National Security Division, Federal Bureau of Investigation. Information Analysis and Infrastructure Protection Directorate. Marine Corps Intelligence Activity. National Geospatial Intelligence Agency. National Intelligence Council. National Reconnaissance Office. National Security Agency. Office of Naval Intelligence. United States Secret Service.

The Covert Action Staff. The Department of Homeland Security, Office of Intelligence and Analysis. The Directorate of Operations. Drug Enforcement Administration. Office of National Security Intelligence.

The United States Intelligence Community (a cooperative federation).

Out on his run with Edgardo the next day, he said, "Are there really as many intelligence agencies as they say there are?"

"No." Pause for a beat. "There are more."

"Shit." Slowly, haltingly, Frank told him about the situation with Caroline and the dead drop. "She said she would use it. So I'm worried. I feel helpless."

They ran on in silence from the Washington Monument to the Capitol, and then back to the Washington Monument again; an unprecedented span of silence in Frank's experience of running with Edgardo. He waited curiously.

Finally Edgardo said, "You should consider that maybe she is out of town. That maybe she is involved in the effort to deal with these guys, and so has to stay away."

"Ah."

It was like taking a pressure off the brain.

Thoreau said, "I rejoice that there are owls. Let them do the idiotic and maniacal hooting for men. It is a sound admirably suited to swamps and twilight woods which no day illustrates, suggesting a vast and undeveloped nature which men have not recognized. They represent the stark twilight and unsatisfied thoughts which all have."

Ooooooop! And the gibbon chorus at dawn? It represented joy. It was saying *I'm alive.* Bert still started it every morning he was out in the enclosure at dawn. May too was an enthusiast. Sleeping in his VW van parked on Linnean, he could start each day joining the chorus at the zoo. It was the best way possible to start the day.

"While the man that killed my lynx (and many others) thinks it came out of a menagerie, and the naturalists call it the Canada lynx, and at the White Mountains they call it the Siberian lynx—in each case forgetting, or ignoring, that it belongs here—I call it the Concord lynx."

There were no lynxes in Massachusetts now.

But the Rock Creek hominid persisted. Oooop! One could follow Rock Creek from the Potomac all the way up to the zoo, with a few little detours. North of that came the beaver pond, and then Site 21. Back out to Connecticut, to an early dinner, pay with cash on the check, big tip, so easy; off again into the park.

There he ran into Spencer and Robert and Robin, as planned; hugs all around. They were an affectionate group. Sling the friz, running and hooting through the dim yellow world, quickly working up a sweat. The flight of startled deer, their eponymous tails. Stand around afterward, feeling the blood bump through the body.

The autumn colors in Rock Creek were not like those in New England, they were more muted, more various—not Norman Rockwell, but Cezanne—or, as Diane suggested when Frank put it that way to her, Vuillard.

Vuillard? he asked.

She took him on a lunch break back to the Mellon room at the National Gallery. Eating hot dogs sitting on the steps, and then going in to examine the subtle little mud-toned canvases of Vuillard. Wandering side by side, arms bumping, heads together. Was that tan or umber or what. Imagine his palette at the end of the day. Like something the cat threw up.

She too was affectionate. She took his arm to propel him along. "So how does your head feel today?" she would ask.

"About the same as yesterday."

She squeezed his arm. "I don't ask *every* day. Are you still feeling better?"

"I am. You know, Yann's doing some amazing things out there in San Diego." It probably sounded like a change of subject, but it wasn't.

"Yeah, like what?"

"Well, I think they've worked out how to get their DNA modifications into human bodies. The insertion problem may have been solved, and if that happens, all kinds of things might follow. Gene therapies, you know."

"Wow. Nice to think that something's going right."

"Indeed."

"It would be ironic to think that just as we were inventing real health care we burned the planet down instead."

He laughed.

"Don't laugh or I'll bleed on you," she said dourly, quoting him from the time of his accident. She too had lost someone young, he remembered; her husband had died of cancer in what must have been his forties or fifties. "So," she persisted, "have you got the feeling in your nose back?"

"No."

"Maybe they'll learn to regrow nerves."

"I think they may. There are some angles converging on that one."

"Cool." She sighed.

"I've gotta get back," Frank said. "I've got a call time in with Anna, to talk about coordinating all her Fix-it agencies into the mission architecture, you should drop in on that."

"Okay I will." And as they started back: "I'm glad you're feeling better."

Mostly he left the VW van in a driveway behind the feral potluck house on Linnean. If he drove it at all, mostly out to the farm, he checked it thoroughly first. Dry cleaning, Edgardo called it. It always proved free of all chips, tags, and transponders. Easy to believe when you looked at it: VW vans as a class were getting kind of old and skanky. But what a fine house. And sitting in the curved vinyl seat at night, reading his laptop on the curved little table, Thoreau seemed to second the thought:

In those days when how to get my living honestly, with freedom left for my proper pursuits, was a question which vexed me even more than it does now, I used to see a large box by the railroad, six feet long by three wide, in which the workmen locked up their tools at night; and it suggested to me that every man who was hard pushed might get him such a one for a dollar, and, having bored a few auger holes in it, to admit the air at least, get into it when it rained and at night, and shut the lid and hook it, and so have freedom in his mind, and in his soul be free. This did not seem the worst alternative, nor by any means a despicable resource. I should not be in so bad a box as many a man is in now.

He had understood entirely. Put such a box in a tree, and you had your treetop view as well. Put the box in a book and you had *Walden*. Put the box on wheels and you had your VW van. Frank printed the passage out and stuck it on the wall the next time he was at the fregan potluck. They too had found the key. He ate with them about three nights a week, all over Northwest, in house after house. There were feral subcultures: there was a farmers' market wing, and a hunters' crowd, and dumpster purists, and many other ways of going feral in the city.

At work Frank was making wonderful strides with the guy from OMB who was administering the Fix-it program that Anna had rediscovered. His name too was Henry, and he worked with Roy and Andrea and the rest of the White House brain trust. Right now, he and Frank were teaming up on the clean-energy part of the mission architecture. The Navy had made an agreement with the Navajo nation to build and run a prototype nuclear power plant that would reuse fuel rods and was overengineered for safety. Meanwhile Southern California Edison had agreed to build a dozen more Stirling heat engine solar-power generators, for themselves and other energy companies around the American West, and for some federal plants that were going to be built on BLM land, using a federal grant program. SCE had also won the contract to build the first big generation of fully clean coal plants, which would capture both the particulates and the carbon dioxide and other greenhouse gases on firing, so that all they would be releasing from the pipe was steam. The first plants were to be built in Oklahoma, and the CO_2 collected in the process was to be injected into nearby depleted oil wells. Oil wells nearby that were still working would look to see if they got any uptick in pressure differentials, making for a complete systems test.

"Sweet," the OMB Henry commented. He was about thirty, it seemed to Frank, utterly fresh and determined. He was unfazed by the past, even unaware of it. The defeats and obstructions, the nightmarish beginning to the century, so balked and stupidified; none of that meant a thing to him. And Washington had hundreds of these kids ready to rip. The world was full of them. He said, "That's a good big subunit of the whole mission architecture, up and running."

"True," Frank said. "I think the question now is how quick we can ramp production up to what we need."

"I wonder how much investment capital is out there. Or whether trained labor will be the real shortage."

"I guess we'll find out."

"That's a good thought." And young Henry grinned.

Evening in the park, and Frank buzzed Spencer and joined him and Robin and Robert at a new fregan house. East, into a neighborhood he had never been in before, a kind of border between gentrification and urban decay, in which burned or boarded-up buildings stood mutely between renovated towers guarded by private security people. An awkward mix it seemed, and yet once inside the boarded-up shell of a brownstone, it proved to be as sheltered from the public life of the city as any other place. Home was where the food was.

Same crowd as always, a mix of young and old. Neo-hippie and postpunk. Some new thing that Frank couldn't name with a media label. The fregan way. Mix of races, ethnicities, modes of operation. A potluck indeed. It was like this every night in so many different places around Northwest. What was happening in Washington, D.C.? What was happening anywhere else, everywhere else? No one could be sure. The media was a concocted product, reporting only a small fraction of the culture. What would they do for a sense of the zeitgeist when the culture had fractalized and the media become not a mirror, but one artifact among many? Had it ever been any different? Was this somehow new? If people walked away from the old mass culture of mass consumption, and everybody did something homegrown, what would that look like?

"How many fregan houses are there altogether, do you suppose?" Frank asked Spencer as they sat on the floor over their plates.

Spencer shrugged. "Lots I guess."

"How do you choose which to go to?"

"Friends spread the word. I generally know by five, or Robert."

"Not Robin?"

"Robin usually just goes where we go. You know Robin. He barely knows what city we're in."

"What *planet* is this?" Robin asked from behind them.

"See? He doesn't want to be distracted with irrelevancies. Anyway, you can always call me."

"I only have my FOG phone now," Frank said. "And even that I'm trying not to use too much. I want to stay off the grid when I'm not at work."

"I know," Spencer said as he chewed, glancing at Frank speculatively. He swallowed. "I should tell you, no one can guarantee this group doesn't have all the various kinds of informants in it. You know. It's loose at the edges, and law enforcement is kind of nervous about the feral concept. I've heard there are people taking money from the FBI just to make some bucks, and they tell them all sorts of things."

"Of course." Frank looked around. No one looked like an informant.

Spencer went back to wolfing down his meal. There was a big crowd tonight and there wasn't going to be quite enough food. At the start of every potluck they had all started to say a little thanksgiving. In most houses, they all said together, "Enough is as good as a feast," sometimes repeating it three or four times. Maybe that was the third great correlation, enough and happiness. Or maybe it was science and Buddhism. Or compassion and action. No, these were too general. It was still out there.

Some of Spencer's friends sat down, and he introduced them to Frank, and Frank leaned forward squinting, repeating their names. He joined their chat about the windy autumn, the park, the cops, feral gossip. Apparently this group was going back over west of Connecticut the next night.

"Do you ever see the jaguar?" Frank asked them.

"Yeah, I saw it once I think, but it was at night you know."

The young women were happy to have Spencer's attention. Frank was regarded by them in the same way they regarded the other older single males in the room, meaning a bit distantly if at all.

Eventually Frank left. His treehouse had been nearby. Long walk down Piney Branch Parkway to his VW van, sleep on that nice mattress, cold breeze flowing down the window at the back of the pop-up.

Thus the feral life, the most extreme set of habits Frank had lived so far. A life on foot, hand to mouth, among friends and strangers. Maybe this was how people lived, no matter what. He googled to see if any studies had been done to determine how quickly new habits were internalized as a norm. Every Wednesday he went by the dead drop and found his note from the week before. It was disturbing, but there was nothing he could do about it. He had to remember what Edgardo had said about that, and trust that he had been conveying to him the actual facts of the situation, rather than merely speculating. He had made it clear enough. Time to refocus on the moment. Ride the wave.

CUT TO THE CHASE
Response to response 4:

Yes, I suppose it was hard to talk about, because it seemed like it broke down in one of two ways, because people were asking: Is it too late or not? And it seemed like this:

If it isn't too late, we don't have to do anything.

On the other hand, if it is too late, we don't have to do anything.

So either way, don't do anything. That was the problem with that way of putting the question. What we came to realize was that it was a false problem or a question put the wrong way, because there was never going to be a too late. It was always going to stay a question of better or worse. It was more a question of, okay, how fast can we act? How much can we save? Those are the questions we should be asking.

Response to Response 5,692:

Because there was no liberal media bias, that's why! That was all a myth. The rules of capitalism favor size and the economies of scale, and so the big corporations, following all relevant legal opportunities, bought up all the mainstream media. Then the message went out coordinated by constant feedback and dialogue using only a certain limited vocabulary and logic, all within a kind of groupthink, until all the media said the same thing: buy things! This moment in history is a good one and will last forever! Nothing can change, so buy things.

But then this weather thing came along. It put the lie to the reality we believed in. So that all began to look a little fishy.

Response to Response 1 to Response to Response 5,692:

Lots of reporters are young, and so they're locked into an Oedipal hatred of the baby-boomer generation. They hated the boomers for what we were given when we were young, the world gone for just the briefest moment out of its mind into a realm of sex drugs and rock and roll, of revolution and war and history right there in our hands, a time of excess and joy, a feeling that things could still change—a freedom that was so extreme no one who was there can even remember it properly, and no one who wasn't there can imagine it, because it was before AIDS and crack and meth and terrorism had returned everything to something like the weird and violent Victorian repression/transgression state of fear that we've all been living in these past years. So I see a fair bit of resentment. You old Vietnam vet, I see their eyes saying, you old hippie, you got lucky and were born in the right little window and got to grab all the surplus of happiness that history ever produced, and you blew it, you stood around and did nothing while the right reaganed back into power and shut down all possibility of change for an entire generation, you blew it in a ten-year party and staggered off stoned and complicit. You neither learned to do machine politics nor dismantled the machine. Not one of you imagined what had to be done. And so the backlash came down, the reactionary power structure, stronger than ever. And now we're the ones who have to pay the price for that. You can see why there might be a little resentment.

Okay—say we did. Well, no wonder. We didn't know what we were doing, we didn't have the slightest idea. There was no model to follow, we were out in the vacuum of a new reality, blowing it and then crashing back to Earth—it was a crazy time. It went by too fast. We didn't really get it until later, what we needed to do. Where the power was, and how we could use it, and why it was important to spread it around better.

So. No more blaming the past. Be here now. Now we know better, so let's see if we can do better. After all, if we boomers try to get it right now, it could be better than ever. We could make it right for the grandkids and get a late redemption call. That's my plan anyway.

ONE DAY SPENCER CALLED FRANK on his FOG phone. "Hey Frank, did you check out your Emerson for the day?"

Frank had everyone reading it now: Diane, Spencer, Robin; even Edgardo, who only rolled his eyes and questioned the intelligence of any optimist. "No," he said now to Spencer.

"Well here, listen to it. 'I remember well the foreign scholar who made a week of my youth happy by his visit. "The savages in the islands," he said, "delight to play with the surf, coming in on the top of the rollers, then swimming out again, and repeat the delicious maneuver for hours." Well, human life is made up of such transits.' —Did you hear that, Frank?"

"Yes."

"Ralph Waldo Emerson, saying that *life* is like *surfing*? Is that great or *what*?"

"Yes, that's pretty great. That's our man."

"Who was this guy? Do you think somebody's making all these quotes up?"

"No, I think Emerson made them up."

"It's so perfect. He's like your Dalai Lama."

"That's very true."

"The Waldo Lama. He's like the great shaman of the forest."

"It's true, he is. Although even more so his buddy Thoreau, when it comes to the actual forest."

"Yeah that's right. Your treehouse guru. The man in the box. They are *teaching you*, baby!"

"You're teaching me."

"Yes I am. Well okay then, bro, surf your way up here and we'll tee off at around five."

"Okay, I'll try to be there."

In all the wandering, work was his anchor, his norming function. The only thing that was the same every day. These days he put in his hours focusing on the many problems cropping up as they tried to convince all the relevant agencies and institutions to act on their various parts of the mission architecture. They were also obtaining UN and national approvals for the sea water relocation projects. Holland was taking the lead here, also England, and really most countries wanted the stabilization, so the will was there, but problems were endless. The war of the agencies had gone incandescent in certain zones, and was coming to a kind of climax of the moment, as resistance to Diane's mission architecture and the Fix-it coordinating efforts flared up in the Treasury Department and Interior and Commerce, big agencies all.

The technical issues in powering a massive relocation of sea water were becoming more and more naked to them. They mostly involved matters of scale or sheer number. Floating platforms like giant rafts could be anchored next to a coastline, and they could move about, they did not have to have a fixed location. Pumps were straightforward, although they had never wanted pumps so large and powerful before. Pipelines could be adapted from the oil and gas industry, although they wanted much bigger pipes if they could power them. Power remained the biggest concern, but if the rafts held an array of solar panels big enough, then they could be autonomous units, floating wherever they wanted them. Pipelines in the northern hemisphere had to be run overland to the playas they wanted to fill. China and Morocco and Mauritania had been the first to agree to run prototype systems, and other countries in central Asia had jumped on board.

Down in Antarctica, they could set them anywhere around the big eastern half of the continent, and run heated pipelines up to the polar plateau, where several depressions would serve as catchment basins. Cold made things more complicated down there technologically, but politically it was infinitely easier. SCAR, the Scientific Committee on Antarctic Research, had approved the idea of the project, and they were as close to a government as Antarctica had, as the Antarctic Treaty signatory nations never met, and never kept to the treaty's rules whether they met or not. In many senses NSF was the true government of Antarctica, and the relevant people at NSF were good to go. They saw the need. Saving the world so science could proceed: the Frank Principle was standard operating procedure at NSF. It went without saying.

After another long day at work, about a week later, Diane asked whether he wanted to get something to eat, and he said of course.

At dinner in a restaurant on Vermont Avenue she talked about work things that were bothering her, especially the tendency for innovation to bog in groups of more than a few people, which she called reversion to the norm. Frank laughed at that, thinking it would be a good joke to share with Edgardo.

He ate his dinner and watched her talking. From time to time he nodded, asked questions, made comments.

Phil Chase was too busy with other things to give much time to their issues, and he was having trouble getting legislation and funding through Congress. Access to him was controlled by Roy Anastophoulus and Andrea Blackwell, and while they said he remained interested in climate and science, he was still going to trust Diane and the agencies to do their jobs, while he focused on his, which ranged all across the board; his time was precious. Not easy to get any of it, or even to contact him properly. Get on with it, they seemed to be saying. Diane wasn't pleased with their priorities. She asked Frank if he would mind asking Charlie to ask Roy to ask Chase about certain things more directly; she laughed as she said this. Frank smiled and nodded. He would talk to Charlie. He thought word could get passed along. Maybe in Washington, D.C., he suggested, six degrees of separation was not the maximum separating any two people, but the minimum. Diane laughed again. Frank watched her laugh, and oceans of clouds filled him.

ANNA QUIBLER HAD BEEN RESEARCHING the situation in China, and she found it troubling. Their State Environmental Protection Administration had Environmental Protection Bureaus, and environmental laws were on the books. There were even some nongovernmental organizations working to keep the crowded country's landscape clean. But the government in Beijing had given power for economic development to local governments, and these were evaluated by Beijing for their economic growth only, so laws were ignored and there was nobody who had a good handle on the total situation. It sounded a little familiar, but in China things were amplified and accelerated. Now an NGO called Han Hai Sha (Boundless Ocean of Sand) was sending reports to the division of the Chinese Academy of Sciences that coordinated or at least collated the information for all the Chinese environmental studies that were being done. For a country of that size, there weren't very many of them. In theory the Academy division was an advisory body, but the Communist Party political command made all the decisions, so the environmental scientists made their reports and had included advice, but as far as Anna's contacts could tell, few major decisions resulting from their advice had ever been made.

Facilitating rapid economic growth had been the ruling principle in Beijing for three decades now, and with a billion people on about as much land as Brazil or the United States, unleashing this engine of human activity had left little room for considerations of landscape. The list of environmental problems the Chinese scientists had gathered was large, but Anna's contact, a Professor Fengzhen Bao, was now writing to her from an e-mail account in Australia, and he was saying that the big areas in the west that had been militarized were going unstudied and unreported. Except for evidence from the windstorms of loess that blew east, they had little to analyze and were not sure what was happening out there. They knew the government had agreed to fill the Tarim Basin, the major dry playa in the Takla Makan, with sea water pumped up from the China Sea, but that was not their worry; indeed some thought it might even help, by covering some of the toxic dustbeds being torn open by the hot strong winds now sweeping the drought-stricken country so frequently. It was the impact of all the other economic activity that was the danger, including strip-mining, coal power generation, deforestation, urbanization of river valleys, cement production and steel manufacturing, and use of dangerous pesticides banned elsewhere. All these factors were combining downstream, in the eastern half of the country, impacting the big river valleys and the coasts, and the many megacities that were covering what farmland they had. Fengzhen said many were seeing signs of a disaster unfolding.

Cumulative impacts, Anna thought with a sigh. That was one of the most complex and vexing subjects in her own world of biostatistics. And the Chinese problem was an exercise in macrobiostatistics. What Anna's correspondent Fengzhen talked about in his e-mails was what he called a "general system crash," and he spoke of indicator species already extinct, and other signs that such a crash might be in its early stages. It was a theory he was working on. He compared the Chinese river valleys' situation to that of the coral reefs, which had all died in about five years.

Anna read this and swallowed hard. She wrote back asking if he and his colleagues could identify the worst two or three impacts they were seeing, their causes and possible mitigations, and clicked *send* with a sinking feeling. NSF had an international component wherein U.S. scientists teamed with foreign scientists on shared projects, and the infrastructure obtained for these grants remained for the use of the foreign teams when the grants were over. A good idea; but it didn't look like it was going to be adequate for dealing with this one.

Early one Saturday morning, Charlie met Frank and Drepung on the Potomac, at the little dock by the boathouse at the mouth of Rock Creek, and they put their kayaks in the water just after dawn, the sun like an orange floating on the water. They stroked upstream on the Maryland side, looking into the trees to see if there were any animals still out. Then across the copper sheen to the Virginia side, to check out a strange concrete outfall there. "That's where I used to bring Rudra Cakrin," Frank said, pointing at the little overlook at Windy Run.

Then he stroked ahead, smooth and splashless. He was not much more talkative here than he had been in the Sierras, mostly looking around, paddling silently ahead.

On this morning, his habits suited Charlie's purposes. Charlie slowed in Frank's wake, and soon he and Drepung were a good distance behind, and working a little to keep up.

"Drepung?"

"Yes, Charlie?"

"I wanted to ask you something about Joe."

"Yes?"

"Well... I'm wondering how you would characterize what's going on in him now, after the... ceremony that you and Rudra conducted last year."

Drepung's brow furrowed over his sunglasses. "I'm not sure I know what you mean."

"Well—some I don't know, some sort of spirit was expelled?"

"In a manner of speaking."

"Well," Charlie said. He took a deep breath. "I want it to come back."

"What do you mean?"

"I want my Joe back. I want whoever he was before the ceremony to come back. That's the real Joe. I've come to realize that. I was wrong to ask you to do anything to him. Whatever he was before, that was him. You know?"

"I'm not sure. Are you saying that he's changed?"

"Yes! Of course that's what I'm saying! Because he has changed! And I didn't realize... I didn't know that it took all of him, even the parts that—that I don't know, to make him what he is. I was being selfish, I guess, just because he was so much work. I rationalized that it wasn't him and that it was making him unhappy, but it *was* him, and he wasn't unhappy at all. It's now that he seems kind of unhappy, actually. Or maybe just not himself. I mean he's easier than before, but he doesn't seem to be as interested in things. He doesn't have the same spark. I mean... what was it that you drove out of him, anyway?"

Drepung stared at him for a few strokes of the paddle. Slowly he said, "People say that certain Bön spirits latch on to a person's intrinsic nature, and are hard to dislodge with Buddhist ceremonies. The whole history of Buddhism coming to Tibet is one fight after another, trying to drive the Bön spirits out of the land and the people, so that Buddhist precepts and, you know, the nonviolence of Buddhism could take the upper hand. It was hard, and there were many contradictions involved, as usual if you try too hard to fight against violent feelings. That itself can quickly become another violence. Some of the earlier lamas had lots of anger themselves. So the struggle never really ended, I guess you would say."

"Meaning there are still Bön spirits inhabiting you people?"

"Well, not everyone."

"But some?"

"Yes, of course. Rudra was often pestered. He could not get rid of one of them. And he had invited them into him so many times, when serving as the oracle, it made him susceptible, you might say. Anyway this one would not leave him. This was one of the reasons he was so irritable in his old age."

"I never thought he was that bad." Charlie sighed. "So where is that Bön spirit now, eh? Is Rudra's soul still having to deal with it in the bardo?"

"Possibly so. We cannot tell from here."

"He'll get reborn at some point, presumably."

"At some point."

"But so . . . Are there ceremonies to call spirits into you?"

"Sure. That's what the oracle does, every time there is a visitation ceremony."

"Ah ha. So listen, could you then *call back* the spirit that you exorcised from Joe? Could you explain it was a mistake, and invite him back?"

Drepung paddled on for a while. The silence lingered. Ahead of them Frank was now drifting into the shallows behind a snag.

"Drepung?"

"Yes, Charlie. I'll see what I can do."

"Drepung! Don't give me that one!"

"No, I mean it. In this case, I think I know what you mean. And I have the right figure in mind. The one that was in Joe. A very energetic spirit."

"Yeah, exactly."

"And I know the right ceremony too."

"Oh good. Good. Well—let me know what I can do, then?"

"I will. I'll have to talk to Sucandra about it, but he will help us. I will tell you when we have made the arrangements, and divined the right time for it."

"The right time for what?" Frank asked, as they had caught up to him, or at least were within earshot. On the water that was often hard to determine.

"The right time to put Joe Quibler in touch with his spirit."

"Ah ha! It's always the right time for that, right?"

"To everything its proper moment."

"Sure. Look—there's one of the tapirs from the zoo, see there in that bush?"

"No?"

"There, it's the same color as the leaves. An animal from South America. But I guess dead leaves are the same color everywhere. Anyway, it's good to see, isn't it?"

"Yeah. So how are the feral animals doing generally?"

"Okay. It all depends their natural range. Some species have been spotted seven hundred miles from the zoo, and up to thirty latitude lines out of their natural range. You must have heard Anna talking to Nick about this. She's helping him and his group to make a habitat corridor map, networking all the remaining wildernesses together. It's a GIS land-use thing."

"So if we want it, we can have the animals back."

"Yeah. We can. It would be cool if the president would back the forest and wilderness initiatives coming out of the animal rights community. Brother to Wolves kind of thing, you know."

Charlie laughed. "He's got a lot on his plate. I don't know if he's got time for that one right now. It's a hard thing to get his attention these days."

For Frank this was a new issue, but Charlie had been dealing with it for years, since long before Phil had become president. It simply was not easy to get any time with someone so powerful and busy. Now Charlie could see that Frank also was running into that limitation. Even though Diane was the presidential science advisor, ensconced in the Old Executive Offices and therefore able to walk over whenever called on to discuss things with the president and his people, she still did not see him very often. He was booked by the minute. No matter how sympathetic Andrea and Roy were to the scientists' cause, there was very little presidential time available to give to meetings with them. On they had to go, flying in formation, and the days ripped away as in the calendar shots of old movies.

But then one afternoon, after Frank had given Charlie a call to beg for some intercession on the nuclear regulations issue, and Charlie had passed the word along in a call to Roy, he got a call back from that so-busy man.

It was right before dinner time. "The boss is ready to call it a day, but he wants to talk to your people about this regulation relief. So he's proposed one of his little expeditions over to the Tidal Basin. We take some takeout to the blue pedal boats, and have a picnic on the water."

"Oh good," Charlie said. "I'll call Frank and we'll meet you down there."

"Not me, I've got stuff to do. Andrea will be going though."

Charlie called Frank and described the plan.

"Good idea," Frank said.

The president would be driven over by his Secret Service detail, and as normal hours of operation for the tourist concession there were done for the day, it would be easy to take over the dock and the tidal pool, and unobtrusively to secure the perimeter. The National Park Service was fine with it; indeed, it was already a little presidential tradition, and from their perspective, being political support from the highest position in government, a good thing. Even the most virulent anti-Chase media had not been able to make much hay out of these expeditions—not that they hadn't tried, but Phil's laughing ripostes had made them look like prigs and fools, and they had mostly given up on that front.

The time being what it was, Charlie decided to take Joe along. He went down to daycare and found him occupied in some game or other with a girl his age, but he was happy enough to join the Secret Service detail in one of their lightly armored black Priuses.

After they parked on 15th Street and got out and walked down to the pedal-boat dock, where Phil and Andrea and some of the Secret Service guys were already standing, Charlie followed Joe a short way up the basin's shore path, agreeing that some rocks to throw in the water would be just the thing. Then Joe found some pea gravel and discovered that throwing it in the water by the handful was just as good as throwing bigger rocks.

Looking north at the Mall Charlie saw Diane, Frank, Kenzo, and Edgardo walking down 17th Street. By coming directly across the Mall, they had almost beaten the car caravan. They were a good-looking group, Charlie thought. Edgardo was gesturing in the midst of some comic soliloquy, making the rest laugh. Frank and Diane walked a bit behind, in step, heads together. As they crossed Independence Avenue at the light, Diane slipped her arm under Frank's, and as they reached the curb he helped her up with what almost looked like a little slap to the bottom. They too were laughing. A couple out on a balmy autumn evening.

They came down to the Tidal Basin on the pedestrian path, and Charlie and Joe joined them on the way to the dock. Some National Park rangers were untying a clutch of the blue pedal boats. The little round lake was empty, the round-topped Jefferson Memorial reflected upside-down in it, the FDR Memorial invisible in a knot of trees on the opposite bank. The late light burnished things. On the dock Charlie saw in the rangers and everyone else that look of contained excitement that surrounded the presidency at all times. This party would make for a story afterward, people's faces said. Another Phil Chase moment to add to all the rest.

Phil was expert in ignoring all that, crying out hellos to rangers he had seen before, making it clear he was a regular. His security people were forming a scarcely visible human barrier, intercepting tourists approaching to rubberneck at the scene, establishing an invisible boundary. Joe rushed to the boats lined up and ready against the dock, attempting to get in the first one, but Charlie caught him just in time by the arm. "Wait a second, big guy, you have to have a lifejacket on. You know that, you're so funny," feeling all the while pleased to see this flash of the old enthusiasm.

"Hey Joe!" Phil exclaimed. "Good to see you buddy, come on, let's be the first ones out! I think I see Pedal Boat One right here in front," stepping down into it.

He reached out for Joe, which meant that Charlie was going to have to join him, and so Charlie took a kid's life preserver from the ranger offering it and tried to get one of Joe's arms through it. A quick wrestling move, similar to the one honed by long practice with baby backpack insertions, got him started, but then Charlie looked up to see that Frank had taken Diane by the upper arm and slipped through the group to the edge of the dock. "Here," Frank said, ushering Diane into Phil's boat, "I've got to be the one who goes out with Joe, I promised him the last time I took out Nick, so I need to go out with them. So here, Diane, you go with the president this time, you guys need to talk anyway." She looked surprised.

"Good idea!" Phil said, reaching out to help her step into the boat. He smiled his famous smile. "Let's get a head start on them."

"Okay," Diane said as she sat down. Frank turned away from them to greet Joe and lead Charlie to another boat.

Phil and Diane pedaled away from the dock. Charlie and Frank got in the next one, held in place by rangers with boathooks, and they took Joe and strapped him in between them. By the time they were ready to go some time had passed; Phil and Diane were already midpond, chomping away like a little steamboat across the coppery water. Frank waved to them, but they did not see; they were laughing at something, their attention already otherwise engaged.

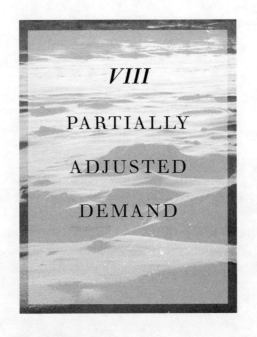

VIII

PARTIALLY

ADJUSTED

DEMAND

PC: Morning Charlie. Have some coffee. Joe, do you want coffee?
JQ: Sure Phil.

CQ: How about hot chocolate.

PC: Oh yeah, that's what I'm having.

JQ: Sure.

PC: Rain on our dawn patrol. Too bad. Although rain has gotten a lot more interesting than it used to be, hasn't it?

CQ: Droughts will do that.

PC: Yes. But now is the winter of our wet content. Here you go, Joe. Here you go, Charlie. These south windows are big, aren't they. I like looking at rain out the window. Here Joe, you can put those right here on the carpet. Good.

(Pause. Slurping.)

PC: So, Charlie, I've been thinking that we can't afford to bog down like we kind of are. We have to go fast, so maybe we can't afford to fight capital anymore. They've rigged the numbers and written the laws.

CQ: So, let me guess, now you want to make saving the world a capitalist project? You make it some kind of canny investment opportunity, with a great six-month rate of return?

PC: This is why you are one of my trusted advisors, Charlie. You can guess what I'm thinking right after I say it.

JQ: Ha Dad.

CQ: Ha yourself.

PC: So yes, that's what you do. Without conceding that private ownership of the public trust is right, or even sensible, but only because it has bought up so much of the next thirty years. Heck it supposedly owns the world in perpetuity. We'll change that later. Right now we have to harness it to our cause, and use it to solve our problem. If we can do that, then the capitalism we end up with won't be the same one we began with anyway. The rescue operation is so much larger than anything else we've ever done that it will change everything.

CQ: Or so you hope!

PC: It's what I'm going to try. I think we are more or less forced to try it that way. I don't see any alternative. Really, if we don't get the infrastructure and transport systems swapped out as fast as is physically possible, the world is cooked. It's like our first sixty days never ended, but only keeps rolling over. It's like sixty days and counting all the time. So we have to look to what we have now. And right now we have capitalism. So we have to use it.

CQ: I don't see how.

PC: For one thing, capital has a lot of capital. And a lot of it they keep liquid and available for investment. It runs into trillions of dollars. They want to invest it. At the same time there's an overproduction problem. They can make more than they can sell of lots of things. And so all capital of all kinds is on the hunt for a good investment, some thing or a service that isn't already overproduced. Looking to maximize profit, which is the goal that all business executives are legally bound to pursue, or they can be fired and sued by their board of directors.

CQ: Yeah, but crisis recovery isn't profitable, so what's your point?

PC: My point is there's an immense amount of capital, looking to invest in new production! Because capital accumulation really works, at least at first, but it works so well it fulfills every necessity for a target population, and then every desire, and so it stops growing so fast, and without maximum growth you can't get maximum profits. So you need to find new markets. And so, this has been what has been going on for the last few hundred years, capital moving from product to product but also from place to place, and what we've got now as a result is hugely uneven development. Some places were developed centuries ago, and some of those have since been abandoned, as in the rust belts. Some places are newly developed and cranking, others are being developed and are in transition. And then there are places that have never been developed, even if their resources were extracted, and they're pretty much still in the Middle Ages. And this is what globalization has been so far—capital moving on to new zones of maximized return. Some national government will be willing to waive taxes, or pay for the start-up costs, and certainly to give away land. And there's usually also a very willing labor force—not completely destitute or uneducated, but, you know—hungry. So capital comes in and that feeds more investment because there are synergies that help everyone. And so the take-off region develops like crazy, growth is in double digits for like a generation or so. China is doing that now, that's what's killing them. And so pretty soon the new area gets fully developed too! People have their basic needs, and they've created local capital that competes for profits. Now they're another labor force with raised expectations. The profit margin therefore goes down. It's time to move on, baby! So they look around to see where they might alight next, and then they take off and leave.

CQ: The World Bank, in other words. That's what I told them. I lost my mind. I took off my shoe and beat on their table.

PC: That's right, that meeting was reported to me, and I wish I had been there to see it. First you laugh in the president's face, and then you scream at the World Bank in a fury. That was probably backwards, but never mind. I'm glad you did it. I think the decapitation is going rather well over there. The midlevel was stuffed with idealistic young people who went there to change it from within, and now they're getting the chance.

CQ: I hope you don't tape these conversations.

PC: Why not? It makes it a lot easier to put them in my blog.

CQ: Come on, Phil. Do you want me to talk or not?

PC: You can be the judge of that, but right now I am enjoying laying out for us the latest from geographic economics. The theory of uneven development, have you read these guys?

CQ: No.

PC: You should. As they describe, capital finds a likely place to develop next, and boom off they go, see? Place to place. The people left behind either adjust to being on their own, or fall into a recession, or even fall into a full-on rust-belt collapse. Whatever happens to them, global investment capital will no longer be interested. That's the point at which you begin to see people theorizing bioregionalism, as they figure out what the local region can provide on its own. They're making a virtue out of necessity, because they've been developed and are no longer the best profit. And somewhere else the process has started all over.

CQ: So soon the whole planet will be developed and modernized and we'll all be happy! Except for the fact that it would take eight Earths to support every human living at modern levels of consumption! So we're screwed!

JQ: Dad.

PC: No, that's right. That's what we're seeing. The climate change and environmental collapse are the start of us hitting the limits. We're in the process of overshooting the carrying capacity of the planet, or the consumption level, or what have you.

CQ: Yes.

PC: And yet capitalism continues to vampire its way around the globe, determined to remain unaware of the problem it's creating. Individuals in the system notice, but the system itself doesn't notice. And some people are fighting to keep the system from noticing, God knows why. It's a living I guess. So the system cries: It's not me! As if it could be anything else, given that human beings are doing it, and capitalism is the way human beings now organize themselves. But that's what the system claims anyway, It's not me, I'm the cure! and on it goes, and pretty soon we're left with a devastated world.

CQ: I'm wondering where you're taking this. So far it's not sounding that good.

PC: Well, think about both parts of what I've been saying. The biosphere is endangered and so are humans. Meanwhile capitalism needs undeveloped regions that are ripe for investment. So—saving the environment IS the next undeveloped country! It's sustainability that works as the next big investment opportunity! It's massive, it's hungry for growth, people want it. People need it.

CQ: The coral reefs need it. People don't care.

PC: No, people care. People want it, of course they do. And capital always likes a desire it can make into a market. Heck, it will make up desires from scratch if it needs to, so real ones are welcome. So it's a good correlation, a perfect fit of problem and solution. A marriage made in heaven.

CQ: Phil please, don't be perverse. You're saying the problem is the solution, it's doubletalk. If it were true, why isn't it happening already then?

PC: It isn't the easiest money yet. Capital always picks the low-hanging fruit first, as being the best rate of return at that moment. Maximum profit is usually found in the path of least resistance. And right now there are still lots of hungry undeveloped places. And we haven't yet run out of fossil carbon to burn. Heck, you know the reasons—it would be a bit more expensive to do the start-up work on this country called sustainability, so the profit margin is low at first, and since only the next quarter matters to the system, it doesn't get done.

CQ: Right, and so?

PC: So that's where government of the people, by the people, and for the people comes into the picture! And we in the United States have the biggest and richest and most powerful government of the people, by the people, and for the people in the whole world! It's a great accomplishment for democracy, often unnoticed—we have to call people's attention to that, Charlie. We the people have got a whole lot of the world's capital sloshing around, owned by us. The GOVERNMENT is the COMMONS. Heck, we're so big we can PRINT MONEY! It took Keynes to teach the economists how that power could be put to use, but really governments of the people, by the people, and for the people have known what this means all along. It's the power to do things. So, we the people can aim capitalism in any direction we want, first by setting the rules for its operation, and second by leading the way with our own capital into new areas, thus creating the newest regions of maximum profitability. So the upshot is, if we can get Congress to commit federal capital first, and also to erect certain strategic little barriers to impede the natural flow of capital to the path of least resistance but maximum destruction, then we might be able to change the whole watershed.

CQ: How many metaphors are you going to mix into this stew?

PC: They are all part of a heroic simile, obviously, having to do with landscape and gravity. A very heroic simile, if I may say so.

JQ: Heroic!

PC: That's right Joe. You are a good kid. You are a patriotic American toddler. So Charlie, can you write me some speeches putting this into inspiring and politically correct terminology?

CQ: Why do you have to be politically correct anymore? You're the president!

PC: So I am. More coffee? More hot chocolate?

ONE DAY AN E-MAIL CAME FROM LEO Mulhouse, out in San Diego, forwarding a review paper about nonviral insertion. The RRCCES lab had gotten some really good results in introducing an altered DNA sequence into mice using three- and four-metal nanorods. In essence, Frank judged, the long-awaited targeted delivery system was at hand.

He stared at the paper. There were a bunch of other reasons piling up to go out to San Diego again. And San Diego was only one of several places he wanted to visit in person, or was being asked to visit. Taken together they implied much more travel than he had time to accomplish; he didn't know exactly what to do, and so went nowhere, and the problem got worse. It wasn't quite like his indecision fugue state; it was just a problem. But it was Diane who suggested that he string all the trips together in a quick jaunt around the world, dropping in on Beijing, the Takla Makan, Siberia, and England. He could start with San Diego, and the White House travel office could package it so it would only take him a couple of weeks at the most. A meeting, two conferences, and three on-site inspections.

So he agreed, and then the day of his departure was upon him, and he had to dig out his passport and get his visas and other documents from the travel office, and put together a travel bag and jump on the White House shuttle out to Dulles.

As soon into his flight as he could turn on his laptop, he checked out a video attachment in an e-mail that had come in from Wade Norton right before departure. The little movie appeared boxed in the middle of his screen, miniaturized so that Wade could show quite a lot. There was even a soundtrack—the opening shot, of the Antarctic coastline, was accompanied by a hokey high-wind and bird-cry combination, even though the sea looked calm and there were no birds in sight. The black rock of the coastline was filigreed with frozen white spume, a ragged border separating white ice and blue water. Summer again in Antarctica. The shot must have been taken from a helicopter, hovering in place.

Then Wade's voice came over the fake sound: "See, there in the middle of the shot? That's one of the coastal installations."

Finally Frank saw something other than coastline: a line of metallic blue squares. Photovoltaic blue. "What you see covers about a football field. The sun is up twenty-four/seven right now. Ah, there's the prototype pump, down there in the water."

More metallic blue: in this case, thin lines, running from the ocean's edge up over the black rocks, past the field of solar panels on the nearby ice, and then on up the broad tilted road of the Leverett Glacier toward the polar cap. At this pixel level the lines very quickly became invisible to the eye.

"Heated pumps and heated pipelines. It's the latest oil tech, developed for Alaska and Russia. And it's looking good, but now we need a lot more of it. And a lot more shipping. The pipes are huge. You probably can't tell from these images, but the pipes are like sewer mains. They're as big as they could make them and still get them on the ships. Apparently it helps the thermal situation to have them that big. So they're taking in like a million gallons an hour, and moving it at about ten miles an hour up the glacier. The pipeline runs parallel to the polar overland route, that way they have the crevasses already dealt with. I rode with Bill for a few days on the route, it's really cool. So there you have your proof of concept. It's working just like you'd want it to. They've mapped all the declivities in the polar ice, and the oil companies are manufacturing the pumps and pipes and all. They're loving this plan, as you can imagine. The only real choke points in the process now are speed of manufacture and shipping and installation. They haven't got enough people who know how to do the installing. That'll all have to ramp up. I've been running the numbers with Bill and his gang, and every system like this one can put ten cubic kilometers a year of water up on the polar cap. So depending on how fast the West Antarctic Ice Sheet breaks up, you would need some thousands of these systems to get the water back up onto the polar plateau, although really they should be spread out elsewhere in the world, because these will only run during the six months the sun is up."

Here Frank got curious enough to get on the plane's phone and call Wade directly. He had no idea what time it was in Antarctica, he didn't even know how they told time down there, but he figured Wade must be used to calls at all hours by now, and probably turned his phone off when he didn't want to get them.

But Wade picked up, and their connection was good, with what sounded like about a second in transmission delay.

"Wade, it's Frank Vanderwal, and I'm looking at that e-mail you sent with the video of the prototype pumping system."

"Oh yeah, hi Frank. How are you? Isn't that neat? I helo'ed out there day before yesterday, I think it was."

"Yeah it's neat," Frank said. "But tell me, does anyone down there have any idea how frozen sea water is going to behave on the polar cap?"

"Oh sure. It's kind of a mess, actually. You know, when water freezes the ice is fresh and the salt gets extruded, so there are layers of salt above and below and inside the new ice, so it's kind of slushy or semifrozen. So the spill from the pumps really spreads flat over the surface of the polar cap, which is good, because then it doesn't pile up in big domes. Then in that layer the salts kind of clump and rise together, and get pushed onto the surface, so what you end up with is a mostly solid fresh water ice layer, with a crust of salt on top of it, like a devil's golf-course-type feature. Then the wind will blow that salt down the polar cap, and disperse it as a dust that will melt or abrade surface ice, and whatever stays loose will blow off the polar cap in the katabatic winds. So, back into the ocean again! Pretty neat, eh?"

"Interesting," Frank said.

"Yeah. If we build enough of these pumping systems, it really will be kind of a feat. I mean, the West Antarctic Ice Sheet will eventually all fall into the ocean, it looks like, or most of it. No one can see that stopping now. But we might be able to pump the equivalent in water back onto the East Antarctic Ice Sheet, where it'll stay frozen and stabilized."

"So what about the desert basins in the north thirties?" Frank said. "A lot of those are turning into salt lakes. It'll be like a bunch of giant Salton Seas."

"Is that bad?"

"I don't know, what do you think about that? Isn't the Salton Sea really sick?"

"I guess so, but that's because it's drying up again, right? And getting saltier? Run one of these systems to the Salton Sea and its problems would be over. I think you have to keep pumping water into this kind of a sea, to keep it from getting too salty and eventually turning back into a playa. Maybe in a few hundred years you could let that happen, if you wanted. I bet by then you wouldn't. They'll be hydrating the areas downwind, don't you think?"

"Would that be good?"

"More water? Probably good for people, right? It wouldn't be good for arid desert biomes. But maybe people figure we have enough of those already. I mean, desertification is a big problem in some regions. If you were to create some major lakes in the western Sahara, it might slow down the desertification of the Sahel. I think that's what the ecologists are talking about now anyway. It's a big topic of conversation among the beakers down here. They're loving all this stuff. I sometimes think they love it that the world is falling apart. It makes the earth sciences all the rage now. They're like the atomic physicists were in World War Two."

"I suppose they are. But on the other hand..."

"Yeah, I know. Better if we didn't have to do all this stuff. Since we do, though, it's good we've got some options."

"I hope this doesn't give people the feeling that we can just silver-bullet all the problems and go on like we were before."

"No. Well, we can think about crossing that bridge if we get to it in the first place."

"True."

"Have to hope the bridge is still there at that point."

"True."

"So you're flying where?"

"I'm on my way around the world."

"Oh cool. When are you going to meet with Phil about these pumps?"

"Diane will do it."

"Okay good. Say hi to him, or have her say hi to him. It's been a lot harder to get him on the phone since he got elected."

"I'll bet."

"I keep telling him to come down here and see for himself, and he always says he will."

"I'm sure he wants to."

"Yeah he would love it."

"So Wade, are you still seeing that woman down there?"

"It's complicated. Are you still seeing that woman in D.C.?"

"It's complicated."

Satellite hiss, as they both were cast into thoughts of their own—then short and unhumorous laughs from both of them, and they signed off.

In San Diego, Frank rented a van and drove up to UCSD, checking in at the department to collect mail and meet with his remaining grad students. From there he walked up North Torrey Pines Road to RRCCES.

The labs were back, fully up and running, crowded, not messy but busy. A functioning lab was a beautiful thing to behold. A bit of a Fabergé egg; fragile, rococo, needing nurturance and protection. A bubble in a waterfall. Science in action. In these, they changed the world.

And now—

Yann came in and they got down to the latest. "You have to go to Russia," Yann said.

"I am."

"Oh! Well good. The Siberian forest is amazing. It's so big that even the Soviets couldn't cut it all down. We flew from Cheylabinsk to Omsh and it just went on and on and on."

"And your lichen?"

"It's way east of where we spread it. The uptake has been just amazing. It's almost even scary."

"Almost?"

Yann laughed defensively. "Yeah, well, given the problems I see you guys are having shifting away from carbon, a little carbon drawdown overshoot might not be such a bad thing, right?"

Frank shook his head. "Who knows? It's a pretty big experiment."

"Yeah it is. Well, you know, it'll be like any other experimental series, in that sense. We'll see what we get from this one and then try another one."

"The stakes are awfully high."

"Yeah true. Good planets are hard to find." Yann shrugged. "But maybe the stakes have always been high, you know? Maybe we just didn't know it before. Now we know it, and so maybe we'll, I don't know. Do them a little more..."

"Carefully? Like by putting in suicide genes or other negative feedback constraints? Or environmental safeguards?"

Yann shrugged, embarrassed. "Yeah sure."

He changed the subject, with a look heavenward as if to indicate that what the Russians had done was beyond his control. "But look here, I've been working on those gene-expression algorithms some more, and I've seen a wrinkle in the palindrome calculation. I want you to take a look at it see what you think."

"Sure," Frank said.

They went into Yann's office, a cubicle just like any other office cubicle, except that the window's view was of the Pacific Ocean from three hundred feet above sea level. Yann clicked his mouse as rapidly as a video game player and brought up pages that worked like transparencies, one colored pattern after another, until it looked like the London tube map replicated a few times around a vertical axis. As he continued to click, this cat's cradle rotated more on the axis, so that a really good false sense of three dimensions was established. He squished that image into the top of his huge screen and then on the bottom began to write out the equations for the middle steps of his algorithm. It was like working through a cipher set in which the solution to each step cast a wave of probabilities that then had to be explored and in some cases solved before the next step could be formulated; and then again like that, through iterations within sets, and decision-tree choices to determine the steps that properly followed. Algorithms, in short; or in long. They dug in, and Yann talked and drew on a whiteboard and clicked on the mouse, and typed like a madman, speed-talking all the while, free-associating as well as running a quick tutorial for Frank in his latest thinking, Frank squinting, frowning, asking questions, nodding, scribbling himself, asking more questions. Yann was now the leader of the pack, no doubt about it. It was as it would have been watching Richard Feynman chalkboarding quantum chromodynamics for the first time. A new understanding of some aspect of the unfolding of the world in time. Here they were in the heart of science, the basic activity, the mathematics of alchemy, discovered in the equations, matched against reality, and examined for its own internal logic as math.

"I have to pee," Yann announced midequation, and they broke for the day. Suddenly it was dinnertime.

"That was good," Frank said. "Jesus, Yann. I mean, do you know what you're saying here?"

"Well, I think so. But you tell me. I only learn what this stuff might mean when you tell me. You and Leo."

"Because it depends on what he can do."

"Right. Although he's not the insertion guy, as he's always saying."

"Which is what we need now."

"Well, that's more Marta and Eleanor. They're doing their thing, and they're hooked into a whole network of people doing that."

"So those nanorods are working?" Frank said, looking at one of the shot-gun sequencers.

"Yeah. They'll tell us about it if we go up to the Paradigms for drinks. The gang usually meets there around this time on Fridays."

"Nice."

"But first let's go talk to Leo, and then we can tell him to join us too."

"Good idea."

Leo was in his office reading an online paper with lots of tables and false-color photos. "Oh hi guys, hi Frank. Out here again I see."

"Yes, I'm doing some other stuff too, but I wanted to check in and see how things are coming along."

"Things are coming along fine." Leo had the kind of satisfied, paws-dug-in look of a dog with a bone. Still looking at the screen as he spoke with them. "Eleanor and Marta are putting the triple nanorods through all kinds of trials."

"So it's nanotechnology at last."

"Yeah, that's right. Although I've never seen how nanotechnology isn't just what we used to call chemistry. But anyway here I am using it."

"So these nanorods are taking your DNA into mice?"

"Yes, the uptake is really good, and the rods don't do anything but cross over and give up their attached DNA, so they're looking like very good insertion agents. The best I've seen anyway."

"Wow."

Yann described to Leo some of his new work on the algorithm.

"Combine the two advances," Frank murmured. "And . . ."

"Oh yeah," Leo said, smiling hungrily. "Very complementary. It could mean—" And he waved a hand expressively. Everything.

"Let's go get that drink," Yann said.

Marta was looking good, although Frank was inoculated. She had been out in the water that day, and it was a truism among surfers that salt water curled hair attractively. Bad hair became good hair, good hair became ravishing. People paid fortunes to salons to get that very look. And of course the sunburn and bleaching, the flush in the skin. "Hi, Frank" she said and pecked him hard on the cheek, like taking a bite out of him. "How's it going out in the nation's capital?"

He glowered at her. "It's going well, thanks," Ms. Poisoner.

"Right." She laughed at his expression and they went into the bar.

Eleanor joined them; she too was looking good. Frank ordered a frozen margarita, a drink he never drank more than a mile away from the California coastline. They all decided to join him and it became a pitcher, then two. Frank told them about developments in D.C., and they told him what they had been hearing from Russia, also the lab news, and the latest on North County. Leo took the lead here, being utterly exposed by events; he and his wife lived right on the cliffs in Leucadia, and were embroiled in the legal battle between the neighborhood and the city of Encinitas as to what should be done. The city was a political fiction, made from three coastal villages, Leucadia, Encinitas, and Cardiff, which gloried in the full name of Cardiff-by-the-Sea (now often changed to Cardiff-in-the-Sea, even though only its beach restaurants had actually washed away). Now it was beginning to look like a civic divorce was in order, Leo said. All the cliffside houses in Leucadia had been condemned, or at least the cliff legally abandoned by the city, and it was uncertain really what was going on given all the lawsuits, but for sure it was making for huge insurance and liability problems, and the involvement of the California Coastal Commission and the state legislature. A lot of Leucadia depended on the outcome.

"It sounds awful."

"Yeah, well. It's still a great place to live. When I'm lying there in bed and I hear the surf, or when the hang-gliders come by our porch asking about tide times—or we see the green flash, or the dolphins bodysurfing—well, you know. It makes the legal stuff seems pretty small. I figure we've already seen the worst we're likely to see."

"So you're not trying to sell?"

"Oh hell no. That would be an even bigger problem. No, we're there for good. Or until the house falls in the water. I just don't think it will."

"Are other people there trying to sell?"

"Sure, but that's part of the problem, because of what the city's done. Some people are still managing to do it, but I think both parties have to sign all kinds of waivers acknowledging the lawsuits and such. Those that do manage to sell are getting hardly anything for them. They're almost all for sale by owner. Agents don't want to mess with it. People are freaked out."

"But you think it will be okay."

"Well, physically okay. If there's another really big storm, we'll see. But I think our part of the street is on a kind of hard rib in the sandstone, to tell you the truth. We're a little bit higher. It's like a little point."

"Sounds lucky." Marta was looking at him, so he said, "How is your lichen doing in Siberia?"

She crowed. "It's going great! Get ready for an ice age!"

"Uh oh."

But she was not to be subdued, especially not after the second pitcher arrived. The lichen had taken hold in the Siberian forest east of Cheylabinsk, with coverage estimates of thousands of hectares, and millions of trees, each tree potentially drawing down several hundred kilograms of carbon more than it would have. "I mean, do the math!"

"You might have to release methane to keep things warm enough," Leo joked.

"Unless the trees die," Frank said, but under his breath so that no one noticed. Yann was looking a little uncomfortable as it was. He knew Frank thought the experiment had been irresponsible.

"It's getting so wild," Eleanor said.

Leo's wife Roxanne joined them, and they ate dinner at a beach restaurant by the train station. A convivial affair. Wonderful to see how results in the lab could cheer a group of scientists. Afterward Leo and Roxanne went home, and Frank nodded to Marta and Yann's invitation to join them and Eleanor again at the Belly-Up. "Sure."

Off to the Belly-Up. Into the giant Quonset, loud and hot. Dance dance dance. Don't take any pills from Marta. Eleanor was a good dancer, and she and Marta bopped together as a team. She had an arm tattoo which Frank saw clearly for the first time: a Medusa head with its serpentine hair and glare, and a circle of script around it; above it read *Nolo mi tangere,* below, *Don't Fuck With Me.* Yann disappeared, Eleanor and Marta danced near Frank, occasionally turning to him for a brief pas-de-troix, hip-bumping, tummy-bumping, chest-bumping, oh yes. Easy to do when you had eaten the antidote!

Then off into the night. A pattern already. The habit was formed with the second iteration. Frank drove to his storage locker and then out to the coast highway and south to Black's, remembering the wild ride with the horrible hard-on. So much for Marta. He laid out his bed on the cliff in his old nook. He sat there slowly falling asleep. Maybe the third good correlation was the simultaneous development of the proteomics algorithm with the targeted insertion delivery. It was the best night's sleep he had had in months.

H IS FLIGHT OUT THE NEXT DAY left in the afternoon, so the next morning he went back to his locker to stash his night gear and pick up his water stuff, then drove to the department office on campus to finish all his business there.

When he was done he gave Leo a call. "Hey Leo, when Derek was on the hunt right before Torrey Pines got sold, did you ever go out and do the dog and pony with him?"

"Yeah I did, a few times."

"Did you ever meet anyone interesting in that process?"

"Well, let me think. . . . That was a pretty crazy time." After a long pause he said, "There was a guy we met near the end, a venture capitalist named Henry Bannet. He had an office in La Jolla. He asked some good questions. He knew what he was talking about, and he was, I don't know. Intense."

"Do you remember the name of his firm?"

"No, but I can google him."

"True. But I can do that too."

Frank thanked him and got off, then googled Henry Bannet and got a list in 2.3 seconds. The one on the website for a firm called Biocal seemed right. A couple more taps and the receptionist at Biocal was answering the phone. She put him through, and no more than fifteen seconds after he had started his hunt, he was talking to the man himself, cell phone to cell phone it sounded like.

Frank explained who he was and why he was calling, and Bannet agreed to look into the matter, and meet with him next time he was in town.

After that Frank put his bathing suit and fins in his daypack and walked down to La Jolla Farms Road, and then down the old asphalt road to Black's Beach.

Being under its giant sandstone cliff gave Black's a particular feel. Change into bathing suit, out into the swell, "Ooooop! Oooooop!" Fins tugged on and out he swam, tasting the old salt taste as he went. Mother Ocean, salty and cool. The swell was small and from the south. There weren't any well-defined breaks at Black's, but shifting sandbars about a hundred yards offshore broke up the incoming waves, especially when the swell was from the south. Presumably the great cliff itself provided the sand for the sandbars, as it did for the beach, which was much wider than most of North County's beaches these days, even Del Mar's.

Outside it was classic Black's. Swells reared up suddenly, hollowed slowly, broke with sharp clean reports. Long slow lefts, short fast rights. Frank swam and rode, swam and rode, swam and rode. It was like knowing how to ride a bicycle—no thinking to it, once you got back into it. What had Emerson said about surfing? All human life was like this.

On the beach a young couple had just arrived. The guy had on long flowing white pants and a long-sleeved white shirt, also a wide-brimmed white hat, and a long yellow scarf or burnoose wrapped high around his neck. He even had on white gloves. Some issues with sun, it appeared, and what Frank could see of his face was albino pink. His companion was twirling around him in ecstatic circles, swinging her long black hair around and pulling off her clothes—shirt over her head and thrown at him, pants pulled off and handed to him. She danced around him naked, arms extended, then dashed out into the surf.

Well, that was Black's Beach for you. Frank stroked out and caught another wave, singing Spencer's song about the VW van: I would fight for hippie chicks, I would die for hippie chicks. Inshore the woman dove into the broken waves while her companion stood knee deep, watching her impassively. An odd couple—

But weren't they all!

After that, it was on to Asia. First a flight up to Seattle, then a long shot to Beijing. Frank slept as much as he could, then got some views of the Aleutians seen through clouds, followed by a pass over the snowy volcano-studded ranges of Kamchatka.

The Beijing meeting, called Carbon Expo Asia, was interesting. It was both a trade show and a conference on carbon emissions markets, sponsored by the International Emissions Trading Association, and among those speaking were governmental representatives involved in establishing and regulating them. Carbon, of course, was a commodity with a futures market (as Frank himself had been, and maybe still was). With Phil Chase in office, the world had assumed the U.S. would be joining the global carbon cap and trade market, dragging Australia and the other recalcitrants in their AP6 with it, and so the value of carbon emissions on the carbon futures market had soared. All countries would set caps and then the trading would be fully globalized, and in theory trading and prices would take off. Now, however, the futures traders were beginning to wonder if carbon might become so sharply capped, or the burning of it become so old-tech, that emissions would be abandoned outright and lose all value in a market collapse. So there were countervailing pressures coming to bear on the daily price and its prognosis, as in any futures market. Discussions at this very meeting had caused the price on the European market to rise a few euros, to 22 euros a share.

All these pressures were on display here for Frank to witness. Naturally Chinese traders were especially prominent, and behind them the Chinese government appeared to be calling the shots. They were trying to bump the present value of emissions futures, the local American trade representative explained to Frank, by holding China's potential coal burning over everyone else's head, as a kind of giant environmental terrorist threat. By threatening to burn their coal they hoped to create all kinds of concessions, and essentially get their next generation of power plants paid for by the rest of the global community. Or so went the threat. Thus the Chinese bureaucrats wandered the conference halls looking fat and dangerous, as if explosives were strapped to their waists, implying with their looks and their cryptic comments that if their requirements were not met they would explode their carbon and cook the world.

The United States meanwhile still had the biggest carbon burn ongoing, and from time to time in the negotiations could threaten to claim that it was proving harder to cut back than they had thought. So all the big players had their cards, and in a way it was a case of mutual assured destruction all over again. Everyone had to agree on the need to act, or it wouldn't work for any of them. So all the carbon traders and diplomats were in the halls dealing, the Americans as much as anyone. Indeed they, as the newcomers to the table, seemed the ones most desperate for a global deal. It was like a giant game of chicken. And in a game of chicken everyone thought the Chinese would win. They were bloody-minded hardball players in general, and only ten or a dozen guys there had to hold their nerve, rather than three hundred million; that was an eight-magnitude difference, and should be enough to guarantee China could hold firm the longest. If you believed the theory that the few were stronger in will than the many.

It was an interesting test of America's true strength, now that Frank thought of it that way. Did the bulk of the world's capital still reside in the U.S.? Did the U.S.'s military strength matter at all in this other world of energy technology? Was it a case of dominance without hegemony, as some were describing it, so that in the absence of a war, America was nothing but one more decrepit empire, falling by history's wayside? If America stopped burning 25 percent of the total carbon burned every year, would this make the country geopolitically stronger or weaker? One would have to find a perspective to measure situations which took into account many disparate factors that were not usually calculated together. It was a geopolitical mess to rival the end of World War II, and the delicate negotiations establishing the UN.

Then the meeting was over, with lots of emissions trading done, but little accomplished toward the global treaty that would replace Kyoto, and which hopefully would limit very sharply the total annual amount of emissions allowed for the whole world. That was becoming the usual way with these meetings, the American rep told Frank wearily at the end. Once you were making what could be called progress (meaning another way to make money, it seemed to Frank), no one was inclined to push for anything more radical.

Frank then caught a Chinese flight down to the Takla Makan desert, in far western China—a turbulent couple of hours—and landed at Khotan, an oasis town on the southern edge of the Tarim Basin. There he was loaded with some Hungarian civil engineers into a minibus and driven north, to the shores of the new salt sea. Throughout the drive plumes of dust, as if from a volcanic explosion, rose in the sky ahead of them. As they approached, the yellow wall of rising dust became more transparent, and finally was revealed as the work of a line of gigantic bulldozers, heaving a dike into place on an otherwise empty desert floor. It looked like the Great Wall was being reproduced at a magnitude larger scale.

Frank got out at a settlement of tents, yurts, mobile homes, and cinder block structures, all next to an ancient dusty tumbledown of brown brick walls. He was greeted there by a Chinese-American archeologist named Eric Chung, with whom he had exchanged e-mails.

Chung took him by jeep around the old site. The actual dig occupied only a little corner of it. The ruins covered about a thousand acres, Chung told him, and so far they had excavated ten.

Everything in sight, from horizon to horizon, was a shade of brown: the Kunlun Mountains rising to the south, the plains, the bricks of the ruin, and in a slightly lighter shade, the newly exposed bricks of the dig.

"So this was Shambhala?" Frank said.

"That's right."

"In what sense, exactly?"

"That was what the Tibetans called it while it existed. That arroyo and wash you see down the slope was a tributary of the Tarim River, and it ran all year round, because the climate was wetter and the snow pack on the Kunluns was thicker, and there were glaciers. They're saying that flooding the Tarim Basin may bring glaciers back again, by the way, so that this river would run again, which is one of the reasons we have to get the dig at the lower points done fast. Anyway, it was a very advanced city, the center of the kingdom of Khocho. Powerful and prominent in that time. It was located on a precursor of the Silk Road, and existed on trade and so on. A very rich culture. So the Bön people in Tibet considered it to be the land of milk and honey, and when the Buddhist monasteries took over up there, they developed a legend that this was a magical city, and Guru Rimpoche started the Shambhala motif in their iconography. It reminds me of the Atlantis myth, in that Plato wrote a thousand years after the explosion at Thera, but still described certain aspects of the Minoan colony on the island pretty well, especially the circular shape of the island. In this case the time lag is about the same, and Shambhala was always described in the literature as being square, with the corners at the four cardinal points, and surrounded by water. What we're finding here are irrigation ditches that leave the riverbed upstream from the site, and circle it and rejoin the river downstream. And the city is platted in a square that is oriented north-south-east-west. So it fits the pattern, it has the name, it's the right period. So, that's the sense in which we call it Shambhala."

"Wow. So it's like finding Troy, or Thera."

"Yes, exactly. A very exciting find. And the Chinese so far are being pretty good about it. The dike holding in this part of the new sea has been rerouted to keep the site out of the water. And between the site and the new lake it looks like they are hoping to create a new tourist destination, linked to the Tibet tour. We're already seeing some Shangri-La hotels and travel companies springing up out here."

"Amazing," Frank said. "I wonder if it will catch on."

"Who knows? But at least we won't have to hurry to excavate a site that's going to be drowned. I did that in Turkey, and it's a terrible experience."

Frank walked around the site with the man. "How old is it, did you say?"

"Eighth century."

"And was it founded by a Rudra Cakrin?"

"Yes, that's right. Very good."

"But I read that he founded the city in sixteen thousand BC?"

"Yes," Chung said, laughing, "they do say that, but it's the same with Plato saying Atlantis was ten thousand years old and a hundred miles across. These stories appear to get exaggerated by a factor of ten."

"Interesting." They walked past a big cleared area of the dig. "This was a temple site?"

"Yes, we think so."

Frank took from his daypack a pill bottle containing some of Rudra's ashes that Qang had given him. He opened it and cast the fine gray ash into the wind. The little cloud puffed and drifted away onto the ground, more dust to add to all the rest. Maybe it would skew some numbers if they ever did any carbon-14 dating.

"Enough," Frank said.

An Aeroflot flight then, during which he caught sight of the Aral Sea, which apparently was already twice as big as before its own flooding project had begun, thus almost back to the size it had been before people began diverting its inflow a century before. All kinds of landscape-restoration experiments were being conducted by the Kazakhs and Uzbeks around the new shoreline, which they had set legally in advance and which now was almost achieved. From the air the shoreline appeared as a ring of green, then brown, around a lake that was light brown near the shoreline, shading to olive, then a murky dark green, then blue. It looked like a vernal pool.

Later the plane landed and woke Frank with a cacophony of creaks and groans. Frank got off and was greeted by an American and Russian team from Marta and Yann's old company, Small Delivery Systems. It was cold, and there was a dusting of dirty snow on the ground. Winter in Siberia! Although in fact it was not that cold and seemed rather dry and brown.

They drove off in a caravan of four long gray vans or tall station wagons, something like Soviet Land Rovers, it seemed, creaky like the plane, but warm and stuffy. People were starting to drive them on the frozen rivers again, he was told. Now they progressed over a road that was not paved but did have fresh pea gravel spread over it, and a coating of frost. The vehicles had to keep a certain distance from each other to avoid having their windshields quickly pitted.

Not far from the airport the road led them into a forest of scrubby pines. It looked like Interstate 95 in Maine, except that the road was narrower, and unpaved, and the trees therefore grayed by the dust thrown up by passing traffic. They were somewhere near Cheylabinsk 56, someone said. You don't want to go there, a Russian added. One of Stalin's biggest messes. Somewhere southeast of the Urals, Frank saw on a cell-phone map.

Their little caravan stopped in a clearing that included a gravel parking lot and a row of cabins. They got out, and the locals led the rest of them to a broad path leading into the woods. Quickly Frank saw that the roadside dust and frost had obscured the fact that all the trees in this forest had another coating: not dust, but lichen.

It was Small Delivery Systems' lichen. Frank saw now why Marta had been not exactly boasting, nor abashed, nor exuberant, nor defensive, but some strange mixture of all these. Because she and Eleanor were the team that had engineered this tree lichen for the Russians, manipulating the fungal part of the symbiote so that it would colonize its host trees more quickly, and then alter the lignin balance of the trees in ways that changed their metabolism. Tree lichens had always done that to their hosts for their own purposes, but these did it faster and to a greater extent. The more lignin that got banked in the tree, the better the lichen did, but also the bulkier the root system became, and this increased the net carbon drawdown of individual trees by 7 or 10 percent. Cumulatively, a very big potential drawdown indeed.

And the lichen were obviously doing well, to the point where a balance had clearly been lost. There were forests Frank had seen in Canada where moss or lichen covered most of the trunks and branches. In particular he recalled a frondy, day-glo green moss that in places was very widespread. But this lichen plated everything: trunk, branches, twigs—everything but the pine needles themselves.

Such a thorough cloaking looked harmful. A shaft of sunlight cut through the clouds at an angle and hit some trees nearby, and their cladding of lichen made them gleam like bronze trees with their needles painted green.

The Small Delivery people out there with Frank were sanguine about all this. They did not think there would be a problem. They said the trees were not in danger. They said that even if some trees died, it would only be a bit of negative feedback to counter the carbon drawdown that was already working so well. If a certain percentage of trees also took on lignin so fast they split their trunks, or had roots rupture underground, or others were suffocated by the lichen growing over the budding points of the new needles, then that would slow any further runaway growth of the lichen. Things would then eventually reach a balance.

Frank wasn't so sure. He did not think this was ecologically sound. Possibly the lichen could go on living on dead trees; certainly it could spread at the borders of the infestation to new trees. But these were not the people to talk to about this possibility.

The new lichen started out khaki, it appeared, and then caked itself with a second layer that was the dull bronze that eventually dominated. Like the cructose lichen of the high Sierra that you saw everywhere on granite, it was quite beautiful. The little bubbles of its surface texture had an insectile sheen. That was the fungus. Frank recalled a passage in Thoreau: "The simplest and most lumpish fungus has a peculiar interest to us, because it is so obviously organic and related to ourselves; matter not dormant, but inspired, a life akin to my own. It is a successful poem in its kind."

Which was true; but to see it take over the life it was usually symbiotic with was not a good thing. It looked like the parts of Georgia where kudzu had for a time overgrown everything.

"Creepy," Frank remarked, scraping at an individual bubble with a fingernail. These were the tiny plutons of a different kind of batholith.

"Yes, it is kind of, isn't it?"

"How do the roots look?"

"Come see for yourself." They took him to an area where the soil had been removed from beneath some sample trees. Here they saw both before and after roots, as some trees had been girdled and killed and their roots exposed later, to give them baseline data. Near them some still living trees, or trees in the process of being killed by the root exposure, were standing in holes balanced on their lowest net of fine roots, leaving most of the root balls exposed. The root balls were still shallow, in the way of evergreens, but the lichen-infested trees had roots that were markedly thicker than the uninfested trees.

"We started by treating an area of about a thousand square kilometers, and now it's about five thousand."

"About the size of Delaware, in other words."

Meaning some tens of millions of trees had been affected, and thus in the neighborhood of tens of millions of tons of carbon drawn down. Say a hundred million tons for the sake of thinking—that was about one percent of what they had put into the atmosphere in the year since the lichen was released.

Of course if it killed the forest, a lot of that carbon would then be eaten by microbes and respired to the atmosphere, some of it quickly, some over years, some over decades. This, Frank's hosts assured him, given the situation they were in, was a risk worth taking. It was not a perfect nor a completely safe solution, but then again, none of them were.

Interesting to hear this reckless stuff coming from the Russians and the Small Delivery Systems people about equally, Frank thought. Who had persuaded whom was probably irrelevant; now it was a true folie à deux.

He had stood a thousand feet tall on the floor of the Atlantic; now it looked like he had been miniaturized, and was threading his way through a forest of mold in a Petri dish. "Really creepy," he declared.

Certainly time to declare limited discussion. It was impossible to tease out the ramifications of all this, they depended so heavily on what happened to the various symbioses feeding each other, eating each other. There would need to be some kind of Kenzo modeling session, in which the whole range of possibilities got mapped, then the probabilities of each assessed. Feedback on feedback. It was very possibly incalculable, something they could only find out by watching what happened in real time, real space. Like history itself. History in the making, right out there in the middle of Siberia.

Then it was on to London, by way of Moscow, which he did not see at all. In his London hotel after the flights, he was jetlagged into some insomniac limbo, and could not sleep. It felt strange to have such a big bed at his command, and a room—oppressive, even decadent.

He checked his e-mail and then the internet. His browser's home page news had a little item about Phil Chase and Diane opening a National Academy of Sciences meeting together. He smiled ruefully, almost a grimace, and clicked to Emerson, where a search using the word *traveling* brought up this:

> Traveling is a fool's paradise. Our first journeys discover to us the
> indifference of places. At home I dream that at Naples, at Rome, I can be

intoxicated with beauty and lose my sadness. I pack my trunk, embrace my friends, embark on the sea and at last wake up in Naples, and there beside me is the stern fact, the sad self, unrelenting, identical, that I fled from. I seek the Vatican and the palaces. I affect to be intoxicated with sights and suggestions, but I am not intoxicated. My giant goes with me wherever I go.

From "Self-Reliance." Frank laughed, then showered and went to bed, and in the midst of his giant's weary buzzing, the luxury of lying horizontally suddenly took him away.

The conference he was attending was being held in Greenwich, near the Observatory, so that they could inspect in person, as an integral part of the conference, the Thames River Barrier. Witness the nature of the beast. The barrier was up permanently these days, forming a strangely attractive dam, composed of modular parts raised up from the river bottom, in a curve like a longbow. Ribbed arcs. One could walk out onto the first part of the broad concrete crescent, and from there it was very obvious to the eye that the seaward side, still a river, but opening like a funnel outward into the broader Thames estuary, was a plane of water distinctly higher than the plane of water on the London side. It was the opposite of the usual reservoir view, and reminded Frank of the walk he had taken with the Quiblers on the dike of Khembalung, right before the monsoon had returned and drowned the island.

Now he walked in that deracinated state characteristic of profound jetlag: sandy-eyed, mouth hung open in sleepy amazement, prone to sudden jolts of emotion. It was not particularly cold out, but the wind was raw; that was what kept him awake. When the group went back inside and took up the work on the sea-level issues, he fell asleep, unfortunately missing most of a talk he had really wanted to see, on the latest satellite-based laser altimetry measurements. An entire fleet of satellites and university and government departments had taken on the task of measuring sea level worldwide. Right before Frank fell asleep, the speaker said something about the sea-level rise slowing down lately, meaning their first pumping efforts might be having an effect, because other measurements showed the polar melting was continuing apace, in a feedback loop many considered unstoppable. This was fascinating, but Frank fell asleep anyway.

When he woke up he was chagrined, but realized he could see the paper online. The general upshot of the talk seemed to have been that they could only really stem the rise by drawing down enough CO_2 to get the atmosphere back to around 250 parts per million, levels last seen in the Little Ice Age from 1200–1400 AD. People were murmuring about the nerviness of the speaker's suggestion that they try for an ice age, but as was said immediately in rejoinder, they could always burn some carbon to warm things if they got too cold. This was another reason to bank some of the oil that remained unburned.

"I can tell you right now my wife's going to want you to set the thermostat higher," someone prefaced his question, to general guffaws. They all seemed much more confident of humanity's terraforming abilities than seemed warranted. It was a research crowd rather than a policy crowd, and so included a lot of graduate students and younger professors. The more weathered faces in the room were looking around and catching each other's eye, then raising their eyebrows.

On the flight back from London, Frank saw that the plane had telephones in the back of the middle seats, and when he spotted the tip of the astonishing icescape that was Greenland, it occurred to him to give Wade Norton another call. He punched in the number, waited. Soon he would be talking to an acquaintance in Antarctica, while flying thirty thousand feet over the tip of Greenland. The technological sublime could be so trippy.

Wade picked up. "Hi Frank. Where are you?"

"I'm in an airliner going from London to New York, and I can see the tip of Greenland, and it still looks icy. It looks the same as always."

"You need lasers to see the difference, except in certain fjords."

"Is that the way it is down there too? Can you *see* the differences down there?"

"Well, the Ross Ice Shelf being gone is the main thing you can see. There's still lots of ice on the land. And more all the time because of us, right?"

"Right, is that still going well?"

"Yes it is. There's some maintenance to be done at the intakes, but by and large the prototypes are all pumping away, and they're set to add more next season. They're talking cubic kilometer this and cubic kilometer that—they've sure ramped up from gallons and cubic feet per second, did you notice?"

"Yeah sure. They had to—it was getting to be like Italian *lira*."

"That's right. Also, if you take away a few zeroes it doesn't look out of control."

"That's true. Maybe that's why the modelers at this conference were so confident we had some chance of climate stabilization."

"Maybe so. Maybe they need to come down here and see some of the tabular bergs coming off."

"Do you think just having that experience would change their calculations though?"

"Well, good question. But I think a lot of calculations are really trying to quantify certain assumptions, don't you? Like in economics? Not as bad as that, of course, but still."

"Maybe we can arrange for a conference in McMurdo."

"Good idea! I mean, NSF would probably hate it, but maybe not. It might be good publicity. Good for the budget."

"I'll check with Diane about it."

"Good. Hey, how's it going with her?"

"Good. She and Phil seem good for each other."

"Ah yeah, that's nice. Phil needed someone."

"Diane too. So hey, how's it going with Val again?"

"Ah, well, good, good. Good when I see her. I'll see her again in about a month."

"Whoah. So, is she off with . . . ?"

"Yes, I think she's with X, for part of that time, anyway. She's with some kind of polar cap sailing village."

"What did you say?"

"Tents on big sleds, like catamarans. They put up sails when the wind is right and move around."

"Like iceboats?"

"Yes, like that I guess, but they're like big rafts, and there's a little camp's worth of them, moving around together."

"Wow, that sounds interesting."

"Yeah, they're like Huck Finn on the ice cap."

"So—but it's going well when you see her."

"Oh yeah. Sure. I can't wait."

"And the, the other guy?"

"I like X. We get along well. I mean, we're friends. We don't talk about Val, that's understood. But other than that we're like any other friends. We understand each other. We don't talk about it, but we understand."

"Interesting!" Frank said, frowning. "It's—kind of hard to imagine."

"I don't even try. That's part of how it works."

"I see." Though he didn't.

"You know how it is," Wade said. "When you're in love, you take what you can get."

"Ahhh."

His plane landed at JFK in the midmorning, and after that Frank had scheduled in a layover of several hours before his commuter pop down to D.C. The plan had puzzled the woman in the White House travel office, but he had only said, "I have some business in New York that day."

Now he got in a taxi and gave the driver the address of a YMCA in Brooklyn. He sat back in the back seat and watched the infinite city flow by outside the window. It went on and on. Frank felt dumbstruck with jetlag, but as the taxi driver pulled up to the curb, next to yet another block-long five-story building, he was also curiously tense.

The chess tournament was taking place in a gym that had room for only one basketball court and a single riser of stands. Stale old-locker smell. There was a pretty good crowd in the stands.

Frank climbed the metal stairs to the top riser and sat down behind a couple of guys wearing Yankees caps. For some reason he didn't want to be seen. He only wanted to see—

Down there at one of the tables, Chessman was playing a girl. Frank shuddered with surprise, startled by the sight even though he had been (mostly) expecting it. Clifford Archer, the tournament website had said, under-sixteen level, etc. It had seemed like it had to be him.

And there he was. He looked a bit older and taller, and was wearing a checked shirt with a button-down collar. Frank felt himself grinning; the youth held the same hunched position over this game that he had had at the picnic tables.

Maybe he had moved up here with family, as Deirdre had guessed. Or was doing it on his own somehow, following his chess destiny.

Every game in progress was represented as a schematic on a screen set up at the far end of the room, and after Frank identified Chessman's game he could follow its progress move by move. In his jetlagged state and his low level of expertise he found it hard to judge how the game was going; they were in an odd configuration, somewhere in the mid-game, Chessman playing black and seeming to be pushed to the edges a bit more than was usual for him, or safe.

Frank studied the game, trying to get what Chessman was up to. It reminded him sharply of the long winter, when he had first met the bros, and built his treehouse. He hadn't cared then what happened in the games. Now he was rooting for Chessman, but in ignorance. The two players had both lost about the same number and strength of pieces.

Then the girl took one of Chessman's bishops, but it was a sacrifice (Frank hadn't seen it) and after that Chessman's trap was revealed. He had her in a pincer movement of sorts, although she had a lot of pieces in the middle.

The men sitting on the riser just below him were murmuring about this, it seemed. Frank leaned forward and said in a low voice, with a gesture:

"Is that young man doing well?"

They both nodded, without looking back at him. One muttered from the side of his mouth, "He's very patient."

The other one nodded. "He plays black even when he's playing white. He's like good at waiting. He's going to win this one, and she's a junior master."

And though Frank couldn't see it, they were right. Chessman made a move, hit his timer and leaned back. The girl scowled and resigned, shook hands with Clifford, smiling crookedly, and went to rejoin her coach for a postmortem.

Chessman stood. No one joined him, and he was not looking around. He walked over to the officials' table, and some of the people standing there congratulated him. Frank stood, walked down the stairs to the floor of the gym, crossed the court, and approached the officials' table. He paused when he saw the youth in conversation with someone there, talking chess, it was clear. Chessman was animated, even cheerful. There was a look on his face that Frank had never seen before. Frank stopped in his tracks. He hesitated, watching. Finally he turned and left the gym.

T HE NEXT DAY FRANK RAN WITH EDGARDO, and told him about his trip, and then said to him, "You know, I've been thinking about what you said about Caroline, and I've tried contacting her by getting into her surveillance, and it hasn't worked, and I'm getting scared. And it oc-curred to me that maybe your friends might be in some sort of contact with her, if what you said happened to be the case, and if so, that they might be able to tell her that I really, really want to see her. I need to see her, if it's at all pos-sible. Because otherwise it's just too . . . well. I'm scared is the thing."

"Yes, yes yes yes yes," Edgardo said, as if pooh-poohing the idea; and then he went silent, as if thinking it over; and then he made no other response at all, but as they made the turn under the Lincoln Memorial, changed the subject to the difficulties that Chase was having with Congress.

The following Wednesday after dinner, Frank went to the mouth of Rock Creek to check the dead drop, and there was a new note.

OUR FIRST SPOT MIDNIGHT LOVE C

In just a couple of hours, if she meant tonight! Thank God he had thought to check! Thank God and thank Edgardo. Frank ran to his VW van, which he had parked in the boathouse parking lot, and drove north on Wisconsin at speed, in a state of high excitement. In Bethesda he took a right and parked in a dark spot near the little park they had first met in. He got out, walked to the bench under the little statue of the girl holding up the hoop. The empty cipher, there in the dark; he waited; and suddenly there she was, standing before him.

They banged together and hugged. "Where have you been?" Frank said roughly, face in her hair. "I've been so scared."

She shook her head for him to be silent, ran a wand over him. "I heard," she said at last, hugging him again. "I've had to be away. But I've been in contact with your friend's friends, and they told me you were concerned."

"Ah. Good old Edgardo."

"Yes. But you need to understand, I have to stay clear of any possibility of them finding me. And a lot of the time you've been chipped."

"I'm trying to stay completely clean when I'm not at work. I got rid of my van and got a new one, an old one I mean, and it's clean too."

"Did you come here in it?"

"Yes."

"Let's go check it out."

He led her to it, holding her hand. At the van she said, "Ah, cute," and checked it with her wand and another device from her fanny pack. "It's all clear." And then they kissed, and then they were climbing inside the van, kissing their way to the little mattress up in the back.

Once again everything else fell away, and he was lost in the little world they made together, completely inside the wave. There was no sexier space than the little overhead mattress of a VW van. And something about it, some quality—the presence of ordinary sheets and pillows, the fact that she had come out of hiding to reassure him, their complete nakedness, which had never before been true—the comfort and warmth of this little nook—even the fact that Diane was with Phil now and Frank entirely committed, no confusion, mind clear, all there, all one, undamaged and whole—the look in her eye—all these things made it the sweetest time yet. The calmest and deepest and most in love.

Afterward she fell asleep in his arms. For an hour or two he lay there holding her, breathing with her. Then she stirred and roused herself. "Wow, that was nice. I needed that."

"Me too."

"I should go," she said. She rolled over onto him, pushed his numb nose with a finger. "I'm going to be out of touch again. I've still got some things I've got to do. Your Edgardo's friends are looking like they will turn out to be a help when the time comes, so look to word from him."

"Okay, I will."

"There'll come a time pretty soon when we should be able to act on this. Meanwhile you have to be patient."

"Okay, I will."

She rolled off him, rooted around for her clothes. In the dark he watched her move. She hooked her feet through her underwear and lay on her back and lifted up her butt to pull them up and on, a nifty maneuver that made him ache with lust. He tugged at the underwear as if to pull it back down but she batted his hand away, and continued to dress as if dressing in tents or VW vans or other spaces with low headroom was a skill she had had occasion to hone somewhere. It was sexy. Then they were kissing again, but she was distracted. And then with a final kiss and promise, she was off.

O NE AFTERNOON AT WORK, just before she left, Anna Quibler got an e-mail from her Chinese contact, Fengzhen. It was a long one, and she made a quick decision to read it on her laptop on the Metro ride home.

As she read, she wished she had stayed in the office so she could make an instant reply. The letter was from Fengzhen, but he made it clear he was speaking for a group in the Chinese Academy of Sciences that wasn't able to get word out officially, as their work had been declared sensitive by the government and was now fully classified, not to say eliminated. The group wanted Anna and the NSF to know that the ongoing drought in western China had started what they called an ecological chain reaction at the headwaters of the Yangtze and the Yellow Rivers; the "general systems crash" that Fengzhen had mentioned in his last e-mail was very close to beginning. All the indicator species in the affected areas were extinct, and dead zones were appearing in the upper reaches of several watersheds. Fengzhen mentioned maps, but the e-mail had not had any attachments. He referenced her previous question, and said that as far as the group could tell, clean coal plants, a greatly reduced pesticide load, and a re-engineered waterway system, were three things that must be done immediately. But as he had said before, it was a matter of cumulative impacts, and everything was implicated. The coming spring might not come. His study group, he went on, wanted to go beyond the diagnostic level and make an appeal for help. Could the U.S. National Science Foundation offer any aid, or any suggestions, in this emergency?

"Shit," Anna said, and shut down her laptop.

In Bethesda, she made sure Nick was okay and then walked on to the grocery store to see if there were any vegetables left from the day's farmers' market, thinking furiously. In the grocery store's parking lot she called Diane Chang's number at work. No answer. Then her cell-phone number. No answer there either. Maybe she was hanging with the president. Anna left a message: "Diane, this is Anna Quibler. I need to talk to you at your soonest convenience about reports I'm getting from a contact in the Chinese Academy of Sciences concerning environmental problems they're seeing there. I think we need to make some kind of response to this, so let's talk about it as soon as we can, thanks, bye."

She had just gotten home from the grocery store with the fixings for goulash (paprika was good at masking the taste of slightly elderly veggies), and was boiling water and badgering Nick to get to his homework, when Charlie and Joe burst in the door shouting their greetings, and at the same moment the power went out.

"Ah shit!"

"Mom!"

"I mean shoot, of course. Dang it!"

"Karmapa!"

"Heavens to Betsy. I can't make dinner without power!"

"And I can't do my homework," Nick said cheerfully.

"Yes you can."

"I can't, the assignment is online!"

"You've got a syllabus page in your notebook."

"Yeah but tonight was added on, it's only online."

"You can do the next thing on the syllabus."

"Ah Mom!"

"Don't Ah Mom me! I'm trying to find the candles here, Charlie can you help get them out?"

"Sure. Wow, these feel funny."

"I hope they aren't all—yep, they are. Melted like the Wicked Witch of the West. Dang it. Why—"

"Did you find matches there too?"

Charlie shuffled into the dark kitchen and gave her a hug from the side. Joe suddenly limpeted onto her legs, moaning "Momma Momma Momma."

"Hi guys," she said resignedly. "Help and get some candles lit. Some of these should work. Come on you guys, we're in the dark here."

They got some misshapen candles lit and placed them in the living room and the kitchen, and on the dining room table in between. Anna cooked spaghetti on their Coleman stove, heating a jar of sauce, and Charlie got a fire going in the fireplace. They settled in to eat. Nick ran down the batteries in his Gameboy, then read by the light of two candles. Charlie typed on his laptop and Anna did the same. The laptop screens were like directional lanterns, adding blue light to the candles' yellow light. They ate yogurt and ice cream for dessert. Anna tried to restrict how many times they opened the refrigerator door, but it didn't really work. She had the thermometers set up in the two boxes, and took a reading sometimes when people wanted to get food.

It was quiet outside, compared to the normal city hum. It had been a while since the last blackout, and it was comforting to fall into the routine. A sign that winter had come. Although there had been a spate of blackouts in the hottest part of the summer as well. Sirens in the distance. The clouds out the window were dark—no moon, apparently, and no city light coming from below. It would have been interesting to know how extensive the blackout was, and what had caused it, and how long it was expected to last. "Should we turn on the radio?"

"No."

They would wait on the generator too. Crank it if they had to.

After a while they got out the Apples to Apples game, and played a few rounds. Joe joined them in the game while continuing to draw with Anna on a big sheet of poster paper they had spread on the floor. He had recently taken to drawing in a big way, mostly sketching big stick figures of various creatures, often red creatures with a kind of Precambrian look, flying over stick forests of blue or green. Now he continued to add lines, and scribbled in patches, while insisting on being part of the game, so that they dealt him a hand, and Anna helped him to read what his cards said, whispering in his ear to his evident delight. The game—junior level, for Joe's sake—dealt people hands of cards on which were printed various nouns, and then an adjective card was turned up by the player whose turn it was, and the rest provided nouns face down, and that player shuffled them and read them aloud, modified by the common adjective, and picked which combination he or she liked the best. The adjective now was SLIMY; the nouns read aloud by Nick were SLIMY ANTS, SLIMY MARSHMALLOWS, and SLIMY PIPPI LONGSTOCKING. You picked nouns tailored to that particular judge, or else just gave up and tried to be funny. It was a good game, and although Joe was somewhat out of his depth and would not admit it, his choice of nouns often had a Dada quality that seemed inspired, and he won about as frequently as any of them.

On this night he was into it. He got a hand he didn't like for some reason, and threw the cards down and said "These are bad! I poop on these cards!"

"Joe."

"I gotta win!"

"It doesn't matter who wins," Charlie said as always.

"Why do we keep the adjectives we win then?" Nick would always ask.

"We do that because they describe us so well when we read them aloud at the end," Charlie would always respond. This was his addition to the game, as for instance, at the end of this one: "I'm noisy, soft, happy, strange, slimy, and old!" he read. "Pretty accurate, as usual."

Nick said "I'm weird, wonderful, useful, skinny, slippery, and sloppy."

Anna was good, hard, spooky, sharp, and important. Ever since she had won the cards for dirty and fat she had been unenthusiastic about Charlie's addition to the game.

Joe was great, short, smooth, fancy, jolly, strong, creepy, and loud. He had won the most.

"What does it mean when an illiterate person wins a game that's written down?" Charlie wondered.

"Be nice," Anna said.

After that they sat and watched the fire. The rumble of other people's generators sounded almost like traffic on Wisconsin. The chill air outside the front door smelled to Charlie of two-stroke engines, and fires in fireplaces. The smell of last winter. Sirens still wafted in from the city distance.

Inside they huddled by the fire. It had been well below freezing for the last week, probably the cause of the blackout, and it was going to be very cold upstairs, with the wind rattling the windows. And in the morning the fire would be out. After some discussion they decided to sleep in the living room again. The couches would do fine for Nick and Joe, and Anna and Charlie hauled the tigers' mattress up the stairs from the cellar. All this was a ritual now; sometimes they did it without the excuse of a blackout.

Faces ruddy in the flickering firelight. It reminded Charlie of camping out, although they never got to have fires in the Sierra anymore. Anna read "Goodnight Moon" to Joe yet one more time (on nights like this he demanded old favorites), while Nick and Charlie read books silently to themselves. This put all four of them out pretty quickly.

The next morning they saw that a little snow had fallen. They were just settling in for the day, Charlie planning to roast some green firewood over the flames of drier wood, when the power came back on with its characteristic click and hum. It had been eleven hours. On the news they found out that electricity for essential services had been provided to Baltimore by the nuclear aircraft carrier USS *Theodore Roosevelt*, and that this had helped the power company to get back online faster.

The day was already disarranged, so Charlie took Nick to school, then returned home, where he and Anna and Joe tried to settle in. None of them seemed to be enjoying this situation, Anna and Charlie trying to work in quick shifts while the other occupied Joe, who was curious to know why he wasn't at daycare; and after a couple hours' struggle, Charlie suggested he take Joe out for a walk while Anna continued to work.

It was a crisp, clear day. According to the little backpacking thermometer hanging from the bottom of the baby backpack (Anna's idea, more data) the temperature outside was very near zero. It would have been perfect conditions for the baby backpack, because with Joe on his back they kept each other warm. But Joe refused to get in it. "I wanna walk," he said. "I'm too big for that now, Dad."

This was not literally true. "Well, but we could keep each other warm," he said.

"No."

"Okay then."

It occurred to Charlie that it had been quite a while since Joe had been willing to get in the thing and take a ride. And it was looking a little small. Possibly Joe had gotten into it for the last time, and the final usage of it had passed without Charlie noticing. With a pang Charlie put it into the depths of the vestibule closet. How he had loved carrying Nick and then Joe around like that. He had done a lot of backpacking in his life, but no load on his back had ever felt so good to him as his boys. Instead of weighing him down they had lifted him up. Now that was over.

Oh well. They set out together on a walk through the hilly neighborhoods east of Wisconsin Avenue.

ON A BRIGHT CHILL SATURDAY MORNING not long after that, Charlie once again joined Drepung and Frank down on the Potomac, this time at a put-in just downstream from Great Falls, on the Maryland side.

Mornings on the river were filled with a blue glassy light unusual elsewhere in the city at that time of year. The deciduous trees were bare, the evergreens dusted with snow.

Frank generally paddled ahead of the other two, silent as he so often was, absorbed in the scene. Charlie and Drepung followed at a distance, talking over the events of the week and sharing their news.

"Did Frank tell you that he visited the original Shambhala?" Drepung asked Charlie.

"No, what do you mean?"

Drepung explained.

"It seems a funny place for Shambhala to have begun," Charlie said. "Out there in the middle of nowhere."

"Yes, doesn't it? But in the eighth century it was different, and, well, howsoever it came about, that's where it happened."

"But eventually it ended up in Khembalung."

"Yes. That is simply the Sherpa word for Shambhala. It came into use when the city was in a hidden valley east of Everest."

"But then the Chinese came."

"Yes. Then the inhabitants moved to the island."

"Now under the Bay of Bengal."

"Yes."

"And so what becomes of Khembalung now?"

Drepung smiled and waggled his paddles. "Always here and now, right? Or at the farm in Maryland, in any case."

"Okay, if you say so. And what about this original site, is it going to be drowned too, you said? Won't that make three for three?"

"No, Frank said it will be close to the shore of the new lake, but they are going to build a dike that will keep it dry."

"Another dike?"

Drepung laughed. "Yes, it does sound a bit too familiar, but I've looked at the maps and heard the plans, and it sounds as if the dike will be rather huge, and more than enough to serve the purpose."

"Why are the Chinese doing this?"

"I think they see it as a tourist attraction, basically. They are going to excavate the ancient city thoroughly, and clean it up for visitors, and call it Shangri-La, and hope that many tourists will come to see it. Then also, maybe go boating or swimming when the sea is filled."

"Amazing."

"Yes, isn't it? But a good thing too. Shambhala is the Buddhist idea of utopia. So, the more this idea is alive in the world, the more people will think about why they are not living in some version of such a place. It stands for a different way of life."

"Yes."

"Also, in the political sense, it seems to me that it's a little bit of a Chinese concession to the Dalai Lama. It's part of their campaign to reconcile with the Dalai Lama."

Charlie was surprised. "You think there is such a campaign?"

"Yes, I think they want it to happen. Even if it is only to serve their own purposes, they seem to be serious about it."

"I'm surprised to hear you say that. Are you sure?"

Drepung nodded. "I've been made aware of informal talks with the Chinese."

For a while they paddled hard to catch up with Frank, who was crossing to the Virginia side to look into the gap between Arlington and Theodore Roosevelt Island. Charlie watched Drepung paddle ahead of him, looking smooth and effortless.

"Drepung? Hey, can you tell me what's going on with Joe and what we talked about?"

"Oh yes. I meant to tell you. Sucandra says that he and Qang can serve as the voice of Milarepa. Qang has done a divination to locate the spirit we exiled from Joe, and she says it is ready to come back. It was not happy to be expelled."

Charlie laughed at that; it sounded like Joe. What if his spirit came back even angrier than before? But he forged on: "Qang...?"

"Yes, she is the servant of Tara, and has taken on much of the work of Rudra Cakrin, now that he is gone on."

"And so—do you know when this can happen?"

"Yes." Drepung glanced over at him. "We are having the ceremony that marks the recognition of the Maryland farm as the current manifestation of Shambhala, next Saturday."

"Oh yeah, we got your invitation in the mail, thanks. I thought it said it was a housewarming."

"Same thing. So, if you could come early, in the morning, we could have these private ceremonies. Then the afternoon could be devoted to celebrating all these things."

"Okay," Charlie said, swallowing hard. "Let's do it."

"You are sure?"

"Yes. I want Joe back. The original Joe."

"Of course. Original mind! We all want that." Drepung smiled cheerfully and called, "Hey Frank!" And dug his paddle tips in, to catch Frank before he disappeared around the tip of Roosevelt Island.

So that Saturday the Quiblers dressed up again, which was unusual enough to put them all in a fun mood, as if they were preparing for a costume party, or even Halloween: the boys and Charlie in shirts with collars, Anna in a dress: amazing!

Charlie drove them out the Canal Road to the Khembali farm, concocting the need for some meeting with Drepung to get them out there early. It was not far from the truth, and Anna did not question it.

So they arrived around ten, to find the farm compound decorated with great swatches of cloth dyed in the vivid Tibetan hues, draped over and between all the buildings, and weaving together on tall poles to form a big awning or tent on the lawn sloping down to the riverside.

Joe said, "Momma! Dad! It's a color house! It's a sky fort! Look!" He took off in the direction of the tent.

"Good!" Charlie said. "Be careful!"

"Will you go with him and watch?" Anna asked. "I want to see what Sucandra and Qang did with the kitchen remodel."

"Sure, go check it out. I think I see them down in the tent right now, actually. But I'll tell them that you're checking it out and they'll be on up I'm sure."

"Thanks."

Off she went inside. Charlie stood by Nick, who was looking at the party preparations, still ongoing. Nick said, "I wish Frank still lived here."

"Me too. But I'm sure he'll be here soon."

"Do you think I can go up in the treehouse anyway?"

"Sure, sure. No one will mind. Go check it out. Don't fall out."

"Dad, please."

"Well. Be careful."

Off went Nick. It was all working out very well.

Charlie walked down to the big suspended awning, his heart pounding with trepidation.

Joe was standing in the middle of a circle of elderly Khembalis, looking around curiously. Sucandra was the youngest one there; Qang was chanting, her voice lower than most men's. Joe nodded as if keeping time to her chant. White smoke billowed out of giant censers and bowls set around a low candle-covered table, on which stood a big statue of the Adamantine Buddha, the stern one with his hand outstretched like a traffic cop.

The candle flames danced on some breeze that Charlie could not feel. An old man on the opposite side of the circle from Qang shouted something. Joe, however, did not seem to notice the shout. He was staring at Qang and the others around her with the same absorption he displayed when watching one of his favorite truck videos. He raised a hand, and seemed to conduct Qang in her singing. She stared fiercely at him, cross-eyed and looking a bit mad. Charlie wondered if she were possessed by the spirit in question.

Finally she took some saffron powder from a bowl held before her by the man on her right, and held it out for Joe's inspection. He put his finger in it, regarded the tip of his finger, sniffed it. Qang barked something and he looked up at her, held his hand out toward her. She nodded formally, theatrically, and took up a bowl of flower petals from the woman on the other side of her. She held the bowl out to Joe, and he took a fistful of pink flower petals, staining them saffron with his finger. The circle of elderly Khembalis joined the chanting, and began shuffling in a clump-footed dance around Joe, punctuating their chant with rhythmic short exclamations, somewhat like the "HAs!" that Rudra had shouted in Joe's face the previous year. Some of them smacked their hand cymbals together, then held the vibrating little disks over their heads. Joe began a little two-step, hands clasped behind his back, reminding Charlie of the dance of the Munchkins welcoming Dorothy to Oz. Then as the chanting rose to a peak, Qang stepped forward and put her hand on Joe's head. He stilled under it. The woman beside Qang put the rest of the flower petals on the back of Qang's hand, and Qang flicked them into the air when she moved her hand away.

Joe sat down on his butt as if his hamstrings had been cut. Charlie rushed to his side, cutting through the dancers.

"Joe! Joe, are you okay?"

Joe looked up at him. His eyes were round, they bugged out like the eyes of the demon masks up at the farmhouse. Wordlessly he struggled to his feet, ignoring Charlie's outstretched hand offering help. He took a swipe at Charlie:

"No, Da! Do it MY SELF. Wanna GO OUT! Wanna go!"

"Okay!" Charlie exclaimed. Instantly he worried that Anna would be concerned by this linguistic regression. But it happened sometimes to young kids, and surely it wouldn't last for long. "Hey there, Joe. Good to see you buddy. Let's go outside and play."

He glanced up at Qang, who nodded briefly at him before she returned her gaze to Joe. She seemed herself again.

"Daaaaaaaaaaaaaaaaaa! Come! ON!"

"Okay sure! Let's go! Let's see if we can find Nick up in the treehouse, shall we? Treehouse? What do you say?"

"Treehouse? Good!" And his face scrunched into a climber's scowl before he marched out the tent door, like Popeye on a mission.

"Okay!" Charlie looked at Qang. "I better go catch up. Hey Joe! Wait a second!"

When Anna came out from the Khembali farmhouse, where she had been conferring with Padma about the re-establishment of the Khembali Institute for Higher Studies, and the possibility of transferring the Khembali/NSF collaborative funds to studying the Chesapeake Bay rather than the Bay of Bengal, she found all three of her boys up in the treehouse, running from one room to the next on a network of catwalks. One of the catwalks was as flexible as a bouncy bridge, and the three of them were busy finding the sweet spot that would cast Joe the highest when Charlie and Nick jumped. Anna could have told them from many previous ground observations that there would be two sweet spots, one each about halfway between the midpoint and the ends, but they seemed to have to rediscover that physical fact every time.

Charlie had gone exuberant, as he often did in these situations. He was getting to be more Joe's age than Joe himself. Although it would have been hard to tell at that moment, given Joe's helpless giggling, and his shrieks of delight at every sprung launching. He had always loved weightlessness. Even in his first weeks, when colic had so often left him wretched and inconsolable, if she had tossed him lightly up and then gently supported him on the way down, never quite releasing her hold on his body and head, he would goggle and go still, then rapt. At the time she had postulated that the weightlessness reminded him of being in the womb, in a swimmer's world, before the outer world had inflicted colic and all its other trials on him. Now, watching him fly, she thought maybe it was still true.

Charlie, on the other hand, just liked playing. Anything would do. In the absence of anything else he would pitch pennies against a wall, or flick playing cards into a pan set across the floor. Wrestle with the boys, especially Joe. Make paper airplanes out of the newspaper. Throw rocks, preferably into water. They all liked that. Very likely during some part of this day she would find them down on the banks of the Potomac, grubbing for pebbles to throw in the stream.

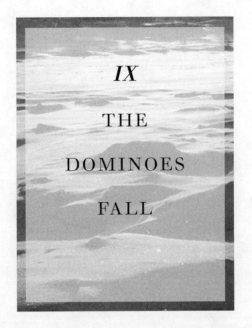

IX

THE

DOMINOES

FALL

"You must not only aim aright,
But draw the bow with all your might."

Tuberculosis progressed in Thoreau until it was clear he was dying. He was forty-four, and just beginning to become a well-known writer. In the bold if morbid style of the time, people dropped by to visit him on his deathbed. It became a kind of tourist destination for the New England intelligentsia. Stories were told to illustrate his flinty character. God knows what he thought of it. He played his part. A few weeks before he died, a family friend asked him "how he stood affected toward Christ." Thoreau answered, as reported later in the Christian Examiner, that "A snowstorm was more to him than Christ."

His Aunt Louisa asked him if he had made his peace with God, and he replied, "I did not know we had ever quarreled."

Parker Pillsbury, an abolitionist and family friend, dropped by near the end, and said to him, "You seem so near the brink of the dark river, that I almost wonder how the opposite shore may appear to you."

Thoreau said, "One world at a time."

Then he died, and for Emerson it was yet another in the series of catastrophic premature deaths that had struck his loved ones. Wife, child, friend. In reading Emerson's essay on Thoreau, Frank could sense the intense care the old man had taken to give a fair and full portrait. "In reading Henry Thoreau's journal, I am very sensible of the vigor of his constitution. That oaken strength which I noted whenever he walked, or worked, or surveyed wood-lots, Henry shows in his literary task. He has muscles, and ventures on and performs feats which I am forced to decline. In reading him, I find the same thought, the same spirit that is in me, but he takes a step beyond, and illustrates by excellent images that which I should have conveyed in a sleepy generality. 'Tis as if I went into a gymnasium, and saw youths leap, climb, and swing with a force unapproachable—though their feats are only continuations of my initial grapplings and jumps."

Emerson went on, "He knew the country like a fox or a bird, and passed through it as freely by paths of his own. His power of observation seemed to indicate additional senses. He saw as with microscope, heard as with ear trumpet, and his memory was a photographic register of all he saw and heard. He thought that, if waked up from a trance, in this swamp, he could tell by the plants what time of year it was within two days.

"To him there was no such thing as size. The pond was a small ocean; the Atlantic, a large Walden Pond. He referred every minute fact to cosmical laws."

In short, a scientist.

But Emerson's grief also had an edge to it, a kind of anger at fate which spilled over into frustration even with Thoreau himself:

"I cannot help counting it a fault in him that he had no ambition. Wanting this, instead of engineering for all America, he was the captain of a huckleberry-party."

Whoah. Pretty harsh, that. And Frank saw reason to believe that this was not the first time Emerson had used the phrase—and that the first time it had been said right to Thoreau's face. They had argued a lot, and about things they both thought mattered, like how to live in a nation where slavery was legal. And in Thoreau's journal, whenever he was grumbling about the terrible inadequacies of friendship, it was pretty clear that he was usually complaining about Emerson. This was particularly true whenever he wrote about The Friend. It made sense, given the way they were; Emerson had a huge range of acquaintances, and spread himself thin, while Thoreau had what Frank thought would now be called social anxieties, so that he relied heavily on a few people close to him. It would not have been easy for any friend to live up to his standards. Emerson said, "I think the severity of his ideal interfered to deprive him of a healthy sufficiency of human society."

In any case they clashed, two strong thinkers with their own ideas, and so they saw less of each other, and Emerson disapproved of Thoreau's withdrawal, and his endless botanizing.

Only in the privacy of his journal did Thoreau make his rebuttal to Emerson's waspish accusation; this was why Frank thought Emerson had made it directly—perhaps even shouted it: he imagined the two men out in Emerson's yard, Thoreau having dropped by without warning, withdrawn and contrary, headed into the woods, and the lonely old gabster hurt by this, and frustrated to see the potential great voice of the age go missing in the swamps— "You could be engineering for all America, and yet off you go to be captain of a huckleberry-party!"

Thoreau wrote: "To such a pass our civilization and division of labor has come, that A, a professional huckleberry-picker, has hired B's field; C, a professed cook, is superintending the cooking of a pudding made of the berries; while Professor D, for which the pudding is intended, sits in his library writing a book. That book, which should be the ultimate fruit of the huckleberry field, will be worthless. There will be none of the spirit of the huckleberry in it. The reading of it will be a weariness to the flesh. I believe in a different kind of division of labor, and that Professor D should divide himself between the library and the huckleberry-field."

Four days later, still nursing this riposte, he wrote:

"We dwellers in the huckleberry pastures are slow to adopt the notions of large towns and cities and may perchance be nicknamed huckleberry people."

In the end, despite these spats, the two men were friends. They both knew that a twist of fate had thrown them into the same time and place together, and they both treasured the contact. Thoreau wrote of his employer, teacher, mentor, friend:

"Emerson has special talents unequalled. The divine in man has had no more easy, methodically distinct expression. His personal influence upon young persons greater than any man's. In his world every man would be a poet, Love would reign, Beauty would take place, Man and Nature would harmonize."

Interesting how even here Thoreau alluded to that source of conflict between them, the question of how to make an impact on the time. Meanwhile, Emerson thought Thoreau had disappeared into the woods and failed to live up to his promise; he could not foresee how widely Thoreau would eventually be read. It took many decades before Thoreau's journals were transcribed, and only then was his full accomplishment revealed, a very rare thing: the transcription of a mind onto the page, so that it was as if the reader became telepathic and could hear someone else thinking at last; and what thoughts! Of how to be an American, and how to see the land and the animals, and how to live up to the new world and become native to this place. His Walden was a kind of glorious distillate of the journal, and this book grew and grew in the American consciousness, became a living monument and a challenge to each generation in turn. Could America live up to Walden? Could America live up to Emerson? It was a still an open question! And every day a new answer came. Frank, reading them in awe, having found the true sociobiology at last, a reading of the species that could be put to use, that helped one to live, looked around him at all the ferals he lived amongst, at the polyglot conclave of all the peoples in the city; and he watched the animals coming back to the forest, and thought about how it could be; and he saw that it could happen: that they might learn how to live on this world properly, and all become huckleberry people at last.

Emerson, meanwhile, lived on. He carried the burden of grief and love, and his tribute to his young friend ended with the love and not the reproach, as always. "The scale on which his studies proceeded was so large as to require longevity, and we were the less prepared for his sudden disappearance. The country knows not yet, not in the least part, how great a son it has lost. It seems an injury that he should leave in the midst his broken task which none else can finish. But wherever there is knowledge, wherever there is virtue, wherever there is beauty, he will find a home."

Frank tried to make one of those homes. He read Emerson and Thoreau to learn about himself. He forwarded the link to Emersonfortheday in all his e-mails, and passed on their news. And he posted printouts of various passages for the ferals to enjoy at the potlucks, and he read passages aloud to Edgardo and Anna; and eventually a lot of his friends were also reading and enjoying Emersonfortheday.com. Diane was a big fan, and she had gotten Phil Chase interested as well.

Phil's hunt for America's past, and an exemplary figure to give him inspiration and hope, was still focused on FDR, for obvious reasons; but he was capable of appreciating the New England pair as well, especially when Diane shoved a passage in front of his face at breakfast. It had become a part of their morning routine. One day he laughed, beating her to the punch: "By God he was a radical! Here it is 1846, and he's talking about what comes after they defeat slavery. Listen to this:

" 'Every reform is only a mask under cover of which a more terrible reform, which dares not yet name itself, advances. Slavery and anti-slavery is the question of property and no property, rent and anti-rent; and anti-slavery dare not yet say that every man must do his own work. Yet that is at last the upshot.' "

"Amazing," Diane said. "And now we're here."

Phil nodded as he sipped his coffee. "You gotta love it."

Diane looked at him over the tops of her glasses. A middle-aged couple at breakfast, reading their laptops.

"You've got to do it," she corrected.

Phil grinned. "We're trying, dear. We're doing our best."

Diane nodded absently, back to reading; she was, like Emerson, already focused on the next set of problems.

As Phil himself focused, every day, day after day; his waking life was scheduled by the quarter hour. And some things got done; and despite all the chaos and disorder in America and the world, in the violent weather swings both climatic and political, the Chase administration was trying everything it could think to try, attempting that "course of bold and persistent experimentation" that FDR had called for in his time; and as a result, they were actually making some real progress. Phil Chase was fighting the good fight. And so naturally someone shot him.

IT WAS A "LONE ASSASSIN," AS THEY SAY, and luckily one of the deranged ones, so that he fired wildly from a crowd and only got Phil once in the neck before bystanders dragged him to the ground and subdued him. Phil was carried back into his car and rushed to Bethesda Naval Hospital, his people working on him all the way, and they got him into intensive care alive. After that the doctors and nurses went at him. The news outside the ICU was uncertain, and rumors flew.

By then it was around eight in the evening. Phil had been on his way to the Washington Hilton for the annual White House Correspondents' Dinner, also known as the Colbert Hour, at which Phil had been expected to shine. After the shooting many of the attendees stayed, standing around in quiet groups, waiting grimly to hear the news, reminding each other this had happened before, and reminiscing about the previous times.

All the Quiblers were at home. When Roy called with the news they were having dinner. Charlie jumped over to switch on the TV, and then they were confronted with the usual images, repeated over and over like a nightmare you could never escape: reporters outside the hospital, administration spokespeople, including Andrea, looking pinched and white-faced and speaking as calmly as she could. And, of course, jostled and bouncing images of the shooting itself, caught mostly in the immediate aftermath, looking like something from an art film or reality TV.

Charlie and Anna sat on the couch before the TV holding hands, Anna squeezing so hard that Charlie had to squeeze back to protect his bones. Nick sat with his face right before the screen, big-eyed and solemn; Joe didn't understand what the fuss was about, and so began to get angry. Very soon he would begin to demand his proper spot in the limelight. Anna started to cry, bolted up and went into the kitchen, cursing viciously under her breath. She had never shown any great regard for Phil Chase or for politicians in general, as Charlie well knew, but now she was crying in the kitchen, banging the teapot onto the stove as if crushing something vile.

"He's not dead yet," Nick called out to the kitchen. His chin was trembling; Anna's despair was infecting him.

Charlie clung to hope. That was what he had at that moment. Anna, he knew, hated to hope. It was to her a desperate and furious emotion, a last gesture.

Now she stormed past them to the front door, yanked her coat blindly out of the closet. "God damn this country," she said. "I can't stand it. I'm going for a walk."

"Take your phone!" Charlie cried as the door slammed behind her.

The Quibler boys stared at each other.

"It's all right," Charlie said, swallowing hard. "She'll be right back. She just needed to get away from—from all that," waving at the screen.

Already all the channels were deep into the tabloid mode that was the only thing the American media knew anymore. Phil's struggle for life was now that beat that came right before the commercials, that moment when they were left hanging, on the edge of their seats, until the show returned and the story was resolved one way or the other. It was all perfectly familiar, rehearsed a million times, *ER* meets *West Wing*. Charlie watched it feeling sick with fear, but also increasingly with disgust, feeling that all those TV shows somehow brought things like this into being, life imitating art but always only the worst art. His stomach was a fist clenched inside him.

For him, as for all the older viewers, there were other reasons than TV shows to feel this sick familiarity: not just the big assassinations of the sixties, not just 9/11, but also the attempt on Ford, the attempt on Reagan. It happened all the time. It was a part of America. In reaction to it they would all mouth the same platitudes they had said before. The lone assassin would turn out to be a nonentity, hardly noticed by anyone before; and no one would point out that the constant spew of hatred against Phil in the right-wing media had created the conditions for such madmen, perhaps had even directly inspired this one, just as no one had said it about the Oklahoma City bomber back in the interregnum between the end of the Cold War and 9/11, when for lack of anything better to hate the hatred had been directed at the federal government. Their culture was a petri dish in which hatred and murder were bred on purpose by people who intended to make money from it. And so it had happened again, and yet the people who had filled the madman's addled mind with ideas, and filled his hand with the gun, and even now were sneering in the commentaries that Chase had risked it after all, daring so much, flouting so much, the only surprise was that it hadn't happened sooner—these people would never acknowledge or even fully understand their complicity.

These dismal thoughts ricocheted around Charlie's mind as he quivered with the shock of the news and of Anna's sudden revulsion and exit. He was trembling, curled over his stomach. He sat beside Nick, swept Joe up into his arms, then let him struggle free. But for once Joe didn't go too far away, and Nick leaned into him, crouched in his enfolding arm. They watched the reporters breathlessly reporting what they had already reported, waiting right there on camera for more news. Charlie turned down the sound and tried to call Roy, but Roy's cell phone was now busy, and he didn't pick up call waiting. Probably he was deluged with calls. The fact that he had called Charlie at all was a reflexive gesture, a reach for an anchor. Roy needed Charlie to know what he knew. But by now he was no doubt overwhelmed. Nothing to do but wait. "Come on, Phil," Charlie prayed in a mutter. But it didn't feel good to say that. "Hang in there. The longer it goes on," he said to Nick, "the better the chances are that he'll be all right. They can do amazing things in intensive care these days."

Nick nodded, round-eyed. Phrases splintered in Charlie's mind as he watched his boys and tried to think. He wanted to curse, mindlessly and repetitively, but for the boys' sake he didn't. Joe knew he was upset, and so occupied himself in the way he usually did when that happened, getting absorbed in his blocks and dinosaurs. Nick was leaning back against him as if to shore him up. Charlie felt a surge of love for them, then fear. What would become of them in such a fucked-up world?

"What's so wrong?" Joe asked, looking at Charlie curiously.

"Someone tried to hurt Phil."

"A guy shot him," Nick said.

Joe's eyes went round. "Well," he said, looking back and forth at their faces. "At least he didn't shoot the whole world."

"That's true," Nick said.

"You get what you get," Joe reminded them.

Anna barged back in the door. "Sorry guys, I just had to get away for a second."

"That's okay," they all told her.

"Any news?" she asked fearfully.

"No news."

"He's still alive," Nick pointed out. Then: "We should call Frank. Do you think he's heard?"

"I don't know. It depends where he is. Word will have spread fast."

"I can call his FOG phone."

"Sure, give it a try."

Anna came over and plumped down heavily on the couch. "What, you have the sound off?"

"I couldn't stand it."

She nodded, the corners of her mouth locked tight. She put her arm around his shoulders. "You poor guy. He's your friend."

"I think he's going to be all right," Charlie declared.

"I hope so."

But Charlie knew what that meant. Hope is a wish that we doubt will come true, she had once said to him, on a rare occasion when she had been willing to discuss it; she had been quoting some philosopher she had read in a class, maybe Spinoza, Charlie couldn't remember, and wasn't about to ask now. He found it a chilling definition. There was more to hope than that. For him it was a rather common emotion, indeed a kind of default mode, or state of being; he was always hoping for something. Hoping for the best. There was something important in that, some principle that was more than just a wish that you doubted would come true, some essential component of dealing with life. The tug of the future. The reason you tried. You had to hope for things, didn't you? Life hoped to live and then tried to live. "He's going to be all right," Charlie insisted, as if contradicting someone, and he got up to go to the kitchen, his throat suddenly clenching. "If he was going to die he would have already," he shouted back into the living room. "Once they get someone into intensive care they hardly ever die."

This was not true, and he knew it. On TV it was true; in real life, not. He slung the refrigerator door open and looked in it for a while before realizing there was nothing in there he wanted. He had not eaten dinner but his appetite was gone. "God damn it," he muttered, shutting the door and going to the window. In the wall of the apartment wrapping the back of their house, almost every window flickered with the blue light of people watching their TVs. Everyone caught in the same drama. "Fuck. Fuck. Fuck."

He went back out and joined the family.

PHIL SURVIVED. It turned out as Charlie had hoped, which was mere luck; but once they got him into intensive care, they gave him transfusions and sewed up the damage, which luckily was not as bad as it could have been—stabilized him, as they said, and got him through the crisis hours, and after that he was "resting comfortably," although from what Roy told Charlie, in a call at five the next morning, neither of them even thinking yet of sleep, still deep in the horrible hours, it was not comfortable at all. The bullet had ticked the edge of his kevlar vest and then run up through his neck, tearing through flesh but missing the carotid, the jugular, the vocal cords. A lucky shot. But he was in considerable pain, Roy said, despite the sedation. The vice president was nominally in charge, but obviously Roy and Andrea and the rest of the staff were doing a lot of the work.

By the time Charlie got to see Phil, over a week later, they had moved him back to the White House. When Charlie's time came he was sitting up in a hospital-style bed located in the Oval Office, with a mass of paperwork strewn on his lap and a phone headset on his head. It seemed possible he was trying deliberately to look like FDR, headset mouthpiece resembling in its cocked angle FDR's cigarette holder, but maybe it was just a coincidence.

"It's good to see you," Charlie said, shaking his hand gingerly.

"Good to see you too Charlie. Can you believe this?"

"Not really."

"It's been surreal, I'll tell you."

"How much of it do you remember?"

"All of it! They had to knock me out to operate on me. I hate being knocked out."

"Me too."

Phil regarded him. It seemed to Charlie that for a second Phil was remembering who Charlie was. Well, fair enough; he had gone on a long journey.

Now he said, "It always seems like there's a chance you won't wake up."

"I know," Charlie said. "Believe me. But you woke up."

"Yes."

There was a tightness to Phil's mouth which looked new to Charlie, and reminded him of Anna. Also his face was pale. His hair was as clean as usual; nurses must be washing it for him.

"But enough of that." Phil sat up farther. "Have you had any ideas about how we can use this to really take over Congress at the midterm elections?"

Charlie laughed. "Isn't it a bit early for that?"

"No."

"I guess. Well, how about handgun regulation? You could call for it with this Congress, then use their lack of response to beat on them during the campaign."

"We would need poll numbers on that. As I recall it's not a winning issue."

Charlie laughed at Phil's bravura, his everything-is-politics pose. He knew Phil didn't really believe in that kind of style—but then again, Phil was looking serious. It occurred to Charlie that he was looking at a different person.

"I'm not so sure about that," Charlie said. "The NRA wants us to think that, but I can't believe most Americans are in favor of handguns, can you?"

Phil gave him a look. "Actually I can."

"Point taken," Charlie conceded, "but still. I wonder about it. I don't believe it. It doesn't match with what I see."

"People want to know they can defend themselves."

"The defense doesn't come from *guns*. It comes from the rule of law. Most people know that."

Phil gave him the over-the-glasses look. "You have a lot of faith in the American electorate, Charlie."

"Well, so do you."

"That's true." Phil nodded and then winced. He took off the phone headset with his right arm, keeping his head as still as possible. He sighed. "It's good to remind me. All this has left me a bit shaken."

"Jesus, I'll bet."

"All he had to do was shoot a little higher and I would have been a goner. He was only about thirty feet from me. I saw something out of the corner of my eye and looked over. That's probably what saved me. I can still see him. He didn't look that crazy."

"He was, though. He's spent some time in institutions, they say, and a lot more living at his mom's, listening to talk radio."

"Ah yeah. So, like the guy who shot Reagan."

"That's right."

"Same place and all—it's like a goddam rerun. 'Hi honey, I forgot to duck!' "

"That's right. He also said to his surgeons, 'I hope none of you are Democrats.' "

Phil laughed so hard he had to rein himself in. "That poor guy didn't know whether he was in a movie or not. It was all a movie to him."

"That's true."

"At least he thought he was playing the good guy. He was a cloth-head, but he thought he was doing good."

"A fitting epitaph."

Phil looked around the office. "I've been thinking that JFK was really unlucky. A lot of these people are so crazy they're incompetent, but his guy was an expert marksman. Amazingly expert, when you think about it. Long shot, moving target—I've been thinking that maybe the conspiracy folks are right about that one. That it was too good a shot to be real."

Whatever, Charlie didn't say. Instead he said, "Maybe so."

It was a gruesome topic. But natural enough for Phil to be interested in it right now. Indeed, he went methodically down through the list: Lincoln had been shot point-blank, Garfield and McKinley likewise; and Reagan too; while the woman who took a potshot at Ford, and the guy who had tried to fly a small plane into the White House, could hardly even be said to have tried. "And a guy shot at FDR too, did you know that? He missed Roosevelt, and Roosevelt got a good night's sleep that night and never mentioned the matter again. But the mayor of Chicago was hit and later on he died."

"Like John Connally in reverse."

"Yeah." Phil shook his head. "FDR was a strange man. I mean, I love him and honor him, but he's not like Lincoln. Lincoln you can understand. You can read him like a book. It's not that he wasn't complex, because he was, but complex in a way you can see and think about. FDR is just plain mysterious. After he had his polio he put on a mask. He played a part as much as Reagan. He never let anyone inside that mask. They even called him the Sphinx, and he loved that." He paused, thinking it over. "I'm going to be like that," he said suddenly, glancing at Charlie.

"Hard to believe," Charlie said.

Phil smiled the ghost of his famous smile, and Charlie wondered if they would ever see the full version again.

Then there was a knock on the door, and Diane Chang came in.

"Hi honey," Phil said, "I forgot to duck!" And there was the full smile.

"Please," Diane said severely. "Quit it." She explained to Charlie: "He says that every time I come in." To Phil: "So stop. How do you feel?"

"Better, now that you're here."

"Are you still doing Reagan or are you just happy to see me?"

The men laughed, and again Phil winced. "I need my meds," he said. "President on drugs!"

"Rush Limbaugh is outraged about it."

They laughed again, but Phil really did seem to be hurting.

"I should let you go," Charlie said.

Phil nodded. "Okay. But look, Charlie."

Now he had a look Charlie had never seen before. Intent—some kind of contained anger—it would make sense—but Phil had always been so mellow. Hyperactive but mellow. Or seemingly mellow. Maybe before the shooting was when Phil had worn the mask, Charlie thought suddenly; maybe now they would be seeing more of him rather than less.

"I want to put this to use," Phil said. "We've gotten a good start on the climate problem, but there are other problems just as bad. So I want to push the process, and I'm willing to try all kinds of things to make it happen."

"Okay," Charlie said. "I'll think about some things to try." By God I will!

He watched Phil squeeze Diane's hand. Test the limits, make an experiment in politics, in history itself. Just how far would Phil go? And how far could he get?

EVERYONE WAS A LITTLE SHAKEN in those first few days after Phil got shot, although as it became clear he would recover, people tended to return from out of that briefly glimpsed bad alternative history to default mode, to the world they had inhabited before, without any lingering sense that things could be different. Because they weren't different, and it was too hard to imagine what things would be like without Phil Chase there. So it was just something that had almost happened and on they went.

But not everyone. To Frank's surprise, one of those who seemed to have been shaken the most was Edgardo. In the immediate aftermath his saturnine face had been set in a murderous expression all the time, and the first time they went out for a run afterward, with Kenzo and a couple of guys from the OMB they had met in the White House men's locker room, he had run around the Mall twice without saying anything at all, a thing of such rarity that Kenzo and Frank looked at each other, uneasy, even a little frightened.

"What's up Edgardo?" Kenzo finally said. "Cat got your tongue?"

"You people are idiots. You are always killing your best leaders. You might as well be some banana republic in Latin America! You're just as bad as all the juntas you set up down there, I suppose it has to be that way. The good ones you kill and the bad ones you give all your money to. Call them good and kiss their ass."

"Geez. Remember, this time the guy only wounded him. And it was a crazy guy."

"It always is. They are easy to find here. Pick anyone."

"Well, gee. Maybe we should change the subject. Have you thought of a new bestseller to write?"

For a long time Edgardo had entertained them on their runs with accounts of the nonfiction books he would write for the bestseller list, popularizing recent findings in the sciences. "Come on," Kenzo encouraged him, "what was that last one? *Why We Fuck Up*?"

"That would be too long to write," Edgardo said. "That is the *Encyclopaedia Britannica,* at the least."

The OMB guys floated back within earshot. "Edgardo, are you talking politics again?"

"Am I talking politics? What kind of a redundancy is that, when are any of us not talking politics? When you talk, you're talking politics."

"I didn't know that. I don't think of it that way."

"It makes no difference what you think. It's all politics. You people in this country don't even know how good you've had it, to be able to just talk politics all this time rather than shoot it. So you do these kinds of things and don't even notice how dangerous it is. Someday you will unleash the furies of *la violencia* down on your idiot heads, and only then will you know what you have lost."

Phil started sending to Congress a new volley of legislation, all kinds of bills that pressured members of Congress to either vote for his programs or be revealed as obstacles, which would then initiate high-profile midterm election campaigns to remove them from office. It was not that the public would necessarily notice but that the party pols would and then they would direct the attack on obstacle representatives. So there was a lot of leverage there and the balance of the parties in the House of Representatives was close enough that Phil was already getting a lot of things through. If these got any momentum and results then by the time the midterm elections came it might be possible to build a solid majority and then accelerate even further. So: judicial appointments, executive actions, all were intensified and coordinated in a single larger campaign, coordinated by Roy and the brain trust. Fuel-mileage efficiency standards of seventy and eighty miles a gallon. A doubling of the gas tax. A return to progressive tax rates. An end to all corporate loopholes and offshoring of profits. Heavy financial support for the World Health Organization's population stabilization efforts. AIDS and malaria eradication funds. Gun control legislation to give the NRA nightmares. It became clear that his team had taken over the tactic called, ironically enough, flooding, which had been used to such effect by the criminals who had hijacked the presidency at the start of the century. It was like a flurry in boxing, the hits just kept on coming, at a pace of three or four a week, so that in the scramble the opposition could not react adequately, not to any individual slaps nor to the general deluge. Rightwing pundits were wondering if Chase had arranged to get shot to gain this advantage, why had the gunman used a twenty-two, where was the evidence he had actually been shot anyway, could they stick a minicam down the hole? No? Wasn't that suspicious?

But in the committees and on the floor of Congress the hammering went on. Roy said to Charlie, "The media is to legislation as professional wrestling is to Olympic wrestling. The real moves are hard to see. We've got them on the run, so come on what's your latest?" The need for a constant stream of good initiatives was getting such that Roy was now hectoring the brain trust to think faster.

"This is just a start," Phil would say at the end of his press conferences, waving away any questions that implied he had suddenly become more radical. "All this had to be done. No one denies that, except for special interests with some kind of horrid financial stake in things staying the same. We the people intend to overturn those destructive tendencies, so grab this tiger by the tail and hold on tight!"

A FEW SATURDAYS LATER, the three kayakers went out on the Potomac again, putting in just downstream from Great Falls.

The overflow channels on the Maryland side had been so torn by cavitation in the great flood that things had been forever changed there, and one new channel of the falls dropped down stepped layers in the gneiss in a very regular way. This channel had been diverted and a few adjustments made with concrete and dynamite to make it even more regular, leaving it stepped so that kayakers could with a hard push paddle up it, one level at a time, catching a rest on the flats before ascending the drops. "Some people make it all the way up to above the falls, and then ride the big drops back down again."

"Some people," Charlie said, looking over at Drepung and rolling his eyes. "Don't you do that, Frank?"

"I don't," Frank said. "I can't get to the top of the Fish Ladder. It's hard. I've gotten around two-thirds of the way up it, so far."

They rounded the bend leading into Mather Gorge, and the falls came in sight. The air was filled with an immediate low roar, and with clouds of mist. The surface of the river hissed with breaking bubbles.

The lowest rung of the Fish Ladder by itself turned out to be more than Charlie and Drepung wanted to attempt, but Frank shot at the bottom drop at full speed, hit the white flow and fought up to the first flat, then waved at them to give it a try. They did, but found themselves stalling and then sliding backwards down the white-water rapids, plunging in and struggling to stay upright.

Frank shot down the first drop and paddled over to them.

"You have to accelerate up the drop," he explained.

"By just paddling faster?" asked Drepung.

"Yes, very fast and sharp. You have to dig hard."

"Okay. And if it catches you and throws you back anyway, do you try to go backwards, or turn sideways on the way down?"

"I turn sideways, for sure."

"Okay."

Drepung and Charlie gave the lowest flume a few more tries, learning to turn as they stalled, which was in itself quite a trick; and near the end of an hour they both made it up to the first level patch of water, there to hoot loudly against the roar, turn, gulp, and take the fast slide back down to the foamy sheet of fizzing brown water. Yow! While they were doing this, Frank ascended six of the ten rungs of the chute, then turned and bounced down drop by drop, rejoining them red-faced and sweating.

After that they floated back downstream toward their put-in, looking over at the Virginia side to spot climbers on the dark walls of Mather Gorge. Frank got interested in a woman climbing solo on Juliet's Balcony, and led them over to watch her climb for a while. Charlie and Drepung reminisced about their one climbing lesson on these walls as if it had been an expedition to Denali or Everest.

While paddling lazily back across the river, Frank said, "Hey, Drepung, I've got a question I've been meaning to ask you—that day at the MCI Center, what was that with you putting a scarf around the Dalai Lama's neck, before he gave his talk?"

"Yeah, what was that about?" Charlie chimed in.

Drepung paddled on for a while.

"Well, you know," he said at last, looking away from the other two, so that he was squinting into the sunlight squiggling over the river. "Everyone needs someone to bless them, even the Dalai Lama. And Khembalung is a very important place in Tibetan Buddhism."

Frank and Charlie gave each other a look. "We knew that, but like just how important?" Charlie asked.

"Well, it is one of the power spots, for sure. Like the Potala, in Lhasa."

"So the Potala has the Dalai Lama, and Khembalung has you?"

"Yes. That's right."

"So how does the Panchen Lama fit into that?" Charlie asked. "What's his power spot?"

"Beijing," Frank said.

Charlie laughed. "It was somewhere down in Amda, right?"

Drepung said, "No, not always."

Charlie said, "But he's the one who was said to be on somewhat equal terms with the Dalai Lama, right? I read that—that the two of them represented the two main sects, and helped to pick each other when they were finding new ones. Kind of a back-and-forth thing."

"Yes," Drepung said.

"And so, but there's a third one? I mean is that what you're saying?"

"No. There are only the two of us."

Drepung looked over at them.

Charlie and Frank stared back at him, mouths hanging open. They glanced at each other to confirm they were both getting the same message.

"So!" Charlie said. "*You* are the Panchen Lama, that's what you're saying?"

"Yes."

"But—but..."

"I thought the new Panchen Lama was kidnapped by the Chinese," Frank said.

"Yes."

"But what are you saying!" Charlie cried. "You escaped?"

"I was rescued."

Frank and Charlie paddled themselves into positions on either side of Drepung's kayak, both facing him from close quarters. They laid their paddles over the kayaks to secure themselves as a loose raft, and as they slowly drifted downstream together, Drepung told them his story.

"Do you remember what I told you, Charlie, about the death of the Panchen Lama in 1986?"

Charlie nodded, and Drepung quickly recapped for Frank:

"The last Panchen Lama was a collaborator with the Chinese for most of his life. He lived in Beijing and was a part of Mao's government, and he approved the conquest of Tibet. But this meant that the Tibetan people lost their feeling for him. While to the Chinese he was always just a tool. Eventually, their treatment of Tibet became so harsh that the Panchen Lama also protested, privately and then publicly, and so he spent his last years under house arrest.

"So, when he died, the world heard of it, and the Chinese told the monastery at Tashilhunpo to locate the new Panchen Lama, which they did. But they secretly contacted the Dalai Lama, to get his help with the final identification. At that point the Dalai Lama publicly identified one of the children, living near Tashilhunpo, thinking that because this boy lived under Chinese control, the Chinese would accept the designation. That way the Panchen Lama, although under Chinese control, would continue to be chosen in part by the Dalai Lama, as had always been true."

"And that was you," Charlie said.

"Yes. That was me. But the Chinese were not happy at this situation, and I was taken away by them. And another boy was identified by them as the true Panchen Lama."

Drepung shook his head as he thought of this other boy, then went on: "Both of us were taken into custody, and raised in secrecy. No one knew where we were kept."

"You weren't with the other boy?"

"No. I was with my parents, though. We all lived in a big house together, with a garden. But then when I was eight, my parents were taken away. I never saw them again. I was brought up by Chinese teachers. It was lonely. It's a hard time to remember. But then, when I was ten, one night I was awakened from sleep by some men in gas masks. One had his hand over my mouth as they woke me, to be sure I would not cry out. They looked like insects, but one spoke to me in Tibetan, and told me they were there to rescue me. That was Sucandra."

"Sucandra!"

"Yes. Padma also was there, and some other men you have seen at the embassy house. Most of them had been prisoners of the Chinese at earlier times, so they knew the Chinese routines, and helped plan the rescue."

"But how did they find you in the first place?" Frank said.

"Tibet has had spies in Beijing for a long time. There is a military element in Tibet, people who keep a low profile because of the Dalai Lama's insistence on nonviolence. Not everyone agrees with that. And so, there were people who started the hunt for me right after I was taken by the Chinese, and eventually they found an informant and discovered where I was being held."

"And then they did some kind of . . . ?"

"Yes. There are still Tibetan men who took part in the rebellion that your CIA backed, before Nixon went to China. They have experience in entering China to perform operations, and they were happy to have another opportunity, and to train a new generation. There are those who say that the Dalai Lama's ban on violence only allows the world to forget us. They want to fight, and they think it would bring more attention to our cause. So the chance to do something was precious. When these old commandos told me about my rescue, which they did many times, they were very pleased with themselves. Apparently they watched the place, and spied on it to learn the routines, and rented a house nearby, and dug a tunnel into our compound. On the night of my rescue they came up from below and filled the air of the house with that gas that the Russians used during that hostage crisis in a theater, applying the correct amount, as the Russians did not, Sucandra said. So when they rescued me they looked like insects, but they spoke Tibetan, which I had not heard since my parents were taken away. So I trusted them. Really I understood right away what was happening, and I wanted to escape. I put on a mask and led them out of there! They had to slow me down!"

He chuckled briefly, but with the same shadowed expression as before—grim, or pained. Anna had spoken from the very start of a look she had seen on Drepung's face that pierced her, but Charlie had not seen it until now.

"So," he said, "you are the Panchen Lama. Holy shit."

"Yes."

"So that's why you've been laying low in the embassy and all. Office boy or receptionist or whatnot."

"Yes, that's right. And indeed you must not tell anyone."

"Oh no, we won't."

"So your real name is . . ."

"Gedhun Choekyi Nyima."

"And Drepung?"

"Drepung is the name of one of the big monasteries in Tibet. It is not actually a person's name. But I like it."

They drifted downriver for a while.

"So let me get this straight!" Charlie said. "Everything you guys told us when you came here was wrong! You, the office boy, are actually the head man. Your supposed head man turned out to have been a minor servant, like a press secretary. And your monk regents are some kind of a gay couple."

"Well, that's about right," Drepung said. "Although I don't think of Padma and Sucandra as a gay couple."

Frank said, "I don't mean to stereotype anyone, but I lived in the room next to them for a few months, and, you know, they are definitely what-have-you. Companions."

"Yes, of course. They shared a prison cell for ten years. They are very close. But..." Drepung shrugged. He was thinking about other things. Again the tightened mouth, with its undercurrent of anger. And of course it would be there—how could it not? Once Drepung had said to Charlie that his parents were no longer living; presumably, then, he had reason to believe that the Chinese had killed them. Perhaps the search for him had made this clear. Charlie didn't want to ask about it.

"What about the other Panchen Lama?" he said. "The boy that the Chinese selected?"

Drepung shrugged. "We are not sure he is still alive. Our informants have not been able to find him in the way they found me. So he is missing. Someone said, if he is alive, they will bring him up stupid."

Charlie shook his head. It was ugly stuff. Not that it didn't fit right in with centuries of bitter Chinese-Tibetan intrigue, ranging from propaganda attacks to full-on war—and now, for the previous half century, a kind of slow-motion genocide, as the Tibetans were both killed outright, and overwhelmed in their own land by millions of Han colonials. The amazing thing was that the Tibetan response had been as nonviolent as it had been. Maybe a full-on terrorist campaign or an insurrection would indeed have gotten them farther. But the means really were the ends for these guys. That was actually kind of an amazing thought, Charlie found. He supposed it was because of the Dalai Lama, or because of their Buddhist culture, if that wasn't saying the same thing; they had enough of a shared belief system that they could agree that going the route of violence would have meant losing even if they had won. They would get there on their own terms, if they could. And so Drepung had been snatched out of captivity with a kind of Israeli or Mission Impossible deftness, and now here he was, out in the world. Taking the stage in front of 13,000 people with the Dalai Lama himself. How many there had known what they were seeing?

"But Drepung, don't the Chinese know who you are?"

"Yes. It is pretty clear they do."

"But you're not in danger?"

"I don't think so. They've known for a while now. I am a kind of topic in the ongoing negotiations with the Chinese leadership. It's a new leadership, and they are looking for a solution on this issue. The Dalai Lama is talking to them, and I have been involved too. And now Phil Chase has been made aware of my identity, and certain assurances have been given. I have a kind of diplomatic immunity."

"I see. And so—what now? Now that the Dalai Lama has been here, and Phil has endorsed his cause too?"

"We go on from that. Parts of the Chinese government are angry now, at us and at Phil Chase. Parts would like the problem to be over. So it is an unstable moment. Negotiations continue."

"Wow, Drepung."

Frank said, "Is it okay if we keep calling you that?"

"No, you must call me Your High Holiness." Drepung grinned at them, slapped a paddle to spray them. Charlie saw that he was happy to be alive, happy to be free. There were problems, there were dangers, but here he was, out on the Potomac. They spread back out and paddled in to shore.

CUT TO THE CHASE

Today's post:

I've been remembering the fear I had. It's made me think about how a lot of the people in this world have to live with a lot of fear every day. Not acute fear maybe, but chronic, and big. Of course we all live with fear, you can't avoid it. But still, to be afraid for your kids. To be afraid of getting sick because you don't have health care. That fear itself makes you sick. That's fifty million people in our country. That's a fear we could remove. It seems to me now that government of the people, by the people, and for the people should be removing all the fears that we can. There will always be basic fears we can't remove—fear of death, fear of loss—but we can do better on removing the fear of destitution, and on our fear for our kids and the world they'll inherit.

One way we could do that would be to guarantee health insurance. Make it a simple system, like Canada's or Holland's or Denmark's, and make sure everyone has it. That's well within our ability to fund. All the healthiest countries do it that way. Let's admit the free market botched this and we need to put our house in order. Health shouldn't be something that can bankrupt you. It's not a market commodity. Admitting that and moving on would remove one of the greatest fears of all.

Another thing we could do would be to institute full employment. Government of the people, by the people, and for the people could offer jobs to everyone who wants one. It would be like the Works Progress

Administration during the Depression, only more wide-ranging. Because there's an awful lot of work that needs doing, and we've got the resources to get things started. We could do it.

One of the more interesting aspects of full employment as an idea is how quickly it reveals the fear that lies at the heart of our current system. You'll notice that anytime unemployment drops below 5 percent the stock market begins to flag, because capital has begun to worry that lower unemployment will mean "wage pressure," meaning management faces a shortage in supply of labor and has to demand it, has to bid for it, pay more in competition, and wages therefore go up—and profits down.

Think for a minute about what that means about the system we've agreed to live in. Five percent of our working population is about ten million people. Ten million people out of jobs, and a lot of them therefore homeless and without health insurance. Destitute and hungry. But this is structural, it's part of the plan. We can't hire them without big businesses getting scared at the prospect that they might have to compete for labor by offering higher wages and more benefits. So unemployment never dips below 5 percent without having a chilling effect on the market, which depresses new investments and new hiring, and as a result the unemployment rate goes back up. No one has to say anything—it works as if by itself—but the fear keeps being created and profits stay high. People stay hungry and compliant.

So essentially, by these attitudes and responses, big business and stock owners act as a cartel to keep the economy cranking along at a high rate but with unemployment included as an element, so that the bottom wage earners are immiserated and desperate, and the rest of the wage earners will take any job they can get, at any wages, even below a living wage, because that's so much better than nothing. And so all wage earners and most salary earners are kept under the thumb of capital, and have no leverage to better their deal in the system.

But if government of the people, by the people, and for the people were offering all citizens employment at a real living wage, then private business would have to match that or they wouldn't be able to get any labor. Supply and demand, baby—and so the bids for labor would get competitive, as they say. That all by itself would raise the income and living standards for about 70 percent of our population faster than any other single move I could think of. The biggest blessing would be for the lowest 30 percent or so— what's that, a hundred million people? Or could we just say, working America? Or just America?

Of course it's a global labor market, and so we would need other countries to enact similar programs, but we could work on that. We could take the lead and exert America's usual heavyweight influence. We could put the arm on countries not in compliance, by keeping out investment capital and so on. Globalization has gotten far enough along that the tools are there to leverage the whole system in various ways. You could leverage it toward justice just as easily as toward extraction and exploitation. In fact it would be easier, because people would like it and support it. I think it's worth a try. I'm going to go to my advisors and then Congress to discuss it and see what we can do.

Previous post:

People have been asking me what it's like to get shot. It's pretty much as you'd expect. It's bad. It's not so much the pain, which is too big to feel, you go into shock immediately, at least I did—I've hurt more than that stubbing my toe. It's the fear. I knew I'd been shot and figured I was dying. I thought when I lost consciousness that would be it. I knew it was in my neck. So that was scary. I figured it was over. And then I felt myself losing consciousness. I thought, *Bye, Diane, I wish I had met you sooner! Bye, world, I wish I were staying longer!* I think that must be what it's going to be like when it really does happen. When you're alive you want to live.

So, but they saved me. I got lucky. At first it seemed miraculous, but then the doctors told me it happens more often than you might think. Bullets are going so fast, they zip through and they're out and gone. And this was a little one. I know, they're saying I paid the guy to use a little one. Please give me a break. They tell me George Orwell got shot in the neck and lived. I always liked *Animal Farm*. The end of it, when you couldn't tell the pigs from the men—that was powerful stuff. I always thought about what that ending said, not about the pigs and how they had changed, but about the men from the other farms. That would be us. People you couldn't tell from pigs. Orwell still has a lot to say to us.

FRANK SPENT SUNDAY AFTERNOON WITH NICK and the FOG people, manning a blind north of Fort de Russey. It overlooked a deer trail, and sightings of deer predators as well as other big mammals were common: bear, wolf, coyote, lynx, aurochs, fox, tapir, armadillo, and then the one that had brought them there, reported a few days back, but as a questionable: jaguar?

Yes, there were still some sightings of the big cat. They were there at de Russey, in fact, to see if they too could spot it.

It didn't happen that evening. There was much talk of how the jaguar might have survived the winters, whether it had inhabited one of the caves in the sandstone walls of the ravine, and eaten the deer in their winter laybys, or whether it had found a hole in an abandoned building and then gone dumpster diving like the rest of the city's ferals. All kinds of excited speculation was bandied about (Frank stayed quiet when they discussed the feral life), but no sighting.

Nick was getting a ride home with his friend Max, and so Frank walked south, down the ravine toward the zoo. And there it was, crouching on the overlook, staring down at the now-empty salt lick. Frank froze as smoothly as he could.

It was black, but its short fur had a sheen of brown. Its body was long and sleek, its head squarish, and big in proportion to the body. Gulp. Frank slipped his hand in his pocket, grasped the hand axe and pulled it out, his fingers automatically turning it until it nestled in its best throwing position. Only then did he begin to back up, one slow step at a time. He was downwind. One of the cat's ears twitched back and presented in his direction; he froze again. What he needed was some other animal to wander by and provide a distraction. Certainly the jaguar must have become extremely skittish in the time since the flood had freed it. Frank had assumed it had died and become just a story. But here it lay in the dusk of the evening. Frank's blood had already rushed through him in a hot flood: big predator in the dusk, total adrenal awareness. You could see well in the dark if you had to. After his tiptoed retreat gained him a few more yards, Frank turned and ran like a deer, west toward the ridge trail.

He came out on Broad Branch and jogged out to Connecticut. Everything was pulsing a little bit. He made the call to Nancy and gave her the news of the sighting.

After that he walked up and down Connecticut for a while, exulting in the memory of the sighting, reliving it, fixing it. Eventually he found he was hungry. A Spanish restaurant on T Street had proven excellent in the past, and so Frank went to it and sat at one of its porch tables, next to the rail, looking at the passersby on the sidewalk. He was reading his laptop when suddenly Caroline's ex sat down across from him. Edward Cooper, there in the flesh, big and glowering.

Frank, startled, recovered himself. He glared at the man. "What?" he said sharply.

The man stared back at him. "You know what," he said. His voice was a rich baritone, like a radio DJ. "I want to talk to Caroline."

"I don't know what you mean," Frank said.

The blond man made a sour face. Aggrieved; tired of being patient. "Don't," he said. "I know who you are, and you know who I am."

Frank saved, shut down, closed the lid of his laptop. This was strange; possibly dangerous; although the encounter with the jaguar put that in a different perspective, because it didn't feel as dangerous as that. "Then why would I tell you anything about anybody at all?"

He could feel his pulse jumping in his neck and wrists. Probably he was red-faced. He put his laptop in his daypack on the floor by his chair, sat back. Without planning to, he reached in his jacket pocket and grasped the hand axe, turned it over in his hand until he had it in its proper heft. He met the man's gaze.

Cooper continued to stare him in the eye. He crossed his arms over his chest, leaned back in his chair. "Maybe you don't understand. If you don't tell me how to get in touch with her, then I'll have to find her using ways she won't want me to use."

"I don't know what you mean."

"But she will."

Frank studied him. It was rare to see someone display aggravation for an extended period of time. The world did not live up to this man's standards, that was clear in the set of his mouth, of his whole face. He was sure he was right. Right to be aggrieved. It was a little bit of a shock to see that Caroline had married a man who could not be fully intelligent.

"What do you want?" Frank said.

Cooper gestured that aside. "What makes you think you can barge into a situation like this and know what's going on?" he asked. "Why do you even think you know what's going on here?"

"You're making it clear," Frank said.

The man waved that away too. "I know she's fed you a line about us. That's what she does. Do you really think you're the first one she's done this kind of thing with?"

"What kind of thing?"

"Wrapped you around her little finger! Used you to get what she wants! Only this time she's gotten in over her head. She's broken the National Security Act, her loyalty oath, her contract, federal election law—it's quite a list. She could get thirty years with that list. If she doesn't turn herself in, if she's caught, it's likely to happen."

Frank said, "I can see why she would stay away from you."

"Look. Tampering with a federal election is a serious crime."

"Yes it is."

The man smiled, as if Frank had given something away. "You could be charged as an accessory, you know. That's a felony too. We have her computers, and they're full of the evidence we need to convict. She's the only one who had the program that turned the vote in Oregon."

Frank shrugged. Talk talk talk.

"What, you don't care? You don't care that you're involved in a felony?"

"Why should I believe you?"

"Because I don't have any reason to lie to you. Unlike her. What I don't understand is why you'd keep covering for her. She's lied to you all along. She's using you."

Frank stared at him. He was squeezing the hand axe hard, and now he started tapping it lightly against his thigh.

Finally he said, "Just by the way you're babbling I can tell you're full of shit."

The man's cheeks reddened. Frank pressed on: "If I knew a woman like that, I wouldn't cheat on her, or spy on her, or try to get her arrested for things that I did."

"She's got you hoodwinked, I see."

This was pointless; and yet Frank wasn't sure how to get away. Possibly the man was armed. But there they were in a public restaurant, out on the sidewalk. Surely he could not be contemplating anything too drastic.

"Why are you bothering me?" Frank said. "What's she to you? Do you know her? Do you know anything about her? Do you love her?"

Cooper was taken aback; his face reddened further. Thin-skinned people, Frank thought, were so often thin-skinned. "Come off it," he muttered.

"No, I mean it," Frank insisted. "Do you love her? Do you? Because I love her."

"For Christ's sake," the man said, affronted. "That's the way she always does it. She could charm the eyes off a snake. You're just her latest mark. But the fact remains, she's in big trouble."

"*You're* in big trouble," Frank said, and stood. He was still squeezing the hand axe in his jacket pocket. Whatever happened, he was at least ready.

Cooper shifted in his chair. "What the fuck," he complained, feeling the threat. "Sit down, we're not done here."

Frank leaned over and picked up his daypack. "You're done," he said.

Frank's waiter approached. "Hi," he said to Cooper, "can I get you anything?"

"No." Caroline's ex stood abruptly, lurching a little toward Frank as he did. "Actually, you can get me away from this guy," and he gestured contemptuously at Frank and walked out of the restaurant.

Frank sat back down. "A glass of the house red, please."

But that was only bravado. He was distracted, even from time to time afraid. His appetite was gone. Before the waiter returned for his order he downed the glass, put a ten under it and left the restaurant. After checking out the street in both directions, he headed back into the park.

He was not chipped, as far as he could tell by the wand Edgardo had given him. He did not see anyone tailing him. He had not let any of the White House security people see which direction he went after he left the compound and crossed the street. He had not used his FOG phone. He had not eaten with the fregans for a while.

Still, Cooper had known where he was.

So the next day he called Edgardo, and they made a run date for lunch. From the 17th Street security gate they ran south, past the Ellipse and out onto the Mall. Once there they headed toward the Lincoln Memorial.

Edgardo took a wand from his fanny pack and ran it over Frank, and then Frank ran it over him. "All clear. What's up."

Frank told him what had happened.

Edgardo ran for a time silently. "So you don't know how he located you."

"No."

Edgardo puffed as he ran for a while, as if singing under his breath, "*Too-too-too-too-too, too-too-too-too-too.* That's bad."

"Also, even though I've seen her twice, I still don't have a way to get hold of her. She's only used the dead drop that once." For which, thank you forever.

Edgardo nodded. "Like I said. She's got to be somewhere else."

They ran on for a long time. Past the Vietnam Memorial, past Lincoln; turn left at the Korean War memorial, east toward the Washington Monument.

Finally Edgardo said, "I think this might mean we can't wait any longer. Also, if he is trying to force you to act, then if you do something that looks rash, there will be a reason for why you would do it.... So that may make it a good time. I want to get you together with my friend Umberto again. He knows more about your friend, and I want him to tell you. She's out of town, as I suggested to you."

"Okay, sure. I'd like to talk to him."

Edgardo pulled a cell phone out of his fanny pack and squeezed one button to make a call. A quick exchange in Spanish, followed by "Okay, see you there." He put the cell phone away and said, "Let's cross and go back. He'll meet us down by the Kennedy Center."

"Okay."

So when they passed the Vietnam Memorial this time, they continued west until they reached the Potomac, then headed north on the riverside walk. As they approached one of the little bartizans obtruding from the river wall, they came on Umberto in a black suit, putting a big ID tag away in his inner pocket. Frank wondered if he was just coming down from the State Department at 23rd and C.

In any case, he walked with Frank and Edgardo upstream, until they could stop at a section of railing they had to themselves, within the shadow and rumble of the Roosevelt Bridge. Umberto wanded them, and Edgardo wanded Umberto, and then they spoke in Spanish for a while, and then Umberto turned to Frank.

"Your friend Caroline has been away from here, working on the problem of the election tampering from a distance. We have reason to worry for her safety, and recently we've also been concerned that the people we're trying to deal with might have had something to do with the attempt on the president's life. So in the process, we have contacted another unit that can help to deal with problems like this."

"Which one?" Frank asked. That list of intelligence agencies, going on and on . . .

"They're an executive task force. A part of the Secret Service that is working together with the Government Accountability Office."

"The GAO?"

"It's a unit of theirs that stays out of sight and works on the black programs."

"You're getting your help from the GAO?"

"Yes, but we are stovepiped to the president. The Secret Service reports to him, and he is overseeing all this work now."

"Well good." Frank shook his head, trying to take it all in. "So what's happening with Caroline?"

"Lots. As you may or may not know, before she disappeared, she was in charge of a Homeland Security surveillance program that combined with the unit we are worrying about, the so-called Advanced Research Development

Prime. Then she came to us, or we found each other, when she got the election disks to you, and through you and Edgardo, to us."

"So you've been working with her since then, is that it?"

"Yes. But we haven't had much more contact with her than you have, from what Edgardo tells me. She's been very concerned to be sure she is working with people she can trust, and understandably so, given what's happened. So we've had to do things her way, to show her she can trust us. She's been doing some work on her own that she's gotten to us, some data mining and even some physical surveillance of some of the problem people, so we can make the case against them stick. And now we feel we are ready to do a root canal on these guys, or I hope we can. In any case this confrontation with you may force our hand."

"Good," Frank said.

Umberto glanced at Edgardo, then said, "The problem is, they've gone inactive since the assassination attempt. I think that wasn't their idea, but it scared them. Now they are very quiet. But still a threat, obviously. So, we know who they are, but they've been clever about distancing themselves from their activities, and they aren't doing anything now that we can stick them with. So, we think your friend is dealing with this same problem, from her side. She doesn't have anything to use, and she wants to stay away from her husband."

Umberto stopped then, and looked at Frank as if it were Frank's turn to say something.

Frank said, "He came right up to me in a restaurant and asked me where she was."

"So Edgardo said."

"And, well, she's not leaving anything at our dead drop."

"Yes. But—I can get a message to her."

Frank nodded briefly. This he knew. It was irritating that she was contacting them but not him—that he needed the black wing of the GAO to contact his girlfriend for him. And she was part of that world. "And say what to her?" he asked.

"We were thinking that, since this group wants to find her, that might be the means to pull them out of their quiet mode."

"Make her the bait in a trap, you mean?"

"Yes. Both of you, actually. We would plan something with the two of you, because you are under their surveillance, while they seem to have lost her. So, we would arrange something in which it looked like you were contacting each other, and trying to be secret, but accidentally revealing to her husband where you are going to meet. Then if they responded to that, and tried to kidnap her, or both of you—"

"Or kill us?"

"Well, we would hope it would not start with that, because they would not want to risk such a thing, or really to draw any attention to her until they have her. We think they want to frame her for the tampering, so they don't have that out there and hanging over them. In any case, we would have people in place such that they would be apprehended the moment they showed up. The exposure would be minimal."

"Can't you just arrest them and charge them with what they've done? Election tampering, illegal surveillance?"

Umberto hesitated. "The surveillance may be legal," he said finally. "And as for the election tampering, the truth is, it seems as though they have succeeded in framing your friend pretty thoroughly. As far as we can tell from what we see, it all came from her office and her computer."

"But she's the one who gave it to you!"

"We know that, and that's why we're going with her. But the evidence we have implicates her and not them. And ARDA Prime is a real group, working legitimately under the NSC umbrella. So we have to have something substantial to go on."

Frank tried to remember if Caroline had mentioned taking the vote-tilting program out of her own computer or not.

Disturbed, he said, "Edgardo? If I'm going to go along with something like this, I have to be sure it's for real, and that it's going to work." He remembered the SWAT team they had run into in the park, busting the bros with overwhelming force. "That it's being done by professionals."

Edgardo nodded. "They can brief you. You can judge for yourself. And she'll be judging it too. She'll be in on the planning. It's not like you will be deciding for her."

"I should hope not."

"We would also have to study the situation very thoroughly, until we understood how they have been tracking you, so we can deal with that and put it to use."

"Good."

"Stay late tonight at work," Umberto said. "I'll try to get you a confirmation."

"Confirmation?"

"Yes. I can't guarantee it for tonight, but I'll try. Just stay late. So we can get you the assurances you require."

"Okay."

"Let's get back to the office," Edgardo suggested. "This has been a long run."

"Okay."

On the way back, after a long silence, Frank said, "Edgardo, what's this about it all coming from her computers?"

"That's what they're finding."

"Could they have set her up like that?"

"Yes, I think so."

"But, on the other hand, *could* she have done the whole thing herself?

Written the tampering program, I mean, and then leaked that to us, so we would counteract it ourselves, and thus tip the election to Chase?"

Edgardo glanced at him, surprised perhaps that such a thing would occur to him. "I don't know. Is she a programmer?"

"I don't think so."

"Well, then. That would be a very tricky program to write."

"But all the tampering comes from her computer."

"Yes, but it could have been done elsewhere and then downloaded into her computer, so that this is all we can see now. Part of a frame job. I think her husband set her up from the start."

"Hmmm." Frank wasn't sure now whether he could trust what Edgardo was saying or not; because Edgardo was his friend.

So Frank went back to his office, and tried to think about work, but it was no good; he couldn't. Diane came by with news that the Netherlands had teamed with the four big reinsurance companies to fund a massive expansion of the Antarctic pumping project, with SCAR's blessing. The new consortium was also willing to team with any country that wanted to create salt water lakes to take on some of the ocean excess, providing financing, equipment, and diking expertise.

Frank found it hard to concentrate on what Diane was saying. He nodded, but Diane stared at him with her head cocked to the side, and said suddenly, "Why don't we go out and get lunch. You look like you could use a break."

"Okay," Frank said.

When they were in one of the loud little lunch delis on G Street he found he could focus better on Diane, and even on their work. They talked about Kenzo's modeling for a while, his attempt to judge the effect of the new lakes, and Diane said, "Sometimes it feels so strange to me, these big landscape engineering projects. I mean, every one of these lakes is going to be an environmental problem for as long as it exists. We're taking steps now that commit humanity to like a thousand years of planetary homeostasis."

"We already took those steps," Frank said. "Now we're just trying to keep from falling."

"We probably shouldn't have taken the steps in the first place."

"No one knew."

"I guess that's right. Well, I'll talk with Phil about this Nevada business. Nevada could turn into quite a different place if we proceeded with all the proposals. It could be like Minnesota, if it weren't for all the atomic bomb sites."

"A radioactive Minnesota. Somehow I don't think so. Does the state government like the idea?"

"Of course not. That's why I need to talk to Phil. It's mostly federal land, so the Nevadans are not the only ones who get to decide, to say the least."

"I see," Frank said. And then: "You and Phil are doing well?"

"Oh yes." Now she was looking at her food. She glanced up at him: "We're thinking that we'll get married."

"Holy moly!" Frank had jerked upright. "That's doing well, all right!"

She smiled. "Yes."

Frank said, "I thought you two would get along."

"Yes."

She did not show any awareness that his opinion had had any bearing on the matter. Frank looked aside, took another bite of his sandwich.

"We have a fair bit in common," Diane said. "Anyway, we've been sneaking around a little, because of the media, you know. It probably would be possible to keep doing it that way, but, you know—if we get caught then they will make a big deal, and there's no reason for it. We're both old, our kids are grown up. It shouldn't be that big a deal."

"Being First Lady?" Frank said. "Not a big deal?"

"Well, it doesn't have to be. I'll keep on being the science advisor, and no one pays any attention to them."

"Not before, they didn't! But you already made it a high-profile job. Now with this it will be a big deal. They'll accuse you of what do you call it."

"Maybe. But maybe that would be good. We'll see."

"Well—whatever!" Frank put his hand on hers, squeezed it. "That's not what matters, anyway! Congratulations! I'm happy for you."

"Thanks. I think it will be okay. I hope so."

"Oh sure. Heck, the main thing is to be happy. The other stuff will take care of itself."

She laughed. "That's what I say. I hope so. And I am happy."

"Good."

She gave him a searching look. "What about you, Frank?"

"I'm working on it." Frank smiled briefly, changed the subject back to the salt lakes and the work at hand.

And he went back to work, and stayed late. And around eleven, as he was falling asleep at his desk, there was a knock at his door, and it was Umberto and Phil Chase himself, and a tall black man Frank had never seen before, whom they introduced: Richard Wallace, GAO.

They sat down and discussed the situation for most of an hour. Chase let the others do most of the talking; he seemed tired, and looked like he was in a bit of pain. His neck was still bandaged in front. Not once did he smile or crack one of the jokes that Charlie had said were constant with him.

"We need to clean this up," he said to Frank in concluding the meeting. "Our intelligence agencies are a total mess right now, and that's dangerous. Some of them are going to have to be sorted out confidentially, that's just the nature of the beast. These are my guys for improving that situation, they report directly to me, so I'd appreciate it if you'd do what you can to help them."

"I will," Frank promised. They shook hands as they left, and Chase gave him a somber look and a nod. He also had no idea that Frank might have played any part in him getting together with Diane. There was something satisfying in that.

ONE AFTERNOON WHEN CHARLIE WENT down to the White House's daycare center to pick up Joe, the whole staff of the place came over to meet with him.

"Uh oh," Charlie said as he saw them converging. Joe was meanwhile looking studiously out the glass doors into the playground.

Charlie said, "What's he done now?"

What a pleasure it was to say that. He knew that the part of him that was pleased was not to be revealed for the moment, and suppressed it. The result was probably a certain defensiveness, but that would be natural no matter what he was feeling; and in truth his feelings were mixed.

The young woman in charge that day, an assistant to the director, listed Joe's infractions in a calm, no-nonsense tone: knocking down a three-year-old girl; throwing toys; throwing food; roaring through naptime; cursing.

"Cursing?" Charlie said. "What do you mean?"

A young black woman had the grace to smile. "When we were trying to get him to quiet down he kept saying, 'You suck.' "

"Except some of us heard it differently," the assistant director added.

"Wow," Charlie said. "I don't know where he would have heard that. His brother doesn't use that kind of language."

"Uh huh. Well anyway, that was not the main problem."

"Of course."

"The thing is," the young woman said, "we've got twenty-five kids in here that we have to give a good experience. Their parents all expect that they'll be safe and comfortable while they're here with us."

"Of course."

The quartet of young women all looked at him.

"I'll see what I can do," Charlie promised.

Then Joe crashed into him and wrapped himself around his right leg. "Da! Da! Da! Da!"

"Hi Joe. I'm hearing that you weren't very nice today."

Joe stuck out his lower lip. "Don't like this place."

"Joe, be polite."

"DON'T LIKE THIS PLACE!"

Charlie looked at the women beseechingly. "He seems kind of tired. I don't think he slept very well last night."

"He seems changed to me," one of the other women observed. "He used to be a lot more relaxed here."

"I don't know if I'd ever describe Joe as being what you'd call relaxed," Charlie said.

But it was no time for quibbling. In fact it was time to extricate the Quiblers from the scene of the crime ASAP. Charlie went into diplomatic mode and made the exit, apologizing and promising that it would go better in the future. Agreeing to a meeting time for a strategy session, as the assistant director called it.

On the Metro home Charlie sat with Joe trapped between him and the window of the car. Joe stood on his seat and held the bar on the back of the seat before him, rocking forward and back, and sideways when the train turned, into Charlie or the window. "Watch out, Da! Watch out!"

"I'm watching out, monkey. Hey, watch out yourself. Sorry," this to the man in the seat ahead. "Joe, quit that. Be careful."

Charlie was both happy and unhappy. This was the Joe that he knew and loved, back full force. Underneath everything else, Charlie felt a profound sense of relief and love. His Joe was back. The important thing was to be gung ho, to tear into life. Charlie loved to see that. He wanted to learn from that, he wanted to be more like that himself.

But it was also a problem. It had to be dealt with. And in the long run, thinking ahead, this Joe, his beloved wild man, was going to have to learn to get along. If he didn't, it would be bad for him. Over time people had their edges and rough spots smoothed and rounded by their interactions with each other, until they were like stream boulders in the Sierra, all rounded by years of banging. At two years old, at three, you saw people's real characters; then life started the rounding process. Days of sitting in classes—following instructions—Charlie plunged into a despair as he saw it all at once: what they did to kids so that they would get by. Education as behavioral conditioning. A brainwashing that they called socialization. Like something done to tame wild horses. Put the hobbles on until they learn to walk with them; get the bit in the mouth so they'll go the direction you want. They called it breaking horses. Suddenly it all seemed horrible. The original Joe was better than that.

"You know, Joe," Charlie said uncertainly, "you're going to have to chill out there at daycare. People don't like it when you knock them over."

"No?"

"No."

"I knock you over, ha."

"Yes, but we're family. We can wrestle because we know we're doing it. There's a time and a place for it. But just the other kids at daycare, you know—no. They don't know how tough you are."

"Rough and tough!"

"That's right. But some kids don't like that. And no one likes to be surprised by that kind of stuff. Remember when you punched me in the stomach and I wasn't expecting it?"

"Da go owee, big owee."

"That's right. It can hurt people when you do that. You have to only do that with me, or with Nick if he feels like it."

"Not Momma?"

"Well, if you can get her to. I don't know though. It might not be a good habit, or . . . I don't know. I don't think so. You can ask her and see. But you have to ask. You have to ask everybody about that kind of stuff. Because usually rough-housing is just for dads. That's the thing about dads, you can beat on them and test your muscles and all."

"When we get home?"

"Yeah, sure. When we get home." Charlie smiled ruefully at his younger son. "You get what you get, remember?"

"You get what you get and you don't throw a fit!"

"That's right. So don't throw any fits. We'll make it work, right Joe?"

Joe patted him on the shoulder solicitously. "Good Da."

But this was only one of many such occurrences. Charlie began to dread the trip down to the daycare center to pick Joe up; what would he have perpetrated this time? Fitting a Play-Doh hat to a sleeping girl; climbing the fence and setting off the security alarm; plugging the sink with Play-Doh and climbing in the little "bath" that resulted . . . he was very creative with Play-Doh, as a sympathetic young black woman named Desiree noted, trying to reduce the tension in one of these postmortem sessions.

But reducing the tension was getting harder to do. The woman in charge asked Charlie to take Joe in to their staff doctor for an evaluation, and that led to an evaluation by a child psychiatrist, which led to a sequence of un-illuminating tests; which led, finally, to a suggestion that they consider trying one of the very successful ameliorating drug therapy regimens, among them the paradoxical-sounding but clinically proven Ritalin.

"No," Charlie said, politely but firmly. "He's not even three years old. A lot of people are like this at his age. I was probably like this then. It isn't appropriate."

"Okay," the doctors and daycare people said, their faces carefully expressionless.

Charlie was afraid to hear what Anna thought about it. Being a scientist, she might be in favor of it.

But it turned out that, being a scientist, she was deeply suspicious that the treatment had been studied rigorously enough. The fact that they didn't know the mechanism by which these stimulants calmed certain kids made her coldly contemptuous, in her usual style. Indeed, Charlie had seldom seen her so disdainful of other scientific work. No drug therapies, she said. My Lord. Not when they don't even have a suspected mechanism. The flash-freeze of her disrespect—it made Charlie grin. How he loved his scientist.

"Look," Charlie said to the daycare director one time, " I like the way he is."

"Maybe you should be the one taking care of him, then," she said. Which he thought was pretty bold, but she met his eye; she had her center to consider. And she had seen what she had seen.

"Maybe I should."

On the Metro ride home, Charlie watched Joe as the boy stared out the window. "Joe, do you like daycare?"

"Sure, Da."

"Do you like it as much as going to the park?"

"Let's go to the park!"

"When we get home."

THE THREE KAYAKERS WERE OUT at Great Falls again, testing the Fish Ladder. Charlie and Drepung were getting better at it; they could rush up three or four drops before they tired and turned and rode the drops back down. Frank was getting almost all the way to the top.

When they were done, and just riding the current downstream to their put-in, they discussed all that was happening, first the new stuff Phil Chase had introduced, and then the latest in the ongoing negotiations between the Dalai Lama and the Chinese government. Drepung was excited about the possibilities opening up.

As they closed on shore, Frank said, "So, Drepung, do you, you know—believe in all the reincarnation stuff?"

"What do you mean?"

"Do you think you are the reincarnation of that last Panchen Lama, and all the ones before?"

Even as Frank was saying it, Charlie was seeing a bit of physical resemblance between the youth and photos he had seen of the previous Panchen Lama, despite how obese the previous one had gotten (although Drepung worked hard to hold down his weight). It was a look in the eye—somewhat like the look on Drepung's face when Frank had given them climbing lessons. A wary, worried look—even a repressed fear—and sharp concentration. Of course it made sense. The Chinese government considered itself to be the master of the Panchen Lama.

"So are you part of these negotiations with the Chinese?" Charlie said.

"Yes."

"But could you get, you know, remanded to them?"

"No, that won't happen. The people and the Dalai Lama are behind me."

"Shouldn't you be announcing who you are, as a safeguard?"

"That's one of the bargaining chips still out there, of course."

"You wouldn't want to be too late with that!"

"No."

Charlie thought it over. "My Lord. What a world this is."

"Yes."

"So," Frank persisted, "have you ever had any, like, memories of your previous incarnations?"

"No."

Frank nodded. "That's what the Dalai Lama said too, in the paper. He said he was an ordinary human being."

"I am even more ordinary, as you know."

"So why should you continue to believe you are the reincarnation of some previous person?"

"We are all such. You know—one's parents."

"Yes, but you're talking about something else. Some wandering spirit, moving from body to body."

"We all have those too."

"But identifiable, from life to life?"

Drepung paused, then said, "I myself think that this is a heuristic device only."

Charlie laughed. "A teaching device? A metaphor?"

"That's what I think."

Charlie began to think about that in the context of what had been happening to Joe.

"And what does it teach us?" Frank asked.

"Well, that you really do go through different incarnations, in effect. That in any life your body changes, and where you live changes—the people in your life, your work, your habits. All that changes, so much that in effect you pass through several incarnations in any one biological span. And what I think is, if you consider it that way, it helps you not to have too much attachment. You go from life to life. Each day is a new thing."

"That's good," Frank said. "I like that. The theory of this particular Wednesday."

Charlie was still thinking about Joe.

A few weeks later, by dint of some major begging, Charlie got Roy to give him ten minutes of Phil's morning time. Dawn patrol, as it turned out, because it was not only the best time to fit something in, as Phil himself remarked, it was also the traditional time for him and Charlie to meet. On this occasion, however, a Sunday morning.

Charlie showed up at the White House having slept very little the night before. Phil met him in a car at the security gates, and they were driven down Constitution and past the front of the Lincoln Memorial. "Let's walk from here," Phil suggested. "I need the exercise."

So they got out and were followed by Phil's Secret Service team through the Korean War Memorial. It was a foggy morning, and still so early that the sun was not yet up. The pewter statues of the patrol hiked uphill through a wet mist, forever frozen in their awful moment of tension and dread. A long black wall on the Potomac side of the statues was filled with little white faces peering out from what seemed to be different depths within the stone, all bearing witness to the horrors of war. At the top of the memorial a small stone basin was backed by a retaining wall, on which was carved the message "FREEDOM IS NOT FREE."

Phil stood for a while staring at it. Charlie left him to his thoughts and walked over to the apex of the statues. *We here honor our sons and daughters who answered the call to defend a country they did not know and a people they never met.*

Then Phil was beside him again. "It's strange, isn't it?"

"Yes."

"So many wars. So many people died."

"Yes."

"I wonder if we can make it all worth it."

"Sure we will," Charlie said. "You're leading the way."

"Can anyone do that?"

"Sure. People like being part of a cause. And Americans like to like the president."

"Or hate him."

"Sure, but they'd prefer to like him. As with you. Your numbers are really high right now."

"Any time you get shot your numbers go up."

"I suppose that's so. But there you are."

Phil shook his head. "Doesn't it seem like these memorials are getting better and better? This place is a heartbreaker."

"They found a really good sculptor."

"Let's walk down and see FDR. He always cheers me up."

"Me too."

It took several minutes to walk from the Korean to the FDR Memorial, skirting the north bank of the Tidal Basin and heading for the knot of trees around it. On first arrival it looked unprepossessing; one felt that FDR had been shortchanged compared to the rest. It was a kind of walled park or gallery, open to the sky, with the walls made of rough-hewn red granite. Little pools and waterfalls were visible farther ahead, but it was all very unobtrusive, like a kids' playground in some suburban Midwestern park.

But then they came to the first statue of the man—in bronze, almost life-sized, sitting on a strange little wheelchair, staring forward blindly through round bronze spectacles. He looked so human, Charlie thought, compared to the monumental gravity of the statue of Lincoln in the Lincoln Memorial. This, the statue said very obviously, had been another ordinary human being. Behind the statue on a smoothed strip of the granite were words from Eleanor Roosevelt that underscored this impression:

"Franklin's illness gave him strength and courage he had not had before. He had to think out the fundamentals of living and learn the greatest of all lessons—infinite patience and never-ending persistence."

"Yes," Phil murmured as he scanned the words. "To think out the fundamentals of living. He was forty when the polio hit him, did you know that? He had had a full life as a normal person, I mean, unimpeded. He had to adapt."

"Yes," Charlie said, and thought of what Drepung had said on the river. "It was a new incarnation for him."

"And then he got so much done. There were five separate New Deals, did you know that?"

"Yes, you've told me about that."

"Five sets of major reforms. Diane has done a complete analysis of each."

"He had huge majorities in Congress," Charlie pointed out.

"Yeah, but still. That doesn't guarantee anything. You still have to think of things to try for. People have had big majorities in Congress and totally blown it."

"That's true."

"What would he do now?" Phil asked. "I find myself wondering that. He was a pretty creative guy. The fourth and the fifth New Deals were pretty much his own ideas."

"That's what you've said."

Phil was standing before the statue now, leaning a bit forward so that he could stare right into the stoical, blind-seeming face. The current president, looking for guidance from Franklin Delano Roosevelt; what a photo op! And yet here were only Charlie and the Secret Service guys to witness it, as well as a runner who passed through with a startled expression, but did not stop. No real witness but Charlie; and Charlie was about to jump ship.

He was feeling too guilty to let the walk go on any further without reference to this. So as they moved to the next room of the open gallery he tried to change the subject to his own situation, but Phil was absorbed in the Depression statues, which Charlie found less compelling despite their inherent pathos: Americans standing in a bread line, a man sitting listening to a fireside chat on a radio. "I see a nation one-third ill fed, ill housed, ill clothed."

"It's almost like the problem is the reverse now," Phil observed. "I see a nation one-third too fat, too clothed, too McMansioned, while the third that is ill fed and ill housed still exists."

"And they're all in debt, either way."

"Right, but what do you do about that? How do you talk about it?"

"Maybe just like you are now. These days, Phil, I think you get to say what you want. Like on your goddam blog."

"You think?"

"Yes. But look—Phil. I asked for some time today so I could talk to you about my job. I want to quit."

"What?" Phil stared at him. "Did you say quit?"

"Well, not quit exactly. What I want is to go back to working at home, like I was before."

As Phil continued to stare at him, he tried to explain. "I want to take care of Joe again. He's having some problems getting along at the daycare center. It's not their fault at all, but it just isn't working very well. I think it would be better if we just stayed home for another year or so, until he gets to the normal preschool age. It would be better for him, and the truth is I think it would be better for me, too. I like spending time with him, and I seem to do better with him than most people. And it won't last long, you know? I already saw it with Nick. It just flashes right by. A couple of years from now everything will be different, and I'll feel better about leaving him all day."

"These are critical years," Phil pointed out.

"I know. But maybe they all are."

In the memorial they were moving from the Depression to the Second World War, as if to illustrate this thought. In this open room there was a different statue of FDR, bigger and in the old style, draped in the dramatic sweep of a naval cape, free of glasses and looking off heroically into the distance.

"I don't want to stop helping you out," Charlie said, "not at all, but the thing is, most of what I'm doing I could do over the phone, like I did before. I thought I was doing okay then, and you've got all the technical advice you could ever want, so all I'm doing is political advice."

"That's important stuff," Phil said. "We've got to get these changes enacted."

"Sure, but I'm convinced I can do it over the phone. I'll work online, and I'll work nights after Anna gets home."

"Maybe," Phil said. He was not pleased, Charlie could tell. He approached the big second statue, which included, off to one side, a statue of the Roosevelts' dog, a Scottie. Phil scolded it: "And your little dog too!"

The bronze had gone green on this version of FDR, everywhere except for the forefinger of the hand stretched out toward viewers. So many people had touched it that it was polished until it looked golden.

Phil touched it too, then Charlie.

"The magic touch," Phil said. "How touching. Every person that touches this finger still believes in America the beautiful. They believe in government and justice. It's a kind of religious feeling. Do you think any Republicans touch it?"

"I don't think they even come here," Charlie said, suddenly gloomy. He recalled reading that FDR had been pretty ruthless with aides who no longer served his purposes. They had disappeared from the administration, and from history, as if falling through trapdoors. "We're two countries now I guess."

"But that won't work," Phil said, holding on to the statue's gleaming finger. "May the spirit of FDR bring us together," he pretended to pray, "or at least provide me with a solid working majority."

"Ha ha." Again Charlie marveled at the photo ops being missed. "You should bring the press corps down here with you, and invoke all this specifically. Why is this not the great moment in American history? You should say it is—up until now, anyway. Give people a tour of FDRness, and a look into your thinking. Into what you admire about Roosevelt, and America in those years. Remember the time we were at the Lincoln Memorial with Joe, and that TV crew was there for some other reason? It could be like that. For that matter you could do Lincoln again. Do them both. Take people around all the memorials, and talk about what matters to you in each of them. Give people some history lessons, and some insights into your own thinking about where we are now. Keep calling these years now another rendezvous with destiny. Call for a new New Deal. These are the times that try men's souls, and so forth."

"I don't think there are any monuments to Thomas Paine in this town," Phil said, smiling at the thought.

"Maybe there should be. Maybe you can arrange for that."

"In my copious spare time."

"Yes."

Phil slapped hands with FDR and moved on. They went around a corner into the final room of the gallery, where an amazingly lifelike statue of Eleanor Roosevelt stared out from an alcove embossed with the emblem of the United Nations.

"The UN was his idea, not hers," Phil objected. "She worked for it after it was established, but he had the idea from even before the war. World peace, the rule of law, and the end of all the empires. It was amazing how hard he tweaked Churchill and de Gaulle on that. He wouldn't lift a finger to help them keep their old empires after the war. They thought he was just being a lightweight, or some kind of a card, but he was serious. He just didn't want to come off as all holier-than-thou about it. Like his lovely wife here used to."

"But he was holier-than-thou, compared to Churchill and de Gaulle."

"No, de Gaulle was the holy one in that crowd. Roosevelt was an operator. And everyone was holier than Churchill."

"This is what you should be saying. So—what do you say?"

"About becoming a memorial tour guide?"

"No, about whether I can do my job from home again."

"Well, Charlie, I think you're doing good work. We need to get to sustainability as fast as we can, as you know. There's a lot riding on it. But, heck. If your kid needs you, then you've got to do it."

"I think he does. Him and me both."

"Well, there you are."

"I can still do the daily phone thing with Roy, and come in with Joe like I used to. And we'll get a big majority in Congress at the midterms, and then you'll get re-elected—"

"You think so?"

"I'm sure of it. And by then Joe will be in kindergarten and beyond, and this phase will have passed. I'll be really anxious to get back to work then, so I don't want you to hold this against me and drop me, you know? That's what FDR did to his aides."

"I'm not as tough as he was."

"I don't know about that. But I'll want to come back."

"We'll see when the time comes," Phil said. "You never know what'll happen."

"True."

Charlie felt disappointed, even worried; what would he do for work, if he couldn't work on Phil's staff? He had been doing it for twelve years now.

But he had wanted to stay with Joe. Actually, he wanted it all. But no one got to have it all. He was lucky he had as much as he had. He would have to keep working hard to stay innovative from home, over the phone. It could be done; he had done it before.

Phil gestured to his guys, following them at a not-so-discreet distance, and a car came to pick them up less than a minute later. Back to the White House; back to work; back to the world; back home. Phil was silent on the drive and appeared to be thinking of other things, and Charlie didn't know what he felt.

ONE STRANGELY BALMY WINTER DAY Frank got the word from Edgardo during their run. It was time to go. They had everything staked out and rehearsed, the time was now. Good. But between lunch and dinner the thunderheads had grown, and big news had arrived from China: there had been some kind of crisis declared, ordinary law and all the normal actitivities there had been suspended. The American nuclear submarine fleet had turned up en masse in Chinese harbors, along with several aircraft carriers; but this was by Chinese invitation, apparently, and the fleet had immediately plugged into the Chinese electrical grid and taken over generating electricity for essential services in certain areas; the rest of the country's grid had been shut down. And Phil Chase had landed in Beijing, apparently to consult with the Chinese leadership. The secretary-general of the UN and dignitaries and representatives from other countries had also flown in. From the sound of it, the Chinese appeared to be attempting a kind of near-instantaneous transformation of their infrastructure—the Great Leap Forward At Last, as one of the news strips at the bottom of the TV screens put it—but only to escape falling into a bottomless pit. And so the attention of the world was transfixed.

All that was very interesting; and maybe good, maybe bad, as far as any potential impact on their own operation was concerned. But there was no mechanism for bailing that Frank knew of, and all he could do was grit his teeth and wait for the time to arrive.

Finally the hour came. He was in his office, his door was closed; he knew just how his FOG phone was bugged, and by whom. Time to play his part. He picked up the phone, dialed the number he had been given.

Caroline picked up.

"Hey," Frank said.

"Oh hey! What's up? Why are you—"

"I've got to see you, I've got the proof you wanted. Meet me down where we met before, by the river, about nine."

"Okay," she said, and hung up.

He stood. Took the Kevlar vest from his desktop and put it on. Kevlar. This was what Phil Chase had to deal with all the time. The feeling of being a potential target. Of having been shot and then going out there again.

He left the White House compound, aware of just which one of the security guys at the gate had been tacking a new kind of chip on him. It had taken them a while to figure it out and get up to speed. The guard hadn't been there all the time, but he had been there a lot, and they had made sure he was there now: thin face, impassive look, didn't meet the eye quite. Do it again, asshole. This time they needed it.

Once out on the sidewalk he put the earbuds of his iPod lookalike in his ears. "Did he do it?"

"Yes," he heard in his right ear.

He walked west on G Street to the Watergate, then across the Rock Creek Parkway, through the Thompson boat club parking lot, where his VW van was parked; then past the van, over the little bridge crossing the creek, and onto the Georgetown waterfront. It was about eight-thirty.

Then the city lost power. "Shit," Frank said. The waterfront was now dark, and people were calling out and wandering in the sudden gloom.

"This is bad," he said.

The voice in his right ear said, "—proceed for now. She says she can make it over no problem."

Frank went down to the water's edge and watched the cars' headlights make an uneven line on the Virginia side. George Washington Parkway, Arlington streets above. Generators were bringing light back here and there across the city, on both sides of the river.

In this partial light Caroline appeared, looking flushed and intent. They met and hugged, then spoke like amateur actors, their voices extra-expressive—at times almost cutting each other off in their eagerness to say their lines. They rolled their eyes at each other, tried to pace themselves better. Two bad actors in the dark. He could see she was wearing the vest under her blouse, and thought her ex might be able to too. He handed her a little key-chain zip drive.

Awkwardly he put his arm around her shoulder, and they rested at the river rail for a moment, itching at the unfelt transference of the new type of surveillance tick that had been lofted onto him by the security guard—a thing of plastic and quartz, pinging at a frequency the wands didn't cover. A programmable mobile chip, programmed to jump on first contact and then stay put: a nano-event neither of them could feel except in the set of their muscles, a kind of itch on the inside of the skull.

Together they hiked back over the little bridge, and stopped by Frank's van. They embraced and drew apart, looking helplessly at each other, just barely visible to each other, and that only by the light of the passing cars on the parkway. This was a dark part of town even when the power was turned on. Frank let go of her hand and watched her walk away.

Now she was walking in a crowd of Umberto and Wallace's people, disguised as ordinary citizens and as tourists, which explained their daypacks and camera gear, their iPod earbuds, their aimless gawking and walking. It was a very professional team, far more expert than an ordinary SWAT team. Special ops—

And yet.

Frank hopped up in his van's driver's seat, prepared to be carjacked or shot; the presence of Umberto's guys quietly sitting in the back of the van was little comfort. The blackout was a factor they had not planned on, it was dark out there and blackouts always induced a little chaos. Caroline was headed for the Watergate and then to the Kennedy Center. The special ops teams were going to follow her for as long as it took. They knew Cooper's group had overheard the call from Frank, they knew Frank had been followed. Because they numbered almost everyone in the area, they were confident they would spot anyone approaching her with intent long before they neared her. At that point they would close in, and act in the same moment as any approach.

Frank's part in the cover story had had him passing along vital information, indeed proof of a crime, so he sat there uncomforted by his guards in back, expecting to be shot or blown up, but of course the van and the area were fully secured, and now one of the guards was wanding him with a bigger device than any he had seen before. Still a nanochip there on the back of his jacket. A tick, smaller than a tick. They would never find it in the fabric.

"I'm going to leave that here and follow her," Frank said.

The man frowned.

"Is there anyone following me?" Frank asked.

"No," the one in back said. "It looks like they're just going for her."

"I'm going over there," he said, and snatched the hand axe out of his jacket pocket and jumped back out into the dusk.

"Stay out of the way."

He was still hearing the team comms in his right ear. Someone said her tick was now taking pings. Source not yet IDed. These devices had to be pinged from within a couple hundred yards. Frank started to run, dashing across Rock Creek Parkway during a too-small gap in the traffic, then racing across the black grass to Virginia Avenue, so much darker than usual, it was normally a very well-lit street. The headlights of passing vehicles destroyed night vision without illuminating much outside the road; they made things worse. Another voice complained that dense ping traffic in the area was making it difficult to identify sources; possibly there were decoys. Frank felt a stab of fear and ran harder still. Decoys? Had Caroline's ex seen this ambush coming, and taken steps to circumvent it?

It was hard to tell who was saying what. A police car with siren screaming

zoomed through the momentarily still traffic. Some of the buildings with generators were lighting up. Frank said, "Can you patch me into her wire?"

"Yeah." There was a click, and then he could hear her whisper: "I'm going
past the Watergate. I'm not sure what to do. It's well-lit here."

"Stick to the plan," someone said.

"I just saw them," she said. "I'm going to step into this espresso shop on the
southeast side of the Watergate, they've got a generator going."

"Okay. Stay cool now. They won't want any fuss."

Someone else said, "We have visual."

"On her or the tail?"

"Both!"

By now Frank was running as hard as he could around the northeastern
curve of the Watergate complex, hand axe at the ready, thinking that a man hit
by tasers might spasm so violently as to pull a trigger, or might shoot for the
head on sight—

Caroline was being escorted out the shop door by two men, one on each
side of her, both holding her by the arm. Their backs were to him; Frank drew
up short as he would have in the woods. Cooper was to her right, looking
down at her, saying something though his jaw was set. Frank hefted the hand
axe, grasped it like a skipping stone. "Come on guys," he whispered.

Then Cooper stopped and looked around, and began to pull something
from his jacket. Figures leaped from the dark as Frank threw the stone over-
hand. It was a perfect throw, but by the time it had flashed through the night
to its target, Cooper had been flattened to the ground; the stone flew over him
and his tacklers and hit one of the SWAT guys square in his flak-jacketed chest.
The man's rifle came up and pointed right at Frank, and three or four others
did as well. For a moment everything froze; Frank found his hands were up
over his head, palms out.

No one shot him. Then fifty yards down the road a brief scrum erupted.
Some of the rifles got redirected that way. Off to the side another sudden
group coalesced out of the dark, men holding guns trained on a pair of other
men. Finally everything went still.

Caroline was stepping back gingerly from their own rescuers. She looked
around, eyes wide; saw Frank. He came to her side and briefly they clasped
hands, squeezed hard. She was white-faced, her gaze fixed on her trussed and
prone ex as if on a beast that might still break free and leap at her.

Umberto appeared before them, rotund in his flak jacket. "Into the Watergate," he said. "We have one of the condos, and they've got their generator
going."

NEAR THE END OF THEIR DEBRIEFING, with Cooper and his crew long gone, and Umberto and his people absorbed in the progress of other parts of the root canal, Frank and Caroline realized they were no longer needed. Umberto noticed them standing there and waved them away. The operation was going well, he indicated. There would be no one left to bother them.

As they were leaving, the man Frank had hit with his hand ax gave it back to him, frowning heavily as he thumped it into Frank's palm. "You could hurt somebody," he said. "Maybe leave it on your mantelpiece."

"On my dashboard," Frank promised.

They found themselves alone, standing outside the Watergate's old hotel lobby entrance. The blackout was ongoing, although generators now lit many buildings in this part of town. Sirens in the distance sawed away at the night.

"So you threw your rock at him again."

"Yes. I corrected for my release and almost got him."

"You could have wrecked everything."

"I know, but we'd gone off the plan. I didn't want him to shoot you or get tasered and spaz out and shoot you by accident. I just did it."

"I know, but that guy was right. You should put it away."

"I'll put it in my glove compartment," Frank said. "It'll be like my home defense system."

"Good."

Frank said, "You know, your ex kept saying that you tweaked the election all by yourself."

She stared at him. "I'm sure he did! That's how he tried to set it up, too. But I've got the evidence of how he framed me along with everything else. And now these guys have it."

"Well good. But why didn't you tell me from the start that you were working with these guys?" Frank gestured in the direction of the mouth of Rock Creek. "You could have told me back in the summer, or even up in Maine."

"It's best never to say any more than necessary in situations like that. I was trying to keep you out of it."

"I was already in it! You should have told me!"

"I didn't think it would help! So quit about that. It's been tough. It's been over a *year* since I had to go under, do you realize that?"

"Yes, of course. It feels like it's been about ten." Frank put up a hand. Clearly time for limited discussion. Gingerly he reached for her, palm out. Her hand met his, and their fingers intertwined. "Okay," he said, "I'm sorry. I've been scared."

"Me too."

They walked down the driveway under the awning to Virginia Avenue. They could see the cars' lights on the Key Bridge. Their cold hands were having their own quick conversation. For a long time they just stood on the sidewalk there, looking around.

"Do you think it's really over?" she asked in a low voice.

"I think maybe so."

She took a deep breath, shuddered as she let it out. "I can't even tell anymore. The group he was part of was pretty extensive. I don't know if I'm going to feel comfortable, just—you know. Coming back out into the open."

"Maybe you don't have to. They'll help you set something new up, like in the witness protection thing. I asked them about it."

"Yeah, me too."

"I want to show you San Diego."

She looked hard at him, eyes searching his face, trying to read something. Their hands were still squeezed hard together. Things were not normal between them, he saw. Perhaps she was still angry at him for asking about the election stuff. For wanting to know what was going on. "Okay," she said. "Show me."

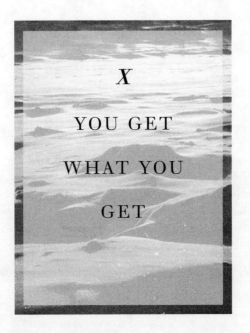

X

YOU GET

WHAT YOU

GET

"But our Icarian thoughts returned to ground
And we went to heaven the long way round."

—*Thoreau*

CUT TO THE CHASE

Today's post:

I think for a while we forgot what was possible. Our way of life damaged our ability to imagine anything different. Maybe we are rarely good at imagining that things could be different. Maybe that's what we mean when we talk about the Enlightenment. For a while there we understood that the ultimate source of power is the imagination.

"Through new uses of corporations, banks and securities, new machinery of industry, of labor and capital—all undreamed of by the Fathers—the whole structure of modern life was impressed into the service of economic royalists. It was natural and perhaps human that the privileged princes of these new economic dynasties, thirsting for power, reached out for control of government itself. They created a new despotism and wrapped it in the robes of legal sanction. In its service new mercenaries sought to regiment the people, their labor and their property. And as a result the average man once more confronts the problem that faced the Minute Man. For too many of us life was no longer free; liberty no longer real; men could no longer follow the pursuit of happiness. Against economic tyranny such as this, the American citizen could appeal only to the organized power of the Government."

That was Franklin Roosevelt, talking as president to the nation in 1936. In the same speech he said, "There is a mysterious cycle in human events. To some generations much is given. Of other generations much is expected. This generation of Americans has a rendezvous with destiny."

But then we forgot again. We went back to imagining that things could only be as they were. We lived on in that strange new feudalism, in ways that were unjust and destructive and yet were presented as the only possible reality. We said "people are like that," or "human nature will never change" or "we are all guilty of original sin," or "this is democracy, this is the free market, this is reality itself." And we went along with that analysis, and it became the law of the land. The entire world was legally bound to accept this feudal injustice as law. It was global and so it looked like it was universal. The future itself was bought, in the form of debts, mortgages, contracts—all spelled out by law and enforced by police and armies. Alternatives were unthinkable. Even to say things could be otherwise would get you immediately branded as unrealistic, foolish, naive, insane, utopian.

But that was all delusion. Every few years things change completely, even though we can't quite remember how it happened or what it means. Change is real and unavoidable. And we can organize our affairs any way we please. There is no physical restraint on us. We are free to act. It's a fearsome thing, this freedom, so much so that people talk about a "flight from freedom"—that we fly into cages and hide, because freedom is so profound it's a kind of abyss. To actually choose in each moment how to live is too scary to endure.

So we lived like sleepwalkers. But the world is not asleep, and outside our dream, things continued to change. Trying to shape that change is not a bad thing. Some pretend that making a plan is instant communism and the devil's work, but it isn't so. We always have a plan. Free market economics is a plan—it plans to give over all decisions to the blind hand of the market. But the blind hand never picks up the check. And, you know—it's blind. To deal with the global environmental crisis we now face without making any more plan than to trust the market would be like saying, We have to solve this problem so first let's put out our eyes. Why? Why not use our eyes? Why not use our brain?

Because we're going to have to imagine our way out of this one.

That's why we made the deal with China. It's one of the greatest win-win comprehensive treaties of all time. Consider that we had a massive trade deficit running with China, and they had bought a lot more of our debt as well. And because of their population, and their manufacturing capabilities, and their low wages, which by the way depressed wages for every other worker in the world, there wasn't an obvious way out of that huge imbalance. They had us. We were getting whipped in the so-called free market by a communist command-and-control political structure that could inflict austerity measures on their own people, which allowed them to win that game. That just goes to show you how free the free market really was, by the way; dictatorships did better at it than democracies! I leave it as an exercise for the blog's responders to hash over what that might mean, but in the meantime, in the real world it was a big problem!

And yet at the same time this so-called success of the Chinese was achieved in part by treating their people and landscape like disposables, and it simply wasn't true, and those false economics were beginning to backlash on them in bigger and bigger ways. They were creating terrible physical problems, worse problems than ours, really, because we've been cleaning up our land and air and water for decades now, as part of the smart planning of government of the people, by the people, and for the people, so that our troubles were mostly on paper. But the Chinese had trashed China itself, and they were headed right to the brink of a major ecological systems crash. Maybe global warming and the giant drought that has afflicted central and east Asia was the final push, but certainly their own poisonous habits had pooled up around them, and the cumulative impacts were going to kill entire regions and endanger the lives of one-sixth of humanity.

That wouldn't have been good for any of us. I know there's a fringe in the response columns saying that the worse things went for the Chinese the better off we would be, but it doesn't work that way. The carbon and particulates that they were putting into the air were going everywhere on Earth, even if China took the brunt of them. And in any case they were desperate enough to be in need of our aid, and to ask us for it—so we were obliged to help, just as fellow human beings. The fact that it gave us bargaining leverage that we hadn't had before with them was just the silver lining on a very big black cloud.

So, we all had an interest in helping the Chinese to escape what was really looking to the Chinese and American scientific communities like an imminent regional acute extinction event. The Chinese Academy of Sciences contacted our National Science Foundation with the relevant data and analysis, and NSF came to me and made the situation clear. We needed to help and the situation was so urgent that ordinary procedures weren't going to do it. So I talked to President Hu (and yes, he was on first, and yes, we cut to the Chase), and our diplomatic teams hammered out a deal in record time—a deal that the Senate immediately approved 71 to 29, because it was that good a deal.

At the invitation of the Chinese government, we docked some sixty ships of our nuclear fleet in Chinese ports, and provided them with almost five hundred megawatts of power for essential services. This helped them to shut down their dirtiest coal plants in the affected watersheds, and replace them with new clean plants built at high speed, sometimes in two weeks. We also helped to pay for these plants. We agreed also to give China all the scientific and technological help we could, everything our environmental science community has learned, from integrated pest management and organic agriculture to toxic waste removal from streams and soil. Americans from our Army Corps of Engineers and the Department of Agriculture went there to consult, and our teams that were already helping with their drought problems and their Salton Sea projects continued with their aid. We'll also be sending over a crack team of security experts to help keep track of expenditures and such, so that we don't have any of the contract corruption that occurred under some lax previous administrations. My recent reorganization of our nation's intelligence services (see previous post) has created some redundancies that give us the personnel to fulfill some of these crucial Chinese-American cooperative security responsibilities, both in Beijing and on-site in the drought-affected areas themselves.

So we're doing a lot for them, and yes, they're doing a lot for us, and everyone is benefiting. What are they doing for us? They've agreed to a cap on their carbon emissions that is impressively low, making them buyers in the carbon trading market, at least for a while longer. They will be challenging the rest of the Asia Pacific Six, which is us, Australia, Japan, South Korea, and India, to match their low cap, and are committed to helping achieve that reduction by investing in clean renewables in the other five countries in the group. As part of that effort they will be building a full set of their clean coal-burning plants for us in the United States, to be built on federal land and run by the Department of Energy. Quickly clean renewables will become part of the public trust.

The Chinese have also negotiated a successful compromise with the Dalai Lama, so that Tibet will take its rightful place as one of the semi-autonomous ethnic regions that are an important feature of both China and the United States, in the form of our Native American reservations. I think you could say that the Chinese leadership, in this part of the deal, has "embraced diversity." The world rejoices at the Tibetan settlement, and I particularly appreciate the extension of civil liberties and personal security to the Falun Gong and all other Chinese religious groups, including Buddhist monks and nuns and their leaders, in Tibet and elsewhere. That's all been very good accommodation of everyone's interests.

I'll add more on that later, but now Diane says it's time for bed. Thanks to everyone for their best wishes, by the way!

Response to response 3,581,332:

I will definitely appreciate the big gains in the House and Senate that will be given to us in the midterm elections. I'll take it to be a vote of confidence from the American people in the programs that we have been trying to enact together ever since the first sixty days. And I know people have been saying I have put my foot to the gas pedal on many of these matters ever since I got shot, and you know what? It's true. So sue me! (But don't.) I know people also say I've gotten to be like Paul Revere—you know, a little light in the belfry—but that is not true. I am more sane now than I have ever been.

So, thanks in advance. A major part of our work will continue to be aiming the amazing productivity of the American people and the global community toward stabilizing the Earth's climate, as you know. That will remain true for many years to come. But now, well before the election, I want to repeat what I've been saying all along, so that no one can later claim to misunderstand:

A major part of sustainability is social justice, here and everywhere. Think of it this way: justice is a technology. It's like a software program that we use to cope with the world and get along with each other, and one of the most effective we have ever invented, because we are all in this together. When you realize that acting with justice and generosity turns out to be the most effective technology for dealing with other people, that's a good thing.

Previous post:

What I do is mix soy sauce and a dry white wine about half and half, and then add a big dash of tarragon vinegar, and some heaping spoonfuls of brown sugar, and a tablespoon of olive oil, about a teaspoon each of ginger and mustard powder, and a dash of garlic powder. Mix that up and the longer you marinate things in it the better, but just dipping it in will do too. Best on veggies, chicken, and flank steak. Sear the meat and then cook at a lower heat.

56,938,222 responses. Cookbook to follow.

Response to response 34:

Why, you ask? Why? Because we were burning a quarter of the world's burn of carbon when we were only five percent of the world's population, that's why! That was only possible because we were so rich and stupid. We were like the guy who uses Franklins to light cigars and blow smoke into everyone's face. We only did it to show we could. Our imaginations had atrophied from disuse. Because power corrupts, and absolute power corrupts absolutely, and a little bit of power corrupts a little bit, and a lot of power corrupts a lot. So, we were pretty corrupt. Empires always are. And read some postcolonial studies if you want to know how long the damage lasts in the colonies after the empire is over! The historical record seems to indicate that the damage lasts for about a thousand years. Empires are one of the most evil and destructive of human systems. We could not become an empire and stay the America that had been up until that point one of the great achievements of history, in that we were the country made up of people from all the other countries, the country that had a new idea of justice and tried to live by it. It was so successful that we became an empire by accident. Then we had to stand down. We had to divest.

   13,576,990 responses

Response to response 589:
   Because in our system there's no such thing! There is only capital accumulation. You know the drill: the rich get richer and the poor get poorer. There is no word or phrase in the language to describe the opposite process. That's part of the emptiness of our imagination. Once or twice I've seen the phrase capital decumulation, but that means a kind of accident or mistake, which isn't what I have in mind. I'm talking about a deliberate act, a positive act. I've tried calling it capital dispersal—capital dissemination—capital disbursement—capital dispersion—you see the problem. Nothing sounds right even at the level of language. Profit redistribution; but see how all our words for it describe actions that come after the capital accumulation. Dispersing capital right at the moment of its creation—it almost seems to contradict reality, and in a sense that's right; in our system there is no word or theory to explain dispersing capital without it being some kind of payment due.
   Preemptive dividending? Usufruct? I leave it as an exercise to the responders to find the right words for this.
   33,322,518 responses

Previous post:

I say it's simple, at least at the level of fundamentals. Everyone's part of the team and should have a part to play. Capital is created by everyone, and should be owned by everyone. People are owed the worth of what they do, and whatever they do adds to humanity somehow, and helps make our own lives possible, and is worth a living wage and more. And the Earth is owed our permanent care. And we have the capability to care for the Earth and create for every one of us a sufficiency of food, water, shelter, clothing, medical care, education, and human rights.

To the extent our economic system withholds or flatly opposes these values and goals, it is diseased. It has to be changed so that we can do these things that are well within our technological capabilities. We have imagined them, and they are possible. We can make them real.

Of course they can happen. You thought they couldn't happen, but why? Because we aren't good enough to do it? That was part of the delusion. Underneath the delusion, we were always doing it.

That's what we're doing in history; call it the invention of permaculture. By permaculture I mean a culture that can be sustained permanently. Not unchanging, that's impossible, we have to stay dynamic, because conditions will change, and we will have to adapt to those new conditions, and continue to try to make things even better—so that I like to think the word permaculture implies also permutation. We will make adaptations, so change is inevitable.

Eventually I think what will happen is that we will build a culture in which no one is without a job, or shelter, or health care, or education, or the rights to their own life. Taking care of the Earth and its miraculous biological splendor will then become the long-term work of our species. We'll share the world with all the other creatures. It will be an ongoing project that will never end. People worry about living life without purpose or meaning, and rightfully so, but really there is no need for concern: inventing a sustainable culture is the meaning, right there always before us. We haven't even come close to doing it yet, so it will take a long time, indeed it will never come to an end while people still exist.

All this is inherent in what we have started, which is why I hope the American electorate delivers big progressive majorities in the congressional elections. We have to become the stewards of the Earth. And we have to start doing this in ignorance of the details of how to do it. We have to learn how to do it in the attempt itself. It is something we are going to have to imagine.

"This generation has a rendezvous with destiny." Our time has to be understood as a narrow gate, a window of opportunity, a crux point in history. It's the moment when we took responsibility for life on Earth. That's what I say. And I'll have more to say about it later.

F RANK AND CAROLINE FLEW TOGETHER out to San Diego.

There was an awkwardness between them now that Frank didn't understand. It was as if, now that they were free to do what they wanted, they didn't know what it was. It reminded Frank in a rather frightening way of his old inability to decide—of how that had felt. They had no habits. They sat side by side, and long silences grew.

Before they had left, Frank had dropped by the office. He had walked into Edgardo's office and given the Argentinian a big hug, his cheek crushed against the tall man's skinny chest. "Thanks Edgardo."

Edgardo had smiled his wry smile. "You are welcome, my friend. It was my pleasure, believe me."

They had then discussed the situation as conveyed by Umberto; it sounded like things would be okay. Phil was untangling the intelligence community, though that would take some doing. Frank then explained his plan, and Edgardo had raised a finger. She might not want to talk about this last year, he had warned. She may never want to. A lot of us are like that. I don't know if she is, but if so, be ready for it. It may always be a case of limited discussion.

Frank had nodded, thinking it over.

Besides, Edgardo had continued—even if she did fix the election single-handedly, and frame her ex to make it look like he framed her, what's anyone to do about that now?

Frank's uneasy shrug had sparked Edgardo's most delighted and cynical laugh. It echoed in his mind all the way across the country.

In San Diego, Frank drove their rental car up to La Jolla. First to the top of Mount Soledad, to show her the area from on high; then down to UCSD, where he found parking and walked her through the eucalyptus groves in their ranks and files and diagonals. Then up the great promenade between the big pretty buildings, the ocean often visible out to the west. Up the curving path on the east side of the library, an inlaid piece of sculpture made to resemble a snake's back. An inscription from Milton carved into the snake's head made it clear just which snake it was. Central Library as the forbidden Tree of the Knowledge of Good and Evil: very apt.

Caroline smiled when she saw it, and kissed Frank on the cheek. "Want an apple?" That was the best sign he had gotten from her all day, and his spirits expanded a bit.

Then out across the street, onto the bluff overlooking the Pacific. He pointed out his bedroom nook, and watched her look out at the view. You could see San Clemente Island on the horizon, seventy miles out to sea. He could see that she liked it. Then they returned to the streets, and up Torrey Pines to the new institute.

Into Leo's lab. Leo regarded Caroline with interest as Frank introduced them.

"Leo, this is my friend—"

"Carrie Barr," Caroline said, and put out her hand.

"Hi," Leo said, taking it. "Leo Mulhouse. Good to meet you."

After a bit of chat about their trip out:

"Are the insertions still going well?" Frank asked.

"They're good," Leo said. "Results are really good right now."

Frank explained to Caroline some of what they were doing, and tried to answer her questions with the right amount of technical detail, never an easy thing to judge. She looked different to Frank now, as if she had instantly become a Californian now that she was here. Maybe it was that he had seldom seen her in the sun. It was hard to believe how little time they had actually spent together. He didn't know how much biology she knew, or whether she was interested in it.

After that, Frank had a meeting on campus. "Do you want to join me for it, or do you want to have a look around while I talk to him?"

"I'll have a look around."

"Okay. Let's meet back at Leo's lab in an hour, okay?"

"Fine." Off she went.

Frank walked over to the coffee kiosk in the eucalyptus grove at the center of campus, where he had arranged to meet with Henry Bannet of Biocal. They shook hands, and in short order were looking at Frank's laptop and the Power-Point show that Frank had cobbled together for him. As Frank spoke, he added stuff Leo had just told him a few minutes before. Bannet proved to be much as Leo had said: pleasant, professionally friendly, all in the usual way—but he had a quickness of eye that seemed to indicate some kind of impatience. Once or twice he interrupted Frank's explanations with questions about Yann and Eleanor's methods. He knew a lot. This guy, Frank thought, wanted gene therapy to work.

"Have you talked to your tech transfer office about this?" Bannet asked.

"It's Eleanor Dufours who is the P.I.," Frank said. "She'll be the one leading the way with any start-up."

"Okay," Bannet said, looking a bit surprised. "We can discuss that later."

By the time Frank got back to Leo's lab, Caroline was already there, and so were Marta and Eleanor, with Marta looking most intrigued.

"Frank!" Marta said. "I didn't know you were going to be out here again so soon."

"Yes, I am. Hi, Eleanor. Have you guys met my friend—"

"Yes," Caroline said. "Leo introduced us," and for a second everyone was saying something at once.

After a brief laugh, they fell silent. "Well!" Marta said. She had a gleam in her eye that Frank had seen before. "What a lucky coincidence! We were just going to grab Leo for dinner in Del Mar, to celebrate the latest results—did he tell you about those? Why don't you two join us?"

Frank said, "Oh, well—"

"Sure," Caroline said, "that sounds great."

So there they were at one of the beach restaurants in Del Mar, talking away cheerfully. Given the results in the lab, they had a lot to be cheerful about. Caroline was seated on one side of Frank, Marta on the other. It made him uneasy, but there was nothing he could do. And besides he too had cheerful news, in the form of his meeting with Henry Bannet.

"So does that mean you're moving back?" Marta said to Frank when the others were all talking among themselves.

"Yes, I think so."

"You've been out there a long time—what has it been, three years?"

"Almost," Frank said. "It feels like more."

After dinner, Marta invited them to come along with them to the Belly-Up, and again Caroline agreed before Frank could beg off. So there they were, in the crush of dancers on the floor of the Belly-Up, Frank dancing with three women, watching Marta and Caroline shouting over the music into each other's ears and then laughing heartily, before excusing themselves and going off to the ladies' room together. Frank watched this appalled. He had never even imagined Marta and Caroline meeting, much less becoming friendly. Now he was surprised to see that they looked somewhat alike, or were in some other way similar. And really, now that he thought of it, it was gratifying that Marta liked Caroline—a kind of approval of his judgment, or his D.C. life. Part of a more general amnesty. But it also felt like trouble, in some obscure way Frank could not pin down. At the very least it probably meant he was going to get laughed at a lot. Well, whatever. Nothing to be done about that. There were worse fates.

Frank had made reservations for the night at a motel in Encinitas, but for some reason he was nervous about that; and besides, he wanted to take Caroline up to Leucadia. He wasn't going to be able to sleep until he did.

So he explained as they left the Belly-Up, and she nodded, and he drove north on the coast highway.

"So?" Frank said. "How are you liking it?"

"It's beautiful," she said. "And I like your friends. But, you know—I'm not sure what I would do out here."

"Well—anything you want, right? I mean, you're going to have to do something different anyway. You aren't going to be going back into intelligence...."

But maybe she thought she was. Maybe that was it.

She didn't say anything, so he dropped the matter, feeling more uncertain than ever.

He turned left off the coast highway in Leucadia, onto the street that led to Neptune.

He parked a little down from Leo's house. As they walked up the street, gaps to their left again revealed the enormous expanse of the Pacific, vast and gray under the marine layer, which was patterned by moonlight. Like something out of a dream. He had her here at last. Breaking waves cracked and grumbled underfoot, and the usual faint haze of mist salted the air.

He stopped in the street in front of one of the cliffside houses. The cliff here had given way in the big storms, and even the streetside wall of this particular house was cracked. It appeared that one corner of its outer foundation overhung the new face of the cliff. There was a FOR SALE BY OWNER sign stuck in the Bermuda grass of a narrow front lawn.

Frank said, "I followed up on something Leo said, and checked the USGS study of this part of the coast, and he's right—this is a little buttress here, a little bit of a point, see? We're a touch higher, and the iceplant doesn't grow as well on the cliff, and there was this erosion, but the point itself is strong. I think this will be the last erosion you see here for a while. And there are things you can do to shore things up. And, you know, if worse came to worst, we could tear down this house entirely and build nearer the street. Something small and neat."

"Like in this tree?" Caroline said, gesturing at the big eucalyptus tilting over them.

Frank grinned. "Well, incorporating it maybe. We'd have to save it somehow."

She smiled briefly, nodded. "My treehouse man."

She walked out to the edge of the cliff, looked down curiously. Anywhere else on Earth this would be a major sea cliff; here it was a little lower than average for North County, at about seventy feet. Everywhere sea cliffs were eroding at one rate or another.

"There's a staircase down to the beach, just past Leo and Roxanne's," Frank told her, pointing to the south. "There's a bike lane on the coast highway that runs from here all the way down to UCSD. I think it's about twelve miles. You could get a job down there on campus, or nearby, and we could bike down there to work. Take the coast cruiser when we need to. We could make it work."

"Well good," Caroline said, staring at him in the moonlight. "Because I'm pregnant."

FRANK DREAMED THAT CHARLIE CAME to him at the end of a day's work and said, "Phil wants to see Rock Creek," and off they went in a parade of black Priuses. In the park it was as snowy as in the depths of the long winter, and they crunched on snowshoes through air like dry ice. At Site 21 the bros had a bonfire going, and Frank introduced the bundled-up Phil as an old friend and the bros did not notice him, they were focused on the bonfire and their talk—all except Fedpage, who looked up from the *Post* he was feeding to the fire. He studied Phil for a second and his eyebrows shot up. "Whoah!" he said, and knocked his glasses up his nose to have a better look. "What's this, some kind of Prince Hal thing going on here?" He jerked his head to the side to redirect Zeno's attention to the visitor. "Oh, hey," Zeno said as he saw who it was. Frank was afraid he would go all blustery and false like he often did with Frank himself, but Phil slipped through all that and soon they were adding fuel to the fire, and talking about Vietnam, and Zeno was fine. Frank felt a glow of pleasure at that. But otherwise it was cold, unless you sat too close to the fire, and the hour grew late, and yet on the Viet vets reminisced; Frank shared a glance with the Secret Service man sitting beside him, a black man he had never seen (and on waking he would remember this man's face so clearly, it was utterly distinct, a face he had never seen before—where did the faces like that come from, who were they?) and their shared glance told them that they both had realized that the president liked this kind of scene, that he was a bullshitter at heart, like Clinton, like—how far did it go back? Washington? And so they were going to be there all night, talking about Vietnam.

But then Spencer and Robin and Robert came roaring through and Frank leaped up to join their night golf. They were going long, they said. It was too beautiful not to. They were shooting new holes all the way down Rock Creek and past the Watergate, curving one shot into the Lincoln Memorial to smack Abe's left knee, then across to the Korean vets, where one of the doomed statues had his hand out as if to make a catch; then on to the Tidal Basin, threading the cherry trees lining the west bank, so that it took finesse as well as brute distance to do well; and then out to the FDR Memorial, where the final hole was declared to be the gold forefinger of Roosevelt's second statue. Frank threw his frisbee and realized as it curved away that its flight was so perfect that it would hit the finger right on the tip, and so he woke up.

THEY GOT BACK TO D.C. JUST IN TIME for the Saturday of another party at the Khembali farm. It was a day on which Frank had a zoo morning scheduled with Nick, so he showed up at the Quiblers' house at around ten.

"How was San Diego?" they asked him. They knew that he was planning to move back there.

"It was good." He smiled what Anna called his real smile. "I found out that my girlfriend is pregnant."

"Pregnant?" Anna cried—

"Girlfriend?" Charlie exclaimed.

The two of them looked at each other and laughed at their nicely timed response, also their mutual ignorance.

Then Anna snapped her fingers and pointed at Frank. "It's that woman you met in the elevator, I bet."

"Well yes, that's right."

"Ha! I knew it! Well!" She gave him a hug. "I guess you're glad now that you went to that brown bag talk at NSF!"

"And came to your party afterward. Yes, that was quite a day. You did a good thing to set that up." Frank shook his head as he remembered it. "Everything changed on that day."

Anna clapped her hands a little. "Frank that is *good* news, so when do we get to meet her?"

"She's coming to the party this afternoon, so you'll meet her out there. She couldn't make it to the zoo, though, she had to do some stuff."

"Okay, good then. Off we go."

They walked up to the Bethesda Metro, trained down to the zoo. In through the front gates—an entry Frank and Nick rarely used—past the pandas, then down toward the tigers, Joe racing ahead in perpetual danger of catching a toe and launching himself into a horrible face-plant. "Joe, slow down!" Charlie cried uselessly as he took off in pursuit.

Frank walked between Nick and Anna, all three looking for the golden tamarind monkeys and other little ferals squirreling around freely in the trees. By the time they had dropped in to see which gibbons were out, and continued down to the tiger enclosure, Joe was up on Charlie's shoulders, and dangerously canted over the moat.

Their swimming tigers were basking in the sun. The male was draped against the tree like a tiger rug, his mouth hanging open. The female lay *en couchant*, long and sleek, staring sphinxlike into emptiness.

For a long time no one moved. Other people drifted by, passed on to other things.

"I saw the jaguar," Frank told them. "It was casual at the time, or, I don't mean casual—I was totally scared and ran away as soon as I could—but I didn't fully get it, how great it was to see it, until a few days later."

"Wow," Nick said. "Did you get a GPS?"

"It was at the overlook."

"No."

"Yes."

"Wow."

After a while longer they went to get snowcones, even though it was just before lunch. Frank got lime; Nick got a mix of root beer, cherry, and banana.

Then Frank took off to go pick up his girlfriend, and the Quiblers went back to the house before continuing out to the farm.

The Khembalis' party was a big one, combining as it did several celebrations, not just the Shambhala arrival, but also the Buddhist plum-blossom festival, which now would always mark the auspicious day when the Dalai Lama and the Chinese government had agreed on his return to Tibet. The treaty had been signed there in Washington, at the White House, just the day before. And now also it was Frank's going-away party as well, and even a sort of shower; and last but not least, Phil and Diane were going to drop by for a bit. Their presence added to the crowd, as well as making the party into a kind of wedding reception, because the first couple had made their actual nuptials a completely private affair some days before. Parts of the punditocracy were squawking that this fait accompli was an unholy alliance of science and politics, but Phil had only laughed at this and agreed, adding "What are you gonna do?"

So when they arrived, there was the usual stir. But as soon as they had accepted a toast from all they insisted that the party refocus on the Khembalis, and the return of the Dalai Lama to Tibet, and to what that meant, which was the return to the Tibetan people of some kind of autonomy or, as Phil reminded them briefly, semi-autonomy. "No one person or institution or nation is more than semi-autonomous anyway," Phil said in his remarks, "so it's very good, a welcome development that truly dwarfs any personal cause for celebration we might have. Although the personal causes in this case are all quite glorious."

To which everyone said, "Hear hear."

Frank and Caroline wandered the compound together, running into people Frank knew and chatting with them over cups of champagne and unidentifiable hors-d'oeuvres. Padma led them through every room in the much-articulated treehouse, and Caroline laughed to see Frank's face as he contemplated the new upper reaches of the system. He took her out on the old limb to show her where he and Rudra had lived, and then he was given a tour of the farm's current crops, and the orchard of apple saplings, just recently planted, while Caroline was taken in hand by Qang to meet some of the other Khembali women.

When Frank rejoined her, she was still deep in conversation with Qang, who was answering her questions with a smile.

"Yes," Qang was saying, "that is probably what they have always stood for. We call them demons, but of course one could also say that they are simply bad ideas."

"So sometimes, when you do those ceremonies to drive out demons, you could say that in a sense you're holding a ceremony to drive out bad ideas?"

"Yes, of course. That is just what an exorcism of demons is, to us."

"I like that," Caroline said, looking over at Frank. "It makes it kind of explicit, and yet—religious. And it—you say it works?"

"Yes, very often it does. Of course, sometimes you need to do it more than once. We had to exorcise Frank's friend Charlie twice, for instance, to drive out some bad ideas that had taken root in him. But I believe it worked in the end."

She turned to Frank to include him in the conversation.

"It sounds like something I could use," Frank said.

"Oh, no. I think you have never been infected by any bad ideas!"

Qang's merry look reminded him of Rudra, and he laughed. "I'm not so sure of that!"

Qang said, "You are only infected by good ideas, and you wrestle with them very capably. That's what Padma says."

"I don't know about that."

"It sounds right to me," Caroline said, slipping an arm under Frank's. "I, on the other hand, could use a thoroughgoing exorcism. In fact I'd like to order up a full-on reincarnation, or not exactly, but you know. A new life."

"You can do that," Qang said, smiling at her. "We all do that. And especially when you have a child."

"I suppose so."

Sucandra joined them. "So, Frank," he said, "now you go back to your old home."

"Yes, that's right. Although it will be different now."

"Of course. The two of you together—very nice. And you will work for the institute you helped to start out there?"

"I'll work with them, but my job will be back at the university. I've been on a leave of absence, so I have to go back."

"But your research will connect to that of the institute?"

"Exactly. Some of my colleagues there are exploring some new possibilities. There's an old student of mine who is doing remarkable things. First there was genomics, and now he's starting what you could call proteomics. It looks like they'll be starting up a small company of their own. In fact, I've been talking to Drepung about the idea of you guys investing in this company. If Khembalung has any kind of investment portfolio, you might want to talk with them. Because if things pan out for them the way I think they might, there'll be some very important medical treatments to come out of it."

"Good, good," Sucandra said, and Qang nodded too. "Qang here heads that committee."

"Yes," Qang said, "I will talk to them. If we can make investments that help health, it's a good thing. But Sucandra is our doctor, so he will have to take a look too."

Sucandra nodded. "What about you, will you be investing in this new company?"

Frank laughed. "I might if I had anything to invest. Right now all I have is my salary. Which is fine. But we're buying a house, so there won't be much extra. But that's okay. If it works there'll be enough for everybody."

"A nice thought."

Then Drepung joined them. He was wearing his Wizards basketball shirt and his enormous Reeboks, and the cord to his iPod was entangled in his turquoise and coral necklaces.

"What about you, Drepung?" Frank asked. "Will you be moving back to Tibet?"

"Oh no, I don't think so!" Drepung grinned. "Only room for one lama in Lhasa! Besides, I like it here. And I am obliged to stay in any case. It's part of the deal with the Chinese, more or less. And besides, this is Khembalung now! And not just the farm, but really the whole D.C. area. So I have work to do here as an ambassador."

"Good," Frank said. "They can use you."

"Thank you, I will give it a good try. What about you, Frank? Won't you miss this place when you go back to San Diego?"

"Yes, I will. But I need to get back. And people always visit D.C. All kinds of reasons bring you back."

"So true."

"Maybe I'll see you out there too."

"I hope so. I'll try to visit."

Neither man was under any illusion as to how frequently this was likely to happen.

Frank looked around at the crowd. He knew a lot of the people there. If he had stuck to his plan and stayed just a year, and lived that year like a ghost, he would have passed through and gone home without regrets. No one would even have been aware of his passing. But it had not happened that way. It all came down to the people you ran into.

This was accentuated when the Quiblers arrived. Charlie pretended to be cheery about Frank's departure, but he also shook his head painfully—"I don't know who'll get us out on the river now."

Anna was simply sad. "We'll miss you," she said, and gave him a hug. "The boys will miss you."

Nick was noncommittal. He looked off to the side. He spoke of the latest developments in their feral research program, steadfastly focused on the details of a new spreadsheet Anna had helped him set up, on which he could record all their sightings by species, and not only keep an inventory, but enter range parameters, to gauge which species might be able to go truly feral. There was also a GIS program that let you identify or design habitat corridors. It was very interesting.

Frank nodded and made some suggestions. "We'll keep in touch by e-mail," he said at one point when he saw Nick looking away. "Then hey—maybe when you go off to college, you can come to UCSD. It's a really fun school."

"Oh yeah," Nick said, brightening. "Good idea."

Anna was startled at this suggestion, and Charlie actually winced. Neither were used to the idea of Nick growing up. But there he stood, almost as tall as Anna, and four or five inches taller than when Frank had met him. He was changing by the day, almost by the hour.

The Quiblers wandered the party. Nick and Anna talked about the swimming tigers with Sucandra as they all stood under the treehouse, looking up to watch Charlie chase Joe around the various catwalks.

"It's gotten so big."

"Yes, people like to live up there. People like to work on it too."

"It would be cool," Nick said.

Sucandra nodded. "You all should consider moving out here with us," he said to them. "We would be so happy to have you here with us. You are already Khembalis, as far as we are concerned. And I think you would like it. A community like this is a kind of extended family. And of course group living is very thrifty," he added with a smile at Anna. "Energy consumption would be only a fraction of that used by an ordinary suburban house."

"That's true," Anna said.

"Hey MOMMA!" Joe shouted down at her from the highest catwalk.

"Hi monkey," she called up. "Did you lose Dad?"

"Yeah, I did!"

"Oh my," Anna muttered.

Actually Charlie was not far below Joe, although on a different catwalk; he had gotten lost at an intersection. He retraced his last steps, and turned a corner— and there was Roy Anastophoulus.

"Roy!"

"Charlie!"

They gave each other a hug.

Over Roy's shoulder, Charlie saw Andrea Blackwell. Charlie had not been aware that they were on again, but by her smile it appeared to be so.

"It's good to see you!" Charlie said. "I didn't know you were going to be here."

"No, well, when we heard about Phil and Diane coming out to get a marriage blessing from the Dalai Lama, we asked if we could tag along and join in."

"So—you mean—"

Roy nodded. "Yes. We got married yesterday at the courthouse." They showed him their shiny new wedding bands. "Now we're here for the blessing."

"Wonderful!" Charlie said. "Wait till Anna hears!"

He yelled down to the ground: "Hey Anna!" Then: "Just a second, I have to catch up to Joe. In fact, if you could take this catwalk across to over there, and wait? Maybe you can help me cut him off."

"Sure."

Back on the ground Anna was indeed delighted with their news. They gathered with the rest of the guests on the lawn in front of the main house, and cheered the appearance of the Dalai Lama, entering the big tent with Drepung, and followed by Phil and Diane, then Roy and Andrea. A troop of Khembalis in their best Tibetan finery performed a brief dance, accompanied by the drums, horns, and swirls of incense that reminded Anna all of a sudden of the first time she had seen the Khembalis, performing a similar ceremony before their little office in the NSF building.

The Dalai Lama, cheerfully sublime as always, led Phil and Diane through a brief set of Buddhist wedding vows; then did the same for Roy and Andrea. While they were still up there, Drepung gestured to Frank and Caroline to come up to the front, and they came out of the crowd to applause. Diane gave Frank a quick high five.

Drepung was the one who led Frank and Caroline through their vows, ending with a blessing on them:

"This couple has come together at last.
There is a presence that gives the gifts.
The spirit of Tara has saved us from demons.
You are the wind. We're dust blown into shapes.
You are the spirit. We're intertwining hands.
You are the clarity. We're this language that tries to say it.
You are joy. We're all the different kinds of laughing.
When the ocean surges, don't let me just hear it.
Let it splash inside my chest!"

Then he and the Dalai Lama stood side by side, and reached out together to join the hands of the three couples. For a moment everything was still; then with a blast on the long Tibetan horns, the party began in earnest.

"Here," Nick said as the Quiblers prepared to leave, and he shoved an envelope into Frank's hand. "FOG made a going-away card out of your phone log. Almost everybody signed it. Jason was out of town."

"Thanks," Frank said. Most of those people he had never met in person; they had been voices over the phone, or names on the sighting board. "Tell them I'll miss them. Tell them I'll try to get something like this started out in San Diego."

"Will there be any animals to see out there?"

"No, not really. You're lucky with what you have here. Out there it's down to birds and rabbits, I'm afraid. Maybe I'll have to arrange a breakout at the San Diego Zoo."

Joe, nearly asleep on Charlie's shoulder, heard the word "zoo" and rolled his head to the side.

"Tiger," he murmured, and pounded Charlie's chest with a single solid tap.

Charlie put his chin on the round blond head. "You're my tiger," he said. Joe drifted back off.

WHEN THE QUIBLERS GOT HOME they changed out of their party clothes and went out in the yard to work on the garden. At five their doorbell rang, and Frank's friend Cutter appeared at their door, a burly black man with big scarred hands and a friendly smile. Behind him his crew were already unloading gear from their truck. The PV panels had arrived at last. Joe ran around the house to investigate, and he and Charlie watched fascinated as the ladders were assembled and scaled. The nimble climbers disappeared onto the roof and then dropped ropes beside the ladder, to help stabilize their climb and also to haul things up. The struts and wiring had been installed weeks ago, but there was a waiting list for the solar panels themselves. Now they were hooking them to a hoist line. Soon what Charlie and Joe could see of the south side of the roof was covered with gear. It was going to be a grid of sixteen photovoltaic panels, capable of generating all the house's electricity when the sun was shining. Whenever more electricity was generated by the panels than they used in the house, the excess would be fed back into the grid, and they would be paid for it by the utility district that had recently replaced the private company as their power provider. This was going to give them a big drop in their carbon-burn numbers, and Charlie was sure Anna and Nick would be very pleased.

With a wave to Joe, Cutter and his team took off.

The photovoltaics were indeed very good for their carbon-burn score, and their garden helped a little; but still they were scoring pretty high, and Anna was getting frustrated. "You just can't do it in a suburban home, when you own a car and a phone and all the stuff."

"We're doing better," Charlie reminded her.

"Yeah, but we're hitting limits." Anna stared at her spreadsheet. "I don't see what else we can do here, either, given the infrastructure and all. I wonder if we should take up the Khembalis' offer and move in with them."

Charlie rolled his eyes. "It seems to me they're crowded enough out there."

"Well, they've sent some of their group back to India. They say there's room."

"I don't know. Would you want to do that?"

"I don't know. In a way I think it would be nice."

Charlie did not reply. He knew that Anna was concerned about the carbon burn of their house. The numbers there had hooked her in their usual way. For the sake of an elegant result she would contemplate almost anything. And to be fair, Charlie recalled now how involved she had been with the Khembalis from the very start—inviting them over, becoming friends with Sucandra and Qang, helping their Institute of Higher Studies—learning more Tibetan than any of the rest of them.

"Let's talk to the boys about it," he temporized.

"Sure. And maybe check it out the next time we're out there for dinner. See what it might really entail."

"If we can. We might not be able to tell in a visit."

"Well, of course."

"And, you know," he reminded her, "we're doing better here than most people who live in a single family house."

"True. But maybe that isn't good enough anymore."

After that Charlie wandered around the house, feeling strange. It was almost sunset outside, and inside the house it was getting dark. The others were out in the kitchen, clattering about as they got dinner started.

Charlie stood in the living room looking around. Something about it caught his eye. A quality of the evening light. It looked like a place that had been lived in long ago. There was a tangle of trucks on the carpet, but otherwise things were cleaned up. It looked spare. Perhaps Frank's comment about Nick going to UCSD had put him in an odd frame of mind. Of course all these things would happen. But the years after Nick's birth had been so intense; and since Joe's arrival, even more so. It had filled his mind. It had crowded everything else out; it had seemed the only reality. He could have said, Once there was an island in time, just off Wisconsin Avenue: a mother, a father, two boys, two cats; and it seemed like it would last forever. But then...

That was all it took, just *then* and *then* and then another *then*. Enough thens and then the island was gone. Someday other people would live in this house. It was an odd thought to have. Charlie sat down, looked around at the room as if it might vanish. One day he would break the couch under him into splinters so it would fit in the trash cans to be hauled away. Island after island went under, and the little Khembalung moved somewhere else.

The phone rang.

"Charlie, can you get that please? I've gotta—Joe! No Joe, we'll get that—oh—oh, okay. Okay! Charlie, never mind! Joe's got it!"

FRANK WENT DOWN TO THE POTOMAC for one last trip out before they left.

It was a hot spring day, the world green and steaming. Charlie couldn't make it; Drepung couldn't make it. Caroline was driving down from the farm later with a picnic lunch; she too was busy, and said she would get to Great Falls before he was finished. She planned to sit on the bluff overlooking the downstream end of Mather Gorge, near the put-in, while he paddled up the Fish Ladder.

An hour later, while taking a rest from his salmon leaps up the Ladder, he looked up at the bluff but did not see her.

When he looked back at the falls, the woman kayaker he had seen twice before was already three steps up the Ladder and ascending like a kingfisher or a water ouzel. As before, the sight of her leaped in his vision, it was like being nudged by the side of the world: broad shoulders, big lats, a thick braid of black hair bouncing on her neck—for an instant, a profile—maybe that was it—or the way she moved. Beautiful. He took off after her, he didn't know why; he intended nothing by it, he knew his Caroline would soon be there; it was just a curiosity that put him in pursuit, some itch to see.

Hard paddle into the first white drop, punching into the flow to get enough acceleration to slide up onto the flat spot above. Do it again. Do it again. Each flat spot had a slightly different length, leading to a different speed of water at the infall. The drops got harder, though in truth they were almost as even as stairs—but not quite—and near the top, the ones that were just a bit taller took a terrific effort to ascend.

But he made it to the top. His lungs were burning and his arms were on fire. He had never managed it before and here he was, on the big sweep of the upper Potomac.

But there she was, rounding a bend upstream, still paddling hard. Frank set off in pursuit, confident now he had ascended the ladder that there were no impediments to catching her. He took off at a racing pace.

But so had she. When he rounded the first bend she was already at the next one; and when he rounded that, his arms in a hot lactic scream, she was even farther ahead, in the long straight section that came there. And yet it wouldn't be that long before she made it to the next bend; and she was still paddling hard. Frank pushed one last time, breathing hard now, sweating until his eyes stung, trying to ignore the lactic acid in the pulling muscles of his arms and chest, until the time came that they felt like blocks of wood. His kayak was slowing down.

When he rounded the bend at the end of the straight, she was disappearing ahead. Gone. He had to give up.

He stopped and sucked down air, sweating, wiping sweat off his eyebrows with the backs of his hands. Cramps flickered through his muscles. He let the kayak drift downstream on the current. He had given it his all. Chasing beauty upstream until he couldn't anymore. A very fast goddess. Oh well.

Now there was the Great Falls of the Potomac to attend to. Very few took the biggest drops in a kayak; they could be fatal. Only the best professionals would even think of it. Everyone else ran the various alternatives, not just the Fish Ladder but other parts of the complex of falls on the Maryland side, more or less difficult.

He took the drop called The Ping Pong, struggling with the big bounces in the midsection, his arms burning again, almost too tired to perform the absolutely necessary course corrections—but too tired to risk an overturn either. He had to stay upright, he was panting as he worked, and would not be able to hold his breath for long. He had to stay upright!

He got through the drops. In the hissing white flow of re-collecting water at the bottom of the falls he floated thankfully, spent. He had just enough strength left to paddle to the Virginia shore. On the bluff overhead, Caroline was watching him.

He grabbed the put-in boulder on the shore, wearily hauled himself in. Undid his apron and struggled to follow his paddle up onto the rocky jumble at the bottom of the bluff. Stiff and sore. Sweat poured out from his head. He stumbled back into the shallows and sat down in the river, then lay back and let the water pour over him. Ahhh, cool water. Just what he needed. Up again, spluttering and gasping. Cooler already.

He hiked up the steep little cleft in the bluff. Sat beside Caroline with a squish. Dripped river water. He was still sweating.

Caroline regarded him. "So," she said. "You came back."

"What do you mean?" Frank said. "I never left."

"I guess that's true."

They sat there, looking down at the river. Below them a pair of kayakers were putting in; one paddled backwards upstream. A wind threw a quick cat's paw across the surface of the river, and on the opposite shore the wall of green trees bobbed and flailed. In the sky to the north a cloud was rearing high into the sky, its white lobes aquiver with the promise of storms to come.

"I love you."

ACKNOWLEDGMENTS

Thanks for help this time from:

Charles V. Brown, Joy Chamberlain, Rita Colwell, William Fox, Doug Fratz, Anne Groell, Jennifer Holland, Jane Johnson, Mark Lewis, Rich Lynch, Lisa Nowell, Michael Schlesinger, Jim Shea, Darko Suvin, Ralph Vicinanza, Paul J. Werbos, and Donald Wesling.

ABOUT THE AUTHOR

KIM STANLEY ROBINSON is a winner of the Hugo, Nebula, and Locus Awards. He is the author of nineteen previous books, including the bestselling Mars trilogy and the critically acclaimed *Forty Signs of Rain, The Years of Rice and Salt,* and *Antarctica*—for which he was sent to the Antarctic by the U.S. National Science Foundation as part of their Antarctic Artists and Writers' Program. He lives in Davis, California.

ABOUT THE AUTHOR